HACIENDA

HACIENDA

A Novel By Albert R. Booky

SUNSTONE
PRESS

SANTA FE

*This is a work of fiction. Any resemblance of any of the
characters to persons living or dead is strictly coincidental.*

Sunstone books may be purchased for edcational, business, or sales promotional
use. For information please write: Special Markets Department, Sunstone Press,
P.O. Box 2321, Santa Fe, New Mexico 87504-2321.

FIRST EDITION

10 9 8 7 6 5 4 3 2 1

Library of Congress Cataloging in Publication Data:
Booky, Albert R., 1925–
    Hacienda / Albert R. Booky. — 1st ed.
        p. cm.
    ISBN: 0-86534-251-2
    I. Title.
PS3552. 06436H33   1966
813' .54—dc20   96-31644
                                     CIP

Published by   SUNSTONE PRESS
                    Post Office Box 2321
                    Santa Fe, NM 87504-2321 / USA
                    (505) 988-4418 / *orders only* (800) 243-5644
                    FAX (505) 988-1025

This book is dedicated to my brothers,
Joe and Ernie
and their wives, Barbara and Cecilia.

<u>*Other Books by Albert R. Booky*</u>

APACHE SHADOWS

THE BUCKSKINS

SON OF MANITOU

PINKERTON ACADEMY

REMEMBER US

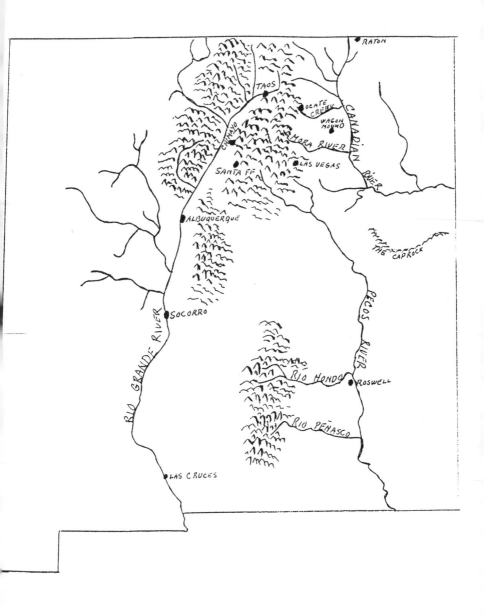

CHAPTER I

The tall, slim young man stood near the bank of the little Mora River and gazed up at the majestic Sangre de Cristo Mountains which towered over him. "The blood of Christ," he murmured half aloud as he made the sign of the cross. His eyes skirted the mountain until they came to rest on Truchas Peak. Behind it, the New Mexico sky was its usual radiant, turquoise blue and puffs of snowy white clouds floated serenely across the sky. The colors of the mountain blended majestically, the grey of the rocky cliffs and ledges merging with the blue and green shadows of the trees, and the heavy mist lent a blue, mysterious tint to the mountainside.

The young man was in his early twenties and his thoughts continued to wander as he stared up at the mountain. His skin was a golden brown and was complimented by his jet black hair and brown eyes. His features were finely cut, some inherited from his mother. The intelligence of the boy was evident in his eyes, and he was not the only one on the hacienda who had also seen the resemblance between the patron and himself, but such thoughts were best kept to themselves.

"Simoñ!" The voice calling to him penetrated his quiet musing.

"Dreaming again? You imagine yourself high on Truchas Peak and looking down toward Chimayo and the Rio Grande, and possibly beyond? How long will it be before you leave the hacienda to satisfy that wandering appetite of yours?" The woman's voice was light with laughter. Simoñ turned to face his mother, whose appearance was that of a woman many years younger than her real age. She was small in stature, had great exuberance, and much zest for life. She was extremely light on her feet and quick in her motions. Her eyes danced with inquisitiveness and excitement and her smile was so contagious, so brilliant and happy that her soft laughter and optimism cheered many of the other hacienda peons when they were despondent.

Simoñ looked down at his mother fondly and he bent to embrace her and kiss her on the cheek. "You know me so well," he chuckled, "You seem able to read my thoughts as if they were your own."

She smiled back and remarked airily, "Well, I am your mother!"

"How could I ever forget, or forget your beauty and your grace? The angels could hardly be an improvement on you."

They both made the sign of the cross at his words and then Maria grabbed her son's hand and cried, "Come, it is time for supper and no doubt your father is waiting for us. He'll be very hungry. We do not want to keep him waiting, for he has put in a hard day irrigating."

As they walked down toward their little casa, they could see the sprawling one story roof of the big house of the patron. The builder had chosen the perfect location for the patio as well as the house, when he selected the site. The beautiful garden of flowers, trees, and shrubbery, which was so carefully nurtured by the gardeners, was even lovelier in the golden twilight and the scent of the flowers almost hypnotic.

The corrals and maintenance buildings were located at some distance south of the patron's house while the dwellings of the peons were located north of the big house and were lined in a row running east and west. All of the buildings on the hacienda were constructed of adobe bricks.

Simoñ and his mother entered the kitchen of their three room casa which consisted of two bedrooms and the kitchen. Benito was seated at the rough, scrubbed table waiting patiently for them. He was a huge man although not exceptionally tall. His greying hair was thick and covered most of his forehead. His eyebrows were also thick and his mustache completely engulfed his upper lip. His skin was weather worn and his hands were the large hands of a peasant. But his eyes shone with kindness and compassion, the traits which had first drawn his wife to him.

The walls of the interior of the little house were unplastered, and exposed the adobe bricks to the warm glow of the candles. The floors were of compacted clay. The kitchen, as well as the other two rooms had only small windows which were furnished with heavy, wooden shutters. The only decorations on the walls were crude, brightly colored paintings of saints on rough boards, and a crucifix also hung in each room.

"Welcome, my son," Benito said in a weary voice.

"Be seated, Simoñ," Maria said. "I will bring our supper."

She bustled to the small open fireplace. A small iron rod extended across the opening and an iron kettle was hung upon the rod. Maria scooped from this kettle with a wooden ladle some of the spicy, delicious chili which her family loved. The chili contained small chunks of pork and frijoles mixed with her special mixture of red chile and herbs and spices. Maria placed a wooden bowl of this chili in front of each of her menfolk and one for herself and on a small platter she placed the stack of tortillas she had made earlier. She now joined her husband and son and they bowed their heads as she said grace. As they began to eat, she spoke but continued to look down at her bowl as she stirred her chili. "Tomorrow, the priest comes and it will be a time of merriment, baptisms, marriages, and confessions, and guests from other haciendas and ranchos will begin to arrive at the house of the patron early in the morning. They will bring their workers and after mass we will have time to visit with them and hear the news." She smiled as she said this, and her eyes sparkled in anticipation.

"I always welcome a Holy Fiesta," Simoñ said simply. Bonito glanced at each of them and he nodded in agreement as he took up another spoonful of chili. Then he folded a tortilla and before he took a bite, he said, "It should be a joyous day, a time for prayer and afterward sporting and games. Laughter from the little ones always lightens my heart. It has been nearly six months since a priest has visited our hacienda. We will keep him busy!" He grinned broadly before he again attacked the chili with gusto.

It was midmorning before the people from the outlying haciendas, villages, or small ranchos began to arrive. The dons and doñas came in their fancy carriages and behind each carriage rode mounted horsemen who were ready to lend assistance if their patrons required it.

The peons were on foot, on burros, or in wagons drawn by mules or oxen. The Gomez peons mingled with the visiting peons and the sounds of voices and laughter floated through the crisp, morning air. Happy voices also echoed from within the walls of the patron's house until the bell from the chapel summoned them to mass. The peons moved slowly toward the chapel, their faces suddenly grave, and reverent, for New Mexicans were a devout people. When they arrived at the fence which protected the cemetery around the chapel from the animals, they halted to allow the patrons to enter before them, and when they had done so, genuflecting as they entered and found their places at the front of the chapel, the peons followed with bowed heads.

When mass was concluded, the patrons left the chapel, again followed by the peons. Now the patrons moved toward the big house where they would be served chicken cooked with rice, lamb or beef and vegetable platters, and for desert there might be a custard or sweet rolls with coffee or chocolate.

The shutters of the windows in the dining room would be thrown open to let the light in for they had been closed during the early morning to keep the cool mountain air within.

From the chapel, the working people had gathered in groups at the corrals or under the giant cottonwoods, seeking the welcome leisure and shade before partaking of their midday meal. Simoñ was part of a group which gathered at one of the corrals.

"What are Americanos like, Manuel?" The questioner was one of the freighters from the Baca Hacienda.

"The ones I have met are very independent," Manuel replied as he raised an elbow and let it rest on a rail of the corral.

"They sure make our governor nervous and I can't say that I blame him, either. Those Americanos sure have the upper hand with their weapons," put in another freighter.

"I don't feel sorry for the governor," Hector interrupted with anger in his voice. "He's a cruel scoundrel and it is he who has helped to keep us New Mexicans under bondage. He will not allow us to own modern weapons so we can protect ourselves from the Indians, especially the Apaches or the Comanches. Heaven knows, the Indians don't suffer under that handicap, for they are armed with weapons which they obtain somehow, how I don't know. Have the Americanos cheated us as he said they would if we traded with them? No. He lied to us, for he knew from the beginning that the Americanos would not make slaves of us, but he told us that, didn't he? He and his kind want to keep all of the trade for themselves."

"What will become of us?" Lorenzo wondered aloud.

"What do you mean?" Manuel asked.

"I can't speak English," Lorenzo replied, "and I know nothing, absolutely nothing about the Americanos, their country, or their ways. What will become of people like me if they should take over New Mexico?"

The men stared at one another, but said nothing until a voice asked, "Are the Americanos anything like the arrogant English?" Lorenzo asked, as he again looked at the freighter from the Baca Hacienda.

"I guess we'll just have to wait to see," replied the freighter. "It is possible that New Mexico may never become part of the United States, but will continue to remain a domain under Mexican rule."

"Can birds fly?" Lorenzo asked seriously. "You know better than we that some day New Mexico will be annexed to the Americanos."

Mañuel turned to Simoñ and remarked, "You have said nothing, mi amigo, what are you thinking?"

Simoñ smiled and spoke for the first time, "I don't intend to wait and see what these Americanos are like. I am going to Santa Fe the first chance I get, to observe and study them for myself. Then I will give you my answer."

"Simoñ," a Gomez peon yelled as he rushed up to join the group, "the patron told me to tell you that he will journey to Chimayo early next week and he wishes for you to accompany him!"

"Why me?" asked the surprised Simoñ.

The peon shrugged his shoulders confusedly and turned to walk away.

"Adios, mi amigos," Simoñ called back to the others as he ran to look for his mother. When he finally found her, he removed his hat, but said nothing. His mother turned from visiting with the other women when she found him at her side and asked, "Yes, my son? What is it?"

"I have just received a message from the patron and he wishes for me to accompany him to Chimayo." Simoñ told her in excitement.

"Not now, we'll talk more about it tonight, Simoñ." His mother wore an expression of deep concentration. Simoñ turned to leave and his mother touched his arm, "Wait, we had better discuss it now. Tonight might be too late."

Simoñ turned back to face her in surprise, "Too late? Too late for what, mother?"

As they walked slowly toward their small, adobe casa, neither said a word until Simoñ finally stopped and turned toward his mother. "You know I love you with every breath I breathe, and nothing which has happened in the past can change that."

Maria looked into her son's eyes for a moment and then looked away, as she continued to walk. Simoñ hurried to catch up with her and continued, "It is difficult for you to talk about, isn't it? Never mind, there is nothing to explain, mother. I understand and my love for you remains the same. It is strong with respect and admiration. No one could love his mother any more than I do you, please believe me."

"Oh, Simoñ," Maria turned and hugged her tall son. "I am so sorry to have marked you in such a way. It is such a terrible burden for you to have to carry for the rest of your life."

"No, mother, do not talk in this way. I will not permit you to do this to yourself."

They entered the house and she sank into a chair as she began, "It happened when I was a very young and very foolish girl, before I met Benito and before the patron was married."

The youth knelt and grasped his mother's hands. "I meant it when I said that I understood. Please, I beg of you, let us not talk about this ever again."

Tears shone in his mother's eyes as she reached to place both hands on his cheeks. "You are so sensitive, and so intelligent, you give me so much pride!"

"Now let us return and continue with our visiting and enjoy our friends while they are here." Simoñ rose, smiled, and drew his mother to her feet.

"You are right," Maria conceded. "You join the young men and I'll return to my friends." She brushed the tears from her cheeks with the back of her hand.

The night before they were to leave for Chimayo, Simoñ lay on his straw filled bed with his hands folded behind his head as he stared at the ceiling through the darkness. All was completely still throughout the hacienda as he wondered what the patron might say to him on their journey, and what his response should be. How long he lay sleepless he did not know, but a noise in the kitchen caught his attention and he turned his head in that direction. The rustling of footsteps and the sounds of wood being placed in the fireplace could be heard and presently a small light appeared as the wood caught fire and a glow shone through the thin serape which served as a door to his room. Now the first rays of the sun entered the cracks of the shutter in his window and Simoñ pushed the handwoven woolen blanket which covered him to one side and began to dress. When he entered the kitchen, his father had just seated himself at the table.

"Buenos dias, padre y madre," Simoñ greeted them.

His parents smiled at him and replied, "Buenos dias."

Their faces were drawn, proof that they also, had had little sleep.

"Maria was warming the frijoles which had been left from the evening meal and fresh tortillas were stacked by the fire. "You must not keep the patron waiting," she said softly.

"And remember," Benito added quickly in a gruff voice, "show him the respect deserved by a man of his breeding."

Simoñ glanced at his mother who turned to her cooking and then answered, "Si, padre."

Maria now opened the shutter of the kitchen window and looked toward the big house. "The lanterns over there are lit and it is time for you to go. Today you will eat breakfast with the patron at the big house."

Simoñ kissed his mother on her cheek, shook hands with Benito and walked out into the early morning. When he reached the back door of the patron's house, he took off his black widebrimmed hat and knocked on the heavy door. The door opened quickly and Patricia, one of the servants, said, "Buenos dias, Simoñ, entras."

"Gracias," Simoñ replied as he extended his hand for the customary handshake. "Como esta usted, Señora Polaco."

"Muy bien, gracias, y usted." she asked courteously.

"Esta bien," Simoñ replied nervously as he entered the large kitchen.

"Follow me, please, Simoñ, and I will show you to the dining room."

When they reached the dining room, no one was there as yet and Simoñ saw for the first time where the doña and don ate their meals and entertained their guests. A long table of burnished, dark wood dominated the room. There were six chairs on either side of the table and one at each end. The chairs were high, straight backed, and were carved with intricate designs. Lovely skyblue draperies hung at the long windows. Paintings of the patron, his wife, and other members of his family hung at intervals around the room. A massive painting of the crucifixion hung on the wall directly behind the chair at the head of the table. Before Simoñ could finish surveying the room in wonder, Patricia pulled out the first chair to the left of the head of the table and told him, "Please sit down until the don and doña arrive, which will be soon."

"Gracias," Simoñ spoke in a low voice as his eyes continued to gaze around the room, and Patricia smiled as she bustled away.

Simoñ was startled by a commanding voice as it said, "Buenos dias, Simoñ."

As he rose hastily to face the patron, Don Victor turned to indicate his wife and said politely, "This is my wife, the Doña Vivian Gomez."

"Buenos dias," Simoñ now bowed slightly and smiled. Three attendants had entered the room behind the doña and don and pulled their chairs out for them to be seated.

Don Victor then said grace and the servants began to serve breakfast. A sort of wheatmeal was served first with cream and while that was being eaten, small servings of meat were placed at the left of each plate and small bowls of frijoles at the right.

"We have eggs if you wish, Simoñ, or would you care for a little honey, perhaps?" The patron spoke kindly.

"No, thank you, Don Victor, this is fine," Simoñ replied nervously.

The patron touched his lips lightly with his napkin and smiled as he eyed the young man on his left. After breakfast, the two men walked to the stables and as they did, the patron said, "Please, my boy, don't be nervous, relax, let formality remain here at the hacienda. I want an equal companion on our trip to Chimayo. Can you do that for me?"

"I'll try, Señor," Simoñ replied.

"I'll address you as Simoñ and you address me as Victor," the patron said.

"But Señor Gomez," Simoñ protested.

"Now, now," Victor interrupted, "that is how I want it to be, once we have left the hacienda, that is, and when we return, we'll continue in the old tradition. I think you know why we must do that?"

"Si, Señor," Simoñ answered.

When they reached the stables, they found that two horses had been saddled for them and a laden packhorse stood nearby.

"Raul, give the spurs to Simoñ, please," Señor Gomez told the stable attendant. "Oh, and don't forget to give him the new boots which go with them!"

Simoñ gasped as the boy brought out the fine, handsewn riding boots and the silver inlaid spurs with the heavy rowels. He had often admired the boots and spurs which the vaqueros wore, but had never dreamed of having anything so splendid as this himself. "They are very fine," he gasped as he inspected them unbelievingly.

"Put them on, my boy, you'll have need of them on our ride. When one rides, one must dress for the occasion."

The hacienda boasted its own bootmaker and he was a master of his trade. Simoñ could justly be proud of such workmanship and fine leather. The spurs were hand forged and the silver inlay was intricately engraved in the shape of birds and leaves, for the blacksmith on the hacienda took much pride and used imagination in his work.

The two men mounted their horses and Raul slid a rifle into each of their saddle scabbards. As they trotted away from the stables, Señor Gomez outlined their trip. "Once we reach La Cueva, we will turn westward and head for Mora and then on to Tres Ritas where we will make camp for the night."

Maria saw the reflection of the sun on Simoñ's new spurs as she watched from her kitchen window. She saw Simoñ glance toward the house and seeing his mother, wave goodbye. She returned the wave and then went back to her chores thoughtfully.

As they rode, Victor began to talk. "I am going to visit Señor Polaco at Chimayo to learn what the Americanos might do with New Mexico if they ever annexed it. I wish to find out if they will permit the haciendas to continue their existence. I received word yesterday that Señor Polaco visited Santa Fe recently and presumably he has found the answer to those questions and others. I am taking you and you alone, with me Simoñ, because I want you to hear first hand what Ricardo Polaco has found out. The doña and I have no children, although heaven knows we have wanted them, and you know that you are the only living heir that I have. The Gomez Hacienda will be yours someday if the Americanos allow it, which is why I wanted you to accompany me on this mission."

Simoñ rode in silence, for he hardly knew what to reply. He had heard from Victor himself, for the first time, what he had long known, that he was indeed the son of the patron.

Victor broke into his revery. "How long have you known, Simoñ?"

"For quite a few years, fa..." Simoñ had started to say father, but stopped before he could finish the title, for he had thought of Benito.

"It's all right, Simoñ, time will help both of us on that score. Let us do what we feel comfortable with."

"Si," Simoñ answered gratefully.

They continued past the little village of La Cueva and two hours later they approached Mora. "We'll stay on the south side of the river, Simoñ." Victor urged his horse across the river just south of the village. "There are more meadows on that side and fewer obstacles for our horses. A good horseman always thinks of his horse and tries to save him all he can. We'll have some rough climbing before we're through."

As they climbed higher, they began to see elk and deer herds numbering perhaps fifty to one hundred animals and then the horses picked up the scent of and a moment later, spotted a bear and their fright was almost uncontrollable as the huge, furcovered creature lumbered from the meadow into the forest.

Don Victor began to reminisce as he watched the bear disappear into the forest, "Our ancestors can be traced back to before Spain became a country," he told his son. "Members of the Gomez family were at the sides of the king and queen when the Moors were finally driven from their last stronghold on the Iberian Peninsula at a place called Granada on the southern coast of what is now Spain. As time goes by, I'll tell you more about your heritage."

"How far back do you know about, Señor?"

"Well, Simoñ, way back there, hundreds of years before the birth of our Lord, Jesus Christ, some of our people lived in the mountains of northern Spain and the way it was related to me, those mountains made our Sangre de Cristos appear as foothills. They were studded with snow capped peaks and dangerously high with perpendicular cliffs, deep cuts and ravines, and beautiful lush valleys.

It was in that harsh, yet beautiful setting that the ancestors of present day Spain lived."

"Do you know the names of any of those people, Señor?"

Simoñ's interest gladdened the heart of Victor as he continued, "One tribe was called the Asturian and I've heard they occupied the northwest corner of the mountains. They believed in Xanas."

"Xanas?"

Victor smiled, "They believed that there were small, very small fairies who lived in the springs and small creeks and that during the night they came out of the water to sit on the rocks and dry their long hair in the moonlight."

"Did they think that they were good fairies, representing goodness?"

"I don't know, or maybe I should say I've forgotten what has been told to me, "Victor admitted.

"Were there many different tribes?" Simoñ asked with interest.

"There were the Basques and the Cantabrians who lived near each other, but east of the Asturians. The Basques had a unique language and I've heard there is no other language similar to it in the whole world. Some people have wondered if it was the language which Adam and Eve spoke, but that is pure speculation I suppose. Then there were the Galicians who lived along the eastern fringe of the mountains, and farther south lived the Lusitanians who are now called the Portuguese. The Lusitanians and the Cantabrians followed a religion called Druid which was an ancient faith. Even today, there are remnants of that religion to be found in rocky ruins throughout their tribal grounds. It is believed that they worshiped a single god, perhaps similar to our Lord. To them, mistletoe was sacred, especially if it grew on the trunks of oak trees. I've heard that their priests, dressed in long white robes, would hunt for mistletoe and when it was found it was harvested with a golden knife, but of course this is probably just legend. I'm afraid I don't know much else about that ancient faith. Ah, we approach Tres Rita and it is time to make camp and see what Patricia has prepared for us to eat. We'll get a good night's rest here and continue on our journey early in the morning."

They cared for their horses and then built a small fire to heat their food. Patricia had provided them with a plentiful supply of meats, frijoles, chile, and a sack of tortillas. While the food was warming, the two men sat nearby on a large log and talked further.

Suddenly Simoñ was silent and then he asked, "Do you hear anything?" Victor rose and listened intently and asked curiously, "What did it sound like?"

"There, I heard it again."

Now Victor exclaimed, "It sounds like voices in the distance."

"It is voices," Simoñ agreed as they withdrew into a cover of thick brush away from their fire and waited. After some minutes passed, they could more readily distinguish voices and hoofbeats approaching. Suddenly from out of the trees and into the meadow which stretched down the slope, a string of burros came into view and they could see men accompanying them on horse and mule back.

"Welcome!" Señor Gomez called as they drew near. The sound of his voice jolted the men and they reined their horses in sharply and reached for their weapons automatically.

"It's all right, we're from the Gomez Hacienda, and are on our way to visit the Polaco Hacienda," called Simoñ.

Upon hearing Simoñ, a voice replied, "Buenos noches, señores, we are from the Polaco Hacienda and are on our way to rotate our patron's sheepherders high up above us on the mesa."

The Polaco men had reached the Gomez camp by now and the overseer gave his men instructions to unload the burros and prepare to camp. This done, he rode toward them, holding out his hand, "My name is Vicente Salcido, señores, and whom do I have the honor of addressing?"

"I am Don Victor Gomez," Victor responded as he shook Vicente's hand. "And this is my son, Simoñ."

Startled at what he had heard, Vicente stammered, "Please forgive our intrusion, Señor Gomez; if we had known it was you who occupied this campsite, we would not have disturbed you. We will leave immediately and make camp farther on."

"No, please stay," Victor answered in a warm, friendly tone. "We would be honored if you would join us and tell us the news of what is happening at your hacienda."

"It is we who are honored, patron," Vicente replied in a nervous voice. He stood hat in hand. He was relieved somewhat to have his men approach the fire after caring for the animals. They carried packs and bedrolls and began to make preparations for their evening meal.

"Please, Don Victor, permit us to have the pleasure and honor of serving the evening meal," Vicente said eagerly.

Victor nodded agreeably and walked back to the log where he and Simoñ had been seated earlier. He noticed that two of the peons from the Polaco Hacienda had removed santos from their packs. They had been carried in leather slings which resembled the cradle boards which the Indians used to carry their young. The peons carefully removed the santos and with the greatest reverence they walked to where they could see their back trail and thus see the country over which they had just come and they stood holding the santos high above their heads so that the santos could see how far they had come.

"They want to show the santos where they have just come from so that they will not get lost on the return trip," Victor surmised in a whisper as he watched them. "This must be their first trip to the mesa, and they fear they could get lost."

"Surely Vicente knows the way," Simoñ commented as he too kept his eyes fixed on the Polaco peons. "Surely Señor Polaco and his mayordomo wouldn't send inexperienced men to the mesa."

"You are right, Simoñ, Vicente shows by his behavior that he, at least, knows where he is going, and he seems confident, but that does not prevent the others from asking for the guidance from a santo as further assurance of a safe return."

They watched as the two peons made sure that the santos had ample time to study the terrain over which they had just passed and then they walked up the hillside a little way, carrying their santos in both hands and high above their heads to show them the direction in which they would be traveling the following day.

It was still dark the next morning when Victor and Simoñ were awakened by the sounds of Don Polaco's crew making preparations to leave. They rose and were stomping into their boots when Vicente approached. "Please forgive our awkwardness, señores, we did not intend to wake you until we were about to leave," he apologised.

"Esta nada," Victor assured him.

"We have prepared and left breakfast for you by our fire," Vicente told them politely. "I hope you have a safe journey to the hacienda of my patron."

"Gracias mi amigo," Simoñ said in return.

"We must be on our way, señores, please forgive our early departure. We must be about the business of our patron. Adios." With a wave of his hand, Vicente walked to where his horse stood, mounted and rode to where his men waited.

"Adios," Victor and Simoñ waved and watched the line of burros and riders move up the hillside above them.

When they had eaten, they gathered their belongings and packed them securely on their pack horse and headed down the western slope of the mountain for a few miles, edging on an angle until they reached the small village of El Valle. They then proceded on to Truchas and then to Cordova. As they reached the river which separated Chimayo and Potrero, they came upon a number of women, apparently from the Polaco Hacienda, washing their clothing. Each woman had selected her favorite large rock upon which to spread and wash her clothing and as the men rode near the river, they watched the women rinsing the clothing and pounding it on the rocks, an age old custom among them.

Now they could see the home of Don Polaco, and its earth colored walls contrasted pleasantly with the green of the many huge cottonwoods which grew profusely both within and outside of the patio walls. A long, narrow portal extended the length of the front wall of the house, the roof of the porch being supported by massive ponderosa pine logs spaced at even intervals in front of the house.

They urged their horses across the river and some of the women greeted them cheerfully while others simply straightened their backs, placing their hands on their hips and watched as the riders splashed across the river below them.

A wide stone wall, waist high, completely surrounded the old casa with gates conveniently situated at intervals. At one point, tall juniper posts had been buried deeply into the ground and supported a heavy, carved gate which opened onto the main entrance.

As Victor and Simoñ rode nearer, they saw Don Ricardo Polaco stride out to meet them. He was accompanied by his son, Modesto, who was about the age of Simoñ and approximately his height and weight. He was a striking figure in his flat crowned, broad brimmed sombrero which was secured with a chin strap. His brown vest was of beautifully worked needlepoint and his trousers were of a lighter shade to compliment the vest. Their tightfitting legs were decorated with silver buttons. A wide, blue velvet sash and soft, handmade boots completed his costume. He strode proudly beside his father as his father emphasized his welcoming remarks with gestures of his hands and a wide smile. "Victor! Compadre! How good to see you! Get down! Modesto, call the stable boy to come for our guests' horses."

Modesto turned away momentarily to call and then advanced also to meet their guests. "Modesto, you remember Don Gomez and this is his son, Simoñ."

As they greeted one another, the two young men appraised their counterparts closely as they listened to their fathers speaking together. Simoñ judged that in spite of his fine clothes, Modesto appeared friendly and not excessively spoiled by his position. He might even like him.

For his part, Modesto was somewhat surprised at the attire of the young man who was Don Gomez's son, but who knew what the people on the other side of the mountain might be wearing these days! He must recommend his tailor, however, in case Simoñ saw fit to mend his habits. Although his dress was not distinguished for its style, he looked like a good enough fellow.

They followed their fathers into the house and Simoñ offered somewhat shyly, "This is a beautiful hacienda."

Modesto smiled. "Thank you for the compliment. It's nice of you to say that."

Dinner was soon served and as they ate Simoñ cast many an admiring look at the lovely, dark eyed Sylvia, Modesto's younger sister. After dinner, the women went to their rooms to rest and the quiet of the siesta settled over the hacienda. But the two young men seated themselves on one of the verandas to become better acquainted.

"Modesto," Simoñ began, "Have you seen or heard much about the Americanos?"

"I've heard about them, of course, but I've never had the pleasure of meeting any of them. The ones that I've heard about are the ones who trade in Taos. They are the trappers who trade for their furs there. I'm told they are a scruffy looking bunch, with long hair and beards and wear animal skins for clothing. Some say that if it were not for their beards, they might be mistaken for Indians, they look so wild. They must be a feisty bunch to live in the wild as they do—they probably wouldn't know how to live in civilization any more." Modesto glanced down at his elegant boots complacently as he spoke.

"You speak of the trappers, but what have you heard of the other Americanos who do not trap, but want only to trade?" Simoñ glanced over at Modesto and then leaned back comfortably and tilted his hat to shield his eyes from the strong midday glare.

"Are you trying to tell me something, or are you asking me?" Modesto also tilted his hat forward as he stared at Simoñ.

"Both, I'm very interested in the Americanos and their way of life, which must be very different from ours. For instance, do they take siestas as we do, or, as I've heard, are they too busy to spend their time at rest?"

"I can't answer that, Simoñ, you'll have to find the answer to that somewhere else." He sat up alertly and looked expectantly at Simoñ. "Are you thinking what I think you are thinking?"

Simoñ pushed back the brim of his hat and grinned, "And what are you thinking, mi amigo? Am I correct that you, too, have been thinking as I have?" He leaned forward earnestly, "We could find some answers if we rode to Santa Fe!"

Modesto wore a broad smile as he answered eagerly, "I am not very well traveled, Simoñ, I have been to Santa Fe a few times, but I have never seen any Americanos there and I have never traveled north to Taos where most of them go. The farthest I have been to the north is Peñasco and up the Chama River as far as El Rito."

"Which is farther than I've been," Simoñ assured him with a grin. "This is the first time I've left the Gomez hacienda, but before I return, I'd like to visit Santa Fe for sure, and Taos, if possible, and even other places. My feet are itching to see what's out there. I believe my destiny is out there somewhere and I can only learn about it if I stay away from the hacienda for a time."

The two young men fell silent for a few moments as they thought, and then Modesto said abruptly, "Let's do it—let's go and see what's out there! Are you game? Will you join me?"

"Join you? I'm way ahead of you, and with you of the same opinion, I have an even stronger desire to travel!"

After the siesta period had ended, the two young men approached their fathers eagerly and after much discussion, the two fathers gave in and approved of their plans.

"Your mother will never forgive me," Victor said with a rueful smile, "but I totally understand your desire to seek adventure, for it is in your blood. The Gomez family has always been in the forefront since the battle for Granada in

1492. In a way it has been my misfortune to have been saddled with my father's hacienda, and it has kept me pretty much at home, but one of your ancestors was with Captain-General Don Juan de Oñate, as an advance scout, and the Gomez family has been in the thick of it ever since." Don Victor continued, gravely now, "But before you go, however, I wish that you would both go to the church and pray for guidance." He considered a moment and then added, "And I want you to be outfitted in the manner befitting the son of a don when you reach Santa Fe."

The next morning before it was fully light, the two young men entered the church, and walking to the altar, knelt and in silence prayed to their Saviour. When they had concluded their prayers, they each lit a candle and then, when they were about to leave, Modesto turned and walked to a small statue of Christ which rested in a niche by itself. "You, who watch over everyone in Chimayo," he said in a low voice, "have worn your shoes thin once again so that once more it is time for the women to replace them."

Simoñ now approached reverently and Modesto told him of the legend of the woman who had fallen into the river and not being able to swim, cried out for Christ to save her. Later, when she reached dry land, she immediately came to the church to thank Him and found that He was as wet as she was.

Simoñ studied the small statue for a few moments and then fell to his knees and crossing himself, said a prayer. Modesto also knelt and when each had finished his prayer, they crossed themselves once more and left the little church. A few minutes later they mounted their horses and rode in the direction of Santa Fe. For protection they each had an old muzzle loading rifle.

CHAPTER II

A few miles out of Chimayo, they overtook a string of freight carretas ponderously rolling southward. The wheels of the carts were nearly six feet in height and as they turned, the friction of the wooden wheels rotating around their wooden axles emitted loud, screeching noises. The screeching sound of the ten carretas could surely be heard far in advance of the slow moving caravan.

"Where are you headed?" Simoñ asked of the the fellow who walked beside the last team of oxen.

"Santa Fe."

"Who's the boss?" Simoñ asked.

"Señor Candelaria, up front," the bull whacker replied. "He rides a big grey horse so you can't miss him. Are those rifles real?" He eyed them longingly.

"Of course," Modesto retorted indignantly.

"Huh," came the bull whacker's reply. "If you were attacked by Indians they wouldn't do you much good in their scabbards!"

"What do you mean?" Simoñ was puzzled.

"You two are young fledgings, aren't you? You're barely out of the nest." The man spoke scornfully as he approached the nigh oxen with his prod pole.

Simoñ looked down at the bull whacker as he walked his horse beside him and asked once more, "What are you aiming at?"

"Experienced travelers carry their rifles, if they're lucky enough to have them, that is, at the ready. Attackers aren't going to give you notice before they attack, you know." The bull whacker grinned broadly as he administered this bit of advice.

Simoñ and Modesto glanced at one another ruefully and then spurred their horses forward. "That must be Candelaria up ahead," Modesto pointed to the head of the line.

"Mind if we ride along with you?" Simoñ asked as they reined in beside the rider on the tall grey horse.

Señor Candelaria glanced quickly from one to the other and then relaxed as he asked, "Where are you headed?" He then fell silent.

"To Santa Fe. Aren't you going to ask us some questions?" Modesto looked inquisitively at the wagon master.

Candelaria glanced around, "One look at you two and the first thing I want to do is wipe your noses, you're so green. What are you doing out without your papas?

"What?" Simoñ and Modesto spoke simultaneously in anger.

"Take those rifles out of the scabbards and keep them at the ready," Candelaria advised sternly, "or if you don't want to do that, at least permit two of my men to carry them. Most of my men don't have the luxury of owning a rifle. They must depend on bows and arrows and the steel tipped lance, and not even all of them have a lance." Even as he spoke, he reined in his horse sharply and was still, as he listened.

"What's the matter?" Modesto asked nervously.

Candelaria whirled his horse and raced back toward the carretas yelling, "Indians! Indians!"

Simoñ and Modesto raced after him as the first shot was heard, and the yelling Apaches charged toward the carretas from behind a thick stand of willows which fringed the meadow they had been crossing. A number of bull whackers fell at the first Apache volley and the Apaches rode right through the string of carretas and on into the brush at the far side of the meadow.

"Everyone get on the east side of the carretas," Candelaria shouted at the top of his lungs as he stood in his stirrups. "They will make another charge any minute!"

Simoñ and Modesto were amazed as they saw the bull whackers prepare to defend themselves and their caravan with the crude weapons which Señor Candelaria had mentioned earlier. Only two of them, in addition to the wagon boss, had rifles. Simoñ and Modesto now had their rifles in their hands and were crouched and waiting with the rest for the return of the Apaches. Finding themselves near Candelaria, Modesto acosted him, "Why don't your men also have weapons to defend themselves? The Apaches have them!"

"If everyone who wanted to own a rifle, was permitted to have one do you think we would put up with that corrupt government in Santa Fe?" Candelaria yelled in anger. "Now stop asking stupid questions and find a better place of concealment."

"They'll kill the rest of us on their next charge," Simoñ replied.

"And what do you propose?" Candelaria asked sarcastically.

"Charge them just before they reach the carretas," Simoñ suggested.

"On foot? Are you crazy?"

"Maybe, but there is one thing for sure, and that is the Apaches will be surprised by such a move and that element of surprise could give us a chance at least."

Candelaria considered a moment and then called to his men, "Come here, everyone—listen to this man and we'll try what he suggests."

Instructions were issued quickly by Simoñ and they got into position as the Apaches began their second charge. The Apaches were obviously startled when the Mexican traders did not shoot or release their arrows, but waited until the Indian attackers were within perhaps thirty yards and then they made a charge toward the mounted Apaches with their pointed lances, yelling at the top of their lungs as they charged.

One after another of the Apaches fell from their horses as the gunshots and lances struck home and the remainder wheeled their mounts and returned to the shelter at the edge of the meadow.

"Will they make another charge?" Modesto asked breathlessly.

"It is obvious that you do not know Apaches," Candelaria said as he studied the retreating Indians. "Your firepower helped turn the tide," he admitted, "but the Apaches are not fools, so don't mistake their prudence for cowardice. There is not one drop of cowardly blood in the Apaches, but they fight only when they believe that the odds are heavily in their favor. Right now I'll bet they will care for their dead and wounded and wait to catch us at a later date." He thought a moment and then continued, "If we move out now, and don't bother their dead, it's my guess they will let us pass. Move the oxen!" he yelled to his men.

The men quickly got their oxen under way once more after gathering their dead, all the while keeping a close watch out for another possible attack.

Three miles down the trail, Candelaria gave orders to halt and Modesto immediately asked, "Why are we stopping?"

"To bury our dead and to give the Apaches time to bury their dead," the freight master answered.

"I think we'll move on, Señor Candelaria," Simoñ told him. "Unless you think we can of further assistance here? If we are needed, we will remain with you."

"No, you go on," Candelaria replied as he pointed his hand toward Santa Fe. "We can manage from here on. Pojoaque isn't too far ahead, and from there to Santa Fe should pose no further danger. The Apaches no doubt will gather their dead and disappear into the mountains. I want to thank you for the assistance you gave us and hope that someday we can return the favor."

"It was our pleasure," Simoñ told him earnestly. "Until we meet again then, Vaya con Dios."

"The same to you both!" Candelaria called after them, as they reined their horses toward Pojoaque.

"We're not going to Pojoaque, are we?" Modesto asked.

"Why not? Is there a better route to Santa Fe?" Simoñ looked at his friend inquiringly.

"Boy!" Modesto shook his head. "I hope God watches over us, or at least assigns one of his angels to do so because we're ignorant of everything!" He followed his remark by making the sign of the cross and Simoñ followed suit.

"Do you think we're as green as Candelaria said?" queried Simoñ.

"Well, here we are, two young sprouts leaving the nest for the first time. I've never been farther away from home than Chama and you've never even traveled that far. If any two people needed watching, it's us!"

"Young sprouts grow," Simoñ countered with a chuckle. "And we'll do just that. Sure we are ignorant of the ways of the world, but we will learn fast. Everyone has to start somewhere and it is time we were out seeking adventures as did our ancestors."

"Let's bypass Pojoaque and head due south to San Diego," Modesto suggested. "We will save time and reach Santa Fe sooner. San Diego isn't too far from Santa Fe."

"Is that the route you people from Chimayo travel when you go to Santa Fe?" Simoñ asked in surprise.

"If we are in a hurry, yes," Modesto assured him with a grin.

It was late afternoon which they reached the outskirts of Santa Fe. "Welcome to Santa Fe," Modesto told his friend as they rode up a dusty street toward the plaza.

"So this is where I will meet the Americanos," Simoñ watched with interest the people going about their business.

"Is that the only reason you've wanted to come to Santa Fe, just to see the Americanos?"

"Modesto, the Americanos I will see in Santa Fe will be only a symbol to me, a symbol of the future, a symbol of how my children and grandchildren will live."

"I take it then that you are convinced that New Mexico will be annexed to the United States some day."

"From the little I have heard about the Americanos, Modesto, I believe it is inevitable, but if it does not come about, I will not have lost anything by looking into the temperament of these Americanos to try to find out what they are thinking, and planning, and seeing for the future. No one ever knows what the future will hold, but the future belongs to those who prepare for it. I intend to be one who is prepared." He broke off in excitement, "Look at all those mules, Modesto! There must be over a hundred of them, up ahead. Some are loaded, while others have nothing on their backs."

"We're entering Burro Alley," Modesto said with a chuckle. "This is one of the trading sections of the village."

As they passed the slow moving beasts, Simoñ studied them with interest, wondering what their packs contained and from where they had originated. Some carried what appeared to be top heavy stacks of pinon wood which swayed as the little beasts minced down the street.

"Those packs contain anything their owners think might sell here in Santa Fe," Modesto explained.

Simoñ noticed how poorly dressed the keepers of the burros were as some of them removed their sombreros as the mounted strangers passed by.

"Most are peons, obviously," Modesto said softly.

"Peons today, Modesto, kings tomorrow," Simoñ said as he glanced at his friend.

Modesto was startled. "And what is that supposed to mean?"

"One day you'll understand my friend," Simoñ replied as they approached the plaza. "So this is the end of the Santa Fe Trail. I wonder when the next wagon train will arrive with the Americanos?"

They sat their horses and studied the area. "I suppose those buildings over there are the government buildings?" He turned for confirmation to Modesto.

"Yes, over there is the Palace of Governors, which is the official residence of the governor and where the officials who help him govern also have their offices. As you can see, the whole area is enclosed within a wall. The soldiers are quartered behind the Palace or Casa Real as it is called for it has a compound of its own which houses the governor's personal guards, and includes stables, kitchens, and buildings for carriages. Of course the governor lives there as well as governs from there. The entire compound is a fortress in itself, don't you think, Simoñ?" He watched as his friend inspected the massive outer walls surrounding the thick walled adobe structure within it.

"I can see now why our Spanish ancestors chose that compound to hold out against Popé and his followers during the revolt of 1680, for it looks impregnable," Simoñ said at length.

"Tortillas, señores? Would you like to buy some tortillas?" The voice of a small boy interrupted their inspection, and Simoñ turned to the small urchin inquiringly.

"Would you like to buy some tortillas, señor?"

Simoñ looked down at the ragged, barefooted boy and said, "No, we don't want your tortillas, but if you will direct us to the nearest church and tell us of a good place to spend the night you will earn a silver coin."

The thin arm of the boy gestured eagerly, "The nearest church, señor, is across the Rio de Santa Fe, about two and a half blocks south on the Santa Fe Trail. It is called the chapel of San Miguel, and you cannot miss it. The best place to stay is..."

Here Modesto interrupted, "We'll stay where my family always stays when we're here."

Simoñ leaned from his saddle and placed the coin in the boy's eager hand. "Thank you, muchacho, for your assistance."

The boy clasped the coin tightly and grinned, "Vaya con Dios, señors. I will light a candle in the church for your safety and good health."

"Now there is a happy boy, Modesto, but I hope our safety doesn't altogether depend on his lighting a candle!" Simoñ turned to watch the boy scurry into an alley way.

"And you will be one poor hombre if you dispense silver coins to every beggar or poor wretch you come across in Santa Fe."

"Are there that many?"

"Si, and more," Modesto said soberly. "Let's hope that one doesn't tell the rest of them of your generosity."

"Let us go to the church and thank our Saviour for our safe arrival, Modesto," Simoñ suggested as he reined his horse in that direction.

As the two young men left the Chapel of San Miguel, they saw a priest talking with a man and woman. The man held his black, broadbrimmed sombrero in his hand chest high, and they could hear him beseech the priest, "Pray for them, padre."

"I will, my son, I will," the priest assured him as the couple turned to leave. The priest started to enter the church and saw Simoñ and Modesto as they watched the man and woman walk away slowly and Simoñ asked, "Is there anything we can do, padre?"

"I don't think so, my son," the priest replied, "but I thank you for asking. Only God can help, through prayer, which I am about to do as soon as I am inside. The Comanches have captured two of his daughters and have taken them into the Llano Estacado, no doubt. There is no way that they can be rescued from the heartland of the Comanche nation."

"We are truly sorry, padre." Modesto spoke for them both.

"Pray for them, my children." He turned and entered the church swiftly.

Simoñ and Modesto hurried away and overtook the stricken couple. "How long has it been since the Comanches took your daughters?" Modesto asked.

"Two weeks ago." The man removed his sombrero once more and bowed slightly.

"My name is Simoñ Gomez and my friend, here, is Modesto Polaco," Simoñ told them.

"My wife, señores, is Bernadette and my name is Ysidro Garcia. We are from El Rancho de las Golondrinas, which is south of here. Our patron was gracious enough to allow us to come to Santa Fe to see the priest concerning our daughters, but there seems to be little hope."

"We are truly sorry," Simoñ told them, "and I hate to ask because we don't want to raise any false hopes, but could you give us your daughters' names and ages? One never knows, we might chance to have dealings with the Comanches in the future, and if we did we could ask about your daughters."

"Bless you both," Bernadette said with deep respect. "The girls are named Rita, who is twelve, and Lucia, who is fourteen. If you should hear anything, please señores, contact us at the hacienda. We will be eternally grateful for any news, of any kind."

"We will do that," Simoñ told them.

The Garcias bowed their heads once more and turned away sadly.

"Those poor people," Modesto said as he watched them walk away hopelessly. "Since we recently declared our independence from Spain, the Indian raids have become more numerous and bold. Under Spanish rule, the soldiers at least patrolled the Llano Estacado, which had the effect of discouraging the Comanches from venturing too far into the settlements. Upon occasion, the soldiers even followed the Apaches and Utes into their strongholds, causing them to hesitate in their raiding, but now, under Mexican rule, the patrols have been halted and the Indians feel free to raid whenever and wherever they choose.

"Hundreds of men have been killed while tending their flocks and working in the fields, and an equal number of women and children have been carried away to be adopted into the various Comanche bands."

"Tell me," Simoñ asked, "would you rather live under Mexican rule and have our people killed and kidnapped as you have just described, or would you rather live under Americano rule and have Americano forts built at strategic locations to put a stop to the Indian menace?"

"What kind of question is that?" Modesto asked indignantly. "Are you suggesting that we declare our independence from Mexico and join up with the United States? If that's what you're thinking, don't say it out loud if you value your life!" He grinned and added ruefully, "I still cherish mine! And what makes you think the Americanos would build forts and defend our people any better than we have?"

"I'm not suggesting anything, just asking a hypothetical question, that's all," Simoñ protested defensively.

"That's all? You were just asking a hypothetical question? Well, forget that kind of question. You're talking treason, and the penalty for treason in New Mexico is death, Simoñ. Just forget it and I implore you in the strongest terms to forget it. Do I make myself clear? Because if you continue with this line of talk, I'm leaving for home right now. You're not in touch with the real world; you've been tucked away at the Gomez Hacienda all of your life and you have little conception of how things really are and how they really function. We live in a country which is authoritarian, for the government has complete power over every facet of our lives.

"The governor literally has everyone's life in the palm of his hand. He can order us snuffed out by the wave of his hand and we have no recourse, whatever the grievance which might be imposed upon us. We are a totally subjugated people." In his eagerness to convince his friend, Modesto was vehement in his persuasion, but finally paused to draw a deep breath and it was then that he saw that Simoñ wore a broad smile.

"Now it is you who sound like a revolutionary, it is you who should calm down, not I!"

"Now what the hell is that supposed to mean?" Modesto flushed angrily.

"That I agree with your assessment of New Mexico's problem," Simon assured him hastily, "but even though I have been tucked away on my father's hacienda all of my life, I, too, can think and wonder about the future. Modesto, what you have just said about Mexico and New Mexico is quite true, but I take it one step further, a step which you have obviously overlooked. You were raised as the son of a patron and have enjoyed all of those privileges which automatically come with belonging to that social class. Whereas I, however, was born and raised as a peon and belonged to a class which enjoys none, or at most, very few privileges of any kind. To many peons, their patron fits the discription which you have given to the governor, having complete control of their lives. Think about that, Modesto, for a minute."

"Think about what?"

"Calm down, my friend, and let's think this thing through, in a rational way. As more and more Americanos come into New Mexico, how do you think they are going to react to our authoritarian form of government with its monopolized economic system?"

"I suppose that they will want to break the monopolies or at least try to open up this area for free trade, and if..." Modesto hesitated for a moment before he continued, "now I see what you're getting at. You think that the peons will learn of the freedom which the Americanos enjoy and begin to demand those same rights for themselves as more and more Americanos come to New Mexico. It could be just a matter of time before the peons revolt."

"Now you're beginning to think like me," Simoñ said. "Do you think the peons are capable of mounting such a revolution?"

"Not in the near future," Modesto answered slowly, "but eventually someone will capture the loyalty and trust of the peons and then the revolution will come."

"What if no leader emerges soon, at least not before the Americano philosophy of government and economics flood our state and our people begin to show an interest in the Americano system? What then?"

"It could fuel the revolutionary fervor, I suppose," Modesto replied.

"Do you think it is possible that some of our people will begin, at some point down the road, to want to secede from Mexico and be annexed to the United States?"

"That is possible," Modesto answered slowly.

"Modesto, all I have been trying to do, if possible, is decide what the future holds for us. That is why I want to talk with as many Americanos as we can, to try to understand them better. Knowledge is a powerful weapon. It is the key which can unlock many doors, doors which could prevent heartache and suffering. I am searching for the truth, my friend, as best as I can determine what the truth is. Truth can be the bricks which are used to build strong, sturdy and happy homes, countries, and lives. I will continue to search for the truth, evasive as it may be, because therein lies the fulfillment for a serene, happy, and productive existence."

"Are you sure you've never been away from the Gomez Hacienda before?" Modesto asked with a grin. "Surely you must have been exposed to books!"

"I can't even read, what use are books to a person who cannot read? But I mean to remedy that. Now let's see more of Santa Fe and find some Americanos to question."

They spent two months in Santa Fe, and during this period, Simon had the opportunity to speak to many people of all walks of life, from the lowly peons, to the government officials, soldiers, Mexican mountainmen, housewives, traders, and especially to any Americano with whom they came into contact.

These they questioned more intently than any of the others, and when even Simoñ had satisfied his thirst for the knowledge he sought, the two friends left Santa Fe to travel back to the Gomez Hacienda by way of Las Vegas.

CHAPTER III

Twenty miles west of Las Vegas, Modesto turned to Simoñ and said, as he stared and nodded northward, "A few miles in that direction is located what the patrons call La Alambrera, (the cage)."

Simoñ glanced with interest at Modesto and then looking toward the rolling hills to the north asked, "La Alambrera?"

"Somewhere in those forested mountains and hidden valleys, from what I've heard, is a place which is a living hell for those unfortunate enough to be taken there," Modesto explained somberly. He followed this strange statement by making the sign of the cross as he continued to gaze in that direction.

Simoñ followed suit, although he didn't understand the significance of his friend's remark. "A living hell?" He crossed himself once more and looked to the heavens. "Dear Mary, Mother of God, forgive my friend, for he does not know what he is saying."

"What I'm saying is not sacrilegious, my friend, but those who operate that hell hole out there and those of us who patronize it, practice blasphemy and worse."

"Those of us?"

"Yes, those of us in the upper social class who patronize La Alambrera."

"What is this place called La Alambrera?" Simoñ was losing his patience.

"La Alambrera is a correctional institution for rebellious slaves who continue to try to escape or cause trouble at their haciendas. Señor Aguilar, the owner and overseer of this place, breaks the slaves of their bad habits, but sometimes he does not succeed."

"Mercy of the angels!" Simoñ once again crossed himself and his face became very sober as his words drifted off to a mere whisper, saying softly "Surely you are joking."

"No, my friend, I wish I were. I do not joke, for La Alambrera is nothing to joke about."

"Why have I never heard of this place?"

"It is a very tightly kept secret, Simoñ, not all patrons know about it, only some of them know of it and patronize it."

"What about the governor?" Simoñ had reined in his horse and sat gazing at the now forbidding juniper, cedar, and pinon covered mountains to the north. "He knows about it, but forbids anyone to talk of it, for obvious reasons."

"You said earlier that sometimes Señor Aguilar does not succeed in breaking the slaves of their bad habits. What did you mean?" Simoñ asked as he slowly placed his right hand on the horn of his saddle and gazed down at it.

"That sometimes they die as a result of Señor Aguilar's over zealous attempts to succeed."

"Oh, my God," breathed Simoñ. He turned to Modesto and asked in a harsh voice, "Do you think we could locate this La Alambrera?"

"What? Are you crazy? Why would anyone want to visit La Alambrera? Are you a sadist?"

"You insult me with such an accusation, Modesto," Simoñ replied quietly.

"I'm sorry, I didn't mean it the way it sounded—it's just, well, why would you want to visit that horrible place anyway? Isn't just hearing about it bad enough?"

"If we are this close to it, I want to see for myself what it looks like and what goes on there. If, in the future, the matter comes up in conversation, I do not want to be asked, "Have you seen the place of which you speak or has someone else told you about it? Perhaps someone's vivid imagination!" He paused and then went on grimly. "I want to be able to answer that I saw it for myself."

"All right," Modesto said as he considered this viewpoint and then reined his horse northward. "Let's try to find it."

For the remainder of that day the two rode over the rock covered forested hills and across arroyos, small valleys, and meadows, and canyons without finding a trace of La Alambrera.

"Are you sure there is such a place?" Simoñ reined in his horse and dismounted to stretch his legs. "It seems to me that we should have at least come across the trail which these people use to get in and out of the place."

Modesto also dismounted and said with a laugh, "I'm going to do what you have been doing every since we teamed up, and that is, ask you questions until you have answered your own original question. Now, Simoñ, if you wanted to have La Alambrera kept a secret, how would you do this?"

"Swear all of the patrons to secrecy?"

"How would you prevent a returned slave from telling those at his hacienda about La Alambrera?"

Simoñ thought a moment and then offered, "Threaten him with some kind of punishment?"

"What if such threats did not succeed?"

"Then discredit the slave's story," Simoñ answered.

"Who would be the best person to use in discrediting such a tale?" Modesto crossed himself even as he asked.

"The priest!" Simoñ also crossed himself and shook his head in disbelief. "Why would a priest be a willing ally in keeping that place secret?"

"To save the souls of the Indian, if not the Indian himself, because as long as the Indian lives under the roof and protection of the patron, he will eventually be converted to Christianity. It's the old Spanish encomiendas system. Am I right?" Simoñ looked inquisitively at Modesto.

"Riiight," Modesto replied as he strung out the word.

"Continue, my teacher!" Simoñ said with a grim smile.

"Are you serious?"

"Si," Simoñ replied. "How else can one learn?"

"All right," Modesto said. "Continue it will be, but first let's make camp and hunt for something to eat."

As they sat before a little fire later that night, Simoñ asked, "Have you ever attended school anywhere?"

"Si," came Modesto's reply. "My father enrolled me in the University of Mexico when I was fifteen, and I completed my studies there about two years ago. Before that I had been enrolled in a school to learn the fundamentals."

"Well, then, I have a source of information to draw upon as questions arise," Simoñ said with a grin.

"I hope I can answer some of them at least," Modesto chuckled.

"For starters, what kind of Indians do you think we would most likely find at La Alambrera?"

"I've already told you that," Modesto answered. "Rebellious, or otherwise troublesome, high spirited Indians."

"No," Simoñ continued, "I mean from which tribes?"

"Probably mostly from the Apache or Comanche nations, I would guess."

"None from the pueblo tribes?" Simoñ asked.

"I doubt it."

"Why not?"

"Well, it has always been much easier for the Spaniards to assimilate the pueblo tribes into their culture because they have been more stationary, living in durable homes of permanent structure. It was much easier to conquer these people, because once their pueblo cities were captured, they gave in. It's been a different story with the Apaches and Commanches. Whereas the pueblo people are pastoral, the others are nomadic, roaming everywhere. They have no permanent towns or dwellings to hold them, and when the Spaniards attacked them, they melted into the environment, disappearing. It was and still is, impossible to defeat them and so the Spaniards employed the encomienda system of assimilation upon them."

"So that is why we will probably find only Apache or Commanche slaves at La Alambrera," mused Simoñ.

"We could find some Utes, or even some pueblo Indians, Simoñ, for no doubt there are still some pueblo Indians who dream of a time that once was, and wish to return to it, especially the ones who have tried to retain their religion."

"Wouldn't you, if the conditions were reversed?" asked Simoñ quickly.

"Absolutely," Modesto answered, "but the conditions are not reversed, for the Spaniards came, saw, and conquered, and that, my friend is a time honored custom, to the conquerors go the spoils."

"But does that make it right?"

"Until a more humane system is devised, yes," Modesto answered without hesitation. "Right or wrong is not considered. The Spaniards believe that they are right and that their culture is superior to that of the Indians. The Indians, however, believe theirs is superior, but the Spaniards are the conquerors and so the conquerors impose their civilization upon the conquered. It is that simple. It has always been that way."

"Do you apply that theory to the peonage system also, Modesto? The aristocrats dominate so they dictate the social order of our day?"

"I suppose that is correct," Modesto replied slowly.

"In America, from what we have learned in our talks with the Americanos, there is no social class. Everyone is equal, which means that no one class dominates. How do you suppose the peons will react when they learn of the Americano system?"

"Heaven only knows," Modesto replied impatiently. "I'm no gypsy who can peer into a crystal ball and fortell the future."

"Come, come, Modesto, your aristocratic upbringing is beginning to show," Simon told him with a chuckle. "Who in their right minds would choose domination over equality and freedom?"

"You might be surprised how many would," Modesto replied.

"No, I wouldn't, and neither would you, my friend, but change is in the wind. I can smell it, and remember, just as you have said, Modesto, to the conqueror go the spoils. And the time is coming when the Americano system will conquer."

"Maybe so," admitted Modesto who was tiring of this tedious conversation. "But I, for one, will not like to see it come to that."

"You had better begin to change your thinking because it is on the way, just as surely as the sun will rise in the morning. You cannot stop change once the time for that change has arrived."

Modesto brooded for a time and then admitted, "You could be right, for many in history have tried to prevent such change, but they have failed in the end. A lifestyle is a conditioned response, too," he went on, "and regardless of the time or place, many will prefer to hold on to the system which they have lived under all of their lives. To these it is a system that they are comfortable with and can understand. Change brings confusion and breeds mistrust. No,

Simoñ, do not believe that all wish for or want change."

"You have a point there, a good point, my friend. It's time right now for us to get some sleep. We have to find La Alambrera tomorrow, that is if there is such a place."

There is, it's out there somewhere, believe me, "Modesto said grimly. "Though why we haven't found it or a trail which might lead to it, I don't know."

Because there isn't much of a trail?" suggested Simoñ.

"No trail? Why not?"

"For the simple reason that if there is no well marked, well traveled trail to La Alambrera there is nothing for the curious to follow."

Modesto grasped this thought and said, "Those who travel to La Alambrera approach it in such various directions that no actual trail is made. Going to such lengths to conceal it certainly reinforces my opinion of what goes on there!"

"I smell smoke," his friend said suddenly as he sniffed the air. "That smoke may lead us to La Alambrera tomorrow."

They were on their way the following morning just at daybreak, riding in the direction from which the smoke had traveled. They had ridden perhaps twenty minutes when Simoñ pointed off to their left. They could see smoke spiraling lazily into the air over the tree tops on a nearby hill. They reined their horses in the direction of the rising smoke and rode through arroyos, crossed a meadow and over that hill and then another, before, from the vantage point of their height they overlooked La Alambrera. As they sat their horses gazing down into the valley below, Simoñ said, "Aguilar sure selected a beautiful location for his operation. Plenty of grass in the valley and it appears that there is a spring near the buildings. Look how huge the trees are, a sure sign of an abundance of water. Let's go down and introduce ourselves, Modesto." As the two approached the crudely constructed building which was the largest, a sense of fear and embarrassment crept over them. Fear for the inmates and what they must endure and embarrassment that it was the patrons who made such a place possible. The place wasn't what Simoñ had visualized. He had expected a well arranged group of buildings constructed in such a manner that they would show organization and planning. Instead, the only building of any consequence had been built hastily of whatever material came to hand. Constructed of rock, logs, and some adobe bricks, it was only partially plastered with mud. Whoever had been in charge of building this place had given no thought to beauty, thickness or proper dimensions of the walls. The doors and windows were not square, and the pitch of the roof was not even or level. To the east side of the building could be seen three small huts and these also had been thrown up indiscriminately. In front of these structures was a stockade built of cedar posts which extended at least ten feet in height. This stockade was massive and boasted watch towers at each corner. On them the two friends could see guards lazily looking down into the stockade which they guarded.

The only commonplace features to be seen were a garden and a row of fruit trees not far from the stockade, but these did little to relieve the harshness of their surroundings.

"I don't think I'm going to like this place and what goes on here," Simoñ muttered softly as his eyes roamed in every direction.

"Hidalgos approaching!" One of the guards announced their approach in a yell, and within a few seconds two men hurriedly emerged from the large structure. Their appearance left no doubt that they occupied a place much lower on the social scale than the lowest peon. Their clothes were drab and ill fitting, they were unshaven, and their hair extended to their shoulders and was ragged and matted. Their legs were encased in worn and soiled moccasins which extended to their knees.

"Welcome señores, get down," the largest of the two men said with a forced smile as Simoñ and Modesto reached them. "My name is Benito Aguilar. I am the owner and operator of this place." He turned to his companion and said, "Take care of the dons' horses, Enrique, pronto!" After he barked the order he turned back to the newcomers and said, "Come in, señores and tell me what I can do for you."

"We are late for a wedding already, Señor Aguilar, and we cannot stay, but thank you for your warm hospitality just the same," Simoñ told him as he dismounted. "I understand that you can educate slaves who misbehave. Is that correct?"

"That is correct, señores, I educate them as you have said, and if they cannot be educated, then they will have no futher need for education," Aguilar said with complacency.

"I see," Simoñ replied. "I have one such slave who needs such education in the worst way. When can I send him to you?"

"Whenever it pleases you, señor," Aguilar said eagerly

"How long do you estimate it will take to educate him?"

"It depends upon how slow the learner is," Aguilar answered with a grin.

"Would it be possible to see your instruments of learning?" Modesto asked.

"It would be my pleasure to have you observe my classes," Aguilar replied. "Follow me, señores."

Simoñ and Modesto followed Aguilar to the stockade and up a stepladder to the top of one of the guard platforms. When they reached this height, they beheld below them, within the stockade, five slaves shackled to five separate individual posts. All five of them were sitting on the ground leaning their heads or shoulders against the posts. Their hands were locked to iron shackles which were attached to chains which in turn were bolted to the top of each post. They were clad in rags and their lack of food was evident in their physical conditions. Their eyes were cast downward and they were motionless. As first glance one would think that the slaves were not alive or human beings at all, but merely images of humans.

Simoñ turned to Aguilar and asked, "How are these slaves being educated?"

"They are made to do hard, physical work for from fourteen to sixteen hours a day, seven days a week, week after week, until I break their spirits. They are fed a minimum amount of food and water each day, just enough to keep them alive."

"Where are their quarters?" Simoñ asked without taking his eyes from the slaves below.

"Quarters, señor?" Aguilar looked surprised. "There are no quarters. Where they sit at this very moment are the only quarters they will ever have here. That is part of their education. Conditions are made purposely as hard as possible so they will realize how good their masters have been to them, and how wise it would be for them to accept their conditions in life and how futile it is to resist. Once they come to this point in their thinking and are returned to their haciendas, they realize their duties there were not as harsh as they once thought." He grinned wolfishly as he concluded.

"Aguilar, let's get down off of this platform and go for a walk," Simoñ suggested.

Simoñ, Modesto, and Aguilar reached the ground and began to walk slowly away from the stockade. "Aguilar, I must confess to you," Simoñ said, "I do not have a slave to be educated. I am Captain Simoñ Gomez and this is Sergeant Polaco. We were sent to find you and your establishment and arrest you."

Aguilar jolted to a halt looking up quickly, his eyes narrowing.

"Now wait a minute and hear me out before you do anything rash, Aguilar. Pressure, very heavy pressure, has been put on the governor from people high up in the government, including those in Mexico City and even from the Archbishop. The governor ordered me, with a troop of soldiers who are camped not far from here, to arrest you for running a business without a license, among other things, mostly because you have not shared your profits. While you have furnished a service to the patrons, who will not be arrested for breaking the law, you will bear the full brunt of it by yourself. They, because of their social positions, will not be touched. It seems to me to be unjust." Simoñ paused to assess the effect of his words on the silent Aguilar and then continued, "Now if you and your men should happen to leave here, and go to somewhere far from New Mexico, some place like California, say, I could report to my superiors in about a week or two, and tell them that I found La Alambrera, but it was deserted, abandoned. By that time you and your men could be well away."

"You would do this for me? Why?" Aguilar stared distrustfully at Simoñ.

"I have my reasons, Aguilar. I am young and I have political plans for myself. You might say that I am very ambitious and certain persons in positions of importance could prevent my rising to higher office. If I can embarrass them, it will not hurt my chances for advancement. It is as simple as that. As I see it, this action of letting you go would aid me more than my taking you in."

Aguilar stared into Simoñ's eyes for long moments and then said, "We will leave immediately."

"Go south," Simoñ said, "because my soldiers are camped west of here. If they see you, I'll have no choice but to arrest you and take you in. Give me the keys so we can unlock the shackles on the slaves."

Aguilar said no more as he tosed the keys to Simoñ yelling to his men as he did so and began to walk away. Within fifteen minutes they were all on their way.

"They are traveling light," Modesto chuckled as he watched Aguilar and his men disappear into the trees. "that was a big gamble, Simoñ. I think we had better free the slaves and get out of here before Aguilar has second thoughts and realizes that he has been tricked."

"Si, I suspect you're right!" Simoñ tossed the keys in the air and caught them again as he grinned broadly.

The two young men walked over to the gate of the stockade, opened it and entered. The gate was hung on large wooden hinges which made a loud, screeching noise as it swung open. The noise turned the heads of two of the slaves who looked apathetically in that direction. The other slaves made no effort to look up. "Simoñ," Modesto said, "we are in a dangerous position."

"What do you mean, dangerous?"

"We are only two and there are five of them. What will they do when we free them?" Modesto eyed the slaves doubtfully. "Will they leave peaceably or will they turn on us?"

"Why in heaven's name would they turn on us? We are going to free them!"

"Simoñ," Modesto pointed out, "first of all we are Spaniards. It was we who took their land from them. We forced and sold many of them into slavery and forbade them to practice their religion under penalty of death. We also restricted their travel and forced them to live under our laws. There are many other reasons for them, these five at least, to show animosity toward us. We are patrons or sons of patrons, remember it is patrons who are responsible for their being here in the first place. When we free them, they could turn on us and kill us or they could even turn on each other. Those first two appear to be Comanches; the third I would guess belongs to the Acoma pueblo; the fourth is probably from the Cochiti pueblo, and the last one looks very much like an Apache, perhaps a Mescalero. Now the Mescaleros are traditional enemies of the Comanches and the two Comanches and the Apache could turn on the Cochiti and Acoma Indians and kill them. We don't know of the circumstances of their being here or what has happened to them since they have been here. We have weapons and horses, they have neither. What would you expect them to do, walk back to their people? No, Simoñ, we could be in a very dangerous spot."

"You have a good point, what do you propose we do?'

"First, we must talk to them and then I believe we should let them go one at a time except for the Comanches. We could free them together. We should give them ample time to travel a safe distance before freeing another." Modesto thought a moment and then resumed, "And another thing, Simoñ, the Apache and Comanches will, without a doubt, steal some horses or burros and food and clothing from some unsuspecting and unfortunate who happens to live in their path homeward. They might even kill them to get what they need. All this could happen just because we came here to do a good deed."

"I guess we are simpletons," Simoñ said, "or at least I am, for I have acted without thinking through what could come about because of my actions. What should we do? Shall we go after Aguilar and turn the place back to him? Surely not."

"It's too late for that, even if we wanted to. No, we'll have to find another solution," Modesto replied.

"I'll talk to them, maybe that will help us to decide. Maybe something they will say will help us to find a solution," Simoñ finally suggested.

"It won't hurt and we have to do something. Talking to them won't worsen our position at this point. But Simoñ, don't unshackle any of them until we get our horses into the stockade and I am a good distance from them and have my rifle ready."

"I agree," Simoñ began to walk toward the five prisoners, who stared up at the tall, handsome young man who approached them. "My name is Simoñ Gomez and my friend here is Modesto Polaco. We heard about this place and came to see if what we had heard was correct, and it is true, perhaps even worse. We lied to Aguilar, telling him that we were officers in the army with orders to take him back to Santa Fe. I told him our troops were within a short distance of here and to make a long story short, Aguilar has gone and now we want to free all of you."

The Cochiti and the Acoma stared in disbelief at the two young men, but the Comanches and the Apache stared at the ground in front of them, giving no sign that they had either heard or understood.

Not discouraged, Simoñ continued, "I know that you are not clothed properly to make the journey back to your people, nor do you have transportation, but Aguilar might have left some clothing in the building and ..." Modesto interrupted at this point, saying, "There are burros back there. They were near our horses when I went to get them."

"So," Simoñ said in relief. "You will have transportation of a sort. Now I will let the Acoma Indian go first. One hour later I will release the Cochiti. An hour after that I will release the Comanches and an hour later, the Apache."

"Which way do you journey?" The Cochiti spoke slowly as he glanced at the Comanches.

"Toward Las Vegas," Simoñ replied. "Why do you ask?"

"Could I travel with you?" The Cochiti looked hopefully at Simoñ.

Coming closer, Modesto muttered, "He's afraid of the Apache and the

Comanches, and I don't blame him."

"I, too, would like to travel with you," the Acoma said as he rose slowly and looked at their deliverers.

"Don't you want to return to your families?"

"I want to purchase some supplies to take back to my village," said the Acoma.

"I, too," volunteered the Cochiti.

Simoñ turned to Modesto and whispered, "They don't have any money to purchase anything!"

"No," Modesto answered, "but they can have the safety and protection of our company and that will cost them nothing. They just want the Apache and Comanches to know that they will not be returning to their tribal lands for awhile and that way they hope that they won't track them down once they leave here. Away from here they will probably part company with us, going their separate ways. Why don't you tell them that they are welcome to join us?"

On the morning of the third day after they had left La Alambrera, Simo Simoñ and Modesto found that the Acoma Indian had slipped away during the night. "Why didn't you leave also?" Modesto asked the Cochiti.

"I am in no hurry, my people and village will always be there. I still want to travel with you if you will permit me to do so. There is nothing for me at my village. I think that my life will be more exciting and maybe rewarding if I stay with you."

Simoñ looked at Modesto and Modesto smiled and said, "If you like, Cochiti. Let's get packed and be on our way. Is it all right if we call you Cochiti, or do you prefer another name?"

"It is all right, for now, anyway," the Cochiti replied eagerly.

Later, as they neared the Salvador Chavez Hacienda headquarters a few miles from Las Vegas, they came unexpectedly upon a small, one room adobe building. They reined in and Modesto studied the structure for a few seconds and then said softly, "It's a morada."

"It will be in use by the Penitentes during Holy Week," Simoñ said as he made the sign of the cross. His two companions followed suit hastily and they looked at one another soberly, perhaps wondering if any of them were Penitentes. No one wished to question the religious privacy of the others and they proceeded on toward the hacienda. It was only a short time later that they rounded a small foothill and Modesto pointed out the Chavez casa which nestled in some trees in the valley below.

The Chavez Hacienda headquarters was located on the very edge of the Llano Estacado where the foothills of the Sangre de Cristo Mountain Range and the plains met. East of the hacienda lay mile after mile of open, rolling country empty of almost any kind of vegetation except for tall grama grass.

"Just a few miles east of here is the Gallinas River, which has cut its gorge through the rich dirt of the Llano," Modesto told them. "It cannot be seen until you are upon it. You can see for miles and miles in every direction except to the west where..."

"Do you know Señor Chavez?" Simoñ interrupted.

"I have never had the pleasure of meeting him, but my father has. Señor Chavez has filled orders for my parents. You see, Simon, Señor Chavez runs his own wagon train which he sends up into the United States. People go both ways on the Santa Fe Trail, you know."

"It is obvious that he does quite a bit of freighting. Just look at his wagons and repair shops."

Wagons in various stages of repair were scattered over a wide area. The Chavez establishment could be seen more easily as the three riders grew nearer. American made wagons, with their white canvas coverings could be seen parked in neat, orderly rows near a repair and blacksmith shop. The sounds of tools clanking as they struck metal, rang through the air as the blacksmiths went about their work. Off to one side of these buildings could be seen wooden wagon axles stacked neatly as one might stack cord wood. Just west of the axles could be seen an equally large stack of wagon trees. In the distance, hundreds of oxen were grazing on the Llanos east of the headquarters. A few carretas were also scattered here and there within a fenced area, along with a few wagons which had seen better days and were now probably used for spare parts.

As the three riders approached the shops, some of the peons halted their work and looked up to watch them for a few moments, then resumed their tasks once more. One man stepped out from among them, however and walked toward them. "Welcome to the Chavez Hacienda. Can I be of assistance to you, señores? My name is Felix Alvarez. To whom do I have the pleasure of speaking?"

Simoñ introduced himself, Modesto, and Cochiti and asked, "Would you be so kind as to tell us where we can find the patron?"

"Si," Felix turned and pointed to the big house, which was perhaps one hundred yards from the wagon yard. "You will find the patron in his house, working on his books, no doubt."

"Gracias, Felix," Simoñ said as he and his companions reined their mounts in the direction of the house.

"De nada," Felix replied as he returned to his work.

Señor Chavez had been informed by servants that three strangers were approaching the house and he met them as they neared the portal which ran the length of the long building. "Get down and welcome to my home," smiled the owner of the hacienda.

Simoñ and Modesto dismounted and walked to greet Señor Chavez as Cochiti held the horses. "Buenos dias, señor, como esta usted?" Simoñ removed his sombrero as he spoke respectfully to the older man.

"Muy bien, gracias," came the reply as he shook Simoñ's hand and then that of Modesto, who introduced himself as Don Ricardo's son.

"The Indian is traveling with us," Simoñ said as he motioned to Cochiti.

"I understand," the patron said as he called to a servant. "Martin, take care of the Indio."

"I have not seen your father, Don Ricardo, for some time," Salvador said. "How are your mother and father?" He watched as Martin and Cochiti walked the horses away.

"They are fine and they would have sent their warmest regards if they had known we would see you," Modesto replied politely.

"And your brothers and sisters? Are they in good health?"

"Si, gracias."

"Amanda," Salvador commanded in a loud voice, "bring wine for my guests. We will be out here on the portal."

From within a voice could be heard faintly answering the summons of the patron. The men chose chairs and sat down while they waited for the refreshments to be brought. Simoñ told of his family at the Gomez Hacienda and Salvador Chavez politely expressed regret that he did not know Señor Gomez. "It is my loss, I am sure," he concluded as the wine was brought to them. "Now, my young friends, where are you going?"

"We're headed for Las Vegas and then on to my hacienda," Simoñ told him. "My father and I were visiting the Polacos at Chimayo not long ago and while we were there, Modesto and I decided to visit Santa Fe to learn all we could about the Americanos."

"What do you think of the Americanos?" Their host looked with interest at his young guests.

Simoñ detected a dislike of the Americanos in Salvador's tone and he decided to shift the conversation back to Señor Chavez. "I am not sure, señor, that one can make an accurate evaluation of a people by one visit alone. I am afraid that I will have to wait until I have had more contact with them before I can pass judgment on them," Simoñ replied warily.

"I do not have to wait, my young friends, because I have been doing business with the Americanos for some years now, and I think that I have grown to understand their natures and temperament," Salvador said.

"Then what is your evaluation of them?" Both Simoñ and Modesto leaned forward as Modesto questioned their host.

"You know, señores, Spain inherited much from the Moors, who themselves inherited much from the Romans. After the western half of the Roman Empire collapsed, it was overrun by the barbarians, but the eastern half survived for another thousand years. From this eastern half of the empire came a civilization that was more magnificent than any civilization in history. Spain came of age under the tutelage of this civilization. Many of our institutions have their roots buried deep in the Middle East and Northern Africa. After all, the Arabs were in Spain for six hundred years and dominated her for four hundred years. One cannot control a country for so long a time without leaving some of its culture behind. One of the institutions which we inherited from the Moors was the idea of a strong, central government under the complete control of one strong leader. A chosen few would be selected to help guide this leader. They would be members of the highest social class. We, my young friends, belong to this social class. Now, what do I think of these Americanos and their peculiar ideas that everyone is equal, that no one is superior to any other because of his breeding or social background? Such thinking is pure nonsense. Breeding is important in horses and cattle, and so it is in humans. Can a burro outrun an Arab purebred? Of course not. And so it is with people. Only our social class can govern or is equipped by background to rule for the good of everyone."

"Do you think, Don Chavez, that New Mexico will ever become part of the United States?" Simoñ leaned forward.

"Part of the United States?" Señor Chavez asked in a shrill voice which expressed his outrage at such a heretical suggestion. "Don't even mention such nonsense, Simoñ. It could get you into much trouble, serious trouble."

When Señor Chavez was not looking, Modesto kicked his friend lightly on the ankle. Simoñ got the message and stood up. "My friend and I must be on our way, Señor Chavez, you will excuse us?" I have been absent from my father's hacienda for too long."

"I understand, muchachos, I have enjoyed your visit, short though it has been. Vaya con Dios," Salvador Chavez said as he also rose to his feet. "Give my regards to both of your families." Within a few minutes, Simoñ, Modesto and Cochiti were riding north toward Las Vagas.

"You almost got us into trouble back there with your questions about the future of New Mexico, Simoñ. For God's sake, let us not speak of such things again or we'll end up in prison somewhere, or worse."

"Do you actually think that Señor Chavez would do such a thing?"

"Si, why wouldn't he? He is a patron and being a patron puts him in the ruling class and I emphasize `ruling'. Do you think that he wants to share the privileges, which he takes for granted, with the peons? He is the only person from this area who trades with the Americanos, and that means that he enjoys a monopoly given to him by the governor. He is a rico, Simoñ, a very rich and powerful man," his friend concluded soberly.

"I guess I'm learning fast, but not fast enough," Simoñ admitted ruefully. "I'm sorry if I put your safety in jeopardy. Being raised as a peon makes it difficult, very difficult for me to understand how people can willingly and purposefully, hurt other people, without a trace of compassion being shown toward their victims."

"You are a good person, Simoñ," Modesto said in a conciliatory tone. "You are even beginning to convert me, but you must guard against saying what you think at all times. Thinking cannot get you into trouble, but saying what you think to the wrong person, could."

"Modesto, does Señor Chavez really have a monopoly on the Mexican trade on the Santa Fe Trail, or is that just your supposition?"

"I'm not sure, but all of the evidence points in that direction, wouldn't you agree? If he doesn't have a monopoly, he surely has friends in high places who can reduce his competition."

"Surely there must be other ricos who also have friends in high places who could obtain permits to trade on the Trail?"

"Maybe there are. Now you are asking me questions which I have no answer for or even any interest in knowing. I may have spoken out of turn, Simoñ. Señor Chavez may not have a monopoly at all in the Santa Fe trade. All I know is that the governor does give out such favors in return for money. Our system of government is riddled with such corruption. It seems to accompany it naturally."

"And the poor peons carry all of the burden," Simoñ added grimly.

"There you go again, Simoñ," grinned Modesto. He turned back to beckon to Cochiti and asked, "Why are you so quiet? What are you thinking?"

"Thinking will not get me into trouble, but talking about what I am thinking might," grinned the Indian. "That's what you said and I think it is good advice."

"See what you have started," Modesto said to Simoñ with a smile. They were nearing the Gallinas River now, and with it, Las Vegas.

"Let's find something to eat," Simoñ suggested. They rode up a dusty street until they came to a small cantina. As they tied their horses to the hitching rack and prepared to enter, they noticed Cochiti removing his jacket and placing it over his burro's head.

"Why do you do that?" Simoñ grinned in amusement.

"By putting my jacket over his head, it will prevent him from straying and there is another, more important reason," Cochiti assured him.

"And what is that?"

"Señor patron," Cochiti said earnestly, "all burros look alike. When we return, there may be many burros tied to the rails and all will have jackets over their heads. I will know which burro is mine because I will know which jacket is mine."

Simoñ and Modesto grinned as Modesto chided Simoñ in mock reproval. "Remember that today is the burros' feast day. January 17th is celebrated in respect for the burros' Saint San Anton."

"And not just the burros are blessed by the priests," Simoñ told him, "at our hacienda all animals are blessed on that day, although when they are blessed depends upon when the priest reaches our hacienda."

"Good, I thought you were ignorant of that day, also."

"I may be ignorant of many things, but not of that," laughed Simoñ as they entered the cantina.

Several miles north of Las Vegas, they came to several little houses grouped together and they noticed three men loading two carretas. They halted in their tasks when they saw the strangers approaching and two of them walked back to lean against the door frame of one of the dilapidated buildings.

"They may have weapons just inside the door," Modesto judged softly. "They seem to be very nervous about something, something which is illegal?"

"Almost anything peons or poor people do can be judged as illegal, "Simoñ commented drily.

"That they are poor there can be no doubt, but apparently they are not peons," Modesto replied, "I don't know of a hacienda within miles."

"Buenos, tardes, señors," Simoñ greeted them.

"Buenos, tardes," one of the men replied.

"My name is Simoñ Gomez and my compadre here is Modesto Polaco, we call our Indian friend Cochiti." A smile accompanied Simoñ's introduction to show the men that they were not threatened.

"My name is Prudencio, Ramon Prudencio," the stranger said swiftly. He gave no indication that Simoñ and the others were welcome and he did not introduce the other two men. Simoñ glanced at the two by the doorway and then looked back at Ramon and said, "We are not the law, we are on our way to my father's hacienda near Ocate."

"The don and doña have no children," Ramon answered coldly.

"Would you accept his bastard son in place of a legitimate one?" Simoñ asked. Ramon stared at Simoñ in surprise and then said, "Get down and come in. We do not have any conveniences, but what we do have you are welcome to share with us."

He turned to the men by the door and introduced them with a nod of his head, "These are my brothers, Elmon and Frutoso."

They all shook hands and then walked into the little house.

Simoñ glanced around and said, "Nice place you have here."

"Thank you, Señor Gomez, for being so tactful," Ramon said grimly.

"I see that you are getting ready to go out on to the Llanos," Modesto said. What makes you think that, Señor Polaco?"

"You are Comancheros, no?" Modesto asked politely. "We are not opposed to your trade, such trade serves a good purpose. It brings trade to our people and gives them an outlet for their handmade goods."

Ramon looked from Modesto to Simoñ and then answered, "Si, we are Comancheros. My brothers and I are about to journey eastward to trade with the Comanches."

"I know," Modesto said as he glanced out toward the carretas.

"We have a special order of Navajo blankets in those carts," Ramon told them, "and we will bring back cattle in exchange for them."

"So you are ranchers, tambien (also), "Simoñ observed.

"No, we are just Comancheros, "Frutoso answered, "we do not have enough land to ranch."

"We did at one time though," Elmon interrupted and then said no more when his older brother, Ramon, gave him a cold stare.

"Forgive my younger brother, he talks too much sometimes, "Ramon said with a smile.

I understand," Simoñ said, "my father did not recognize me as his son until a few weeks ago. I was raised as a peon by my mother and the man who took responsibility as my father until then."

"Our story is reversed," Ramon said "my family once had a ranchero, but lost it. It seems that my father fell into disfavor with a new governor years ago and his land grant was taken from him."

"You mean stolen from him," Elmon interrupted angrily.

"Please forgive my brother's imprudence, señors, he is still bitter."

I can understand why," Simoñ said. "I would feel the same as he does if I were in his shoes."

"It looks as if you have fallen in with your kind of people, Simoñ," Modesto said with a grin.

"What do you mean?" asked Ramon in surprise.

Modesto spent the next few minutes telling Ramon and his brothers about Simoñ and his search for the truth. After Modesto finished, the Prudencios seemed more open and friendly.

Simoñ and Modesto could see that the Prudencios had indeed fallen into dire circumstances, for the little house was run down, with only two small windows for light. It had only one room and there were signs that the sod roof had not been successful in keeping the rain out. As they walked back outside, they noticed that the two laden carretas were in hardly better shape than some of those already discarded behind the house. A few oxen grazed contentedly in the distance and nearer at hand a three sided lean-to constructed of adobe served as a shed.

"A friend of ours has allowed us to use this small part of his hacienda as our home," Ramon explained.

"The San Miguel area, with Las Vegas as its largest village, has attracted many patrons over the years, most of whom have had dreams of building huge empires, but the Indians destroyed many of their dreams as they did our friend's, the owner of this land," Frutoso told them. "His hacienda was a large one, for it contained as much as half a million acres, but it is no more. Only scattered, small villages remain of that once happy dream. Poor people live in those villages now, people who are exposed to the repeated dangers and suffering of Indian raids.

"The Apaches and Utes come down from the north and west and the Comanches come in from the east and attack them. Life for the villagers is one of constant struggle for survival. They have no money and cannot accumulate large herds of cattle or flocks of sheep because the Indians will steal them. The only stock they have is that which they can pen up at night and even then the Indians continue to make their lives one living hell.

"They are forgotten by or deserted by the govnernment in Santa Fe and even the priests seldom visit those small, miserable villages."

"Who keeps them supplied with stock if the Indians raid them from time to time?" asked Modesto and then continued. "Why you do, don't you? And from the looks of your equipment, you do it at little or no profit for yourselves! You three and Simoñ have much more in common than I realized," he said admiringly. "Your philosophies of life are the same. I'll bet you even look to the coming of the Americanos as unstoppable progress for the future and the betterment of these poor people that you speak about. Simoñ, you are among true friends!"

The Prudencio brothers did not answer Modesto's remarks, but replied instead by walking toward the carretas. Ramon spoke politely but firmly, as he said, "Señors, we must travel to the village of the Yap Comanches, so if you will excuse us, we must finish our preparations and begin our journey."

"Would you mind if we tagged along?" Simoñ asked. "I have never been out on the Llanos and never had any dealing with the Comanches. I would appreciate it if we could travel along with you. It would give me a better understanding of the Comanche people."

Ramon glanced at each of his brothers, who said nothing, and then said, "I suppose it would be all right, but I warn you, it could be dangerous."

"We understand and will not hold you responsible for our safety," Simoñ replied as he looked sideways at Modesto.

Before Modesto could speak, the quiet Cochiti did so. "I think this is where we part company. I have no desire to see the Comanches and I surely will not seek them out. They are not friendly to my people, in fact the opposite is true. We have joined with the Hispanos more than once to make raids upon them in retaliation for the destruction they have brought to both our peoples. No, I think if I were to travel with you, I would be riding to my death."

Modesto and Simoñ talked with Cochiti while the Prudencios finished packing and then Cochiti rode westward with some coins jingling in his pocket while Simoñ and Modesto moved out with the Comancheros, Ramon, Modesto and Simoñ taking the lead.

CHAPTER IV

Should we take turns scouting ahead?" Modesto asked as he glanced at Ramon.

"There is no need of that," Ramon replied, "for we are expected, and it is even possible that a small party of Yaps will be waiting for us to escort us to their camp. You see, my friends, the Comanches are a nomadic people; they roam wherever the food is plentiful, wherever their fancy takes them. The Yap band, which is a small band made up of ten or twelve families, is known to my family and we are also known to most of the other Comanche bands east of here as well, so we are safe from attack. I think Cochiti was wise in not accompanying us, though. If he had wished to do so, I would have had to forbid him to make the journey."

"Why?"

"Because the Indians have always fought each other, even before the arrival of the Spaniards. The nomadic tribes raided the Pueblo tribes for food and carried off women and children for hundreds of years and they still do. It is also not uncommon for Mexican villages, which are located between the pueblos and the nomadic tribes, to permit the Comanche raiding parties to pass by without interference, knowing full well where the Comanches are going. Some of the Comanche raiding parties have traveled as far as Chama, passing many Mexican villages without the slightest hindrance. I have also been told that the Apaches and Comanches both travel in the same way through Mexico with no hindrance from villagers along their way."

"Why do they permit these raiding parties to pass unmolested?" asked Simon, although he had a good idea.

"Survival," Ramon answered. "The villagers have no modern weapons with which to defend themselves for they are forbidden by law from having such arms. The penalty for possessing such weapons can be death, a long prison term, or even a long stretch of forced labor in the mines. Since the Indians have the best rifles available, the odds are heavily in their favor, hence the villagers follow the line of least resistance for the good of their people. Any resistance would only result in their destruction. The only things of value they have are their women and children and they would lose them almost certainly if they tried to place any obstacles in the way of the raiding parties. While the people in the villages might be poor, they are certainly not dumb! Of course, at times they are raided anyway, but that is usually only before the pueblos have harvested their crops. We have always known that during the harvest in the pueblos, we are least likely to have our villages plundered."

"What has all this to do with Cochiti?" Modesto asked.

"That is an easy question to answer," Ramon replied. "He is a pueblo Indian. Some day, as was the Pecos Pueblo, the pueblos will be wiped out by a large Comanche raiding party, or if they are not wiped out, the survivors will abandon their homes and seek safety elsewhere. Survival is what motivates people to behave as they do in these mountains. It has nothing to do with bravery, cowardice, or even religion. Survival determines their behavior, as well it should. In my opinion at least," Ramon added soberly.

"You are about to trade with Comanches who no doubt have killed or carried off women and children from some of these villages in which you have friends," Simoñ objected.

"That is true," Ramon admitted. "Survival," he repeated to himself. "It is a matter of survival. We do what we must to survive. What do you expect us to do? The governor in Santa Fe is too busy filling his coffers with gold and silver to be concerned about the peons. We are expendable, we are not even allowed to purchase American rifles to defend ourselves. We survive the best way we know how and survive we have, under the most difficult conditions. We are a conditioned people, we are a stubborn people, we are a tough people who will not surrender to the Indians our homes, churches, or land. We will survive."

"Are we saving our land, family, churches and culture for the Americanos to add to their melting pot?" Simoñ asked.

"Here we go again," Modesto said as he glanced at Ramon and then back at Simoñ.

"You may be right," Ramon conceded as he returned Modesto's look. "I have met a few Americanos and I have learned from them that they are from a country which has many different nationalities among its citizenry."

"But no Mexicans, right?" Modesto asked.

"There must be a few," Ramon answered. "There must be French Canadians among them also, for that hardy breed can be found anywhere. I have heard that some of those French Canadian trappers founded a settlement south of Isleta over a hundred years ago."

"What was it called?" Modesto hoped that Ramon would not remember and thus put his knowledge in question.

"They called it Canada," Ramon replied as he turned to glance at Modesto. "It's name was later changed to Fuenchara. It shouldn't be too difficult for you to accept the fact that Frenchmen used to live not too far east of here. After all, it was their territory until the United States purchased it. Spain owned it for a short time before that. The French called it the Louisiana Territory and so did the Americanos. The distance from New Mexico to the French Territory was a hundred miles, and to a Canadian trapper, that distance is nothing. If Frenchmen can travel to New Mexico from the Louisiana Territory, it stands to reason that Mexicans can travel that distance also, to the United States. Si, I believe that you could find Mexicans living in the United States and I'm very sure that you will also find many Spanish speaking Americanos in Florida and along the Mississippi River. After all, those territories once belonged to Spain also. So si, I would say that you would find expatriated Spaniards and Mexicans among the Americano citizenry."

"And don't forget the Canadian River, Modesto," Simoñ grinned. "We Mexicans didn't give it its name."

"I suppose you two are right, when I think about it, I've heard of Antione Leroux, myself, and he certainly isn't Spanish."

"And don't forget St. Dennis who married Catin, Ramon's niece, down in Texas somewhere," Ramon added, "Ramon is his last name, you know."

"Water up ahead," Elmon yelled as he pointed to a draw that had a gradual slope toward a spring which had made a small water hole.

"We'll water here!" Ramon called back.

As the animals began to drink, Frutoso whispered, "I hear hoofbeats." He and Elmon quickly held the headstalls of the horses, ready to prevent them from nickering to the other animals.

The others listened and nodded in agreement, and Ramon began to climb to the top of a little knoll above the spring and motioned for the others to do as Frutoso and Elmon. "Apaches!" Ramon whispered as he lowered his head.

Simoñ pulled back and said softly, "How many?"

"It's a scouting party," Ramon whispered. "There are three, but there are probably more behind them."

"What are they doing out here in Comanche territory?" Modesto wondered.

"Hunting buffalo, probably," Ramon guessed.

"What should we do?" Modesto asked nervously.

"Wait." Ramon cautioned.

"Wait? For what?"

"To see if those three are the advance scouts of an Apache buffalo hunting party," Ramon explained patiently. "We shouldn't have to wait long if there are more for they'll be along shortly."

They waited, prone, in silence, and at length they could once more detect hoofbeats in the distance. Telling the others to keep down, Ramon once more moved up the slope and peered over cautiously for long moments and then slid back down to them. "Buffalo hunting party."

"How do you know that?" Simoñ questioned.

"Because they have their women with them, and pack mules laden with buffalo robes and dried meat," Ramon explained. "We'll wait until they have had time to get out of sight. We'll just stay close to the horses until they are out of sight and hearing. The horses could still give our positions away."

"They carry rifles," Ramon whispered. "Much better than our old muzzle loaders. Now you understand what I meant when I told you what our people are up against. We are lucky compared to most of our people, for at least we have rifles, out of date though they may be, and of course you realize we are breaking the law just by having these old rifles in our possessions."

"That will change one day," Simoñ whispered.

Modesto grinned as he listened,"You never give up, do you, mi amigo?"

"I suggest that we all quit talking and be quiet," Ramon whispered, "even though they are a long distance away, let's not take any chances."

After they had waited quietly for a long while, Ramon again slipped to the top of the ridge and cautiously looked over. He saw that one of the horsemen had pulled his horse in and sat looking at the ground. Suddenly he called to some of the others, and when the others joined him, they too, stared at the ground, then looked in the direction of the Comancheros, and pointed with their rifes.

"They've spotted our carreta tracks," Ramon whispered to the others as he continued to watch the Apaches.

Do you think they'll follow the tracks? "Modesto asked.

"I'm sure they can tell the tracks are fresh and that we can't be far off, but maybe they'll mind their oun business and leave us to ours," Ramon said hopefully. "But we'd better be prepared for a fight." He watched for some minutes and then reported that while the main party had gone on ahead, about fifteen warriors had remained behind and were gathering around what must be their leader. "We had better get back to the carretas and get ready for them."

The small party of Comancheros concealed thenselves as best they could beneath the carretas and waited for the approaching Apaches, but nothing happened. Finally Ramon spoke, "What are they doing? What are they waiting for?"

"Quiet," cautioned Frutoso, "I hear hoofbeats, get ready, they're coming!"

"No, the hoofbeats are fading," Elmon said, they must be riding away from us instead of toward us."

"Stay here, all of you,"Ramon commanded. "I'll have a look." He ran in a crouched position to the top of the knoll where he again looked over cautiously and saw the Apaches galloping westward. He came back down the slope grinning. "Come on out muchachas, they've decided for some reason to join the others."

As the others crawled out from beneath the carretas, Simoñ looked eastward and said, "There is the reason they have decided to leave us alone."

As the others looked in that direction, they saw Comanche braves walking their horses toward the Comancheros.

"The Yaps are a welcome sight!" Ramon yelled as he grinned broadly. When the Comanches reached them, one asked, "You Prudencio?" Ramon nodded.

"You come," the brave said as he and his followers reined their horses away from the Comancheros.

The Comancheros followed for two hours until they came to a small Comanche village of about twenty tepees.

"Sharp Knife," Ramon said to a Comanche as he pushed the flap of his tepee to one side and stepped forward.

"Our brothers have arrived," the warrior said gravely as he stepped forward to clasp hands with the Prudencios. He looked skeptically at Modesto and Simoñ, reserving judgment.

"These two strangers, Sharp Knife, are my friends, Simoñ and Modesto," Ramon said in explanation.

"If they are the friends of the Prudencios, then they are our friends, also" the chief said gravely. "Do you bring our blankets?"

"Si, do you have the cattle?"

The chief did not speak but pointed to the cattle which grazed out beyond the tepees. He then walked to the carretas and removed the buffalo robes which covered the Navajo blankets. He inspected the blankets, pulling one of them out from the stack to scan it and throw it over his shoulder. He looked down at it and felt its texture, then turned to Ramon and said with a smile, "Deal—cattle yours, blankets mine."

A commotion was heard and the Comancheros looked to see what could be causing it. What they was a saw a Mexican girl being slapped, kicked, and spat upon by some squaws. Apparently the Mexican girl had tried to attract the attention of the Comancheros and in this she had succeeded.

The chief glanced in her direction and laughed as he said, "The squaws do not like the Mexican girl, but the braves do."

"What does he mean?" Modesto questioned Elmon in a whisper.

"She is a captive and apparently none of the braves want her as a wife so she is used as a slave by any who wish to do so."

Elmon gave Modesto a short version of the girl's fate and then turned to watch the proceedings.

"That is inhuman," Simoñ said softly. "Is there any way we can get her out of here and take her back with us?"

"Why?" Elmon asked. "Who would want her now?"

"Why?" Simoñ asked in anger. "Because she is one of us, that's why. And also because no woman should be mistreated in that manner. Talk to Ramon and see if the chief will throw her in as part of the trade."

"I'll try," Elmon answered, and he walked over to his brother and the chief.

Simoñ and Modesto watched as the three men talked and in a short time,

Elmon turned and pointed to Simoñ. The chief and Ramon also turned to look at Simoñ and a slow grin crossed the face of the chief before he yelled at the Mexican girl. She came sullenly to the chief who spoke to her as he pointed to Simoñ. The poor, frightened girl stared at Simoñ and then walked slowly toward him as the squaws taunted her. When she reached Simoñ, she stopped, and with her head bowed, she stood in front of him saying nothing.

"What is your name?" Simoñ asked gently.

"Lucia, señor," the girl's reply was barely audible.

"And your last name is?" Simoñ spoke in a comforting way, as he endeavored to encourage the girl.

"Garza," the girl whispered.

"Are you from the Rancho de las Golondrinas, by any chance? Are your mother and father Bernadette and Ysidro Garza?" questioned Simoñ eagerly.

"The girl looked up hopelessly with tears streaming down her face and replied, "Si, señor."

"Listen to what I say and do not do anything other than what you are doing right now. Do you understand?"

"Si, señor," the girl replied.

"I am going to get you out of here, but we will have to do some very convincing acting first, if we are to succeed. Now, what did my compadre say to his brother and the chief?"

"He said that you would like to have me as part of the trade if that were agreeable to the chief."

"And what did the chief say?"

"He said that he would be glad to get rid of me because I have caused problems among the squaws and especially among the braves, and that with me gone, the bickering would stop."

Simoñ thought a moment and then said, "Stay here with my friend, Modesto, while I talk with the chief. Do not show any emotion or excitement, for if you do, he may change his mind and refuse to release you. Is your sister Rita here with you?"

"No, señor, she was traded to another band of Comanches a week ago."

Simoñ talked to the chief, and at length convinced him that if Rita could be brought back here to the Yap band and given over to him, Simoñ would send the chief ten new Navajo blankets with the next trip of the Prudencios. The chief studied Simoñ for a few seconds and realizing that Rita was being ransomed, he said quickly, "She is worth twenty blankets."

"Fifteen blankets?" Simoñ asked hopefully.

"No, twenty," the chief said firmly.

"Twenty it is," Simoñ conceded. "I say before you now, that when the Prudencios return, they will bring the blankets. I will get them from the Navajoes or from some other source as soon as we get back home. I give you my word, and

I come from an honorable family who believes that truth is the sacred word of the Great Spirit."

"Do you support your friend's words?" Chief Sharp Knife looked at Ramon. "Does he speak the truth or is his tongue forked?"

"He and I both speak the truth, Sharp Knife. We will keep our word because if we do not, the Great Spirit will send the lightning to strike both of us dead, sending us to be with the evil spirits."

"It is done, then. I will send for the squaw called Rita."

"At the end of the second day, Rita was brought back to the Yap band, and Lucia and Rita had a secret, happy reunion and the Comancheros left the Comanche camp with the two girls and the cattle.

When the girls had been delivered to their joyous parents, Simoñ and Modesto were once more on the trail to the Gomez Hacienda.

CHAPTER V

It was early in the day when Simoñ and Modesto came into view of the Gomez headquarters still several miles ahead of them. When they drew closer, they could hear religious chanting, made eerie by the silence which punctuated it. After the silence was drawn out to a great length, the chanting was resumed, sorrowful in tone. Cries of distress wafted over the still air.

Simoñ and Modesto glanced at each other in alarm and then spurred their horses into a gallop. As they neared the first buildings, they saw the carnage. Some buildings still smoldered from the fires which had raged through them. Doors, shutters, and furniture had been piled to burn in an attempt to destroy the adobe structures. The entire area looked as though a tornado had swept through it as it left almost total destruction in its path.

"Where is everyone?" Simoñ looked about in despair as he walked his horse among the ruins.

"Up there," Modesto pointed.

"The cemetery!" Simoñ spoke in a harsh voice as he wheeled his horse and galloped toward the little cemetery. "Mother...!" He raced his horse and when they reached the cemetery, they saw that the peons of the hacienda had just completed the burial ceremony for at least twenty people. Upon hearing the approaching horsemen, some of the peons began to scream and run, but when one of them realized that it was Simoñ, they recovered themselves, and returned slowly to the gravesites.

"What has happened?" Simoñ asked as he leaped from his horse and rushed forward.

"Comanches, patron," Luis said as he removed his sombrero and approached Simoñ. "They struck just as the sun began to show its light over the hills. Many of us were still eating our morning meal and were struck down in the kitchens, others as they rushed for their weapons, but we were no match for the well armed, fast moving Comanche warriors."

"Where is my mother?" Simoñ glanced around frantically, looking in all directions.

"They took her, patron," Luis answered sadly.

The significance of his use of the term, patron, finally struck Simoñ and Modesto and Simoñ crossed himself as he asked, "What happened to my father?"

"The doña and don were among the first to be killed, and they are buried in the family cemetery, patron, but Benito is buried here," Luis spoke of the only father Simoñ had really known in his young life, and Simoñ again crossed himself sadly and then turned to the more urgent matter of his mother's whereabouts. "How many others did they take with them?"

"She was the only one, patron. The others they left for us to lay to rest."

"Has a priest arrived yet?" Simoñ asked.

"No, patron. The Los Hermanos Mayor of The Brothers of Light conducted the burials."

"The Third Order of St. Francis of Assisi," Simoñ said softly. "The Penitente Mayor," Modesto said as he crossed himself.

"With due respect," Luis told them, "I do not think the priest will come, for he is too far from us. When our turn comes for a visit, I'm sure that he will say mass for them." Luis stood looking at the ground as he spoke and then he looked up as if waiting for Simoñ to decide their future course. The other peons had remained gathered at the grave sites of their friends and family members. The women had their heads covered with the black lace rebozos and their men folks stood beside them, sombreros in their hands. Now they, too, looked at Simoñ, apparently waiting for his orders.

Simoñ remained silent for a few moments thinking and then asked Luis softly, "Which way did they take my mother?"

Luis looked from Simoñ to Modesto and then turned to glance back at the others before he spoke, "They rode toward the Llanos, patron. The chief rode a big Appalaoosa, a sorrel with a spotted blanket on his rump, a magnificent animal. He rode the only such horse."

"You are not going after them, are you?" Modesto asked quickly.

"What would you do if they had your mother?" Simoñ spoke harshly as he looked at Modesto in surprise.

"I will go with you," Modesto said hastily.

"No," Simoñ said decidedly. "You must stay here and take charge of the hacienda until I return. The peons need someone of authority to look to for instruction, guidance,and assurance and you fill that order. Will you do that for me, mi amigo?"

"How can I refuse?"

"If I ride hard, I may catch up with them before they have a chance to harm my mother," Simoñ said as he sprang into the saddle.

He rode at a gallop to the stables to search in vain for a fresh horse and Modesto rode after him to gather fresh supplies for him before he took up his headlong pace once more.

The trail of the Comanches was not difficult to follow, for the grass of the Llano had been bent under the weight of many horses and Simoñ followed in their wake until he reached Valmora, on the Mora River. The village seemed deserted when Simoñ rode into it and he pulled his horse down from its brisk trot into a walk and watched for any sign of life. "Hello!" he called again and again, with no response. Only silence greeted him. Finally a shutter was creaked open timidly and an old man peered out, looking in each direction. He said nothing, but stared at Simoñ vacantly. "The Comanches have gone, señor," the old man whispered. Simoñ rode in the dirction of the old man. "How long has it been since the Comanches passed this way?" he asked urgently.

Muttering something, the old man disappeared and shortly reappeared at the door of the small adobe. "Two, maybe three, hours ago." The old man looked at others who were now appearing from out of the nearby houses for confirmation.

"Si, a good two or three hours, señor," another young man told Simoñ as he walked up to him.

"That would put them at Gonzales, or beyond, by now," Simoñ figured as other people gathered around him. "Did they head in that direction or did they ride toward Sabinoso?"

"Gonzales is where they headed," another man said as he pointed southward. "They were moving at a pretty good speed, considering all of the loot they were packing on a number of burros."

"Did any of you see a Mexican woman with them? A captive woman?"

"Si, I will never forget how that woman struggled to free herself. She did break loose as they came up the street and she ran down that alley there." The speaker pointed between a row of adobe houses. "But she did not get far before a Comanche riding an Appaloosa rode after her and swept her off her feet as he galloped by her. She continued to put up a fight, to scratch and bite until that Comanche slapped her hard across the face. The force of the slap apparently stunned her and that gave the Comanche the time he needed to tie her hands together. They then tied her to the back of a burro. Some of the other warriors yelled to Sitting Buffalo, for that was his name, to kill her because she would cause too much trouble and be impossible to break.

"Sitting Buffalo said that he liked women with spirit and it was his business what he did with the woman and not theirs."

"Who is the captive woman?" One of the men looked up at Simoñ curiously.

"My mother," Simoñ answered as he spurred his horse toward the south.

The villagers shook their heads and the ones who had heard Simoñ, crossed themselves. One of them said in a low voice, "He rides to his death, that one. He is a brave son. Let us pray that in some way he will be able to rescue his mother."

"Such courage should not be wasted," another said softly, admiringly.

Simoñ took care to save the strength of his horse, walking now and then and occasionally loping him, but stayed mostly in a trot. He knew he'd never catch up with the Comanches if he didn't preserve his horse's strength, so he swung to the ground and walked beside him from time to time, petting him and murmuring encouragement. A short time later he stepped off the horse and pulled his saddle and blanket and bridle off, letting him drink from a small spring which bubbled out of a nearby rocky ledge, and then let him roll, stand and begin to graze before he hobbled him.

As Modesto had hoped, Simon had taken time to gather supplies before he rode away from the hacienda, and now he made a small fire and made coffee. That, with a few cold tortillas and some jerky made his meal. He lay down and watched the horse graze beside the little stream and then exhaustion overcame him and he slept.

Several hours later he awoke and both he and his horse were now in better shape as they again took up the trail which lay so clearly before them. When Gonzales was reached, he learned that the Comanches had passed by there only about an hour before and they still had his mother. Apparently they, too, had stopped for a rest.

"They're heading for the caprock," Simoñ muttered to his horse. "We're gaining on them, for they don't expect any pursuit. It can't be over sixty miles to the caprock and I'll bet their band is camped below the rim."

His horse was once more beginning to tire, for he stumbled now and then, and again Simon stopped where there was water and allowed him to drink and eat and get some rest. On this occasion Simoñ was too anxious to sleep, and he restrained his impatience with difficulty until his horse was sufficiently rested to continue. Three or four miles from the caprock the following day, Simoñ muttered to himself, "They have sheltered below the caprock." When he reached the rim, he peered over cautiously and saw many tepees scattered along a nearly dry stream bed. The small stream of water meandered for perhaps a mile before it went underground. A winding trail snaked its way down the slopes of the caprock. Simoñ tossed his hat on the ground and untied the Navajo blanket which was behind his saddle. After removing his spurs, he wrapped the blanket securely around his shoulders. He tied his horse and began his slow descent toward the village. When he was within one hundred yards of the first tepee, he covered his head with the blanket and strode right into the village. Whenever he passed a warrior he touched him lightly, enough for the warrior to notice it and make some comment. As he walked, Simoñ noticed that several braves, at intervals, had entered a tepee at some distance ahead of him. He headed for that same tepee and when he reached it he stooped slightly and entered.

A meeting of some sort was about to take place, for the warriors were seated around a small fire talking among themselves. Simoñ walked around the circle of Indian leaders and touched each one. After he had done this, he lowered himself to sit with them.

"We are called the people," the civil chief began. "As is our law, I am called father of our band." The chief adjusted one of his long braids which had various colored bits of cloth woven into it. At intervals along the braid there were small, colorful beads. Each of the warriors present wore a braided scalp lock on the top of his head. In this scalp lock, each also had placed a colorful feather.

Now the chief turned to Simoñ and asked, "Why do you cover your head?"

Simoñ lowered the blanket and when the braves saw that a stranger had invaded their council, they leaped to their feet and converged on Simoñ. As they held him, he said, "I have counted coup thirty-two times since I entered your village, the village of the People, the Komantcia."

When the chief heard his words he looked in surprise at Simoñ and asked, "How do you know the ancient name of the People?"

"Does it make any difference? It is true, that is what is important. Do you not add berries to your pemmican? And you do not eat dogs, nor do your men ride mares, but only geldings. Do you know the customs of the Mexicans and more importantly of the Americanos?"

"Why do you ask such questions?" the chief asked sternly.

"Because," replied Simoñ, "it is important to know the customs of all people, to know them is important to the peace of all of our people in the future."

"Let him go," the chief told his warriors. "You are a brave Mexican to come among us, as you know, counting coup is considered a very brave deed. You have used wit and skill. You are indeed a very brave man and we admire bravery in a man. You did not come just to count coup because if you did, you would have left our village as you came. What is it you want?"

"My mother," answered Simoñ, "your braves stole her from my hacienda in my absence."

The chief leaned over to a brave sitting next to him and mumbled something, after which the Comanche warrior rose and left the tepee.

"How do you know that it was my band which captured your mother?"

"I have followed the tracks to this camp, "Simoñ replied calmly.

"You know of course, that I can have you killed for asking for the property of one of my braves?"

"The Comanches do not kill brave men," Simoñ answered, knowing full well that the Comanches had done just that, but he knew that he had to use every trick at his disposal to help win his mother's freedom and flattery was not to be omitted.

"You are ignorant of Comanche ways," the chief said derisively, but you are young and that may explain your ignorance of our ways."

The flap of the tepee was flung aside and the Comanche who had left earlier returned, followed by another Comanche brave.

"I see that Sitting Buffalo has followed the Comanche custom of painting his face when he is visited by a stranger, "Simoñ said.

"Who is this man and why is he asking for my captive?" Sitting Buffalo asked harshly as he looked at his chief.

"He is the son of your captive Mexican woman."

Now the flap of the tepee was once more pushed to one side and another Comanche entered. Although Simoñ recognized him immediately as one of the slaves whom they had freed from La Alambrera, he made no sign but waited to see what the Comanche would do when he recognized him.

"My brother, Sitting Buffalo," the newly arrived Comanche said as he turned to face his brother, "this is the man who freed me from captivity. In return for my freedom, you should give his mother her freedom. It is only fair and just that you do this."

"It is not right for my people to hold your people as slaves just as it is wrong for your people to hold my mother as a slave," Simoñ said earnestly. "Chief, from the east, new winds are beginning to blow. These winds bring with them ideas that are not famiiar to either of our peoples, ideas that will not be accepted by your nation or my people without a struggle.

"But these ideas are big medicine, too big and too strong for either of our peoples to stop. The Great Spirit has given this idea new life. The Great Spirit has brought this idea back from the dead and has breathed life into it. The Great Spirit stands at the shoulder of the people who bring His will to us, and He will not permit it to fail. One of these ideas is that one cannot hold another against his will. My people hold many peons in bondage, which is wrong, and these new ideas say that it is wrong.

"Your people hold others against their will, and this also is wrong. These new ideas say that you offend the Great Spirit when you force young Mexican boys to become Comanches. Sitting Buffalo is a great and brave warrior. He carries a lance when he goes into battle. To your people, Sitting Buffalo does this because his courage is great. Sitting Buffalo uses his lance to kill his enemies at close quarters and that also shows his bravery, because he fights the enemy one by one, in single combat. Other brave men must show courage also, the courage it will take to free a slave." Simon now looked straight at Sitting Buffalo and proceeded, "Does Sitting Buffalo possess the courage it will take to free my mother in return for the courage I showed in freeing his brother?"

A scuffle was heard outside the tepee and then the flap was pushed aside and Maria was forced inside. She displayed surprise and then fear, as she moved to embrace her son.

"It is all right, mother, I am not a prisoner. Not yet, anyway." His tired face looked down gravely at hers.

"What are you doing here?"

"I came for you," Simoñ answered as he turned to look at those gathered around them. "Do I have your permission to leave with my mother in peace?" Simoñ asked as he looked at the chief.

"You must be a proud mother," the chief said slowly. "Your son has shown much courage in coming here. He also shows that he possesses big medicine because he can foretell the future. In that future he predicts that the Mexican,

Indian, and American will live as one people under one tepee." The chief drew himself up as he asked, "Do you believe as he does?"

"I do not possess big medicine," Maria replied, "but I believe that my son does."

The chief looked long at the two Mexicans who stood there before him and he finally said, "Go back to your people in peace, both of you, but as I say this, I know that I have not seen and heard the last of you."

"I wish peace with you," Simoñ said in turn. "And may the Great Spirit watch over you and your people."

Simoñ and his mother turned and left the tepee and had begun to walk toward the path which led upward to the top of the caprock when they heard a loud summons, "You have a horse for your mother?"

They turned to see the chief standing beside his tepee and looking toward them. "No," Simoñ called back.

The chief turned to beckon to a warrior and within minutes a horse was led to them. "Take it with my good wishes for your safe journey home. I wish peace with you, also. Let us not fight one another."

Simoñ looked at the chief, smiled, nodded, and waved goodbye as Maria mounted the Indian pony and he began to lead it up the steep trail.

That night, by a campfire, Simoñ and his mother began to make plans for the rebuilding of the hacienda headquarters. "What plans do you have for the future?" his mother asked as she began the conversation. "The hacienda is yours now to do with as you see fit."

"Mother, I haven't worked out the details yet, but I can give you a general picture of what I hope to accomplish and I have a good idea of the direction I want to go."

"Tell me, Simoñ," Maria leaned forward eagerly.

"I think I want to build a fortress type compound which could protect all of us at the headquarters should the need arise in the future. It would cover perhaps five acres in area and would be completely enclosed by a high, thick, adobe wall. Behind that wall would be enough shelter and space for all of the people under our care to have safety and supplies in case of another attack or some other emergency. I would have a fireproof munition building in the center of the compound in which I would store rifles and ammunition with which we could ward off any attack which might be thrown at us. Later I will go to Missouri to purchase the latest rifles and a few cannon to mount at strategic points along the wall."

"Rifles and cannon?" Maria gasped in alarm. "That is illegal and Santa Fe will never permit you to own such weapons. Those in power would fear a revolt!"

"By the time they learn of my armaments, I will already have them in place," Simoñ replied calmly.

"How do you plan to do this without Santa Fe knowing about it?"

"Santa Fe will have no objections to my building defenses after what happened at the hacienda and I will design the structure so that it will accommodate the cannons and rifles once we purchase them at a later date. Platforms high up on the walls for the cannons and peepholes for the men to shoot through will be built. Then when I can, I will bring the rifles and cannons." Simoñ explained.

Maria wasn't convinced and worry was apparent in her voice when she said, "But Simoñ, Santa Fe will send an army to arrest you and dismantle your fortress. If Santa Fe can't accomplish your destruction, she will send a larger army up from the interior of Mexico. The Mexican government will not tolerate such a violation of its laws. Not to mention the threat you will present to its authority."

"Then I'll have to think up some kind of strategy to obtain its approval."

"You had better think through your plan very carefully before you begin this ambitious project of yours," Maria replied with concern written on her face.

"I guess it is pretty ambitious at that," admitted Simoñ with a grin.

"Ambitious to say the least!" Maria retorted.

"Maybe I had better leave that part of my plans until later, then, and build my empire first," Simoñ mused in deep thought.

"Empire! What are you talking about, Simon?"

"Mother, what I want to do also, is to develop a trade with the Indians, especially with the Comanches, on a large scale. When I travel to Missouri, I will also purchase American goods and bring them to the hacienda and invite everyone to come there to trade. I want to be a Comanchero in reverse and I have just the men to run that part of the empire. They are the Prudencio brothers. I met them not long ago. They live a few miles this side of Las Vegas."

"Is that part of your idea for an empire?" Maria asked, concentrating only on that part of her son's dream.

"Si, And I also intend to raise thousands and thousands of sheep, cattle, and perhaps goats out on the Llano Estacado. I will establish little villages at strategic locations as sheep and cattle camps where my men can live with their families."

"Who will buy your livestock?" queried Maria.

"The Americanos," Simoñ said confidently. "I will also drive some of my stock to Chihuahua, San Antonio, and even to New Orleans if need be, wherever I can find a market."

"Do you really believe the Comanches will allow you to do this? You are actually planning to use land they consider theirs to raise your livestock? No, they will drive you off. They will never let you do this."

"Not if they need me as much as I will need their land," Simoñ replied.

"Explain yourself."

"They will want my trade goods, mother, and for them to be able to come in to trade with me, I will extract their permission to use the Llano. The range that I will use will be only a small part of their nation anyway, I believe that they will see the advantages of my proposal and will agree to my terms. Besides, New Mexico may be part of the United States before I finish developing my empire, and if that is the case, the Americanos surely won't stop me from arming my hacienda."

"Simoñ, you have big dreams and I hope you won't bite off more than you can chew," Maria said with amusement in her voice. She thought to herself that only the young could have such far-reaching, incredible dreams and the confidence to try to accomplish them.

"Only time will tell, mother," Simoñ said with a smile.

The next morning snow was beginning to fall as they trotted their horses toward Gonzales. Maria could hardly be seen because Simoñ's Navajo blanket completely engulfed her. She held the blanket together beneath her chin as she leaned into the ever increasing wind.

When they rode up the street of Gonzales, the people emptied their homes in their eagerness to cheer the young caballero and his mother. They wore broad smiles as they watched and waved at one of the first Mexicans in a long time who had defied the Comanches and lived to tell of it. Pride in what Simoñ had done and hope that maybe things were beginning to change were on their faces as they repeatedly called, "God bless you," after them.

Maria uncovered her bowed head at the villagers and a smile creased her lips. "What is this, a welcome for a conquering hero?" She turned to smile proudly at her son.

"Some day, mother, these people will be able to walk the streets of this village without the least bit of fear of attack by the Comanches. That is what this outburst of emotion is really about. It is the hope of a better time ahead, a more safe and secure time."

The people insisted that they stop for food and warmth, if only for a short while, and they were made welcome at one of the small houses bordering the street. While they were eating, their horses were given grain and hay in a lean-to at the back of the house. Such courtesy was natural with these kindly people. No matter how poor they might be, they could be depended upon to share what they had and gladly. It was for people such as these that Simoñ planned, for he hoped to improve their lot in life.

As Simoñ and Maria left the little village, they turned and took one last look behind them and waved at the people who were scattered in the street and waving exuberantly at them.

Maria was again wrapped in her blanket, clutching it to her chin as they once again put their horses to a trot homeward.

When the Gomez hacienda finally came into view a short distance before them, they could hear a chorus of voices. The voices soon changed to shouts of jubilation and joy as more and more of the peons recognized them. They rushed from all directions to join Modesto and to welcome their new don and doña. Modesto stood at the front and center of the gathering, and he wore a large grin combined with pride and amazement in his friend's ability to accomplish the impossible.

"In years to come I will be able to say that I was there at the beginning," Modesto said to his friend as Simón dismounted and turned to help his weary mother. He was the first to shake Simón's hand and embrace him, saying, "Congratulations, you really did it. You brought back your mother."

The women gathered around Maria, taking turns at hugging her, and brushing tears from their cheeks although they were smiling all the while. The men were shaking hands with Simón and the grins on their faces displayed their pride. They also welcomed Maria as they removed their sombreros, bowed their heads and shook her hand.

Simón jumped up into a nearby carreta and raised both hands to gain their attention. When all was quiet, he said, "Thank you for such a warm welcome. I want to give a special thanks to my good amigo, Modesto for his support and for looking after things in my absence."

The peons began to cheer once more and clap their hands as they turned toward Modesto.

Simón now looked grave as he continued, "I want to say now what I didn't have time to tell you before, how sorry I am for the loss of your loved ones. I, too, suffered losses, the loss of the only father I knew for most of my life, for I will always remember his strength and kindness. I also lost the one I recently came to know as my natural father and I will always regret that I didn't have the opportunity to know him better. I will attempt to carry on after him and hope that he would be proud of my efforts in this respect.

"There is going to be a new beginning in New Mexico and we, the people of this hacienda, are the ones who will nurture this new change to maturity. In the spring we will move the headquarters of the Gomez Hacienda to the Ocate Valley where we will start to build our new homes and dreams. Later, I will tell you in more detail why I have decided to rebuild the hacienda on another location although still on my father's land grant, but for now and for this winter, let us make ourselves as comfortable as we can until spring comes. Then we will begin to build our new homes in a new place, with new hopes and new strengths."

When everyone had gone back to their chores, Simón and Maria walked to the cemetery and knelt at the graveside of Benito. They crossed themselves and bowed their heads reverently and closed their eyes, remaining silent as they thought of the husband and foster father who slept beneath the mound. They would miss his quiet goodness, his great strength upon which they had leaned. They rose wearily and stood side by side as they stared down at the grave and finally Simón turned and looked at the devastation of the hacienda, then spoke quietly to his mother. "Let us go now to Victor and his wife, Vivian."

"Si." Maria took Simoñ's arm and they started down the hill toward the small Gomez family cemetery which was behind Victor's partially destroyed house. "We must show our respect to those two good people, to your father. I loved him so and it seems so very long ago."

After their visits to the graves of Don and Doña Gomez, Simoñ escorted his mother to the battered big house for some badly needed rest. He turned her over to Patricia who smiled, bowed, and said, "I will care for the Doña, Don Simoñ. Please do not worry about her. She is at home now and in the best of hands."

Simoñ walked back outside and sought out Modesto whom he found near one of the small adobe buildings which had been spared by the Comanche raid. As they walked around the stricken hacienda, Simoñ told Modesto what he hoped to do. "Will you stay with me and help me build my new hacienda?"

"I wouldn't miss it for the world," Modesto replied. "I'll be back in the spring before you begin. I have many brothers at home and I will not be missed that much. And of course our hacienda is not that large. I'll visit with my family from time to time as our work will permit."

CHAPTER VI

When spring came, eighty-three peons of the Gomez Hacienda, along with Simoñ, Maria, and Modesto began their trek to the valley which bordered the Ocate creek. Their way led along the base of the Sangre de Cristo Mountains, over terrain which was exceedingly rough, with many arroyos and rocky canyons running through it. The area was blanketed with many trees which also made their travel difficult. Carretas which carried most of the heavy cargo were drawn by oxen and urged along by men walking at their sides. Thirty to forty burros packed the remainder of their things.

The cattle, sheep, and other stock which could be driven, followed behind the carretas. The various kinds of fowl which could not be driven, had been crated and were also carried in the carretas. To entice the flock of sheep to follow, rather than be driven, one peon carried a container of salt over his shoulder, thereby encouraging the leader of the flock to follow him.

The land upon which the compound would be built had been selected earlier by Simoñ. It was a cool, February morning when the caravan began to wind its way towards its destination perhaps twenty miles away. It was led by Simoñ and Modesto who rode ahead and picked their way over the best route.

Some men had been sent on ahead earlier to prepare for the arrival of the others. They had taken with them the dismantled portions of the old buildings which could be used in the new. Temporary shelters had been erected by these men during the winter and they were now laboring at the tasks of felling and peeling trees for the use of vigas in the construction of the permanent buildings. Knowing that their compadres were on their way and would reach their destination in two days, the loggers had halted their logging temporarily to dig pits in the ground and build fires in them. When the fires had dwindled into coals, they placed a layer of rocks before placing carefully wrapped venison on them, then more rocks and finally more hot coals and then a layer of dirt, thereby leaving the venison to roast slowly while they resumed their work of felling trees.

When the caravan reached the Ocate Valley, some of the men went to work immediately building forms for the making of adobe bricks.

Simoñ also assigned others the task of quarrying the flagstone which was easily accessible, while others began to build a dry rock building.

Simoñ rode to the men who were making the adobe brick forms and instructed them, "When you are ready for the making of the adobes, follow the advice of Eleberto Romero for he knows the best clay to use to obtain the strongest adobe bricks, and of course he knows the best quantity of straw, grass, weed, etc. to add to the clay mixture."

"Si, patron," one of the men looked up and answered cheerfully. "Eleberto knows what he is doing, for he is the best."

Simoñ wheeled his horse and shouted, "Jose, Jose Jimenez."

"Aqui Patron?" Jose yelled as he dropped what he was doing and began to walk toward Simoñ.

"I would like for you to take charge of building four large, hornos in the places where I have had the rocks piled," Simoñ told him.

"I will begin as soon as the first adobes are cured," Jose assured him.

"Julio Jaramillo," Simoñ next called.

"Si, Don Gomez," came Julio's reply.

"Take good care of the sheep, take your dogs along with you and keep them out of the way."

"Esta bien," Julio answered as he whistled to his dogs and went to relieve Estevan.

One job after another was assigned to individuals by Simoñ as he and Modesto rode among the peons, supervising and answering questions and giving advice as they occurred.

Within a week, fruit trees were planted, ground was plowed up and readied for the planting of crops and the compound area was cleared and the building locations staked out.

An irrigation crew had gone upstream and found a spot on the Ocate creek where it could easily be dammed so that the irrigation ditch which would bring the precious water, could be started.

"This valley will begin to blossom by late spring," Simoñ said with satisfaction. Their paths had crossed in their suspervisory riding and Modesto grinned. "If it doesn't it won't be because we haven't tried." He rode on his way whistling.

"Modesto!" Simoñ called after him. Modesto reined his horse back toward Simoñ and asked, "Si?"

"Chimayo is famous for its carved statues of Christo and saints. Do you know the artisan who is the best at that craft?"

"Si, I know him well," Modesto said quickly.

"Talk with my mother and see how many she would like for our church and then send someone with the order, por favor."

"Si, patron," Modesto laughed as he saluted Simoñ. Simoñ grinned after his friend as he watched him ride away. He had been indispensable in this venture.

"Manuel," Simoñ suggested as Manuel Roybal walked by near him, "Why don't you take another man and cut enough timber to erect one large cross in the field and one to be put up here, also. They will serve us until our church is built."

When fall came the compound had been completed with its three foot thick outer walls and all around the inner part of the walls, extending eighteen feet inward, toward the center of the compound, was built a solid row of rooms. They extended outward toward the plaza of the compound. Inside, the rooms were connected to one another, making it possible for a person to walk all around the inner compound through one room after another without having to step outside into the plaza of the compound.

On the roofs of the dwellings, and behind the firewall was built a wooden platform from which men could defend the compound. This platorm fitted snugly against the outer wall, and would enable defenders to shoot down on any invader. In the center of the compound had been erected a large building with walls at least three feet thick. This fortress would one day house the gunpowder and the arms which could be used to defend the hacienda. With the completion of the rooms which were being used for temporary living quarters for everyone, individual houses were now being built for each family. These were kept within a quarter mile of the compound. The church was located on the highest ground overlooking the village. The belfrey tower was empty at present. The large, two story structure adjacent to Ocate Creek or river, boasted a very large water wheel which turned slowly with the power of the running stream. This was the mill which had not yet ground its first ounce of flour.

The casa of the don and doña was a replica of the one at the old location. It formed a large square with the center being an open patio or courtyard. Over the fireplace in the long living room, or sala, hung a portrait of the old don and doña. A double door led from the living room area into the patio where already bloomed many varieties of flowers, and shrubs, and a few fruit trees had been planted. Niches in the thick walls of the rooms housed candles which lent a soft glow to the whitewashed walls. Paintings on boards or retablos of the crucified Christ were hung on some of the walls as were small crosses. Each of the rooms opened onto the patio and thus the fragrance from the flowers permeated every room.

The giant wooden beams or vigas which crossed the ceilings broke the monotony of the whitewashed expanse. The floors were of hard packed dirt made from a careful mixture of mud and straw and packed with a wooden thumper before being smoothed and leveled lovingly by hand. Large buffalo robes and Navajo rugs were distributed over the floors in each room.

There were no closets in the house, but instead there were many beautifully carved wooden trunks which were bound in copper or brass or leather. A few trunks were constructed completely of bull buffalo rawhide and they, too, were trimmed in beautiful designs. A few tall wardrobes also took the place of the more conventional closets.

The small containers which every household required were made of tin or other metals.

Simoñ had persuaded the Prudencio brothers, Elmon, Frutoso, and Ramon, to move to the Gomez Hacienda as the future managers of the trade with the Comanches.

To Modesto's great surprise, Simoñ revealed to him his love for his sister, Sylvia, whom he had met during his first visit to the Polaco Hacienda. When Sylvia was one of the first members of the Polaco family to visit the Gomez Hacienda, Simoñ had renewed his acquaintance with her and fallen deeply in love, and she with him. They planned to be wed at some time in the future, but after she had returned to her hacienda, Simoñ began to reexamine their plans and found them lacking and so Maria, accompanied by Modesto, rode to Chimayo to make arrangements for the young couple to be married sooner.

In the fall, Modesto, Simoñ, and his mother rode once more to the Polaco Hacienda and he and Sylvia were married at the small church at Chimayo.

When they returned to Ocate, they found the building program about completed and the agricultural portion was in full production with the exception of fruit bearing trees which would require several more years to mature.

Sylvia felt at home immediately, and under Maria's tutelage, she began to take over the supervision of the many household tasks which accompanied life on the rancho. She and Maria watched as a number of small, underground dugouts were constructed throughout the area for the purpose of storing their vegetables such as cabbage, potatoes, and other simi-perishable produce. Each peon would have a designated dugout assigned to his family from which it would draw such foodstuffs.

One of the first tasks which had been performed, of course, when they first arrived, had been the digging of a water well within the area of the future compound. Simoñ felt confident that in the event of a future attack, he had provided well for the safety of his people.

The faces of the peons reflected their satisfaction, for as they went about their work they were happy, contented, and pleased with their young don and doña.

The Gomez Hacienda was once more operating efficiently and Simoñ's plans were ready to be implemented further.

CHAPTER Vll

The years passed uneventfully and Simoñ and Sylvia now had five children whom Maria loved dearly. Although she could also discipline them if it were required. Leandro the oldest was ten years old. His sister Josephine was eight years old, their brother Carlos was almost seven, and the two little ones, Ignacio and Emilo, were five and two years old respectively. For play mates they had the children of Modesto and Ursula who lived at a short distance, but still within the compound. Their children were all girls, Stephanie was the oldest and Josephine's age, and the two younger girls were Anna, almost the exact age of Carlos, and Prestina who was a little older than Ignacio.

It was on an early morning in June when Simoñ and Sylvia were awakened from their sleep by the high pitched shrill of the txistu and an accompanying drum. The shepherds' dogs, who were aware that they were about to head for the high pastures to attend the flocks, were barking joyfully.

"We overslept, my dear," Simoñ hurriedly threw back the bed covers and slid his feet to the floor. "Today is rotation day for the sheepherders, and Manuel, Enrique, and Alex are reminding me of that fact by playing the txistu and the drum."

"Must they rise so early? It's still the middle of the night," Sylvia yawned as she turned on her side and prepared to go back to sleep.

"The herders are accustomed to rising early, dear. The sheep see to that because they begin to graze and move about at approximately three in the morning. For that reason the shepherds must be awake to see that they are safe and do not scatter too widely and so they are accustomed to rising early also."

Sylvia turned over and asked, "But Simoñ, you are the patron. Can't you assign these duties to others?"

Simoñ grinned down at her. "But I want to go with them to the sheep camps to see how things are going up there in the mountains. A good patron keeps in touch with all the facets of his hacienda. We are prospering because we are efficient and efficiency makes us prosper."

"You talk in riddles," said Sylvia grumpily. "I'm going back to sleep. When will you return?" Her voice was muffled by the large, feather stuffed pillow.

"I'm not sure," Simoñ bent to kiss his wife's cheek affectionately. "One flock is over the hills and on the floor of the upper Mora river valley south of here."

He heard his wife give a gentle snore and he laughed to himself as he left the room.

The herders were packed and sitting their horses when Simoñ appeared after a hasty breakfast.

"Buenos dias, patron," the herders greeted him almost in unison.

"Buenos dias." Simoñ put his boot toe in the stirrup and threw his leg over the saddle as he said, "You know the way, you lead off, Manuel."

"Si," Manuel replied politely. He spurred his horse into a trot and Alex and Enrique leading two pack mules followed Simoñ. The four dogs who were accompanying them, frolicked ahead.

Simoñ caught up with Manuel as they hit their stride, and asked, "Have you been the camp tender lately?"

"No. Although Señor Polaco has been sending one tender every week to take supplies and help out if coyotes or wolves are giving trouble or if the flock is beginning to scatter. The last time that I was a tender was two months ago," Manuel replied.

"Which flock did you go to then?"

"Camp number three," Manuel said.

"How were things there then?"

"We lost a few lambs and one ewe over a period of several weeks and that is not unexpected when we first take the flocks to the high country," Manuel told him. "As you know, such losses are not unusual when the flock is moving through rough country. Of course when they are in the meadows, they are much easier to watch."

"Who is the herder at camp number three, the camp which we will visit first?" questioned Simoñ.

"Hernandez, patron, Jose Hernandez, and he is a good one, too."

"Do we have many dogies this year? Have you talked with other tenders?"

"Some, but not many. As you know, when the ewe refuses to nurse her lamb, the herder ties her to a bush, thereby giving the lamb a better chance to nurse. If she continues to kick at the lamb, then the herder looks for a ewe who has lost her lamb and tries to get her to accept the orphan. As you know, by having the bucks in with the ewes the year around, lambs are dropped the year around, making it easier for the herder. A few lambs born all along are easier to watch than hundreds born around the same time."

"I hope that we haven't lost any black sheep," Simoñ mused.

"The black sheep are important to the safety of the flock, all right," Manuel agreed. "The herder can count them easily and if one or more are missing, that means many others are missing also. Are we going to participate in the sheep drive to the mining camps in the Sierra Madres again this year?"

"We have never missed a year yet," Simoñ answered. "We cannot afford to miss it. The sheep are worth only cincuenta centavo up here, but a peso and a half or even two and a half pesos at the mining camps. Which is why most of the families of northern New Mexico band together to get their collective flocks to market in the south."

"Money does speak, doesn't it, patron? But some who sell their flocks down there spend the extra money buying Indian slave girls. If that is true, then we really lose, don't we señor?"

"I'm afraid that is true in some cases, Manuel. And since it cost their captors nothing to capture them, their profit is clear. It doesn't seem very smart on our part," admitted Simoñ, "and they don't get any of my money."

"Nor mine," said Manuel with satisfaction.

"Of course we sell many other things in the south," said Simoñ. "In fact I hope we have enough burros to pack the large amount of goods which we have stored throughout the year in preparation for the annual trip. The store houses are full of the woolen goods which the women have woven, as well as the buffalo hides and robes and this year we will have flour to trade also. I may even trail some cattle this year, not many however, for I want to build up the herd." Simoñ broke off and pointed ahead as the first sight of the sheep came into view. They could hear the dull clonk of a wooden bell and the bark of the shepherd's dogs. "Over here!" Ricardo waved excitedly as he trotted out from under the trees.

Enrique was left at Camp Number Three and Ricardo joined the others as they rode for Camps One and Two. When all supplies and replacements had been delivered to their proper locations, Simoñ and Ricardo, Felix, and Caesar started down the mountainside toward home. When darkness fell, they made camp on the banks of the Ocate Creek, and the three peons scattered to tend the animals, build a fire and cook their meal. They, as had their replacements, talked little. They had a feeling of uneasiness with Simoñ for he was their patron. Simoñ sensed their unease and kept to himself, not wanting them to feel awkward, but every time he moved to do something they rushed to his assistance. Finally, in exasperation he said with a grin, "Someday this division, this gulf which you feel separates us from one another will be no more, and we will no longer feel ill at ease with one another."

"Si, patron," Felix said hastily, but he spoke in rote, and Simoñ knew they did not understand what he was trying to say.

How could they for they had been born under a system which demanded respect for their dons and doñas, they knew nothing else. They feared the power which their patron had over them and who could blame them? Manuel had less fear than they and so if he handled his hacienda right, in time that feeling of subservience would fade. He rose once more and started to walk to the creek. They rose too and looked uncertain, but as he continued to stroll slowly along the creek, they subsided and returned to the preparation of their meal.

When Simoñ came to a deeper portion of the creek, he sat down on the bank, removed his boots and socks, rolled up his trousers and dipped his feet in the cool water. The creek wasn't very wide at this point and the water was only knee deep, but it was as clean as the pristine air he breathed. As he kicked his feet, he noticed a glitter at the bottom of the creek bed, and he leaned over to take a better look, seconds later he bent to pick up the shiny object which had caught his attention. The peons were visiting as they worked by the fire and hadn't noticed him.

"It looks like gold!" Simoñ spoke softly as he examined the coin closely. Again he bent to look along the bottom of the creek bed and at length spotted another piece wedged between two jagged rocks. He pried it loose and placed it carefully in his pocket with the first one. After doing that, he carefully memorized the location and estimated how far up the bank it was from the fire. The remains of the campfire would be easy to find and he would pace off the distance between where he was standing and the fire.

The following day when they had reached the headquarters, Simon rode directly to Modesto's house. "I have what could be tremendous news," Simoñ told him excitedly. He withdrew from his pocket the two gold coins which he had found, and handed them to Modesto.

"Gold!" Modesto examined the coins, but could find no describable markings to indicate what they were. He glanced up at Simoñ inquisitively.

"I have not told anyone, Modesto. If we are lucky and there are more, we could be rich. Rich enough to have the finest hacienda in all Mexico!"

Modesto looked rather skeptical at these grandiose plans, but quien sabe, who knew what might happen? It certainly wouldn't hurt to go have a look!

"With this gold, we can buy rifles and cannons to protect the hacienda and we could begin trade with the Americanos as Chavez has done. There is no limit to what we can do, Modesto!"

"If there is a lot of these gold coins up there in the mountains, all these things you mention could happen," Modesto said slowly. "But first we must go to find out."

"I must tell Sylvia," Simoñ turned and leading his horse, walked briskly toward his own house.

His wife was instructing the household servants in some of their duties when Simon walked into the kitchen. When she had finished, Simoñ asked, "Do you have a moment? I have something to tell you."

"Surely, what is it?" Sylvia looked up into her husband's face fondly. "Is everything all right up at the camps?"

"Let's go out into the patio to talk," her husband said quietly. When he had shown Sylvia the two coins, she gasped, "Where did you find them?"

"Up on the Ocate," Simoñ told her softly.

"Could there be more of them?"

"I don't know, but Modesto and I are going back up to look tomorrow. We'll use the excuse that we need fresh meat."

That evening they could hardly eat their supper, so excited were they over the prospect of finding yet more gold coins.

"Leandro," Simoñ said as he looked across at his oldest son, "I want you to go to bed early tonight, for I want you to come with Modesto and I in the morning. We're riding up into the mountains."

"Si, papa."

"May I come, too?" Carlos asked hopefully.

"Not this time, Carlos, but I promise that one day you will accompany me when I go either to the mountains or out onto the Llanos."

"That's what you always say, papa," Carlos answered disappointedly.

"You are too young," Sylvia interrupted. "In another year or so you will be accompanying your father everywhere and you will be complaining that you would rather stay and play with the other boys instead of doing your share of work."

This Carlos couldn't envision and he returned to his lamb stew disconsolately.

It was difficult for Simoñ and Sylvia to fall asleep that night and when Simon did finally settle down and doze off, he was awakened by his wife who shook him and asked, "What on earth were you dreaming about and who on earth is Alvino? We have no one by that name on the hacienda."

Simoñ sat up in bed and rubbed his eyes. "It was a strange dream," he said slowly.

Sylvia was now wide awake. "Tell me about it," she demanded as she pushed her pillow against the headboard and sat up. "I can't sleep anyway."

"In my dream, I was standing in a recruiting line and a soldier yelled, 'You, there, keep in a single line. The young Spaniard in front of me looked ahead and then turned to look back down the line and then hollered back, 'We are in a single line!'

'No smart backtalk,' the soldier yelled again as he walked up to the young Spaniard and gave him a shove. He then continued down the line yelling, 'Keep in a single line.'

'That's his job,' a slightly older man who stood in front of the young Spaniard turned to explain. 'Don't you know that all Spanish soldiers must follow orders exactly? Soldiers don't think,' he continued, with a smile on his face. 'They just follow orders. My name is Alvino Mendoza.' He extended his hand.

'The young man grasped his hand and replied, "I am Jose Gomez. It is a pleasure to meet you. I hope I get a chance to sign on. I hope you do, too." he added politely.

"We'll both make it," Alvino answered. "You just wait and see."

The line moved slowly, but finally they reached the table where the recruiting officer sat. "Your name?" He glanced up at Alvino.

"Alvino Mendoza, sir." Alvino replied in the military fashion.

"Home?"

"My home was in Barcelona, Spain, señor, before I arrived here."

"Parents' names?"

"Augustine and Josephine Mendoza."

"Your father's occupation?"

"Gunsmith."

"Your occupation?"

"Unemployed at the present time, but back in Spain I helped my father."

"Sign here, and if you can't write, make your mark," the soldier said as he placed his finger on a line in the ledger.

Alvino signed his name and when he had finished, the soldier ordered, "Move on with the others."

Jose Gomez went through the same procedure and Alvino waited for him. "See, I told you we would make it," Alvino said with a grin. "We're both going to be rich."

"If we live long enough," Jose said with a laugh.

"We'll make it. Juan de Oñate is one of the best Indian fighters in all of Mexico and he is a businessman to boot. He operates a silver mine when he is not fighting Indians. His father owns silver mines in Zacatecas which makes Juan an influential person from an influential family. Associated with him, how can we fail? Oñate will become rich and in the process will make us rich also," Alvino said optimistically.

"You forgot to mention," Jose reminded him, "that his wife's family has influence also. After all, his wife is a descendent of the last Aztec emperor, Montezuma, and of Francisco Cortez, the conquerer of Mexico."

"You're right of course," Alvino agreed. "So we're in good hands! What is your background, if I am not being too inquisitive?"

"One of my ancestors was decorated by Queen Isabella herself, for bravery at the fall of the last Moor stronghold in Spain, Granada. For this bravery he also received a title. His son and his son's son followed in his footsteps and also served Spain as soldiers. Now I am to serve as they did, and make a name for myself." He grinned broadly, and added "And I won't object if I get rich in the process."

"The angels are with me," Alvino said. "To have signed on to help colonize northern Mexico and for having fallen in with one such as you."

"We are both lucky," Jose agreed.

When the colonial party was assembled, there were one hundred and thirty people who were farmers, eleven Franciscan friars, two hundred and seventy single men, some of whom were Indians and some who were Negro slaves. Eighty three carretas would be drawn by oxen and some supplies would be carried by pack mules. Seven thousand cattle were to be driven, also.

The carretas were large and cumbersome, with huge wooden wheels which had been cut from giant old cottonwoods and fitted upon wooden axles. They would move slowly, thought Jose and Alvino.

It was a crisp, clear, January morning in 1598 when the carretas moved out, headed for the Concho River and then toward the Pass to the North.

"I've heard that Coronado followed the Concho River until it joined with what he called the La Junta de los Rio," Alvino said.

"Do you suppose that Oñate will also follow that route toward the Indian pueblos, Jose?"

"No, I understand our captain will blaze a new trail."

"It's been forty years since Coronado attempted to find the gold roofed cities of Cibola and failed. Maybe Oñate will find them," mused Alvino. "If there is such a place as Cibola, Juan Oñate will find it, for he will leave no stone unturned until he does," Jose said confidently.

"And we'll be with him!" Alvino said in excitement. "We will become rich. I've heard that De Soto found pieces of gold that were worth five or six million pesos each. Maybe we'll be the owners of large pieces in the not too distant future. Hmmm, Jose?"

"Let's hope so. Some have said that De Soto was so rich that the king, himself, borrowed millions from him to keep Spain afloat. Did you know that De Soto was with Pizarro in Peru? That was before he explored Florida. His share of Atahualpa's ransom was said to be in the millions. That must have been a large room where the gold was stored for you know that Pizarro got the lion's share. I can just see those Incas standing in line with their arms full of gold cups, plates, and vases as they moved slowly toward the Spaniards who stood at the entrance of the room to receive them. Let's hope we find another Peru up north!"

"If there's gold up there, we'll find it. We Spaniards have a keen nose for the stuff," laughed Alvino. "I only wonder why they let forty years pass before organizing another expedition."

"The Mixton War," Jose answered. "That was the last super effort by the Mexican Indians to drive us into the sea. Its taken forty years to quell those attempts. Of course Juan's father, Cristobal, came out of that war a hero and gained the governorship of the state of Neuva Galicia, to boot. From there he went on to discover mines in Zacatecas, and become one of the richest men in all of New Spain. And of course Juan's mother came from royalty, with money of her own, for she is the daughter of Gonzalo de Salazar."

"So that's where our captain got all his money?" Alvino questioned.

"No," contradicted Jose. "When it comes to soldiering, it appears he rivals his father in daring and bravery. He fought many a battle with the Chichime Indians on our northern border, and while stationed on the frontier, he discovered mines of his own in San Luis Potosi, Zichu, and Charcas."

"Governor and Captain General Don Juan de Oñate wants you both to report to his nephew, Sergeant Major Vicente de Zaldivar at once." The soldier sent to relay this order pulled his horse in beside them.

"Yes sir!"

When the two men reached Vicente, the Sergeant Major already had five men gathered around him. Vicente introduced the newcomers to the five men and then continued, "We will be the advance scouts for the general. It will be our responsibility to find a new, and more direct, shorter route to where we will colonize the land, which the governor has decided to call New Mexico. This new route must be good enough to accommodate our wagons. We will not follow the route of the others along the Concho River, but will find a new route. We will be going into unexplored territory, which, if our sources are correct, is nothing but desert. But we are Spaniards who laugh at the dangers of the unknown. Not only do we laugh at them, but we welcome them." He paused to look around the circle of men and then continued firmly, "All good Spaniards are stoic by nature and are born soldiers by necessity. To their regret, the Moors found this out as have the Aztecs, Incas, and any other Indians foolish enough to resist us, rather than submit to the king and to the pope.

"We are Spaniards and we will act like Spaniards, doing what is expected of us, and that is, the impossible, which to us will be the routine. I believe we are all of the same mind on this subject, or else you would not have been chosen as advance scouts. We will leave shortly, so prepare yourselves for departure. That is all for now."

"Is it true?" Alvino asked Jose as they went back for their equipment, "that a Spaniard by the name of Sosa colonized the land where we are headed, but was brought back to Mexico City in chains?"

"Si," replied his friend, "but there was a difference."

"And what was that?"

"Señor Gaspar Castano de Sosa colonized New Mexico without the permission of the vice-roy, and that, my friend, is called breaking the law. Sosa was tried and found guilty of colonizing without permission."

"What punishment did the court administer?"

"He was exiled to China and was told never to set foot on New Spain's soil again. At least that's the way I heard it. Then, when the crown decided to colonize what Sosa had earlier occupied, he was selected from a list of conquistadores to be the best one qualified to head the expedition, but when he was sent for, to become the first governor of New Mexico, the royal court was told that he had been killed in China during a mutiny," Jose said.

"So Oñate was the crown's second choice?" Alvino commented in surprise.

"From what I've heard, that's true."

They reached their supplies and immediately began to pack. One pack mule carried their scanty belongings and as Jose was examining his sword for nicks, Alvino said admiringly, "That is sure a beauty."

"It belonged to my father and to his father before him. The handle is inlaid with gold and silver and the two emeralds are to remind us that our family was present at the surrender of the Moors at Granada. That we had a hand in freeing our country of non-believers." Alvino approached to examine the sword more closely and Jose held it out. "It's Spanish steel, all right." Alvino ran his finger along the smooth, flat surface of the blade admiringly.

"There's not a flaw in its design or a weak spot in the steel. Its blemishes were heated out of it during its manufacture," Jose said proudly. "It has served my family well over the years, and now it is serving me.

"My father told me the story behind the making of it. It was made in Toledo and its maker selected the best steel with which to work, then after he had heated it in his forge, he dipped it into the water for as long as it took to say, 'Blessed be the hour in which Christ was born.' He then reheated it and worked with it again. Reheated it once more, and dipping it again into the water, sang, 'Holy Mary Who bore Him!' He continued to work with the steel, reheating it again after working with it and returning it to the water, this time for long enough to say, 'The iron is hot.' The next time the sword was placed in the water, he said, 'The water hisses.' The next time it was heated and worked and placed once more in the water, he said, 'The tempering will be good.' Once more he heated the sword, and after finishing his hammering, he dipped it into the water for the last time and said, 'If God wills.' There, my friend, you see the finished product before your eyes."

"Spaniards make the best daggers and swords in the world. As you know, swordsmen the world over prefer the Spanish steel." Alvino looked almost reverent as he watched Jose sheath his weapon.

"We Spaniards not only make the best steel, my friend, we lead Europe in almost everything that is manufactured, and we have the best educational institutions also. I suppose we have the Arabs to thank for that. If it had not been for their occupation for hundreds of years, we might still be where the rest of Europe is at the present time. We are united now under one monarch; we all speak the same language and there is only one church, the Catholic Church.

"While other countries struggle and use their energies to try to catch up with us, we use our energy to conquer and spread the Holy Faith."

"And if we don't hurry and join our sergeant, we may have to catch up too." Alvino grinned as he mounted his horse.

When they reached the head of the column, the sergeant gave the charge of their pack mule into the hands of an aide and ordered them to ride out ahead of him and the others.

"Jose and Alvino were equipped with long lances and swords hung at their sides. They, as well as their horses, wore armor, and they rode out to be the point men for Oñate's journey northward."

Simoñ added, "As I watched this dream unfold, I also seemed to be Jose." He grinned at the memory of his vivid dream. "I guess it was finding the gold which made me dream of my ancestor and his journey to New Mexico."

"Do you suppose that your dream was really true?"

"How do I know? You know how dreams are. Some of the time you can figure them out and the rest of the time they are very puzzling."

Suddenly he turned to Sylvia in excitement. "Do you suppose what I dreamed was what really happened?" He thought a moment and added, "Could that have really been the way the sword was forged?

That sword which hung over my father's mantle and now hangs over ours?" He looked doubtful now, "But as I said, dreams leave you asking more questions than finding answers. I suppose it was just a dream."

He rose and began to pace the floor. "But they make you wonder about how much we don't know about the human mind. It was so real, so vivid, more real than any dream I've ever had." He turned toward his wife and said, "I think now that I'm awake, I'll get together what supplies we will need and get started."

'It's only three in the morning! I can imagine what Modesto will say at the very idea of your leaving so early in the morning."

Simoñ bent and peered out the window and said over his shoulder, "It's such a moonlit night that it's almost as light as day. And I'll bet Modesto won't mind leaving early if he's as excited as I am about this." He bent to kiss his wife and said, "You go back to sleep, my dear. I'll wake Leandro and get our breakfast."

"I think I will go back to sleep if you don't mind," murmured Sylvia as she turned on her side and pulled the covers up around her ears.

Simoñ woke Leandro and they were in the kitchen searching for something to eat when Rosita entered. "I will prepare your breakfast, Don Simoñ." She stifled a yawn as she spoke.

"Go back to bed, Rosita," Simoñ said. "We can get our own breakfast for once."

"No, señor, it's my job to prepare the meals at the Gomez Hacienda. Please, señors, take your seats at the table and I'll soon bring you your food."

"Whatever is quickest and easiest," Simoñ said over his shoulder as he and his son walked out of the kitchen.

In a short while Rosita was placing their plates before them, and upon them were eggs, hominy, and ham. "Would you like some batter cakes after you have finished with this?" she asked.

"You spoil us," grinned Simoñ as Leandro spoke up, "Oh, si!"

After breakfast, the father and son walked toward the stables in the bright moonlight and when they entered the stables, they found Modesto currying the horses. "I see that we're not the only ones who rise before the sun!" Simoñ laughed as he took the bridles from the tack room where they were kept. "Do you have gold fever also?"

Modesto grinned as he said, "I could hardly sleep. All I could think of was that gold that you showed me yesterday."

"Let's saddle up and be on our way, then."

The three of them soon had their horses saddled and bridled and the pack mule loaded with the necessary supplies. They were miles from the headquarters by the time the sun showed itself on the Llano horizon. The horses chose their footing carefully as they climbed higher on the rocky slopes of the Sangre de Cristo's, and the morning breeze was crisp and cool as they rode in single file. Simoñ led the way, with Leandro riding between the two men. Leandro was thoroughly enjoying the outing for he felt so adult to be riding with the two men. He felt a fleeting pity for his younger brother, but he had only time for the thought to form before the voice spoke, "They are three miles south of you." It was a strong voice which spoke.

Simoñ and the others reined in their horses abruptly and their eyes searched the trees for a sign of its owner.

"Up here," the voice spoke once more and then a lone figure stepped from behind a large ponderosa pine tree. They sat their horses silently as they studied the figure and neither side spoke for a moment or so until the stranger said, "I'm friendly, more friendly than those Navajoes over yonder." He was striding toward them now and they could see him more clearly.

"He's what they call a mountain man," Modesto said softly as he kept his eyes on the stranger. "Every stitch of his clothing is made from animal skins. He probably traps animals for a living."

"Well, just don't sit there, come on up." The stranger had halted and was beckoning in a friendly fashion.

As they rode nearer, they saw two horses standing in the trees beyond him, one of them a pack horse.

"I'm called Montes, Eloy Montes. And what might be your names? It was time you gave your horses a little breather anyway. Why don't you get down and we'll talk?"

Simoñ introduced himself and his party and they dismounted and loosened their saddle cinches.

"As I said, there is a Navajo war party just a couple of hills over—six of them. Are they what you are looking for?" He seated himself on the ground and leaned against the trunk of a tree.

"No, but we thank you for warning us. We have flocks of sheep up here in the mountains cared for by a single shepherd with each flock. Right now I am more concerned for their safety than ours."

"Then you're a good man, Simoñ, to care for the safety of your sheepherders. You must be a different strain from most patrons I've known over the years.

What do you say we follow the Navajoes to make sure they don't bother your herders?"

"Why do you want to risk your life to help us?" Leandro asked in awe.

Eloy looked at Leandro and chuckled, "Muchacho, I live every day with danger. Danger is a part of my way of life. It accompanies me wherever I go. It is as much a part of my life as my arm or leg. And besides, the Navajoes pose little danger for us...now if they were Comanches or Apaches or the early Chichimecs, then we might have something to worry about."

"I never heard of the Chichimecs of which you speak," Leandro said with interest. "Who were they?"

"Leandro, it is not polite to ask so many questions of Señor Montes," his father chided him.

"No, it's all right," Eloy protested. "Inquisitiveness is a sign of intelligence. But before I tell you about the Chichimecs, maybe we'd better be sure those Navajoes aren't heading for your flocks."

"You lead, for you know where the Navajoes are," Simoñ suggested, "we'd have no idea where to look."

The short line of riders kept in single file as they trotted through the trees toward Cerro Vista Peak.

"I'm sure you know that the Mora River and valley separate us from Cerro Vista Peak," Simoñ said as they stopped to breathe their horses.

"Si, I do know that," Eloy glanced back at Simoñ. "I learned how to trap beaver in that river when I was a boy. When we reach the next rise, we should be able to look down on the Mora Valley and if we are lucky, spot the Navajoes."

When they reached the next high point, they searched the valley and as much of the mountainside as they could see below them, but in vain. Several minutes passed in silence as each of them searched and then Leandro spoke excitedly, "There!"

The others looked over where he was pointing and then Eloy said, "It's all right, they are heading across the river and riding up into the trees east of the valley. They are probably heading for Chacon and beyond." He muttered to himself, "I think your flocks are safe, Simoñ." He reined his horse away from the edge of the hill.

"Where are you heading?" Modesto asked.

"To look for a good camp site," the mountain man said. "My animals could use some rest."

"Would you mind if we camped with you? I'm sure my son would like to hear about the Chichimecs and anything else you'd like to tell him. And to tell the truth," Simoñ said with a grin, "Modesto and I would also."

"There isn't much else to tell except that they were extremely cruel to their captives," Eloy replied. "There's a likely looking spot up ahead," he said with satisfaction.

The others knew that he had probably known that they would find the spring bubbling out of the mossy ledge on the edge of a little mountain meadow. They dismounted, unsaddled, removed their horses' bridles and led them with neck ropes to the spring to drink. They would hobble them for a few hours while they ate also. Leandro chuckled to himself as he thought how much Señor Montes would like Rosita's rice sweets.

They built a small fire and made coffee and gathered around the fire and began to eat some of the food which Rosita had packed. "I haven't had such tasty pollo con arroz, chicken with rice, since I was a little boy," Eloy accepted a second helping.

"If you think that's good," Leandro said, "wait until you eat Rosita's rice sweets."

"If you don't hush, Eloy will follow us home," Simoñ laughed.

"Would you tell us more about the Chichimecs now?" Leandro asked.

"It won't be pleasant," Eloy said as he glanced at the boy's father.

"It's all right," Simoñ said. "Leandro has to grow up some time and I guess there is no better time or better person to tell him."

"The Chichimecs used to live below the Rio Grande and toward the eastern coast of Mexico," Eloy began. "Later, the Spaniards came and found much silver in the area. Silver mines were opened and some of the Spaniards became very rich as a result. The Chichimecs fought for their land, of course, but, as was the case elsewhere, the Spaniards prevailed. Many Spaniards died cruel deaths before then, however, for the Chichimecs were cannibals. They scalped their enemies and tortured them while they were still alive and then ate them. They kept a record of the number of their victims, carving a notch on one of the bones of a victim, usually on an arm or leg bone. Sometimes the victim was still alive when they removed it. Any torture that you could possibly imagine, they probably used and many that you could never imagine.

"And they always fought in the nude, why, I don't know, but before a battle they would disrobe." Eloy paused a moment and then continued, "I've fought with and traded with most other tribes, but none of them are as cruel as what I've heard about the Chichimecs."

Simoñ began to talk of other things, thinking Leandro had heard enough for one day, and then when the conversation began to lag, Eloy slapped the boy on the back and asked, "Now where is that rice sweet you are so proud of? I'd like to sample a little of that!"

Leandro eagerly opened the package which contained the rice sweets, and offered some to the Mexican mountainman. Eloy removed one piece and took a bite and praised it. "You were right, boy, that Rosita sure knows how to cook. It is very tasty."

As they each took another piece, Leandro asked Eloy, "Why did you become a mountain man?" The boy's admiration was plain as he awaited his answer.

Eloy looked from Leandro to Simoñ and Modesto and stammered, "Some day you'll understand, Leandro. It would not be proper or wise to discuss a topic under the present circumstances."

"Why not?" Leandro asked innocently.

Simoñ and Modesto glanced at one another and then Simoñ spoke, "He'll have to learn the truth some day on that issue, also, so why don't you give him your version of the political conditions in Mexico? That is what you are thinking, isn't it?"

Eloy nodded as he turned to the youth. "I became a mountain man, boy, because of the corrupt and unjust political system which governs our country. Justice is a joke in our country and so is `freedom'. The government gives only lip service to it. What we really have in Mexico is a dictatorship by a small group of aristocrats who keep themselves in power by any means available to them, from murder to instilling fear in the people. Obey the law, they say, and most of the people seem to agree."

Leandro crossed himself and looked at his father fearfully as if to say, "Father, say that Eloy is wrong, say that what he has said is not true."

Simoñ looked at his son sadly and said, "What can I say, Leandro, I have told you approximately what Eloy has just told you. Perhaps I have phrased it in more general terms, but the gist is the same. We, Leandro, are patrons, and part of the aristocratic system. Now do you understand why I have spoken of the Americanos so often and admire their system of government? Under their system everyone has the freedom to climb as high as they wish. There are no titles and everyone is equal before the law. Under our system, I am afraid this is not true. When people live under a system such as ours for a number of years, they grow to accept it without question. Look at our peons back at the headquarters. Although I've tried to instill more pride into them, they find it difficult to accept new ideas. Most seem to accede to their lot in life without question. But we are not superior to them just because we were born into wealth or into the upper social class. There are good and intelligent people in every class.

"Our government keeps the ricos in power by force and by keeping people ignorant. Look at Santa Fe as an example. Who lives in the largest and most luxurious dwelling in all of New Mexico? The governor, of course, and who protects him? The army. And who else lives in splendor? The patrons and ricos and the army also protects them and their property."

"Simoñ, you're not a Mexican, you're an Americano struggling to be born," Eloy chuckled. He rose and stretched and declared, "Well, my friends, I think I'll be on my way. I'm heading for the northern Rockies to trap. And this time I plan to take my furs to Missouri to sell." He pondered this and added, "Or I could sell them at a rendezvous. In my line of work, I have freedom. Freedom to sell my pelts to whomever I wish and for the price I consider fair. This is true if I deal with the Americanos, but is not so here in New Mexico. Here I would have to sell my pelts to someone controlled by the governor."

"Why don't you wait now and leave in the morning?" suggested Simoñ. "I'm sure you have many more tales to tell Leandro and to us, also, which we'd like to hear."

"All right, I guess I'm not in that big a hurry," grinned Eloy as he sat down once more.

The remainder of that afternoon and evening was spent listening to some of the adventures which Eloy had experienced in his wandering. Finally Modesto said with regret, "It's time to turn in." He began to unroll his blankets. "We will have a busy day tomorrow." As he spread his blankets, he suddenly froze and then looked toward the others, "Do I hear a tristu? He cocked his head to his left and listened and the others did also.

Leandro was the first to break the silence by saying softly, "I don't hear anything."

Simoñ placed his finger across his lips and shook his head. Again they all listened and all they could hear was the wind whistling gently through the tops of the tall pines, and all they could smell was the pungent odor of the pine needles. They listened and watched for long moments, but heard nothing out of the way. Finally Modesto dismissed his notion and turned once more to his blankets. "I guess I mistook the sound of the wind for a tristu."

"Or it could have been the flute of the Macedonian!" Eloy looked quizzically at the others.

"The Macedonian?" Simon spoke in surprise. "Who is the Macedonian?"

"He is a mythical figure whom the Indians and mountain men believe roams throughout the Rocky Mountains, giving aid to anyone in need, regardless of who they are."

"What do you mean by mythical?" Modesto asked curiously.

"Just that," Eloy answered. "No one that I have ever met has admitted seeing him, but many believe that they have heard his flute. I guess maybe that flute that he is said to play could sound like a tristu or similar instrument."

"Maybe he is a shepherd," suggested Leandro.

"No," said Eloy. "At least not by what we mean by a shepherd."

"Tell us what you've heard about him," suggested Simoñ as he lay down and pulled his blankets up to his chin.

"His lodging is supposed to be on Pike's Peak," began Eloy, as he, along with the others, prepared for sleep. "But no one has ever located it, although many have searched for it, I understand. He is supposed to have come from a village in the Pindus Mountains of Greece near Macedonia which was under an oppressive Turkish rule. The Turks, who were Moslems, regarded the Macedonians and Greeks, who are Christians, as less than cattle. The legend has it that the Macedonian's family suffered much cruelty under the Turks."

"Why didn't the Macedonians resist the Turkish invaders?" asked Simoñ.

"Why didn't our ancestors resist the Moors in Spain?" countered Eloy.

"But they did," Simoñ answered angrily.

"What did it get them? No, my friend, it is not always easy to repel invaders, however much you may try. Just as the Moslems controlled Spain for hundreds of years, so did the Turks control other countries."

"Si," conceded Simoñ. "But finally we triumphed and some of my ancestors were there to take part in the fight to liberate Spain."

"But it took many years to drive them out," Eloy countered. "At the expense of much blood and sacrifice the Moslems were finally beaten and driven back to Africa. No doubt the Macedonians are suffering the same tribulations which our people suffered so long ago, and maybe worse. I have heard that what hurt the Macedonians the most were the Janisaries."

"Who were they?" Leandro sat up in interest.

"Young boys were taken from their Macedonian and Greek families and raised as fanatic Moslems, boys younger than you, Leandro. They took only the very smartest. They also took young girls, the prettiest, to serve in the harems of the officials. You ask why didn't they revolt? If they had, and they did at times, their entire villages could be wiped out."

"That sounds horrible," shuddered Leandro.

"Well, so the story goes," went on Eloy, "the Macedonian somehow escaped after he found that his family had been killed by the Turks and somehow ended up here in the Rockies. It has been said that he befriends those who are suffering because he has seen so much suffering in his part of the world."

"And he plays the tristu?" Leandro asked.

"Si, for his people were mostly shepherds, and they played a homemade wooden flute similar to our tristus."

"Do you suppose what we heard was the Macedonian playing his flute?" asked Leandro in excitement as he looked at Modesto.

"I don't know, Leandro," Modesto answered. "I'm not even sure any more that I even heard a flute. Perhaps I just thought I heard it, so faint it was. But none of you heard it, did you?"

It was quiet as each of them pondered what Eloy had told them about the Macedonian and their quiet voices were replaced by the sound of crickets, and the sound of the breeze which blew through the tops of the pines as it increased in volume. Now the hooting of an owl could be heard nearby and in the distance could be heard the faint howl of a coyote and then others answering his call. The three quarter moon cast its light over the mountainside and the shadows lengthened as the night wore on and the men slept.

The camp became a bustle of activity early the next morning as the eastern sky began to fight back the darkness. Eloy had arisen earlier than the others and was quietly making his preparations to leave.

"You should have awakened us," Simoñ told him as he and the others began to prepare breakfast.

"A peon disturbing the sound sleep of patrons?" Eloy chuckled as he packed his belongings on his pack horse.

"You're supposed to stand with your hat in your hand and with a bowed head in the presence of your superiors," joked Simoñ.

Eloy responded immediately by removing his hat and bowing low before he asked, "Or should I kneel to show the proper respect?" he grinned broadly as he spoke.

"We joke, but joking does not remove what is true," Simoñ said soberly. "Some day our joking will not be so painful, when it is no longer true."

After breakfast was eaten, goodbyes were said and Eloy rode up the slopes toward a destination unknown while the men of the Gomez Hacienda watched in silence until he disappeared from their sight. The silence was finally broken by Modesto, who suggested, "Now let's find that creek and start looking for that gold!"

"We Spaniards are good at locating gold," laughed Simoñ. "Are we to duplicate Pizarro's find today?"

"We might even begin another Potosi," Modesto said with a grin.

"What is a potosi?" Leandro asked.

"A Potosi has made many Spaniards rich, Leandro, rich beyond their wildest dreams. Spaniards have been removing from the many mines at Potosi, precious metals for hundreds of years. There seems to be no end to its rich resources."

"How do you know all these things?"

"He learned them at school," Simoñ told his son.

"What does your schooling tell us about our chances of finding large quantities of gold along Ocate Creek?" The boy asked in wonder.

Modesto and Simoñ couldn't resist chuckling at the question, but then Simoñ answered, "Not very great, I'm afraid, but who knows, it's nice to think and dream about finding more gold. Modesto has studied and can tell you about buried treasure and all of the rest of it, but that will have little bearing upon our case. Now if I knew more of my family's history, I might know whether or not anyone had ever lost any gold at our hacienda, but I know little or nothing about it."

The three packed their belongings and made haste to be on their way, for talking about it had excited them once more.

"Keep your rifle ready at all times," his father warned Leandro. "We could run into another Indian war party."

They again made camp where Simoñ had camped just two days before and after hobbling their horses began to search the bed of the creek beside their camp, and then worked upward to where Simon had found the coins. The remainder of that day was spent in that manner and when night came they returned to their camp and looked over their meager findings.

"It doesn't look too hopeful, does it?" Simoñ bent to lay more wood on the fire.

Modesto didn't reply, but seemed in deep thought. He finally turned to Simoñ and asked, "You're sure you found those coins the other day just below the sharp bend in the creek?"

"Si," answered Simoñ. "And the only one we found today was also this side of the bend."

"I was just thinking that since what we've found so far has been located below that sharp curve, there must be a rational explanation for it."

"Could someone have dropped it there trying to escape from Indians or bandits?" queried Leandro.

"That could have happened," admitted Modesto. "or did someone need to hide it and perhaps buried it near the creek bank?"

"And the creek bank gradually eroded until the gold began to fall out?" added Simoñ. "Then tomorrow we'll walk up as far as the bend in the creek and search carefully along both banks, looking for any such sign."

"What kind of container will we be looking for?" asked Leandro.

"I'd say a wooden or metal strongbox," said his father.

"It could be that it was hidden in a rawhide pouch," suggested Modesto. "After all, whoever hid it wouldn't expect to leave it there for very long."

"Maybe he was killed by Indians before he could come back for it," contributed Leandro excitedly.

"That's possible," said his father with a smile. "But I'll bet we'll find something tomorrow, unless the rest of the container was washed away or is buried in the creek bed. If that should be the case we may never find any more gold than we have already."

The first rays of the sun woke Leandro first as they filtered through the leaves of the trees overhead. Thoughts of their search came immediately to his mind and he brushed aside his blankets and leaped to his feet as he called to his father and uncle, "Time to get up!"

They made hasty work of breakfast and once more began their search. At the bend of the creek, the banks were at least six feet high and from there to their camp there was a matter of between one hundred and fifty to two hundred yards. When they reached the bend, they climbed down and walked along the gravel riverbed which bordered the water, examining the bank on either side of the creek.

"Are you having any luck?" Simoñ looked back up the creek to where Modesto and Leandro were searching. As he did so, he saw a sparkle upon which the sun's rays were reflecting part way between him and the others. His eyes were fixed on that locations as he vaguely heard Modesto's retort. "If we had, don't you think we might have mentioned it?"

"Look here!" Simoñ ran toward the spot where he had seen the shiny object "I think I have found something."

Leandro and Modesto started toward him as fast as they could walk over the rock strewn, dry part of the creek bed. When they reached Simoñ, he was busily prying another coin out of the side of the bank. The bank had eroded heavily in this area and Modesto began to dig systematically in the soft dirt above where Simoñ had found the fourth coin. Suddenly his knife struck something which didn't yield and he shouted, "I've found something! Look, I've exposed part of a leather trunk."

Simoñ and Leandro began to help him loosen the dirt around the trunk. They worked carefully so as to not dislodge any more of its possible contents. They were grinning at each other as they worked, unable to believe that they had really found it. That is, if there were still something to be found in the trunk. As they dug, they exposed more and more of the trunk and while the upper portion seemed to be almost intact, the lower half was badly decomposed, and that had apparently led to the gradual release of the gold coins.

"Keep digging," said Simoñ.

"That's one thing you don't have to encourage us to do," Modesto said as he mopped his face with his neckerchief.

"You're right," conceded Simoñ. "The gold has been here a long time and it won't go anywhere in the next few minutes. I think it might be smart on our part for one of us to stand guard on the creek bank to keep an eye out for danger. In our excitement we have neglected to post a sentry."

Simoñ stood watch while Modesto and Leandro continued to dig around the old trunk and then began to try to loosen it from its base. When that threatened to collapse the trunk completely, they broke into it and found it packed to the very top with linen pouches, each of them secured at its very top. Modesto lifted one out of its nest gingerly, cut the thong which secured it and opened wide the pouch. He gasped in wonder at what he saw and held it out for Leandro to peer into. Leandro let out a squeal and looked up at his father. "It's really so, father! It's really there!"

The next few minutes were spent pouring out the contents of the pouch and counting the coins in order to estimate how many there might be altogether. It staggered them to consider what they had found and they hastily placed the coins back in the pouch. Modesto then handed each of the remaining pouches up to Simoñ and Leandro who packed them away out of sight as speedily as possible. They then looked for sign of any other trunk in the ground near the first one and finally concluded that there had been just the one. But what a one! They had removed thirty-six pouches, twelve to a layer and there were one hundred gold coins in each pouch. Or at least the first one had held that number. The last pouch in the deteriorated portion of the trunk had only a dozen coins remaining in it. They knew the missing coins could be scattered over a large area in the creek bed, and it wasn't surprising that Simoñ had spotted two of them, the wonder was that they hadn't found more of them yesterday when they first began to search.

"Whenever we come this way, I am going to look around the creek," Leandro told his father and uncle. "Wouldn't Carlos enjoy helping me?" He grinned in anticipation and his elders realized that for him the search was at least as enjoyable as the actual finding of the gold.

"How are we to get the gold home?" Leandro asked.

"We'll pack it home on the horses," his father told him, "which means we'll have to go slowly, for we'll have a heavy load."

"Well, let's get to it then," proposed Modesto.

The gold was packed evenly on the pack horse and in the saddle bags of each rider and the three headed back down the mountainside to the headquarters. They camped early that night to rest the animals and continued on the next day, reaching home in the early evening. They quietly unpacked the gold while the peons were at supper and placed it in the leather trunks which were scattered around the walls in Simon's and Sylvia's bedroom. "No one ever opens these except Sylvia or me," said Simoñ. "We'll have a new one made, supposedly for clothing and place them in there, under lock and key. In the meantime as an added precaution I think you'd better store some of our winter clothing over the gold, Sylvia."

"I'll do that right now," Sylvia walked over to a leather trunk which rested at the right of the bed. "I'll remove some from here and some from the others and then I'll place all the rest of our clothing that we removed from the trunks on top of our woolen goods."

"While you're doing that, I'll go tell my mother of our good news. Leandro, you and Modesto go on ahead, I'll be right .along, but will you ask Luis to join us in the dining room also?"

"It's strange," said Sylvia, "although we know we can do many good things for our people and our hacienda, still it places a heavy burden on us, does it not?"

Simoñ sighed as he looked fondly as his wife, "We'll not let it be too heavy a burden, my dear, we'll use it for the good of all." He grinned and whirled her around exuberantly. "I'll buy you whatever you desire, my love."

Some of the others were already assembled in the dining room and when he entered, he looked around the circle and said, "Please be seated. Leandro, get some wine from the cabinet and pour for us."

"What are you planning now?" Modesto questioned with a smile.

Luis, the mayordomo, entered and asked, "Did you send for me, Don Simoñ?"

"Si," Simoñ and Modesto rose as Doña Sylvia entered the room and Modesto hurriedly pulled the chair back for the doña.

"Please tell the Prudencio brothers, Luis, that I wish to see them," Simoñ continued.

"Esta bien," Luis replied and he turned and left the room.

"What is this all about, my husband?" Sylvia settled herself in her chair and looked inquiringly at Simoñ.

Simoñ began to explain just as Doña Maria entered the room, and he rose once again and hastened to escort his mother to a chair. Then he resumed his seat and began once more, "We are going to go to Missouri in the United States to purchase some modern rifles and cannons. And I think we'll also stock up on some goods for the Prudencios to use in their trade with the Comanches." He looked at his mother and then at the others. Doña Maria said nothing, but waited as Simoñ glanced around the circle before he went on. "We have made very little progress here at the hacienda beyond what was accomplished at the beginning, for there was a limit to what we could do with our resources. Now that we have found the gold, this changes the situation. I want to expand the hacienda out onto the Llanos and also expand the trade with the Indians, especially with the Comanches.

The gold has given us the capital we need to make that expansion. What do you think, mother?"

"How do you propose to deliver the gold to Missouri safely so that you can purchase these things?"

"We will lease a wagon from Salvador Chavez and go with his wagon train to Missouri, Simoñ said.

"Are you going to tell him about the gold?" Doña Maria asked doubtfully. "I don't trust him, he could have you killed before you ever reached Missouri. He might be capable of such a deed, you know."

"Patron," Ramon Prudencio and his two brothers entered the room at that point, and Simoñ waved them to the empty chairs at the table. The three men swept their sombreroes from their heads as they bowed to the two señoras before seating themselves rather uneasily and looking toward Simoñ for enlightment.

"Mi amigos," he said, "it is time that we expand our trade with the Indians. We propose to travel to Missouri to purchase trade goods, wagon loads of it. Are you prepared to expand the trade?"

"We have been ready for some years, Don Simoñ," answered Ramon respectfully.

"Good," the patron told them. He proceeded to tell them of the finding of the gold pieces which would enable them to begin their expansion. "My mother was just asking me how I was going to get the gold to Missouri without Salvador Chavez being any the wiser. I had thought of leasing one of his wagons and concealing it beneath buffalo robes or other pelts which we may have accumulated. As you know, his wagon trains pass not far from here on the Santa Fe

Trail, and we can join him and use his train as protection from attack."

"Very good," his mother and wife applauded, and his wife asked, "Who will accompany you to Missouri?"

"Modesto will remain here to care for the hacienda and I will take Leandro and the Prudencios."

"Simoñ," Modesto rose and began to pace back and forth. "Why am I to be left behind yet again?"

"So that I will have a hacienda to come back to," grinned Simoñ. "You, my faithful friend, and brother-in-law, are capable of that task. While I know that you wish to accompany me, I know that you realize that I am correct in leaving the responsibility of the hacienda and all of its inhabitants in your capable hands."

"I understand," said Modesto ruefully. "It will be as you wish."

"Ramon," Simoñ turned to the Comanchero, "will you be ready to accompany me to the Chavez Hacienda to get the wagon?"

"Si, patron." Ramon nodded.

"Elmon, you and Frutoso do whatever you need to do to be ready to modify the freight wagon so that the gold may be concealed safely. Now let us hope that Salvador Chavez is planning to make a trip back to Missouri soon."

After conferring among themselves, Elmon spoke up, "Patron, we were thinking of making a false bottom on the wagon, if that is agreeable to you."

"Whatever you think," Simoñ replied. "Just as long as Salvador or his wagon master do not suspect anything. Remember, the gold is heavy, and so we'll make sure that we pick a good sturdy wagon and one of his best teams of mules to pull it. Whatever number of spans you judge necessary to do the job."

"Si, patron," Elmon replied. "Do not concern yourself, I will take care of the matter."

"Well, then," Simoñ said, "if there is nothing else to be said, let us retire for the night. We'll have a busy day ahead of us tomorrow."

"Bueños noches," the Prudencios rose to their feet. They bowed to the ladies and left the room, and when they had gone, Maria said, "Don't you think that Leandro is a little young to go with you to Missouri?"

"Grandmama!" Leandro protested.

"Mother," Simoñ replied with a polite, but firm smile, "Leandro is no longer just a small boy. He is nearly my height and he does the work of a man around the hacienda."

"But," Sylvia rose to Maria's defense, "he may be approaching a man in height, but he is still a boy inside."

"Ladies," Simoñ said persuasively "it is time for Leandro to take up the responsibilities of a man. Let go of him, give him a chance to show of what he is made. He's a Gomez. Let him prove himself."

"I suppose you are right," Sylvia said hesitantly. She looked from the eager face of her son to that of her husband and then at Maria's dubious expression, and threw up her hands as Maria winked an eye and nodded slightly. "I can see I am outnumbered."

"Thank you, mother," Leandro said as he hugged his mother. "And you too, grandmama." He gave his grandmother a swift hug and rushed from the room excitedly.

"He's like you," Maria said proudly as she looked at her son. "He'll be able to take care of himself."

Simoñ and Ramon rode to the Chavez Hacienda south of Las Vegas and returned with the freight wagon. "The next wagon train will be in two weeks," Simoñ told them jubilantly. "Let's make sure that we are ready to join it."

"Patron," Ramon said softly. "Do you think this is a good time to leave the hacienda?"

Doña Maria looked at Ramon in surprise and then turned to her son. "What did you hear at the Chavez Hacienda? Is something wrong?"

The men looked at one another for a moment and neither spoke.

"Well!" Maria spoke in a tone which was half scolding, "I'm waiting for an answer."

"Mother," Simoñ replied somewhat sheepishly. "It seems that the state of Texas is in revolt against Santa Anna."

"In revolt?" Doña Maria couldn't have looked more astonished.

"Yes, mother, it seems that the Mexican Americano citizenry doesn't agree with the president and his intention to do away with the Constitution of 1824. The Americanos who moved to Texas and became citizens of Mexico, want the constitution restored. Of course Santa Anna disagrees and refuses."

"What else did you learn on your trip to the Chavez Hacienda?" Doña Maria asked indignantly. Indignant that her son had not thought it necessary to tell them at first.

"Apparently many other states agree with the Texans because they too, are in revolt. It is rumored that Santa Anna has taken to the field with his army and is presently in the southern part of Mexico attempting to quell the revolts there. He has sent a General Cos to put down the revolt in Texas."

"With all these revolts going on, don't you think it would be wise to stay at home and protect your family and hacienda?"

Doña Sylvia had entered the room and asked, "Are we in any danger? Will we be safe here?"

Simoñ smiled reassuringly at the women and explained, "That is precisely why I wanted Modesto to stay here. If he judges that things have become too dangerous, he will leave here with all of the occupants of the hacienda and ride toward Missouri to meet us. I don't anticipate any danger soon, and should be on my way back with the means to defend us before any trouble arises this far north. As you know, it is imperative that we have modern weapons with which to defend ourselves. If I succeed in purchasing what I want, and return to New Mexico before the revolt spreads, the revolutionaries will stay clear of us."

"Spreads?" Doña Maria questioned. "What do you mean, Simoñ?"

"There is strong talk of a revolt here in the north, also," Simoñ told them calmly.

"Continue," his mother demanded. "we need to know it all. Please don't leave out the slightest detail."

Simoñ thereupon went into everything he had heard concerning his information thus far. "What is happening has been inevitable. I have seen it coming, which is why I have looked to the United States as our saviour. It is she and she alone, who has the authority to provide us with a stable and free society. Santa Anna and others like him can only bring us more and heavier taxes and send more soldiers to force us to pay them. More and more of the people, especially the peons, resent such arbitrary authority along with the heavy and unfair taxation which accompanies it inevitably. The spirit of revolt has been smoldering for years among these people, which is why the government has refused to permit them to own modern weapons. As I see it," he continued grimly, "it is only a matter of time before what is happening in Texas and Mexico, further to the south, happens here in New Mexico. No one can expect people to submit to such brutal subjugation forever. Sooner or later a leader will emerge and the revolt will begin. I am hoping that I can get to Missouri and back before the flames of revolution are ignited here."

"You don't paint a very pretty picture," his mother told him soberly.

"What the future holds may not be a very pretty picture, mother, unless the Americanos come before the revolution begins here, and we are spared the blood and anguish of war. I still believe that America is our only hope."

Doña Maria listened and was silent for long moments before she finally commented, "Now after many years of watching and listening to you, Simoñ, skeptically, I might add, I am just now beginning to hear what you have been trying to tell us. You have vision and understanding, my son, and you seem to have the ability to grasp a situation quickly and see through the smoke screen around us to see the core behind it all. I am proud of you, very proud."

"Thank you, mother," Simoñ answered softly. "I have more disturbing news and that is that Santa Anna has borrowed money from every country willing to loan it to him and rumor has it that he is in default of his payments. Even the Catholic Church has been used poorly and the Church has been forced to send its capital out of the country. Apparently this borrowed money has been spent by a few to maintain their luxurious life styles. It is even rumored that he is looking for countries who might be interested in purchasing part of Mexico, and even New Mexico is said to be for sale. If that is what he and his ruling class of Gachupines want for Mexico, I say 'viva America'!" He paused as he looked at each of them in turn before he continued. "From the time that the mobs were paid to yell 'Viva Agustin', to our present day, our country has been ruled by greed, and incompetent men. For over thirty years after the first president of our country captured the palace we have run through presidents almost as fast as we brand cattle. Our present president has held that office no less than six times himself. No, my friends, if we are to have stability, justice, and equality, we must look to America." He glanced at his good friend, Modesto, and said, "I quote an Americano, Patrick Henry, who said, 'If this be treason, make the most of it.'"

"It seems to me from where I sit," his mother said quietly, "that purchasing the modern weapons you speak of, Simoñ, is the first thing we should put in motion. Without them we would be vulnerable to any force. With them, we may be left alone. Is there no way that you can convince Señor Chavez to move up his departure date a week or two?"

A knock was heard at the door and Luis entered. "Patron, there is a gentleman here from the Chavez Hacienda with a message."

Simoñ rose from the table and left the room. A man dressed as a caballero stood near the outer door and asked, "Are you Señor Gomez?"

"Si."

"I have a message from Don Chavez." The man handed Simoñ a note. "Shall I carry an answer back with me?"

"Si," Simoñ replied after quickly scanning the message. "Tell your patron that we will be ready."

"Si, señor," the messenger said as he turned and left.

Simoñ entered the dining room once more with a broad smile on his face. "Señor Chavez is complying with your wish, mother, he has sent a message saying that his wagon train has already left his hacienda and should pass east of here tomorrow sometime after lunch. That if we want to accompany his train, we had better meet it near the mound on the Llanos which resembles a wagon. Now if you think it would be dangerous for me to leave the hacienda at this time, I won't go. What do you all think?"

Doña Maria spoke first, "I think you have planned well, son, and I think we should honor your plan. If things do get to that point, we can always do as you say and travel toward Missouri on the Santa Fe Trail. This business in Missouri needs your attention immediately, for it seems to me that our entire future depends on this first trip to America."

"Sylvia?"

She smiled confidently as she said, "I have complete faith in your judgment, Simoñ."

"Modesto?"

"Your remaining here will not render it less dangerous, but on the other hand if you do not get the rifles we know for certain it will be more dangerous later, so I agree with the others. You must go, you need to go!"

"Good," Simoñ turned to Ramon. "You and your brothers prepare the freight wagon for we leave at five in the morning."

CHAPTER VIII

W hen the Chavez wagon train rolled into sight of Westport Landing at midday, Simoñ said to Ramon who rode on his left side, "This is where our future begins, Ramon. If all goes well, we will make the hacienda a safe haven for anyone within fifty miles of us. We will gain a reputation as the protector of the unprotected, a safe harbor where people can anchor until the storm subsides. A fortress of justice, security, and serenity. As time passes, our hacienda will grow to be known as the beacon light of hope and a dispenser of collective courage. It will be a new beginning," Simoñ mused. "A new beginning."

Ramon saw hope and excitement radiating from Simoñ's face and he smiled as he replied, "Si, patron. I, too, believe in your dream for our forgotten people. You will be their knight in shining armor."

Simoñ said nothing for a while and then turned to Ramon. "Without people such as you and your brothers, the dream of a better future for our people would remain only a dream. We are all in this together, my compadre." He turned to his right where Leandro rode and said with a happy smile, "I want you in on my dreams for our people from their conception, because it will be you, my son, who will have to complete that dream. I want you at my side at all times. Remember that. Do not wait to be asked to come with me, I want you there with me. Do you understand, son?"

"Si, papa." Leandro drew himself up a little taller in the saddle as he rode proudly beside his father.

"I think it is time for you to stop calling me papa, Leandro, papa sounds too immature, too unequal, too unsure of yourself. I want others to see you as you are, as I see you, as strong, independent and self assured. Why don't you call me father?"

"All right, father," Leandro agreed with a smile.

The Chavez wagon train continued to sway ponderously toward their destination and as they reached the outlying dwellings, Simoñ said, "Ramon, you, Elmon, and Frutoso stay with our wagon, and I'll ride ahead with Leandro to see what we can find out."

Ramon reined his horse nearer to the huge wagon which Frutoso was now driving. Elmon rode on the off side beside his brother.

The business district of Westport Landing was scattered along the banks of the Missouri River. They could see river boats tied to the docks and large warehouses fronting the landings. Men were busily either loading or unloading the boats.

"The buildings all seem to be constructed of logs or lumber," Leandro observed, as they saw for the first time an American frontier town.

"There don't seem to be any buildings built of adobe, do there?" Simoñ said.

"And look at the people," Leandro said. "Listen to the different languages being spoken. And look at the Indians of various tribes who are going about their business not molesting one another. And their dress! Everything from buckskin to homespun."

"There are even a few Mexicans among them," remarked Simoñ.

"Excuse me, señor," Simoñ spoke to a buckskin clad horseman who had ridden abreast of them. "Where are those boats which are tied along the dock taking their cargoes?"

"You must be new here." The stranger grinned as he reined his horse to a slower pace. He gave Simoñ and Leandro a closer inspection and then continued, "You must have come in with the Chavez train."

"That is right, señor, we did," Simoñ replied politely.

The frontiersman turned in his saddle and glanced toward the docks and then back at the strangers. "Well, some of them go up the Big Muddy and some of them go down. It depends a lot on what freight they are carrying."

"How can boats with such a heavy load be propelled against such a strong current?" Leandro asked with interest.

"Sonny," the frontiersman grinned, "this is your first trip to Missouri, isn't it? Do you see those big wheels which are located either at the sides of the boats or at the rear? Well, those big wheels are turned by steam engines which are located inside the boat.

"When the engines are fired by wood, the wheels turn and move the boat through the water. You see, the wheels have big paddles on them, which make the boats move."

"The boats seem to leave in pairs. Why is that, señor?" Simoñ looked at the frontiersman eagerly.

"For more than one reason, for protection against hostiles, and also, if they experience trouble with sandbars or anything else. From time to time, the river floods and when it does, it washes debris downstream. Sometimes trees are partially buried in the mud and if an end of one of them is protruding toward an oncoming boat, and is concealed under the muddy water, it can gut a boat. The sandbars can be treacherous for they can change, and often do, continually with every flood."

"If they become stuck on a sandbar, what do they do?" Leandro asked.

"Most of the time, if they shift their load, perhaps unload until the boat rises in the water, they can get off all right, but sometimes they have to abandon their boat completely and then there is one more hazzard in the river."

"That sounds like a slow way to transport goods," observed Simoñ.

"You're right there, my friend," the frontiersman agreed. "If they are lucky, they may make eight miles an hour, but that is upstream, and they make much better time, of course, going downstream, barring trouble. And remember, one boat can transport a lot of freight at one time. Slow, though they may be, if they run into difficulty, they still can move much faster than a wagon train."

"Thank you, señor, for being so kind, and removing some of our ignorance," said Simoñ with a smile.

"It was my pleasure," the frontiersman grinned cheerfully.

"Please forgive me for not introducing my son and myself," Simoñ said somewhat belatedly. "My name is Simoñ Gomez and this is my son, Leandro."

"Pleased to make your acquaintance," the frontiersman replied. "My name is Reese Marquette. I will be visiting your country soon."

"My country? If it is not too impertinent, may I ask why?"

"To visit a friend," replied Reese cautiously.

"Oh, I see," Simoñ answered politely. "Maybe we will have the pleasure of your company on our return trip? Please forgive my inquisitiveness one more time, Señor Reese, but would you be so kind as to tell me where I could purchase rifles such as the one which you are carrying?"

"Of course," replied Reese. "I'll do better than tell you, I'll take you to the man who manufactures them, myself."

The three rode down the street and Reese said, "Be careful of the mud holes, they can fool you! They are deeper than they look. To prove my point you can see that wagon up ahead of us."

"It's practically buried up to its axles in mud," said Simoñ with a grin.

"This happens every spring, so I'm told," Reese said with a chuckle.

"You sound as though you are not too familiar with Westport Landing."

"Well, yes and no. I'm familiar with it and then again I'm not familiar with it. Let's let it go at that." He grinned and went on, "Here's my friend's place of business. Follow me and I'll introduce you to him."

They tied their horses at the hitching rack which stretched in front of the long building and followed Reese inside.

"Hello, Reese!" A man called as he saw his friend enter.

"Otto, this is Simoñ Gomez and his son, Leandro. This is Otto Muller, Señor Gomez. They are interested in some of these." Reese raised the rifle which he carried in his right hand.

Otto shook hands with Simoñ and Leandro and said "Pleased to meet you both. So you like Reese's rifle?"

Simoñ glanced at Reese and then back at Otto and Otto saw the hesitation in his eyes and quickly squelched it. "Reese is like a father to me. I would trust him with my life. In fact I have." He glanced at Reese fondly and continued, "So don't be afraid to tell me what you have in mind."

Simoñ spoke quickly, "Forgive me, Señor Reese, but my purpose here in Westport Landing is of extreme importance to me. It could be a matter of life or death, so I'm sure you can understand my caution."

"I understand," Reese replied. "and I will leave if that will make you more comfortable."

"I have to trust someone and my instincts tell me that I should do that with you two. Is there some place where we can talk in private?"

"Of course, come back to my office," Otto went ahead to lead the way and shut the door securely behind them.

Simoñ then told Otto and Reese about his dream for his hacienda and that he expected American annexation of New Mexico.

An hour had passed before the conversation ended and when it had, Simoñ and Leandro were presented with five of Otto's rifles in advance of the full order. Three of them were for the Prudencios.

"You know that you're playing with fire, don't you?" Reese said as they finally left Otto's office. "The Mexican government will not stand idly by and let you fortify your hacienda. Such a fortification will pose a threat to its authority. You will be a challenge."

"You sound like my mother," Simoñ said with a smile. "But I told her that if I am cautious, they will never find out."

"I hope so," Reese replied. "Such a plan can only succeed if all of your people are loyal to you."

"I have confidence in their loyalty," Simoñ said with assurance.

"You had better be right," Otto observed wryly. "Or you're a dead man." He paused and then continued thoughtfully, "I'm sorry that I cannot help you with the four cannons, but I do have a friend who might be able to help you. Come back this evening and in the meantime I'll try to set up a meeting."

"Thank you, my friend," Simoñ said as he shook Otto's hand.

"It was my pleasure," Otto told him. "I, too, have a dream such as yours, which is why I left Germany. However, my dream is not as ambitious as yours. Good luck to you and your people. I'll pray that you'll succeed."

"I must," Simoñ replied confidently.

Reese looked at Otto and then at Simoñ and Leandro and said, "I believe you will. You have my prayers also. Some day you'll be an adopted American such as myself."

Simoñ looked puzzled. "What do you mean. I don't understand."

"I'm a Canadian by birth," Reese told him.

"You're an American by choice."

Reese nodded, "By choice. Freedom is like a drug, once you taste it, you become addicted for life."

"Well, we must be going. My men are waiting for us," Simoñ said.

"Where are you staying?" Otto grinned, "I hope not in one of our inns for they are not very pleasant, for most have many beds in each room and more than one person has rented each bed. This is a rapidly growing frontier town, with many inadequacies, I'm afraid."

"We'll stay with our wagon and sleep under it," Simoñ told him. "And with these new rifles, thanks to you, we will not be molested."

As they started to walk out the door, Simoñ turned back to ask, "We're going to need some freight wagons. Can you recommend someone for me to see about that?"

"McAllister is the one to see about that. You'll find his yards up on the bluffs above us," Otto told him.

"Once again, I thank you."

Otto and Reese watched as their new acquaintances walked out to the hitching rack and then Otto said, "That is quite an order he gave me. I'd better see about getting it started."

Reese nodded and he, too, walked out to his horse.

"Let's ride up to McAllister's and have a look at his wagons, what do you say, Leandro?" Simoñ asked as they rode away from Otto's establishment. They reined their horses in the direction of the bluffs which overlooked the Missouri River and as they rode, a strong odor began to assail them.

"What is that awful smell?" Leandro sniffed in disgust.

"It appears to be coming from that building just ahead of us," his father said as he reined in his horse. "It's my guess that there are green buffalo hides stored in it. Let's circle around the area and climb that bluff east of that large house halfway up the bluff."

The top of the hill was reached and the McAllister wagon yards could be seen not far ahead. They pulled their horses up in front of the office, tied them to the hitching rack and entered the office. A man sitting behind a desk looked up and asked, "May I be of any help?"

"Yes," Simoñ answered. "We're interested in buying some freight wagons."

The man rose from behind his desk and proved to be tall and thin. "You've come to the right place, for we have a large selection of conestogas or the 'road wagon' as it is sometimes called. We also have some 'Dearborn' wagons. Would you like to look at them?"

"Yes," replied Simoñ.

"My name is Tom Harcrow. I manage the yard for Mr. McAllister. He is back in Pittsburgh right now ordering some wagons. None of our wagons are manufactured here. They are all made in Pittsburgh, by master craftsmen and then shipped here by way of steamboat."

"My name is Simoñ Gomez and this is my son, Leandro."

Hands were shaken and Tom said, "Let me show you the wagons. They are out back."

When the yard was reached, Tom stopped beside a large Conestoga and asked, "Are you interested in large wagons such as this, or perhaps a smaller model?"

"This one looks like what we might want," Simoñ said as he and Leandro began to walk around it admiringly.

"This is a very sturdy wagon," Harcrow told them. "It is built of hard woods and as I said, master craftsmen constructed it. This one is twelve feet long, two and a half feet deep, and three and a half feet wide. It is built to carry from eight hundred to a thousand pounds. The wagon has three osnaburg covers over it to help protect your merchandise. To prevent your load from shifting when you're either pulling up a hill or going down one, the wagon is constructed so that the front half slopes up and forward and the rear of the wagon slopes back and up. This keeps your load stable and snug. We also carry a smaller wagon such as this one here. It is called the 'Dearborn' and carries roughly half the load of the Conestoga. As the Conestoga, it is built by master craftsmen who use only the best of the hard wood available."

Simoñ shook hands with Tom Harcrow as he told him, "Thank you for your time, Señor Harcrow. We will want to think about your wagons before we decide."

"The pleasure is mine. The wagons are ready for immediate delivery if you decide to purchase one."

"Thank you again," Simoñ said as he and Leandro turned to leave the yard.

When they got back to their wagon, they proudly presented rifles to each of the Prudencio brothers. The three men inspected their rifles closely and Ramon murmured, "We can keep the entire Mexican army at bay with such rifles! Are these the kind you plan to purchase, Don Simoñ?" He raised his rifle to his shoulder and sighted down the barrel.

"That is what I plan to do. What do you think of them?"

The broad smiles on the faces of the three men told Simoñ what he wanted to know even before they answered.

That night, Simoñ and Leandro returned to Otto's office hoping to cement the deal for the purchase of four cannons, but it was not to be. When the time for the meeting arrived, Otto's promised guest did not appear.

"I was not able to locate my contact man," Otto said ruefully. "It appears that he has not yet returned from a journey up the Missouri, but we do have an alternative."

"And what might that be?"

"Some of the steamboat traffickers have mounted twelve pound guns on their river boats. It is possible that some of them might have some spare guns which they would sell, or they might have some on boats which are in dry dock for repairs. They could sell their guns to you, and have replacements when their boats are ready to go into the water once more."

"I'll look into that in the morning," Simoñ promised Otto.

"Those twelve pounders can shoot grape shot or shells and balls and they might be a good substitute," Otto added.

The meeting was not a complete failure, for in addition to hearing about a possible substitute for a cannon, Simoñ placed an order for the ordnance necessary to accompany the rifles.

Early the next morning, Simoñ and Leandro appeared along the wharf section of Westport Landing, hoping to be able to locate some of the twelve pound guns. They finally found the owner of a small fleet of steamboats who was repairing two heavily damaged boats.

"Good morning, señor," called Simoñ as they walked closer to the boat where men were already working. "Could you tell me who owns these boats?"

"I am the owner," a loud voice answered as a large man walked from the other side of the boat. He was stripped to the waist and it was obvious that he was taking an active part in the repair work. "What can I do for you?" He spit tobacco juice to one side as he spoke.

Simoñ introduced himself and his son to Clyde Lindstrom and said, "I would like to purchase four twelve pound guns and I was wondering if you might consider selling yours?"

"You are Mexican?"

"That's right," Simoñ answered.

"Are you from Texas?" This question was a hostile one.

"No, we're from New Mexico. Why do you ask?"

"Remember the Alamo!" yelled the big man angrily. "I'll be damned if I'll sell my twelve pounders to be used against Sam Houston and his men. I doubt very much if you'll find anyone else who will accommodate you either. So you had better be on your way, sonny, before me and my men give you both a free swim."

Simoñ wasn't intimidated and he asked quietly, "Do you know Otto Muller?"

"Sure," Clyde answered. "Everyone knows Otto, what of it?"

"He will vouch for my intended purpose for those twelve pounders of yours. If I can persuade him to come here, will you take his word for my integrity?"

"Sure!" Clyde replied roughly. "Otto's word is as good as gold around here."

"Leandro?" Simoñ motioned to his son and nodded in the direction of Otto's store.

"Si, padre," Leandro responded as he left to seek Otto.

"Care for a drink?" Clyde seated himself on a wooden crate and took a long pull from a flask.

"What kind of accident did your boats have to cause so much damage?"

"Damned buffalo," Clyde replied as he took another long swig of whiskey. He wiped his mouth before he continued, "They acted as if my boats weren't even in the river. The whole herd, thousands of them, came to the river to drink, but the lead cows were pushed into the river by the others behind them, it seems the others wanted a drink too," Clyde chuckled. "The lead cows did not seem to want to move fast enough so the rest of them pushed them right out into the water. In minutes, those mangy critters had engulfed my boats, and jostled them about until they were nearly sunk. That's what happened to them. Say, are you one of them outfitters, or one of them commission merchants out to make a fast buck?"

"No, neither," Simoñ replied with a polite smile. "I'm trying to establish a trade route, so that I may do exactly as you are doing with your boats. And I give you my word that I am not here to purchase guns to use against Sam Houston. I'm trying to become a business man and at the same time protect my hacienda."

"From what I've heard, that's impossible to do without that fellow, Santa Anna's permission, so don't take me for a chump, mister. I may not have had much schooling, but that does not make me blind to what is happening in your country. You aristocrats treat your people worse than we treat our dogs." Clyde took another pull on his flask and then warmed to his task, "Why that Santa Anna fella is a traitor to his own people. He promised them religious reforms and then went back on his word and sided with the Church and its large land holdings and business interests. In my estimation, religion should not be in business, but care only for the religious needs of the people and how about that fellow, Bustamanti, whom Santa Anna drove out? He was a traitor, too. He stopped Americans who went to Texas from taking slaves, but permitted his friends in the upper class to own peons which is just a fancy name for slaves. He even stationed soldiers in Texas who had been recruited from prison, and gave them the right to declare martial law when it pleased them. Those soldiers committed all kinds of autrocities, from rape to murder, under the protection of martial law. The Americans finally got their fill of them, and forced them to leave most of the areas in which they were stationed."

"I'm afraid you know much more about what is going on in my country than I do, señor," Simoñ said warily. "But believe me, Señor Clyde, I am not like those aristocratic people that you describe so well. When Señor Otto gets here, he'll explain, but until he does, let's talk about more pleasant subjects."

"Sure," Clyde replied gruffly. "What do you want to talk about?"

"Tell me something about your business, Señor Clyde."

"Well, to begin with, we average about ten tons of supplies on a steamboat for every member of the crew and although every kind of transportation has its drawbacks, being on the river suits me. I'd not like the job of using mules to transport goods, with the problem of loading and reloading them every day, I can tell you that. Some places of course, hauling goods over land is the only way to go, but that's not my style." He took another drink after offering it to Simoñ in a perfunctory manner.

"I see that you know your business, señor; you must be very successful."

"In America, yes, but if I were in your country, the answer would be no," Clyde replied.

"I agree with your assessment of the economic conditions in my country, but some day it will change," Simoñ said confidently.

"Some day the peons in your country will rise up and throw out the aristocrats," Clyde said. "They will do it just as they revolted against Spanish rule not too long ago and drove the Spaniards back to where they came from."

"Hello, Simoñ," Otto called as he walked toward them. "What seems to be the problem?"

"There's no problem," Simoñ replied, "Clyde here needs to be assured that I will not use his twelve pounders against Sam Houston. Could you convince him that I would not do such a thing? Leandro and I will take a little walk so that you two gentlemen can talk. Come on, son."

Within a short time Simoñ had his rifles, twelve pound guns, and fourteen Conestoga wagons loaded with trade goods which he believed would be in demand by the Comanches. Otto had helped them to recruit a wagon train crew and a wagon master. The wagon master, Justin Thurman, was a mule man who got the best mule skinners available on such short notice. Reese Marquette was to accompany the wagon train as the head scout.

The Gomez and Prudencio families were happy with the results of their trip to Missouri and were now anxious to get back to the hacienda, for they were worried about the highly inflammable political situation which existed in Mexico, and New Mexico in particular.

At dawn, on May twenty-fourth, Justin's voice could be heard as he yelled with a loud roar, "Stretch 'em out!" The wagon train was on its way. Reese rode out ahead and was not sighted after that very often, perhaps once a day, as he checked in to make a report, or drink a cup of coffee. Sometimes he spent the night with the wagon train, but he was back out before the sun rose, keeping watch for any sign of trouble.

Simoñ, Leandro, Ramon, Elmon, and Frutoso also rode as out-riders, keeping a sharp lookout. Justin rode in front of the train at a little distance. When Simoñ drew within hailing distance of him this day, Justin beckoned to him and Simoñ asked, "What's wrong?"

"Have you noticed the number of rattlesnakes, some of them very large, too? There seems to be more of them this spring than usual. I suggest you assign one or more of your men to ride ahead of the train a ways and either kill or scatter them for if we don't they'll strike at the mules, crippling some and killing others. These snakes could slow us down more than Injuns. They could even bring the train to a halt and force us to return for replacements."

"I'll take care of it," Simoñ said as he reined his horse and loped off to attend to it.

Shortly, Frutoso and Elmon could be seen as they scanned closely the area that the train would soon approach.

That evening Reese joined the men at the camp fire and they talked and joked while they enjoyed their evening meal and when they finished they stayed by the fire relaxing and enjoying one more cup of coffee. "Where are Elmon and Frutoso?" Reese asked as he looked up at Simoñ questioningly over the rim of his coffee cup. Simoñ stool quietly nearby and stared out into the prairie.

"They're taking the first watch," Simoñ replied as he turned his head slowly in Reese's direction. He then walked over and sat down next to Reese and asked in a low voice, "Do you think New Mexico will join Texas in the revolt against the government in Mexico City, Reese?"

Reese finished his coffee thoughtfully, and then finally said, "I've heard that the Californians have revolted a number of times. That government of yours in Mexico City seems to go out of its way to provoke revolts. From what I heard back in Westport, the officials who are sent to govern California are arrogant and completely ill equipped to govern." He hesitated for a moment and then asked, "Is it true that there is a stone platform in Mexico City with an iron pipe embedded in it that is used to burn people alive if they question the authority of the Church? It is said that it is called the Quemadero or some such name."

"I really don't know," Simoñ answered defensively. "I certainly hope not. You see, Reese, I never left my hacienda until I was nearly twenty years old and even then I only traveled to Las Vegas and Santa Fe and a few small villages scattered throughout New Mexico. There is much that is happening now and has happened in the past of which I am completely ignorant, but I must confess that what I have heard has me deeply disturbed."

"Well," Reese continued, "I just heard of the Quemadero for the first time recently. I never heard of it before, but if it is true, it will take more than a Santa Hermandad to calm the people if they are anything like the Americans. We French Canadians are Catholic too, and we hesitate to question the authority, but these Americans do not. They question everything."

"You talk as if you are not an American but a Canadian," said Simoñ.

"I'm sorry if I left that impression, for I am an ex-Canadian and a one hundred per cent American now. I have thrown in with the Americans, and believe wholeheartedly in the purpose and future of my new country. This young country is breathing new life into the concept of liberty, justice, and equality. For the first time in hundreds of years, people are breathing the fresh air of freedom, fresh air which gives those who breathe it, the strength to stand up and face the forces of evil and corruption and overwhelm them.

"You'll notice the difference when you get back to your hacienda. The air of Mexico will seem stifling and depressing as compared to the United States."

"I experienced that when we arrived in Westport Landing," admitted Simoñ. "You mentioned the Santa Hermandad, awhile ago, Reese, what is that?"

"Don't know for sure, Simoñ, but from what I've heard, it's some kind of secret organization which was approved by the king of Spain way back there somewhere. He was supposed to have given it its name, which means Holy Brotherhood. Your people are sure hepped up on the Catholic Church, aren't they? The Church can do no wrong. Maybe I'm wrong about the people of Mexico, maybe they believe the priests have a right to dictate to them and they won't revolt after all."

Simoñ persisted, "What does the Santa Hermandad do?"

"It's some kind of vigilante group," Reese said slowly. "I don't know any more about it."

"You are wrong about the Mexican people being lulled into complete subjugation by the Church, Reese. Yes, we are Catholic, very Catholic, but we can see, think, and act for ourselves, also. Time will show that what I say is correct."

"I hope so."

"I know so," insisted Simoñ.

"I mean no disrespect to the Church, for I am a Catholic too," Reese said slowly. "It's just that the Church, like any other organization, has people in it who take it upon themselves to do whatever pleases them and they sometimes disobey the directions of the church officials. It is said that power corrupts and absolute power corrupts absolutely, and as we know, some people are prone to grasp power at the least provocation and use any method at their disposal to hold onto that power once they have it. I suppose some priests in Mexico use their robes to keep that power." Reese got to his feet, and said, "Well, I guess I'd better get some sleep so I'll be ready to ride in the morning. Good night, I enjoyed our little talk."

"I did too," Simon answered. "We must have more of them."

By the time the wagon train was making preparations to stretch out the following morning, Reese was far out on the high plains scouting. He walked his horse leisurely as his eyes, nose and ears were alert to any sign of trouble. Shortly after sunup, he spotted what he thought was a light cloud of dust to the southwest. He reined in and studied it and then spoke to his horse, "There's no doubt about it, Shiloh, that's dust all right, but the question is what is stirring it up? Could it be buffalo or might it be Indians? He watched it for awhile and then loped his horse in that direction. He had ridden for perhaps two miles when, as he topped a small rise, he could see a Comanche riding toward him. They both reined in their mounts and sat scrutinizing one another. Reese said softly, "Could be that he is the advance scout, Shiloh? One thing for sure, though, he's not scouting for a war party because he doesn't wear war paint. We need to find out what he's up to, though. It's possible he's looking for buffalo. Let's keep moving toward that dust cloud and see for sure what causing it. We'll just stay clear of that scout though." He rode in a direction which allowed him to pass by the Comanche at a neutral distance and saw that the Comanche was following the same procedure. Reese grinned as he continued to trot and then lope his horse toward the dust cloud and after several more miles, he topped another little rise and was surprised to see a wagon train below in the distance. "That's a fine looking train, Shiloh, what in blue blazes is it doing so far south of the Santa Fe Trail? Are they lost and why did they have a Comanche scouting for them?" He leaned forward on his saddle horn and absently rubbed his horse's neck as he thought. As the train drew nearer, Shiloh cocked an ear and Reese again spoke to him, "Well, I'll be. Is that a mirage or am I seeing a Comanche wagon train? Those are sure enough Comanche outriders. Guess I'd better skedaddle back to our train and let them know about this, but they won't believe us."

When he came within sight of his own wagon train, he put his horse into a gallop and waved his rifle in the air. Justin saw him coming and raised his right hand high, signaling for the wagons to halt.

"Comanches," Reese yelled as he rode up. "Maybe five miles southwest of us."

"I figured some were near," Justin replied. "We saw one of their scouts earlier and after he studied us for awhile, he hightailed it over the hill yonder. How many of them are there?"

"It's a Comanche Conestoga wagon train," Reese told him.

"What! Is this some kind of mountain man joke?"

"Nope, it's no joke. It's a train of brand new Conestoga wagons being driven by Comanches." Reese had to grin at Justin's reaction.

Simoñ had left the wagon train when he saw Reese riding in and he rode up to meet them. As he pulled up, he asked, "What's going on, Reese?"

Before Reese could reply, Justin broke in, "He's trying to tell me that there's a wagon train heading our way from the southwest and it is completely manned by Comanches! What kind of hooch did you give him to drink last night, anyway?"

Simoñ turned to look at Reese, but said nothing and Reese spoke, "Do you want to come and take a look for yourself? I know what you're thinking, for I couldn't believe my own eyes at first, but it's true. It's a Comanche wagon train."

"Have the Comanches taken to trading in Missouri?" asked Simoñ doubtfully.

"That's nonsense," Justin scoffed. "I've been traveling the Santa Fe Trail since shortly after Becknell opened it up, and I've never seen or heard of Indians, from whatever tribe, organizing a train. You are seeing things, Reese. Maybe you saw a mirage." He grinned.

"Suit yourself," Reese said as he reined his horse to ride away.

"Wait!" Simoñ called. "I believe you."

"Awww come on, have you gone loco?" Justin protested. "Reese here is just plumb tuckered out. A day's rest will cure him of seeing things that aren't there."

Simoñ shaded his eyes and questioned, "What are those dust clouds southwest of here, then?"

Justin turned in his saddle and looked in that direction. "They look like dust clouds all right," he admitted finally, "maybe we'd better circle the wagons and look into it." He wheeled his horse and rode back to the wagon train. As he rode, he made a circular motion over his head with his right hand and yelled, "Circle the wagons!"

"Where is Ramon? Isn't he the expert on Comanches?" questioned Reese.

"Why don't you ride out to look for him?" Simoñ suggested.

Reese reined his horse toward the west, but he didn't have to ride more than a couple of miles before he met Ramon coming towards him.

"I guess you saw the dust," Ramon said as he neared Reese.

"It's Comanche wagons," Reese said as he watched for Ramon's reaction.

"It's what?" Ramon's response was satisfactory and Reese grinned cheerfully as he asked, "You are the Comanche expert, what does it mean?"

"Can't be," Ramon said with a puzzled expression on his face.

They trotted briskly in the direction of their wagon train.

"Let's not go through that again," Reese said.

"The others didn't believe it either?"

"Hardly," Reese said. "So let's skip over the questions about my having seen things. I have no desire to repeat the answers."

"Well, then," said Ramon with a slight smile, "I guess the only way to get some answers is to ride out there and find out what the Comanches are doing with wagons."

Simoñ watched from afar as the two riders disappeared over the horizon in the direction of the still distant dust cloud.

When the wagon train was spotted, Reese and Ramon pulled their horses into a walk and when they were close enough for the Comanches to see them, they stopped and waited for the Comanches to send a delegation to talk. They didn't have to wait long, for within a few minutes several Comanches trotted their horses toward the two strangers. As they drew near, the Comanche leader made the sign for friendship, extending the first two fingers on his right hand and holding the other fingers flat with his thumb. Reese and Ramon returned the sign and sat waiting.

"They're from the Antelope band," offered Ramon as he glanced at Reese.

Now the Comanche leader raised his right hand and held it chest high, palm down, then moved it across his chest in a snake-like fashion.

"That's the sign for Comanche," said Ramon and he now replied by using the Comanche signs he knew from trading with them, asking them where they were going.

The Comanche leader glanced back over his shoulder and replied in Spanish, "East to Missouri."

"Those wagons are all empty," Reese said in a low voice.

"Yes, they are empty," the Comanche replied in response, and this time he spoke in broken English.

Ramon chose to speak in Spanish because his English was not very good and he wanted no misunderstandings. He then translated for Reese. "The Comanche's name is Many Horses," he told Reese, "and get this, those wagons belong to Otto Muller in Westport Landing. Can you believe that?"

"How did he get them?" Reese wore a puzzled frown.

Many Horses apparently was not at ease having Ramon as an interpreter and he turned to Reese and said slowly, "Otto friend of Comanche, big friend. Him friend of Vlach, too, and Vlach Comanche brother. Vlach marry Snow Skin, Comanche woman. Sister of my big friend, Three Tongues. Comanche and Otto helped Vlach get freedom from Mexican bandits and rewarded wagons' supplies."

A smile crossed Reese's face when he heard the word, Vlach, in connection with Mexican bandits, for Otto had related the bout they had had with the bandits.

"What are you smiling about?" Now Ramon wore the puzzled look.

"We're among friends," Reese replied.

"What do you mean?"

Reese turned to Many Horses and said, "Vlach is like a son to me. I am in search of him right now."

Many Horses extended his hand to Reese and said, "You, me, hands together—show we brothers, American way."

The two men shook hands and Reese turned to Ramon, saying, "You had better ride back to the wagons and tell them everything is fine. I'll join up with you later and fill you in on what I find out. Tell Simoñ that the reason these wagons are in Comanche hands, well you know as well as I do what to tell him. Tell him also, that the Comanches are returning the wagons to Otto."

As Ramon rode away, Many Horses told Reese about their battle with the Tonkawas and how Vlach, Nat Cochran, had masterminded the entire battle, and how they had completely routed their old enemies.

Reese also learned that the Macedonian had joined forces with Nat and they were searching for a ranch site somewhere in New Mexico.

"They no look north New Mexico, too many people there, maybe they look south, near Mountain That Stands Alone (La Sierra)," Many Horses told him.

"I must return to my wagon train now," Reese told Many Horses, but I will always remember my friend, Many Horses."

Many Horses drew himself up, made the sign for friendship and then wheeled his horse around and rode back to his people.

"It's a small world," Reese muttered as he watched him ride away.

"I wonder what the odds are against such an event happening?" mused Simoñ. "One in a million, I'd bet." Reese had just told him what he had learned.

"I don't know the odds, but it was a lucky meeting for me to find out Nat's probable whereabouts," Reese said.

"You are not leaving us, are you Reese? We need you," Simoñ asked anxiously.

"I'm staying with you until you reach home, Simoñ. I've got plenty of time to locate Nat."

This Nat fellow whom you are trying to locate? Is he in New Mexico?"

"It looks that way," Reese replied. "Many Horses seems to think that he's heading for the Jicarilla Mountains in south central New Mexico."

"That's Mescalero country, Reese!" Simoñ protested. "They are reputed to be some of the cruelest Indians in all of New Mexico. They are said to be deceitful, cunning, and worst of all, expert at camouflage. They are able to become invisible, almost right before your very eyes. People have told me that they have stood next to an Apache in broad daylight and within two or three minutes, he seems to disappear. They can reappear in the same amount of time if they choose."

"I don't know anything about the Apaches, but I have the feeling that I am about to learn," Reese said ruefully. "This is the last frontier, Simon, and where there's a frontier, there you will find the Canadian trapper or trader. My father was a trapper and at times a trader, all his life and he, more than once, penetrated into forbidden areas against the warnings of others. He was the first, on more than one occasion, to sit down with the Shawnees, Delaware, Wyandott, Ottawa, and Illinois to smoke the stone pipe of peace. In those early days, a trader had to be able to carry his canoe across portages and carry his provisions and trade goods the same way, to reach rivers whose swift currents and deadly rapids would repel today's traders. We have it easy today as compared to the first traders. We used wagons to carry our trade goods. In my father's day, they, themselves, at times had to carry the trade goods on their backs. They considered themselves lucky if they were able to use pack animals."

"What did your father trade with those Indian tribes you mentioned?"

"In those days there were plenty of beautiful, shiny pelts of prime quality to be found everywhere. The Indians exchanged them for vermilion, coffee, tobacco, sugar, beads, and trinkets of all kinds. They always wanted iron hatchets, sewing awls, brass kettles, rifles, and lead which they could melt down and mold into balls for their musket loaders." Reese fell silent as he relived his early years within the peaceful, quiet sanctuary of his mind.

Simoñ perceived a smile cross Reese's face along with an expression of deep contentment.

"Those were the days of men, freedom, and complete happiness." Reese murmured without realizing that he spoke aloud. "Wilderness everywhere, and civilization was confined to the eastern seashores."

"I envy you," Simoñ's voice brought Reese back to the present and he laughed as he said, "You ruined my dream!"

"Sorry."

"There is an old Cherokee saying, Simoñ," Reese said slowly, "It goes, `the old ways are swift birds, they fly away or die and leave no sign.' My dad's ways and now mine remind me of that saying. I'm turning myself out to pasture. I'll find my friend, Nat, and spend my remaining days with him and his family. They're all I've got now. I have no other whom I feel close to except for Otto and I don't want to spend my remaining days with crowds of people, but my old bones are beginning to ache and other parts of me are beginning to show signs of wear." He chuckled at he thought of all the hardships he had put those bones through.

"Maybe we can visit once in a while after you get settled," Simoñ suggested.

"If there is going to be any visiting, once I'm settled, I'm afraid you are the one who will have to do it," grinned Reese.

"Well, then, guess I'll have to do the visiting," Simoñ replied with a laugh.

"Here we are yapping as if we had nothing better to do," said Reese. "I'd better get back out there and do my job, or we may not have a chance to do any visiting, unless it's down under."

"Now that's my kind of man," Simoñ said softly as he watched Reece ride out. "Free spirited, loyal, and a defender of all which man cherishes. The world will be a much sadder place to live in when his kind are gone. I must some day journey to meet this Cochran fellow too."

"Who are you talking to, father?" Leandro and Elmon had ridden up behind him.

"Just a ghost of the past," Simoñ replied as he watched Reese disappear over the horizon. Leandro and Elmon both crossed themselves when they heard the word ghosts.

"Have no fear," Simoñ told them. "It was just a figure of speech."

"Ramon wanted to see me, I'm told, so if you'll excuse me, patron, I'll go find him." Elmon reined his horse away.

Simoñ and Leandro rode side by side, neither of them saying a word until finally Leandro asked, "What's wrong, father?"

"Nothing, my son. I was talking a few minutes ago with our good friend, Reese, about the past, and now I am thinking about the future, and what it will hold for us. Take a look behind us and tell me what you see."

Leandro turned in his saddle and studied the ten Conestoga wagons slowly creaking their way along the rutted Santa Fe Trail. He saw that some of the mule skinners were riding while other walked beside their mules, giving their backsides a rest. The occasional crack of a whip could be heard and he could see

Justin riding just ahead of the first wagon. He turned back to his father, puzzled. "I don't understand, father."

"What you see, Leandro, are Americans. There are many American wagon trains, but there is only one Mexican train and that is the one managed by Salvador Chavez. The future belongs to the people such as those you see behind us, Leandro. We must also be a part of that future. We must plan for our future. The future belongs to those who prepare for it. Spain developed a huge empire, much too large for her little Iberian geographic location to hold together. Her empire, with her armies and navies, was spread too thinly around the world. As you know, some of the presidios north of the Rio Grande had only twenty or so men in them to protect the citizenry, much too few to be effective. Some of them, I understand, had only five or six, and you can imagine what little respect the Indians had for such a pitiful military presence."

"What are you driving at, father?"

"That the world, our world at least, has reached a time for change, my son. Mexico drove Spain out of this hemisphere as the English drove the French out and men like our friend Reese, were left without a home, without a country, and what did he do? He elected to become an American. The infant nation which is the United States is on the move. They call it their Manifest Destiny. They will swallow all of the territory from here to California and down to the Rio Grande, and possibly more. We will be living under the American flag in the not too distant future, Leandro. The revolt in Texas is a forerunner to what will happen here. Mexico's government is too corrupt and too inefficient to withstand these marching Americans who have this dream of equality, justice, and liberty for all. As an example of what America is like, compared to Mexico, one has only to look at the vast variety of trade goods which the Americans bring to Santa Fe. What do we manufacture that the Americans desire? Nothing. The traders carry animal hides, mules, and a few horses back on their return journey, but hardly the goods one might expect from a country on the move. No, my son, America is destined for greatness and for better or worse, we will be part of that greatness."

"Father, will there be war between Mexico and the United States?"

"Only time will tell, Leandro. Let us hope that the Americans will permit us to have the privilege of sharing the respect they have for equality and justice as their Constitution states."

"Simón," Justin yelled and he galloped up to join the two Mexicans. "Pawnee Rock is just ahead a few miles, we'll stop there for our morning break and give the mules time to water and graze."

"What river will we find there?" asked Simón.

"The Arkansas," Justin replied, "its headwaters are high in the Rockies, probably two hundred miles away," chuckled Justin. "We'll be following her for another forty miles or so until we reach her big bend. We'll ford her there at that point and take the Cimarron Cutoff."

"Why that way?" asked Simoñ.

"It's a good hundred miles shorter for one thing, of course it has its drawbacks," he added quickly. "Well, we could have more trouble with the Indians on that route. And for about sixty miles after we leave the Arkansas, there is no water until we reach the Cimarron River. Once we reach that river, we follow it until we pass Willow Bar and then it's another thirty miles to the north Canadian River. Our next marker after that is Pointed Rock. From there on, actually before we reach Pointed Rock, is your country. You are probably much more familiar with that country than I am."

"We're nearly home once we reach the Canadian River," Simoñ said. I assume we'll rest in Rendezvous Valley with its cool, natural spring water and good grass. Wagon Mound Peak is only a short way from there."

"More like a stone's throw," agreed Justin. "And this is where we join up with the mountain route of the Santa Fe Trail, which comes by way of the Raton Pass."

"Once we reach Rendezvous Valley, we could follow Ocate Creek instead of crossing it and reach my hacienda much quicker that way."

"You're the boss," Justin said. "But couldn't the terrain along the creek slow us down?"

"No, I don't think it would," considered Simoñ.

"All right," agreed Justin. "It's up Ocate Creek then."

A little later they reached Pawnee Rock and Leandro remembered he had been disappointed when they came that way the first time because such a famous landmark was so insignificant.

Justin explained when told that, that out on the prairie when anything rises above the flat plains it is a hill and that particular rise was around one hundred and fifty feet.

"I've forgotten why it's called Pawnee Rock," said Leandro.

"Because this is where the Indians, for some reason, decide to challenge the wagon trains. Many men are buried hereabouts. It's a famous ambush site."

"Where are the grave markers?" Leandro looked around inquiringly.

"We don't mark our graves along the trail anymore," Justin explained, "because if we did, the Indians would come by after we had left and dig up the graves for anything of value which was buried with the dead. When we found that they did this, we discontinued marking the graves. Well, I'll get back to the wagons and make sure everything is tidied up."

"Here comes Reese, father," Leandro pointed directly west along the wide, rutted Santa Fe Trail.

Reese trotted up to Simon and Leandro and reported, "A very large wagon train is headed our way, with a U. S. military escort. There must be over a hundred Conestoga wagons in it. The wagons are drawn by oxen, eight yokes to a wagon. There must be at least a thousand spare oxen mixed with the extra horses."

Simoñ glanced at his son and said, "Go back to camp and tell Justin what Reese has told us."

"Here come the Prudencio brothers, one riding in from the south and the other two from the northwest," Reese pointed out.

"They probably saw what you saw," Simoñ commented.

"No one could miss that train," Reese replied.

The Prudencios also reported seeing the train and guessed that it was still a day's drive west of them.

"That's my guess also," agreed Reese. "Those oxen don't move very fast."

"Let's get back to our train and get our heads together as to what we should do," Simoñ proposed.

"Bull whackers!" Justin yelled. And when the men heard his yell, they quickly gathered around him and the others.

"What did you say about bull whackers, captain?" one of them asked curiously.

"You heard me correctly," Justin told him. "There's a wagon train over a hundred wagons long, coming from the west. They won't reach Pawnee Rock until tomorrow."

"Could they cause us any problems?" asked Simoñ.

"A sizable problem," Justin replied shortly. "Our mules could easily get mixed up with that herd of oxen and horses if both herds are grazing along the river. Or a fuss could dust up over the merit of mule skinners versus bull whackers!" He grinned and continued, "And when men have been on the trail as long as they have, tempers can get pretty short."

"Should we harness up and get out of their way?" Simoñ wore a worried look. "We could head north for a couple of hours or so, and be out of their way altogether."

"We could," considered Justin as he rubbed his stubbly chin and stared into space. "But we should make some kind of contact with them. They might have some valuable information about the trail ahead of us such as the fact that Indians might be sitting and waiting for a small train such as ours to come along, or maybe Mexican bandits could pose a hazzard."

"We'll just make sure that our mules don't get mixed up with their stock," argued Ramon. "Our mules need the rest and we do need any information they might have. The precautions would be worth taking for the information."

"Riders approaching," Reese motioned with his head.

"The name is La Porte, Brian La Porte, and I am captain of the scouts for the caravan a few miles behind me," La Porte said as he rode up to them. "These four with me are part of my Wyandott scout troop."

"Pleased to meet you," Simoñ told him. "I am Simoñ Gomez." He shook hands and then introduced the others of his party.

When Reese's name was mentioned, all five scouts turned quickly to stare at Reese, and La Porte asked with obvious and extreme pleasure, "Reese Marquette?"

"Yes?" said Reese in surprise.

"We are all Wyandotts," Brian said, but quickly added, "I should correct that, for I'm half Wyandott and half French Canadian, and your name, Reese Marquette, is one of the most honored in our tribe's history, along with those of Nat Cochran and Otto Muller. Your name is always spoken of with great reverence when we speak of the days that once were."

"You honor me with your words," Reese said quietly.

"The honor is ours, friend of the Wyandotts," Brian said as he and the others crowded around Reese to shake his hand.

"It seems that you know one another," Simoñ said with a smile.

"Indirectly," was Reese's reply.

"It was he, Nat, and Otto who befriended our people a few years ago and helped us in our search for a new land west of the Father of Waters. Our tribe lived originally on the upper Ohio and even further east, but the white man moved farther and farther to the west in his hunger for the land, thereby forcing my people from their ancestral land," explained Brian La Porte. He looked at Reese as he continued, "The white man and his ways have caught up with us once again. We shall move no more. We now seek peace with the white man, for we must live as brothers. I, myself, am an example of what the future holds for the Wyandott. I carry a white man's name but I am three quarters Wyandott."

"What you are, Brian, is what America will become. The future will reflect upon America's faces the multitude of races which will have spread across this infant nation," said Reese.

Now Simoñ spoke, "I believe this also. Soon the Mexicans will take their place beside the new race called the Americans, and their blood, too, will mingle with those of other nationalities, until the blood will be as one. The world may be taking little note of what is going on here now, but soon it will be scrambling to learn all it can about this new nation which is destined to make itself known in every capital city of the world."

"Where do you plan to make your camp tomorrow during break?" Reese asked.

"Here at Pawnee Rock," Brian replied. "There's plenty of grass for the stock of both our trains. Unless you have plans to move on before we arrive, we would welcome a visit with you. I'm sure I speak for our wagon master. We need to talk, too, about the signs which we have seen for the last three days."

"We will wait for your arrival," Simoñ assured him.

"It is done." Brian spoke to his scouts in their language and they wheeled their horses and rode away, and Reese's companions looked at him with even more respect.

It was near ten o'clock the following morning when Spotswood Williams, the wagon master, led the first wagon to the spot where he wanted the circle to begin. It took nearly an hour before the circle was completed with the tongues of each wagon facing inward, a sign that they might expect trouble with the Indians. When the circle was begun, the first wagon turned to the right, the second veered to the left, the third followed the first and so on until the circle was complete. Each wagon had moved slowly and methodically until it came to a halt with its front wheels along side the rear wheels of the wagon just ahead of it. The front wheels and the back wheels were then chained together. Simon and his crew watched with admiration as the train coiled slowly into its large circle without a hitch.

"They make it look so easy," commented Leandro.

"They are all seasoned bull whackers," Justin said, "if they were not, the whole train would be in one hell of a mess by now."

The bull whackers unhitched their oxen and drove them out to graze and watched as they plodded slowly toward the river to drink. After they had drunk, they moved back and began to graze.

The train had its wagon master, three lieutenants, one for every thirty-five wagons and each lieutenant had his sergeant under him. Such a large train needed numerous cooks and day and night herders. As Simoñ and his men watched the crew settle down, the military escort rode in.

"Lieutenant Morrison of the United States Army," Morrison said as he dismounted, removed his heavy leather gauntlets and extended a hand to Simoñ. Simoñ in turn introduced his men to the lieutenant and then asked, "How long have soldiers furnished escorts on the Santa fe Trail?"

"Congress has passed a law ordering that the part of the Santa Fe Trail which lies within the borders of the United States be surveyed and marked and trains escorted. It is also rumored that a fort will soon be constructed where the trail crosses the Arkansas, so that the wagon trains will have protection," Morrison told him. "Well, I must see to my men," he continued. "Please exuse me. Perhaps we can have a more lengthy visit later."

"Yes," Simoñ replied. "We'd like that."

That evening Simoñ and Reese paid a visit to the large train and looked up La Porte, hoping to find out if there were any Indian war party signs out ahead of them.

"Why don't you ask the lieutenant instead?" Simoñ glanced at Reese inquiringly.

"To understand how an Indian thinks, you should always ask an Indian. If you have any trouble between here and your hacienda, it will probably come from Indians and since La Porte thinks like an Indian, we should talk to him. After all, Williams and Morrison get their information from La Porte, so I think we should get ours from the horse's mouth also, and not second hand."

They found La Porte sitting by a campfire in the company of two of his scouts.

"Are the other scouts keeping the wagon train safe?" Reese grinned as he and Simon walked up to the fire.

"Come, sit down. I was expecting a visit from my brother, Reese," La Porte rose to welcome his guests. "Please honor our campfire with your presence."

"The honor is ours," Reese returned politely as he and Simoñ dropped down near the fire.

"Please, it would make us happy if you would share our food," La Porte continued.

"You are a kind and gracious host," Simoñ said as he helped himself to a piece of one of the rabbits which were roasting over a spit.

La Porte grunted in satisfaction and seating himself, said, "I know why you have come and I will tell you what we know.

"My scouts and I have seen many Kiowa and Cheyenne signs for the past hundred miles or more. The signs were the heaviest between Lower Spring and Lower Crossing. As you know, that stretch of the Santa Fe Trail is the most barren and lacks water. We are a large train with many men, all of whom are handy with their rifles, which is why we were not attacked. We made no mistakes, thereby not giving the Indians a chance to strike a quick blow and then retreat. They are still out there somewhere, hoping that we will let our guard down." La Porte laughed gruffly as he continued, "If they had known that I was the captain of the scouts, they would not have wasted their time waiting for us to make a mistake. La Porte makes no mistakes. Maybe I should have left my Wyandott sign along the trail." He laughed again as he punched Reese playfully. "My brother, Reese, is only one Wyandott scout and he scouts for a small train, too small to be safe from an Indian attack. I think the Kiowa and Cheyenne will not follow us tomorrow when we leave, they will follow you. You will be attacked for sure."

"How large is their war party?" Reese asked cheerfully.

"Thirty," La Porte replied quickly and without hesitation as he sunk his teeth into a piece of rabbit.

"I can see why they did not attack your wagons," said Reese. "They are so few and you are so numerous."

"You have not much more than half of the men in the war party," said La Porte after he took another mouthful. "That will give them all the incentive they need."

"We will be on our guard at all times, La Porte, thanks to what you have told us. I think we can survive. We are a small train, that is true, but we also carry something with us which will be a surprise. We carry in our wagons four twelve pounders."

La Porte who had just lit his pipe and taken one puff, removed it quickly and turned to Reese with a large smile. "You too are a Wyandott! Wyandotts do not make mistakes and no other tribe can out guess us. I wish I could be with you when the battle starts so that I could see the expressions on the faces of those Kiowa and Cheyennes when you open up on them with those twelve pounders. We still talk about the strategy that you used against the river pirates when you guided our people down the Wabash to our present home. Someone always relates that story to our young people around the campfires. I have a better feeling now about your train. I must admit that earlier I had great misgivings about your making it safely. My scouts and I would not have been forgiven if we had knowingly allowed you to ride to your death. We have even considered leaving our train and joining yours. Now I see that you will not need our help. The Kiowa and the Cheyenne will once again face the mighty Wyandott Nation and they will be driven back to their people in shame as the dogs that they are. And we will not tell any of the people in our train about your twelve pounders. Your secret is safe with us."

"We must leave now," Reese said as he and Simoñ rose reluctantly to their feet.

"We must also leave at sunup," said La Porte jovially as he rose and slapped Reese on the back and shook Simoñ's hand in farewell.

"There are many rattlesnakes as you approach Council Grove," Reese warned, "so be on your toes. I know how easily oxen can stampede when they hear rattlesnakes."

"May the Great Manitou watch over you and your friends," La Porte said gravely. "The Wyandott Nation sends its tribal spirit to its other honored son, Nat. Please give him our devoted word and sacred vows for his happiness in the remaining days of his life."

He held his pipe in his outstretched hands slightly higher than his head and began to pray to his gods. The other Wyandotts also rose as Laporte said, "Hear my words, Great Manitou, I am a devoted son and believer in your divine power and spirit. You are the mover of everything that is good, evil flees from your approaching spirit. You are the most powerful, the most generous, the most protective, the most understanding. Smile down upon your sons, Reese and Nat. This I ask as one of your humble and devoted children." Laporte now opened his eyes, lowered his pipe and sat down again, crosslegged by the fire. He said nothing further as he began to smoke once more.

Reese and Simoñ watched for a moment from a few steps away and then left for their wagons. As they walked, Simoñ asked in astonishment, "You are a Wyandott warrior? You are more famous back here than the Macedonian is in the Rockies!"

"The Macedonian?" Reese turned to Simon in surprise. "What do you know of the Macedonian?"

"Not very much, only what the mountain men and some Indians have said.

No one knows for sure if he's real or just a mythical being. Have you heard of him?"

"Yes," replied Reese as he quickened his step.

"Why do you begin to walk faster? Have I said something to offend you? You are not the Macedonian, are you?"

"Don't be absurd, Simon, the man is a myth, no man alive could live up to what is credited to him."

"Why are we practically running back to our wagons?"

"To make sure that no one in our train tells anyone in that east bound train about our twelve pounders." answered Reese.

When they reached their campfire, they found everyone except Elmon and Frustoso leisurely eating supper, and Reese asked about them in a casual manner.

"They've taken first watch," Leandro answered, Why?"

"What did you learn from the scouts?" Ramon looked up with interest at them.

"Have any of you visited the other train?" Reese glanced around the circle.

"No," Leandro answered, "we left the information gathering to you. What did you find out?"

"There is a war party of around thirty Kiowa and Cheyenne out there waiting for us," announced Simoñ.

"Thirty!" Ramon looked up at Simoñ from his position by the fire.

"Yes, thirty. From now on we all stay together and keep our rifles with us at all times. No one is to leave the wagons unless he gets permission from me personally. I want all of you to get as much rest as possible tonight for it may be the last time you will be able to sleep with both eyes shut until we reach the Canadian River. We'll leave at sunup, when the other train pulls out."

CHAPTER IX

Well before sunup, Justin had his men up and busying themselves with harnessing their mules. When all was ready, Justin reported to Simoñ who immediately gave the order for Justin to stretch the wagons out. Reese, Elmon, and Ramon had been in the saddle an hour before the wagon master issued his orders to continue their journey toward New Mexico and the Gomez Hacienda. Frutoso took Leandro with him on his scouting tour whereas the other three went their separate ways. As the Gomez train began to move, the mule skinners could see that the east bound train had already driven its oxen into the circled wagon corral and the bull whackers were beginning to push their way into the mass of moving oxen, seeking the pairs they wanted. The Gomez mule skinners could be heard as they cracked their short blacksnake whips and yelled to their mules to get along. Not to be forgotten in all of the commotion was the friendly but continuous battle of pride and competition between the bull whackers and the mule skinners. A few bull whackers snapped their twenty foot whips in the air as they yelled at the Gomez caravan," Watch yore topknot!" or others yelled, "Hold onto yore hair!"

"Same goes to you all," came the gist of many replies from the mule skinners as they laughed and shouted their goodbyes.

The Gomez wagon train moved slowly westward keenly alert to any sign which might warn them of danger that they all knew was always near. Everything had gone smoothly when Justin called for a halt at midmorning. They would rest the mules and give them time to eat and drink.

"Here comes Reese," Simoñ yelled as he saw him trotting his horse in their direction. When he had reached the wagons, Reese told Simoñ and Justin that the signs were increasing and numerous. "There's around thirty of them, all right," he concluded. "But I think La Porte was wrong about there being some Cheyenne among them. I think they are all Kiowa."

"How can you tell?"

"The moccasin prints of the Kiowa and Cheyenne are very similar, hard to distinguish, but let me show you." Reese dismounted and dropped to one knee. He stirred the earth in front of him and drew two moccasin prints on the ground, both very similar, but different enough for an experienced scout to distinguish.

"This one," Reese pointed to the first one which he had drawn, "belongs to a Cheyenne brave. This other one is that of a Kiowa and you can see the slight difference in the instep and the outer side of the print? I believe all the moccasin prints which I have seen so far belong to Kiowas. We'll know for sure soon, for we are bound to spot them. I think that Ramon had better accompany me when I go back out and Elmon, Frutoso, and Leandro had better not scout more than a mile or two from the train. I think the long distance scouting should be left to Ramon and me."

"Whatever you say, Reese," Simoñ assured him.

"Justin had better be ready from now on to circle the wagons at a moment's notice. The slightest delay in circling them could mean lives. Keep the spare mules as close to the wagon train as possible, also. We don't want to tempt the Kiowas any more than necessary," he cautioned with a grin.

A little later, after a hasty cup of coffee, Reese and Ramon rode back out. Reese grinned as he glanced at Ramon, "You know they are watching us, so it's high time we evened the score a little and began to watch them."

The two rode in silence for over an hour and their eyes and ears were kept busy as they watched for signs. Ramon reined in his horse suddenly and as he peered at the ground, he muttered, "A single rider passed this way not too long ago."

Reese rode over to where Ramon sat and jumped to the ground to examine the pony tracks more closely. "They're fresh all right, real fresh, maybe two hours old." He stood up and searched the horizon in all directions, but saw nothing except the tall prairie grasses bending in the light breeze. "I don't think this scout has spotted us," he decided. "He can't be too far over that rolling country. What do you say we pay the Kiowa a visit, Ramon?"

They had ridden several miles when Reese reined in and asked, "Can you smell them, Ramon?"

"No, I can't," admitted Ramon.

"I can," Reese said softly as he kept his eyes glued northward. "They can't be far ahead. Let's move carefully."

Within a few minutes, Reese waved his hand and both riders halted as Reese motioned to a knoll ahead of them. They dismounted and led their horses cautiously, moving toward the high ground. As they drew nearer, they could hear voices. Reese placed a large rock on the end of his reins to prevent his horse from straying and Ramon did the same before they continued on their hands and knees. When they reached the top of the knoll, they peered over and saw the war party. They were in the process of applying war paint to their horses as well as to themselves. Reese and Ramon had seen enough and they moved back cautiously until they reached their horses where they mounted and moved away at a walk. When they reached a safe distance and could talk, Reese said grimly, "We had better hightail it back to the wagons. They're painting up for an attack."

The men of the train saw them shortly before they could hear them shouting, "Circle the wagons!"

Justin repeated their warning as he turned to watch the mule skinners skillfully begin their circle. While this was being done, Simoñ rode out at a gallop to bring Leandro and Frutoso in.

When the wagons had been circled and the mules safely enclosed within the circle, the men sought protective cover and waited for the attack. Not a word was spoken as the seasoned mule skinners and the others held their rifles at the ready and watched for any sign of the Kiowas. They hadn't long to wait, for the Kiowa war party abruptly appeared on a small rise a short distance from them. None of them appeared to be using saddles, for their legs dangled loosely at the sides of their ponies. They sat there insolently, studying their target calmly. They appeared as still as statues except for the occasional breeze which blew their hair, feathers, and the manes and tails of their ponies.

"They sure have their horses painted up," Simoñ said softly to Reese as he studied them with fascination.

"See that warrior to the left who is mounted on the black and white paint?" Reese asked.

"Yes," Simoñ nodded.

"Can you see those red lighting symbols on his horse?"

"Yes," replied Simoñ.

"The lightning symbols are supposed to give his pony the speed and power of lightning. The brave also carries a coup stick."

"What do the zebra stripes signify?" asked Simoñ.

"That means that they belong to a certain military society. See he has painted the same stripes on his own arms and legs also. That curved lance which he carries is the badge of the military society to which he belongs, the Dog Soldier Society." Reese scanned along the line of warriors and continued, "The warrior in the middle and a few paces to the front, has spots painted all over his face, which means that he is a great warrior, with many coups to his credit. He wears a red painted eagle feather in his scalp lock, which means that he has been wounded during battle. That painted circle on his chest which has lines extending from it designates the location of his old wounds."

"What do the circles around the eyes of their horses signify?"

"By that, they hope to improve the sight of their horses." He broke off to yell, "Get ready, they're about to attack!"

At that moment, the Kiowa battle cry was heard as they dashed toward the wagon train and began to shoot.

The battle continued for over half an hour, after which the Kiowas gathered up the warriors who were either wounded or dead and rode off beyond the range of rifle fire where they halted.

"What do we do now?" Simoñ looked to Reese for guidance.

"They may quit for today and be back tomorrow," guessed Reese. He rolled over on his side so he could see the others. "Has anyone been hit?" he called. After a few second of silence, Justin spoke, "I guess not."

"Good," Reese replied as he rolled back over on his stomach and resumed watching the Kiowas who were gathered around their fallen warriors. The Kiowa chief mounted and stared toward the train and then motioned to his warriors and they melted over the horizon.

"We can stretch our legs now," Reese said as he stood up. "I think they'll leave us alone for a spell."

"How many times do you think they'll attack before they give up and leave?" asked Simoñ.

"It depends on their losses," answered Reese.

"Look!" Ramon pointed to smoke which was rising behind the little hill.

Simoñ again turned to Reese and asked, "What is it saying?"

Reese watched the smoke signals intently, but said nothing until three puffs of smoke rose into the sky, one after the other before they dissipated. A few seconds later, three more puffs occurred.

"They're asking for help from any Kiowas or allies who might be within seeing distance of their signal," Reese answered. "Which is a good sign. That means that they believe that we are not as easy a target as they expected." He stood motionless as he watched the spot where the smoke had originated, and after a few seconds he turned to Simoñ and suggested, "Let's have a meeting with Justin, Leandro and the Prudencios."

The men were shortly gathered around Reese, for they looked to him for guidance. "I have a plan," he began, "hear me out and see what you think. I'm of the notion that we should finish this battle on our terms, not on theirs. If we play it their way, the battle could last for days. I propose to have one battle and finish it with their defeat tomorrow."

Simoñ asked eagerly, "What do you propose?"

"Let's bring them to us in one full scale charge. We could have the four twelve pounders lined up in a row and at the appropriate time we'll remove the camouflage and open fire with everything we have, with the guns as well as our rifle fire."

"How are we to get them to fall for our trap?" Justin looked interested although slightly skeptical.

"We know they have at least one scout watching us and reporting to the chief every move we make. They know that we have just seventeen men, now just suppose that we can convince them that we have only, say nine able bodied men left. This will encourage them to think that we are about finished and that one swift charge by them could finish us off."

Simoñ asked, "How can we convince them that we have only nine men?"

"By burying eight of us," Reese said cheerfully.

"Burying eight of us?" Leandro exclaimed.

His father wore a smile as he said, "It just might work, but we had better be convincing with our burial detail."

Reese took command. "Get a detail of your men and have them dig eight graves just outside the wagon perimeter in full view of the scout."

"Frutoso, you and Elmon load the twelve pounders with grape shot and nails and break some of the glass supplies in the wagons and feed that to the guns as well. We'll wait until after dark to get them into position."

He turned to Ramon and Leandro and said, "When the time is right, I want you to be ready to pull two wagons out of the circle where we'll have the guns camouflaged. Keep the mules harnessed and ready to do that."

While everyone was busy, Reese walked out from the safety of the circle and acted as if he were searching for something, and then in a few minutes, the grave detail arrived with the picks and shovels and Reese pointed to eight separate and distinct locations, making it very clear to the Kiowa scouts that the Gomez crew were preparing to bury their dead. When the men had begun to dig, Reese walked back inside the circle to direct the men who were loading the big guns. "When it gets dark enough, we'll place them behind the wagons we plan to move out of line immediately we see any signs of attack. We'd better keep the mules harnessed all night just in case they decide to pull a sneak attack on us," he added.

After awhile the fake bodies of eight men were laid to rest and covered and Reese read over them. Wooden crosses were forced into the ground at the head of each grave with the use of a sledge hammer, all of which took place in full view of the Kiowa scouts, who watched with great interest.

When darkness came, sentries were posted and the guns quietly placed in position and camouflaged behind the two wagons which were ready to be moved as soon as necessary. Then the remainder of the night, the men took turns at sleeping, but all were awake and eager before daylight, waiting for the anticipated attack. If they had played their parts well enough, they could almost certainly anticipate an attack soon. Not the slightest breeze stirred the grass and the only sound came from the mules and horses as they moved about grazing. All kept their eyes fixed on the rise where the Kiowas had last been seen.

Simoñ glanced at the twelve pounders and their crews and nodded in satisfaction. He looked at the positions of the men who lay holding their rifles in readiness as the sun began to peep over the horizon. Now the sun caused shadows to be cast behind the wagons and further disguised the cannons which stood ready. Suddenly Reese whispered, "I hear hoof beats, be ready."

In seconds, the Kiowas could be seen as they mounted a full fledged charge at the wagon train. War cries echoed as they opened fire, confident that it would be soon be over for the survivors of yesterday's battle.

"Hold your fire," Reese yelled, "until I give the signal."

The men picked their targets and waited for Reese, and the two mule skinners, in charge of moving the wagons at the last moment, waited eagerly for his signal.

"Now!" Reese yelled at the top of his lungs and the men opened fire and the wagons were pulled to one side. The twelve pounders opened up and the riflemen fired their first volley almost simultaneously. The combined fire power brought many horses and riders down and their chief and his remaining warriors withdrew, racing from the field. As the last of them disappeared over the hill Reese rose to his feet and yelled, "Anyone hit?"

"Two," Justin yelled back, "but neither seriously."

"Good," Reese grinned, "we'll patch them up and then get under way!"

Within a short time, the Gomez train had resumed its journey to New Mexico without further incident. Lower Spring was reached, followed by Middle Spring, Willow Bar, Upper Spring, Cold Spring, Rabbit Ears, anbd finally Round Mountain.

"Our next rest stop will be Point of Rocks, New Mexico," Justin yelled to Simoñ with a smile.

"Yes, and from there I'll be able to see the Sangre de Cristo Mountains and home," Simoñ called back light-heartedly.

Leandro rode up beside his father and said, "We made it father, we made it!"

"Yes, my son, we made it. I'm very proud of the way you have handled yourself on this trip," he added. "You have proven beyond a doubt that you can handle the responsibilities of a man. You have accepted every challenge given to you, reacting as a mature man would. Welcome to the ranks of manhood, my son."

Leandro beamed at his father and then, to hide his embarrassment, he spurred his horse lightly and dashed off to join Elmon and Frutoso.

When the Gomez wagon train reached the junction of Ocate Creek and the Canadian River, Simoñ suggested to Justin where they could cross the river. "The terrain on the north side of the creek is much more suitable for the wagons," he told Justin.

"You certainly know the country better than I do," Justin admitted. He turned the wagons in the direction Simoñ had indicated, and Simoñ beckoned to his son. "I want you to ride on ahead and inform your mother and the others that we are coming in so that Modesto will have time to prepare for the wagons."

Leandro's face lit up as he said, "Si, father!" He wheeled his horse and galloped toward the crossing.

The wagon train continued to rumble toward the Sangre de Cristos across the soft, rolling country east of them. Reese rode back to ride beside Simoñ and Justin and said, "We made it and without the loss of a single man or wagon. I'll bet not many trains can make that claim."

"We owe much of it to you, too, Reese," said Justin. "Without your expertise we could have had some losses." He was thinking of the tales they would have to tell at the campfires on their return trip.

About mid afternoon the wagon train reached the headquarters of the hacienda, and Doña Sylvia and Doña Maria, the children and Modesto and his family stood by Leandro at the huge open log gates of the compound. The peons were everywhere cheering and waving their sombreros and scarves. Simoñ spurred his horse into a gallop toward his family and when he reached them, he swung to the ground and caught his wife up into his arms.

"Welcome home, dear," Sylvia leaned back to look up into her husband's face. Then she made way for her husband to embrace his mother who stood with her arms outstretched and tears running down her cheeks. As she embraced him she whispered, "I'm so proud of you, my son."

"Thank you, mother," Simoñ said as he kissed her on the cheek. He released her, gave each of his children a hug, and then turned to shake hands with Modesto and greet his family.

"Welcome back," Modesto said warmly as they clasped hands firmly.

"It's good to be back," Simoñ said with a wide smile.

"Do you want the wagons in the presidio, Simoñ?" Justin called.

Simoñ turned to see Justin motioning as the wagons drew nearer.

"Presidio?' Simoñ questioned. "I've heard it called many things, but never presidio."

"It looks like a presidio to me," Justin commented. "Should I bring the wagons in?"

"Yes," said Simoñ. "Bring them on in."

Justin led the first wagons into the compound, but then reined his horse to one side of the gate and sat there watching the remaining wagons pass by him one by one. When they came to a halt within the compound, the mule skinners immediately began to unharness the mules and the children gathered around to watch.

"Modesto," Simoñ said as he turned once more to his friend, "order some lambs butchered and prepare for a fandango. We will have a feast tonight for everyone. And please have someone show the mule skinners their quarters."

"Shouldn't we unload the wagons first?"

"One more night won't hurt," Simoñ replied.

"You're right," conceded Modesto and he left to carry out Simoñ's orders.

Doña Sylvia and Doña Maria had returned to the house to instruct the house servants to prepare for their two guests, but not before they had been introduced to Reese and Justin.

"This is nice," Reese said admiringly as they walked toward the house.

"I'll show you around more tomorrow, but right now I'll show you to your rooms so that you can refresh yourselves and have an hour or two to rest before dinner," Simoñ told them.

"That sounds like what the doctor ordered," Justin laughed. "A bath wouldn't feel bad about now."

"Can't argue with that," Reese grinned.

A short time later, a knock came on Reese's door and he opened it to find a servant standing in the doorway. "If you need anything, señor, please call for me. I am Luis and it will be my pleasure to serve the friend of my patron." He bowed slightly as he moved to withdraw.

"You are very kind, Luis." Reese motioned behind him at the room and grinned, "This is much better than I'm used to."

Luis bowed once again and said, "Dinner will be at six, Señor Reese."

Reese turned away from the door and placed the catch all sack on a large leather trunk which sat against a white washed adobe wall. He leaned his rifle against the headboard of the bed, pressed down on the thick, fluffy mattress with the palm of his hand and chuckled aloud as he murmured, "Simoñ, such living will ruin a man!" He sat down on the bed gingerly, the weight of his body making a deep indentation. He rose to his feet and muttered, "Such a contraption is not for me. I'll sleep on the floor."

He walked to the beautiful curtains which shielded the patio from his sight and pushed one of them aside. The view of the patio was breathtaking in its beauty. Flagstone paths led between the flowers and had been designed so as not to distract from the beauty of the landscaping, but to enhance it. Reese released the curtain and let it fall back into place and turned to inspect the remainder of the room. A wash basin, with a large pitcher of water by its side, sat on a beautifully carved table. A folded towel lay nearby. A large candelabra hung from the overhead vigas. It contained many candles and Reese could see that it could be lowered with small wooden pulleys when it was necessary to light them. A large mirror was set in an intricately carved frame and it rested on an easel. The furnishings were all of carved wood, except for a huge stuffed chair which was covered in soft, dark red leather. With the curtains closed, a minimal amount of light entered the room and Reese decided to take a nap. He took one of the pillows from the bed, and casually tossed it on the floor, and lowered himself to it and within minutes he was sound alseep.

When he woke, he washed himself and brushed his clothing as best he could, so that he would be ready for the evening meal when they called. While he was brushing his hair, a knock came on the door. "Yes?"

"It is Luis, Señor Reese. You are expected in the dining room in half an hour."

"Thank you, Luis, I won't be late," Reese called.

"Bueno," Luis replied, and walked away.

Reese glanced into the mirror and tried to adjust his clothing so that it showed him in the best light possible. He finally grinned at his reflection ruefully and muttered half aloud, "That's the best I can do...I know I'm a sorry sight, but they'll have to take me as I am."

He finally left his room and walked down the corridor and entered the dining room where the others were already assembled.

"I hope I haven't kept you waiting," he said apologetically.

"Nonsense," Simoñ said heartily. "We ourselves just arrived."

When they were all seated, Simoñ glanced around the table and said, "Shall we say grace?"

He then went on to give thanks for their safe return and the fact that the people who had remained at the hacienda were all in good health, and finally he gave thanks for friends such as Reese and Justin.

When Simoñ had finished giving thanks to the Lord, the servants brought in the meal. As a beginning, each was served a bowl of chicken soup, which was followed by platters of roast beef and lamb, accompanied by a platter of baked chicken, venison meat balls and patties, bowls of Spanish rice, lettuce, cabbage, green beans, tortillas, honey and butter. A choice of hot coffee or chocolate to drink and for desert the servants brought in a rice sweetened pastry and a milk custard.

Simoñ had ordered that their best dinner ware be used on this special occasion and each guest had a silver plate and silver bowls and table ware, also of silver, from which to eat.

"This is much better than tasajo, huh Reese?" Simoñ joked with a smile. He referred to the Spanish name for jerky.

"I'm not so sure," Reese replied with a grin. "I'm used to tasajo, as you call it. But I'm sure not used to this other! No offense of course, for it is all delicious, but such things can ruin a man's appetite for the simple things. I'd better be on my way before I'm spoiled!"

The ladies laughed appreciatively and Doña Maria commented, "That is the most unique compliment we have ever received from a guest. We thank you, Señor Reese, for such a compliment. We will pass your praise on to the cook."

"You do that, please, señora," Reese smiled at Doña Maria.

"Señor Justin will be going back to America soon, but where will you be going, Señor Reese?" Sylvia looked across the table at Reese as she asked, and then added quickly, "Of course we hope that you will stay with us as long as you can."

"I'll be looking for my friend, Nat Cochran, and his family. They are somewhere in New Mexico."

"It shouldn't be too difficult to find him, Señor Reese. There are not that many Americanos in New Mexico," Sylvia assured him.

Suddenly and unexpectedly the strumming of a guitar could be heard from the open windows and then a voice began to sing. They stopped eating and listened with pleasure to the soft music of La Paloma.

Some señor serenading his señorita, no doubt," Leandro said.

The fandango will be beginning shortly," Modesto told Reese and Justin. "Will you be joining us in observing the festivities?"

"Observing?" Justin gave a laugh. "I won't just observe for I plan to take part in the dancing. How about you, Reese?"

"I'm not so sure," Reese replied doubtfully. "I plan to leave before sun up, so I guess I'd better turn in early."

"Before sun up?" Simoñ protested. "Why so soon? Why don't you stay with us for awhile?"

"I'd like to, Simoñ, but I'd like to locate my friend," Reese said quietly. "But I'll be back someday, and I'll bring Nat and his family."

"We'll hold you to that," Simoñ said fervently.

"It's a deal," Reese grinned.

The fandango lasted way into the night, with the mule skinners and the peons dancing on the dusty compound ground to the sounds of guitars, two mandolins, one Indian drum and one tristu. The Gomez family, as did Modesto's, visited the dance a few times and then returned to the Gomez house, for they had more to think about, as Simoñ soon found out.

"We must talk, Simoñ," his mother said as they left the dance the final time.

"Talk? About what?" He looked down at his mother in surprise.

"Much has happened since you left, Simoñ." Modesto answered for Doña Maria as he strolled beside Simoñ. "And none of it good."

When they reached the house, they went straight to the sala and Modesto began by saying, "There has been a revolt in New Mexico, against Mexican rule, similar to that which took place in Texas. There was a battle at San Ildefonso, under the leadership of the rebels. Their leader is called General Chopon. The rebels defeated Governor Perez and just before the governor and his retreating troops could reach Santa Fe, some Santo Domingo Indians blocked his passage and killed the governor. The last we heard, a Taos Indian who goes by the name of Jose Gonzales, sits in the palace and claims the governorship. A number of his sympathizers have approached us and asked for our support. We stalled them, telling them that only you could make that decision and that you would be back shortly.

"They set a time for their return and that time is the day after tomorrow." Modesto paused for a moment and lit his pipe, before he continued gravely, "Many influential men of northern New Mexico support this new government, Simoñ, for better or for worse. Also there is an opportunist by the name of Manuel Armijo, who is behind this revolution. At least that is what we have learned from my father in Chimayo. It seems that Armijo and a very influential priest at Taos had stirred up the people against the new governor, Perez, before he was killed. Perez brought back with him from Mexico City word of a new tax, a direct tax. It seems that the government in Mexico City is getting more blatant and greedy. As you know, we have always had taxes, but never a direct tax. This Armijo and the priest spread rumors that the governor was going to tax people if they even sang, laughed, or did any thing out of the ordinary, and the people believed them, although it wasn't true of course. But although it wasn't true, it shows the people wouldn't be surprised at anything which the government did. Anyway, they revolted, turning on Governor Perez, and killing him."

"Where is this Armijo fellow from?"

"He is a rico from the Albuquerque area, who although born a peon, stole so many sheep and other things that he is now rich. He is a swayer of people, an orator of the first order."

"Why didn't the governor arrest Armijo and the priest when he learned what they were up to?" asked Simoñ.

"They were too clever for him. Although they fomented the revolution, they remained in the background, and the governor could not obtain any proof of their plotting," Modesto answered.

"The people must surely know they cannot withstand the power of Mexico City," protested Simoñ.

"They were assured that the Texans were on their way to render aid," Modesto commented.

"Were they?"

"No."

"What have you heard about the government in Mexico City? What is it doing about this?"

Modesto rose and began to pace back and forth. "It is rumored, and there are many rumors, that an army is being assembled in the south under the leadership of Manuel Armijo, who seems to have Santa Anna's blessing and support."

"I thought that he was behind the revolutuon against the government?" Simoñ said.

"He became a turn coat and Santa Anna supports him or shall I say that he supports Santa Anna." Modesto answered.

"What kind of man is this Manuel Armijo, other than being an orator and a turn coat?" Simoñ asked.

"I'm not sure," Modesto replied, "but it's my guess that he's not the type which we'd want for governor, simply because he has Mexico City's support."

"I think you're probably right there," Simoñ replied with a worried look on his face.

"The Mexican Army of the south has not received its marching orders yet," Modesto said. "At least according to my sources in Santa Cruz, the seat of the revolution. As you know, Chimayo is next door to Santa Cruz."

Now Simoñ began to pace as he thought, and finally said, "We had better be prepared for what could happen the day after tomorrow, when the rebel delegation arrives. I could not get four cannons in America, but I did get the next best thing. I've got four twelve pounders in the wagons, as well as plenty of rifles and ammunition. We won't have time to train our people to use those rifles and cannon, so we'll have to stall that delegation for a few days. In the meantime, maybe I can persuade Justin and the mule skinners to stay with us for awhile until our people know how to use the American weapons. I'll go talk to Justin right now to see what he thinks."

Justin had just finished a dance and was escorting his partner back to her seat when Simoñ approached him.

"Justin, I need to talk with you. It's very important."

"Talk away," said Justin as he wiped his brow.

"Let's go over by the wagons," suggested Simoñ as he led the way in that direction.

Justin followed him and asked curiously, "What's wrong, Simoñ?"

"While I was gone, there was an insurrection here and the insurrectionists have taken over the department of New Mexico. It is said that there is an army coming up from the south to put it down. Some of the insurrection sympathizers came here to my hacienda, in my absence, and asked for my support."

"Did Modesto give it?"

"No," Simoñ replied, "he told them that I was away, but they are coming back the day after tomorrow for my answer."

"I see," Justin replied slowly. "And you want my men and me to stick around until after they leave, right?"

"Something like that, Justin."

"What does that mean?"

"I would appreciate it if you would stay and support me, and I must ask another favor also."

"And what is that?"

"Could you and your men help the Prudencios and me to teach the peons how to use the new American rifles? All it would take is two, or maybe three, days, and it could save our hacienda for us."

"I can give you my answer right now and the answer is yes, but I'll have to talk to my crew before I can give you their answer. I'll ask them after the dance and let you know in the morning, or if you want your answer sooner, we could call off the dance and take a vote right now."

"Oh no, not now," Simoñ protested. "The men have earned the dance. Let them enjoy themselves. In the morning will be fine."

"See you in the morning, then," Justin said as Simoñ turned and headed back to the house.

"Yes, I'll see you in the morning."

In the morning, Simoñ was just finishing his coffee when Luis entered the dining room and said, "Patron, the Americanos are waiting for you."

"Waiting? Where, Luis?"

"Out in front of the house, patron."

Simoñ rose to his feet hurriedly and left the room, saying, "Thank you, Luis. Send for the Prudencios, will you please? Tell them I'd like to see them right away."

"Si, patron," Luis answered as he hurried out of the room.

When Simoñ stepped outside of the house, he saw Justin and the mule skinners lounging around the patio gate. When they saw him, they stopped talking and gave him their attention.

"What did you find out, Justin?"

"We're all here, ain't we?" Justin retorted with a broad grin. "When do we start, boss?"

Simoñ looked at the enthusiastic mule skinners and said, "I knew I could depend on you fellows. We'll start right away. I'll round up some of my people and we'll meet you in the compound. Justin, could you have some of your men begin to uncrate the rifles?"

Modesto ran up at that point and asked, "What do you want me to do?"

"Help me round up some of the men so that we can show them how to use the new rifles, and we'll need them to help unload the wagons."

He turned back to look at the mule skinners and said, "I'm very grateful for your support. I hope that some day I can replay you."

The oldest of the mule skinners stepped to the front and said, "Sonny, when it comes to fightin' tyrants, we Americans need no encouragement...they are like a red flag to a bull to us. We're a free people and we intend to stay that way, and every time we take on a tyrant, it's the same as another blow for freedom."

His companions cheered at this and he grinned at them cheerfully, and encouraged, went on, "The way I see it, it's every American's God given duty to fight tyrants, and if we don't face up to 'em, we could be sent to hell, or ought to be, anyhow. There, I've said my piece and it's more than I've said since I was last drunk." He spit out some tobacco juice and returned to the others.

"He speaks for all of us," another skinner said.

"Them's my sentiments," another skinner also voiced his approval as he glanced around at his friends.

Simoñ had to fight back a tear as he said briskly, "I'll be at the compound shortly with my men."

The mule skinners turned to walk toward the compound and Simoñ left to round up the men he thought best fitted to train in the use of the new rifles.

Within a short time, Simoñ faced his people who were gathered in the compound, and told them, "These Americanos will instruct you in the use of the new rifles which I have brought back from America. Jose Gonzales and his men will be back tomorrow and I want you to be prepared in case of trouble. I won't waste any more time talking, so listen carefully to the Americanos."

Now Justin stepped forward and said, "My men will issue each of you a rifle and show you how to use it. If there is anything you don't understand, please speak up, because tomorrow will be too late."

The mule skinners reached into the crates, unwrapped each rifle and handed it to each of the peons as they filed by and the instruction began immediately.

Simoñ, Modesto, and Justin stood over by the wall watching the exercises and Simoñ said, "Reese said to tell you all goodbye. I saw him off before daybreak. I didn't mention this matter, for I knew he was anxious to be on his way. Did I do right?"

The other two nodded, and then Justin said slowly, "Well, it's too late to think about that now. But he'd have relished the chance to stay and fight! But we can handle it all right."

Simoñ asked for their advice about making plans concerning the arrival of the rebels. They walked over to the main gate of the compound and sat down against the wall.

"What kind of political philosophy does Jose Gonzales follow?" Simoñ looked at Modesto inquiringly. He realized that the more he understood about the rebel, the better he could respond.

"I'm not sure, in fact I don't believe anyone knows for sure, except those who are closest to him," Modesto said slowly. "But if I were to guess, I'd say it won't be to our liking. How could it be with the likes of Armijo mixed up in it?"

We don't want to run off one jackel and replace him with another," Simoñ mused. "But we do not want to support Jose if he wishes to set up an independent country with himself as president, either. New Mexico can't stand alone, for we haven't the resources to be independent. Sooner or later some strong country would take us."

Modesto glanced at Justin when Simoñ finished, but said nothing, although much was on his mind. He waited to see if Justin understood what Simoñ was hinting.

Finally Justin looked at Simoñ and asked abruptly, "Are you waiting for us Americans to move in?"

Simoñ decided to be frank. "That, in my estimation, would be the best solution for everyone concerned. New Mexico is on the frontier of Mexico, it's her northern frontier, about which the officials in Mexico City seem to care little. There have even been rumors that the officials there have been considering using us to pay off their European creditors. It looks to me as though war between the United States and Mexico is inevitable. The Americans won't sit idly by and permit some European power to purchase New Mexico and Santa Anna has threatened war if the Americans annex Texas, which they will do sooner or later. It would already be an established fact if it were not for the slave issue. Jose must know all of this, so why is he acting independently of the Texas movement? It should be a joint effort if he is really serious about wanting to be free.

Or is he acting for personal gain?"

"That is why the rebels have told the people that Texas will join with them," put in Modesto. He said nothing more, again waiting for a response from Justin.

"What you say makes sense, Simoñ, but I must admit that I am not a politician and can't think like one. I'm just a wagon master trying to make an honest living. But, for what it's worth, I have a gut feeling that this Jose fellow is not on the up and up, but an opportunist looking out for himself. And so are the other influential people you spoke about earlier. They don't care about people like me, they just want to feather their own nests at the expense of the rest of us," concluded Justin.

Simoñ glanced at Modesto and he returned the look and then stared at the ground without saying anything.

"You agree with my thinking, then?" Simoñ looked sideways at the tall wagon master.

Justin considered how to answer before he said, "I know you, Simoñ, but I don't know this other fellow. I know you are honest and care about people. You're my kind of people and I trust your judgment or else I wouldn't have thrown in with you. All I can say is that I'm with you when these people come tomorrow. When it's over, we're heading back to the states."

"Thank you for that trust," Simoñ said gratefully. "I'll not betray that trust."

The next day began with anxiety for everyone. The sound of every hoofbeat turned heads. Every yell turned heads, and even every nicker from the corrals turned heads, but it was nearly ten o'clock before a group of horsemen could be seen coming in from the south.

When they were first sighted, Simoñ ordered, "Here they come. You all know what to do, so get to your stations."

They watched as the riders approached, and Modesto said, "There are more of them this time. There must be at least twenty of them and they are well armed."

"They sure are," Simoñ said as he watched the rebels. "I hope that doesn't indicate that they are coming to issue an ultimatum."

He looked along the top of the compound battlement and was pleased that the men were well concealed. The rebels pulled to a stop in front of Simoñ and Modesto and their spokesman said, "Buenos dias, señores, it's a beautiful morning, no?"

"Si, very beautiful," Simoñ replied evenly.

"My name is Felix Jaramillo, and you must be the evasive Simoñ Gomez."

"Si, you are correct. I am Simoñ Gomez, patron of the Gomez Hacienda, but I am not evasive as you suggest," Simoñ said resolutely.

"Many pardons, Señor Gomez, perhaps that was a poor choice of words on my part. Please forgive me."

"What can I do for you, Señor Jaramillo?"

"I see that you and your segundo have those new American rifles. They are illegal in New Mexico, you know," warned Felix.

"I doubt if you have ridden this far just to tell me what is or is not legal," said Simoñ shortly.

"You are so right, I did not."

"Out with it," said Simoñ. "What is your business with me?"

Before Felix could answer, one of his men gestured toward a lone rider who was pushing his horse to the limit as he rode their way. "It's Mario, Señor Felix." No one said a word as they waited for the rider to draw near. As he reined up in front of Felix, he gasped, "It's all over, Felix, Manuel Armijo, with an army from the south, has occupied Santa Fe and has proclaimed himself the legitimate governor of New Mexico. He was reinforced by troops sent up from Zacatecas. Jose retreated to Santa Cruz and Armijo followed him there and defeated him. It is said that Jose was brought to Armijo before Armijo even entered Santa Cruz and Jose, knowing that all was lost, accepted his fate as an honorable soldier should, and said to his captor, `How do you do, companero?' He approached Armijo with outstretched hands to show he was unarmed and also to act as one governor to another, on equal terms. It is said that Armijo replied, `How do you do, companero? Confess yourself, companero.' Then he ordered him shot." The rider looked imploringly at Felix and asked, "What shall we do?"

Felix was jarred from deep thought and jerked his head toward Mario and answered harshly, "We have failed just as Pope failed in 1680. It is all over, the rebellion of 1837 is over. Finished, lost. Our only hope now lies with the Americanos."

Simoñ glanced quickly at Modesto in surprise and then returned his attention to Felix and his men.

"We return to our homes and families," Felix told his men. "Conceal your political affiliations with Jose and if that is not possible, I suggest you leave New Mexico."

He now turned to Modesto and Simoñ and said, "You ask what business I have with you, señores? I have no business, no business whatsoever." He bowed mockingly and he and his men rode away at a gallop.

"That scoundrel, Armijo betrayed those people for personal gain," Modesto said angrily. "Not too long ago he plotted with Felix and others like him, and now he's turned on them as a jackel would. I'm sure when Jose approached Armijo, he did not expect to be shot. Why should he? After all, he and Armijo were companeros in the conspiracy."

"We have learned much about our new governor," Simoñ replied soberly.

CHAPTER X

Simoñ constructed an addition to his house which was to become his office, the nerve center of his enterprises. It was a spacious room, with the equipment, supplies, and personnel necessary for conducting the proper and skillful management of his hacienda. The supervision and management of his affairs kept him close to his office more and more as his domain expanded.

A huge table had been constructed and placed in the center of his office. It was used for the frequent meetings which he had with Modesto, his segundo, and also those in charge of the various flocks, herds. etc. Occasionally he would call in his caporales, or overseers, to hear their reports. He kept in very close touch with the far flung activities of the hacienda, including the trade with the Comanches which flourished under the supervision of Ramon and his brothers. Even the ciboleros, (buffalo hunters) were represented at the meetings by agregados.

It was on a chilly April morning when Orlando came to clean the office and build a fire for the comfort of his patron.

Simoñ had developed a routine over the years in the management of his hacienda. One of these routines was his prompt arrival at his office every morning at eight o'clock sharp except for Sunday which was reserved for church services.

Simoñ's good right hand was Marcello Sandoval, a methodic and meticulously efficient aide.

Marcello turned away from the papers which lay before him on his desk. "Buenos dias, Señor Gomez."

"Buenos dias, Marcello." Simoñ strode briskly to his huge desk which occupied a good portion of the north end of the room. "Como esta usted."

"Muy bien, gracias, y usted?" Marcello replied.

"Muy bien," Simoñ replied absently as he searched through the papers which lay on his desk.

"Buenos dias," Orlando, another of Simoñs office help said as he approached his patron.

Simoñ looked up from his desk and almost as an afterthought, replied, "Buenos dias, Orlando."

"Do you wish anything, patron?" Orlando stood waiting.

"No," Simoñ replied. "Everything seems fine, gracias."

Orlando left the room and Marcello turned in his chair to face Simoñ who stood by his desk studying a paper.

"Have you made a decision about Cerrillos, señor?"

Simoñ sat down behind the desk, and after a few moments of silence he looked up at Marcello and said, "Si, I have. I think we should make our presence at Mount Chalchihuitl more evident by sending a few more men to mine for the turquoise there. For this reason, when the Americans annex New Mexico, I want to be able to prove that we mined part of that area before they came. Our presence there now should make it easier for us to file an American claim in the area.

"Turquoise is a valuable commodity, especially in our trade with the Indians. It could be a bonanza for us in later years."

"I agree," Marcello answered. "As you know, turquoise is believed by the Indians to bring good luck for they also believe that it is a gift from the gods. Potential profit is very great so it would be a sound investment."

"Would you take care of the selection of the men who will go to mine for me, Marcello? And take care of all the other details?"

"It will be done," Marcello answered him.

"Oh, and be sure that you see to it, also, that everyone of the peons receives a copy of my proclamation guaranteeing to them and their descendents the perpetual right to hunt, gather wood, and graze a certain number of livestock, which will be specified in the proclamation, on the Gomez lands."

"Orlando is taking care of that right now," Marcello replied.

"Good. Thank you, Marcello. I don't know what I'd do without your help."

Marcello smiled and returned to his work.

"Do you think we can revive the dream of Don Luis Maria Cabeza de Baca?" Simoñ smiled as he asked this.

"If anyone can, it is you, señor," Marcello replied "you have a good start at it."

"De Baca's Las Vegas Grande was a much larger dream than I ever hope to accomplish," Simoñ protested.

"Maybe so, and maybe not," Marcelloi answered. "Your grant is only part of that which once comprised the huge grant of Don de Baca, but don't forget that the Llanos is claimed by no one now and so the grazing is free for those who dare to send stock out on it. This free grazing could make your grant equal to his."

"Don't forget that it was the Indians who destroyed the Las Vegas Grandes," Simoñ reminded him. "They could administer the same fate to me."

"But don't forget either, señor, that you are on friendly terms with the Comanches, thanks to the Prudencio brothers and their Comanchero trade. The Comanches need you now as much as you need them. I do not believe that they, as a nation, would harass you for it would be too costly for them. And besides, the Llano is large, very large, and the little that you would use for grazing would hardly be missed by them."

"But it was not the Comanches so much who destroyed de Baca's dream as it was the Apaches, Navajoes, and Utes," Simoñ reminded him.

"You'll find a way to limit that also," Marcello replied confidently.

"We will try." Simoñ again bent over the papers on his desk and the large room was quiet until he asked, "How many villages have been established in the mountains west and north of us by some of my former peons?"

Marcello drew forth a ledger from one of the drawers in his desk and looked through it quickly, then replied, "Four thus far, Don Simoñ."

"How are they faring?"

"They are finding that it is still difficult to develop large flocks of sheep and herds of cattle because of the Apache raids. They swoop down upon them and do much destruction, taking many lives. They kill many animals as well as drive them off, but those peons don't give up! They bury their dead and begin again."

"We Spaniards do not give up easily, do we?" Simoñ wore an expression of pride as he continued, "Fear and cowardice are omitted from our vocabulary and we will prevail in the long run. We'll wear the Indians down. Will our people have trouble in living up to their partido contracts?"

"The contracts call for a return after four years, of double that which they have borrowed from you. I believe that they can meet their obligations, señor."

"If they can't, I want to be told about it immediately and if they can prove that they cannot meet their obligations because of the Indian menace, we'll extend their contracts. Although we'll have to be careful in making our decisions because we don't want to set any precedents or encourage some to avoid their contracts for reasons not justified. How large are their flocks and herds?"

"Only large enough to be penned up every night," Marcello replied. "Not any larger than can be watched safely."

"The Indians must be increasing their raids. Make a note for our next general meeting. We should discuss some way to give protection to the people in those isolated communities," Simoñ mused.

"It's not only the Indians who cause them to sustain losses," said Marcello. "The severity of some of the winters account for some of them."

"Well, we'll try to remedy that soon by beginning to send stock out on the Llanos," Simoñ answered. "Out there they should have unlimited feed except in extreme weather. The grama is nourishing even though it dries during the winter months."

"They can have bad storms out there, though, so I have heard," Marcello commented drily.

"You always remind me of the weak points, don't you Marcello? I want you to continue to do so."

"I just want to make sure that you see the entire picture, señor."

"America will give you and people of your ability a chance to see what you can do one of these days, Marcello. But I'd hate to lose you, but that's the price to pay for progress, I guess."

"Si, I guess," Marcello said with a chuckle.

"I suppose I am a hopeless dreamer, Marcello. I keep hoping that people will improve and learn to respect and accept all others just as people and not catagorize them into groups according to their origin."

"All great men were dreamers and movers, señor," Marcello said eagerly. "Without dreamers the world would be stagnant."

"Some dreamers dream the wrong dream, I'm afraid. Some dream greatness for themselves at the expense of others. Santa Anna is such a man and look at how many headaches and suffering he has brought to the people of Mexico. And he does this for personal gain and power. Maybe I'm looking through rose tinted glasses when I look at America. Maybe I see only what I want to see. Maybe her people are no different than Santa Anna."

"You know you are wrong there," Marcello interrupted.

"Not all together, I'm afraid, for no doubt there are men in America just like Santa Anna, but there are more people like you, Marcello, and your kind are in the majority. It is said that good always triumphs over evil. Sometimes it is slow about arriving, but it does. You know a price has to be paid for freedom for it does not come cheaply. Sometimes it's very expensive, and that is why it is cherished by those willing to die for it. Vigilance and sacrifice are the prices people must pay to preserve liberty, for without it, a country can only become a fief for someone like Santa Anna. Tell me, Marcello, what do you think would happen if you fell in love with a rico's daughter and she with you and you asked for her hand in marriage?"

"You know the answer to that question without any help from me," answered Marcello with a grin.

"Would such a marriage be more likely to happen in America?"

Marcello considered a moment and then said, "Si, but I'm sure there are some in America who would object also. Here in New Mexico, every rico would object."

"So what you are saying is that in America anything can happen and does happen," finished Simoñ.

"I suppose so," conceded Marcello.

"We could talk all day and I would enjoy it but we have work to do and we need to get to it. If any one wants me, I'll be with Modesto." Simoñ rearranged the papers on his desk and rose to leave the room.

He found Modesto talking with Graciano Martinez, the mayordomo of the buffalo hunters. "Buenos dias, Graciano," Simoñ said as he approached the two men.

"Buenos dias, patron," Graciano replied as he removed his sombrero.

"Are you doing well in the gathering of buffalo robes?"

"Si, patron, very well."

"And we are not wasting the buffalo meat in the process?"

"That is true, señor, it is made into tasajo and smoked and brought back to the hacienda for the people, Señor Gomez."

"Good, we must never waste the meat when our people are in need of it. Modesto, this fall I'd like to go out with Graciano and his hunters to get a good look at the Llanos first hand. I think it is time for us to consider sending our flocks and herds out there and establishing line camps where the men can live. What do you think?"

"Si, I think it is time to put that part of our plan into operation. Maybe we should have considered it before now," said Modesto thoughtfully.

"Let's not look back and think of what we might have done, for we need to concentrate right now on the future. Which reminds me, we need to train some of our men in Indian fighting."

"Indian fighting?"

"The villages in the mountains have been harassed increasingly by the Indians. Lives are being lost and property is being stolen or destroyed. Some of our shepherds have been killed and their flocks stolen or run off. This has to be stopped."

"My hunters are also good Indian fighters, patron," Graciano said eagerly. "Can we be of any help? During the summer months, as you know, we don't hunt as much, for the buffalo robes are not of prime quality at that time."

Simoñ considered this proposal and said, "We could certainly use your men to make a tour through the mountains. This would encourage the villagers and let them know that we are aware of their problems. In the meantime we need to train a special unit to be used on a permanent basis in patrolling the mountains. We must protect the people. These retaliations are long overdue.

"Modesto, select five good men to accompany Graciano and me on a trip to the villages. We'll plan to leave early this afternoon. Make sure that each of the men you choose has one of the American rifles. Graciano, I'll need ten of your best buffalo hunters! Meet me in front of my office when you're ready and be prepared to be out for several days."

Modesto and Graciano left to prepare for the trip and Simoñ went to the house to tell his wife. On his way he met his son, Carlos and Ramon Prudencio leaving his office.

Carlos had grown into a strong young man and was now taller than his brother, Leandro. Taller by several inches and heavier. He had taken a liking to trading with the Comanches and was doing well under the tutelege of Ramon. He was also becoming quite an expert on the Comanches and their ways. He even dressed more like a Comanche than he did a Mexican, and he knew their language and some of the chiefs personally.

Leandro, on the other hand, had taken to the wagon train end of their business as naturally as Carlos had taken to being a Comanchero. Simoñ's and Sylvia's next younger son, Ignacio, was showing promise in keeping the books, and was under Marcello's feet constantly. Emilo, the youngest, still had not shown in what direction his inclinations would take him, although he was ranging constantly over the hacienda questioning and eager to learn.

Josephine, the only daughter of the family, was Simoñ's pride and joy and her mother's and grandmother's as well. She was a quiet girl, slender and straight. An excellent horsewoman, she was interested in all of the activities of the hacienda, and her beauty was known far and wide.

Carlos and Ramon had been looking for Simoñ and when they located him they greeted him eagerly, "Padre, one of our friends by the name of Facing North has sent word that he has a herd of three hundred and sixty cattle and about half that many sheep which he wishes to trade to us."

"Do we have enough trade goods to strike a deal?"

"Si, patron," Ramon answered. "It might clean us out, but Leandro is due any day now with another wagon train with supplies from Missouri. When he arrives, our store house will be filled once again."

"Do the best you can, then," Simoñ told them. "And see Modesto about getting some of the men to take care of the stock which you get from the Comanches. We'll turn them over to Casimiro and his vaqueros and Emeterio with his herders." He again started to the house, but turned back as he realized that Carlos and Ramon had hesitated. "Is there something else?"

"Si, padre, Facing North wants to know if we will take two little Mexican girls as part of the deal? He says that he does not want them. You know what it means for the little girls if we don't take them."

"I see," Simoñ said. "Of course take the girls and turn them over to Anita at the nursery."

"Si, padre," Carlos and Ramon walked away and Simoñ continued toward the house to ask Sylvia to tell someone to prepare food for their trip to the mountains. He also wanted to tell Marcello that he would be away for a few days.

He next visited the corrals and ordered that his favorite sorrel mare be saddled and brought to the house at noon. When he returned to the house once more, he found Modesto and the five men whom Simoñ had requested.

"These men have volunterred to be Indian fighters, Simoñ. They are young, eager, and capable." Modesto introduced each of them as Gilberto, Juan, Jose, Tito, and Filomeno. Simoñ nodded and shook hands with each of them and said, "I'm looking for men around whom to build a fighting unit. This is not going to be a one journey affair. If you show promise in Graciano's eyes, you will become the nucleus of what I will call The Mountain Riflemen, whose duty will be to protect the villages in the mountains from the Indians. You will be gone from home most of the time as you patrol the area around the villages. If this sort of job does not appeal to you, say so now, and I will understand." His eyes twinkled as he asked, "What do you say?"

The five young men glanced at one another and then one of them answered eagerly, "We understand and we want the job, patron."

"Good, Modesto take them to the compound and issue them rifles and ammunition. Filomeno, weren't you held captive by the Apaches when you were younger until you escaped?"

"Si," Filomeno looked with surprise at the patron for he hadn't realized he knew about his being a captive.

"Because of the knowledge you have learned from your captivity, I will place you in charge of the five of you, with the title of Captain of the Mountain Riflemen, subject to your performance, of course. If you do not show leadership ability, I will have to remove you from that position. The protection of the villagers must be paramount above every other consideration. Do you understand?"

"Si, patron, I understand. You will not have to replace me. I will do the job that you require of me. Muchas gracias, patron, for giving me this chance."

"Now get yourselves ready, for I want you here at noon, ready to travel."

CHAPTER XI

When they were ready to leave, Modesto, Sylvia, and Marcello were there to see them off. Simoñ turned to Graciano and said, "You are in command now, lead the way."

The ten buffalo hunters, dressed in buckskins, the five young recruits, and Simoñ and Graciano trotted their horses west toward the Sangre de Cristos which loomed ahead.

An hour out from the headquarters, the Indian fighters met four carretas being pulled by oxen along the banks of Ocate Creek. A string of pack burros followed behind. The carretas carried wool freshly cut by knife from sheep. Cutting the wool using this method was a slow, backbreaking process, but the villagers were too poor to be able to afford the new hand shears. The burros carried grain which the villagers hoped to convert into flour at the Gomez mill, the pay to be on a percentage basis. The wool would be sold or traded at the Gomez headquarters.

Upon seeing the approaching riders, the small caravan of pobladores (settlers) held up a bultos, a carved image of a saint, asking the saint's protection if the riders intended harm.

Simoñ sensed their alarm and called out loudly, "We are friends—we will not harm you!"

The pobladores crossed themselves and stood by their motionless animals, waiting for the strangers to speak again.

"I am Simoñ Gomez, patron of the Gomez Hacienda."

The settlers immediately removed their sombreros and nervously shifted their weight from one foot to another as they bowed their heads, but said nothing.

"Where are you taking your harvest?"

"To your hacienda, if it pleases you, Señor Gomez," an old grey haired man in his seventies said.

"From what village do you come?"

"El Cojo," the old man replied.

"Martine Silva's village?"

"Si, Señor Gomez," the old man replied.

"Martine was wounded in a skirmish with the Navajoes many years ago. He was a fighter, that one. He and his sons were the first settlers in the village. That is why it is called the 'lame one'," Simoñ explained to Graciano.

"An appropriate name," commented Graciano.

"When you reach the hacienda, tell Señor Marcello, who will be in my office, that I want you to get top price for your wool."

"Marcello...si, Señor Gomez, I will do that, and many thanks for your kindness."

"What is your name?" asked Simoñ.

"Pablo Rivera," the old man replied.

"Pablo, have the Indians given your village much trouble?"

"Si, much trouble. Very much trouble from the Indios."

"Maybe we can put a stop to some of their raids," Simoñ told him. "These men with me are Indian fighters, and they will be scouting the mountains continuously from now on, in hopes of keeping the Indians away from the four villages which are located on my hacienda."

"The El Cojo people crossed themselves and smiled approvingly.

"We are indebted to your kindness, Señor Gomez," old Pablo said.

"Adios, compadres," Simoñ called back as he and the Mountain Riflemen rode up the mountain side and disappeared into the thick forest. Their way grew steeper by the minute and they finally halted to give their horses a breather and dismounted to stretch their legs.

"Filomeno, have you given much thought to your new assignment?" asked Simoñ during the halt.

"I was thinking that I must take alternate routes to the villages in order to avoid ambushes and also to avoid a set schedule so that our visits won't be anticipated," Filomeno said.

"I see that I have selected the right man to be captain," Simoñ said with satisfaction. "Well, let's make tracks."

"It takes an Indian to think like one, Filomeno," Graciano said. "Your years of captivity prepared you well for your assignment."

"Thank you, señor," Filomeno smiled with pleasure.

As they neared the top of the slope which they had been climbing, they could hear the sound of dogs barking and a voice yelling in anger. They covered the remainder of the distance in a rush and looked down on the valley below. A small creek wandered along the valley floor and at that point, the valley was perhaps a quarter of a mile wide. A grassy meadow extended on both sides of the creek, and a flock of sheep grazed there.

The shepherd's dogs were barking and dashing forward in an attempt to help a boy as he struggled vainly with two Indians who were trying to tie him down.

"Utes!" Graciano muttered. "They're after the sheep, but where are the rest of the Indians?"

"The rest?" Simoñ looked surprised.

"Si, the rest, patron. The Utes never raid in parties that small. Especially if they are this far away from their tribal lands. Patron, I suggest that Filomeno take some of the men and rescue the boy."

Filomeno looked at Simoñ and Simoñ nodded. Filomeno spoke to four of the men and within seconds they were on their way down the tree covered mountainside toward the shepherd boy.

Simoñ and the others followed at a slower pace. Suddenly two shots rang out and the dogs stopped barking.

"The Indians have shot the dogs," Simoñ said angrily.

"Barking dogs draw attention," Graciano commented grimly.

"I hope they don't kill the boy before Filomeno gets there," Simoñ said as he urged his horse to a faster pace.

"They will if he doesn't stop fighting them," Graciano replied.

"If there are others, where are they?" Simoñ glanced constantly around as they descended rapidly.

"Probably preparing to raid El Cojo, would be my guess," Graciano suggested.

When they had nearly reached the bottom of the hill, they heard shots and as they looked in the direction where they had seen the boy struggling with the Indians, they saw that Filomeno had shot the Utes, and they were sprawled on the ground near the boy, who was now hunched over and crying.

"You're safe now, muchacho," Simoñ said when he reached the boy and dismounted.

"But they killed my dogs. They killed my dogs!" The boy repeated as he sobbed.

"They won't kill any more dogs." Simoñ placed his arm about the boy's shoulder as he tried to comfort him. "How old are you, muchacho?"

"Nueve (Nine), señor," the boy said as he pulled away from Simoñ and wiped the tears from his face as he did, then asked, "Who are you señor?"

"I am the patron of the Gomez Hacienda," Simoñ answered.

"You lie, you are bandits! You are after my sheep, too!"

The boy began to run for the forest, but before he reached the trees, Graciano had spurred his horse in pursuit, sweeping him off his feet and returning him to Simoñ.

"Why didn't you believe me when I told you who I was?"

"What would Simoñ Gomez be doing up here with all these armed men?" The boy continued to struggle as Graciano dropped him in front of Simoñ.

"Are you going to kill me?"

"What do we have to do to convince you that we mean no harm?" asked Simoñ in frustration. "What is your name?"

"Only banditos and Indians have guns," the boy said sullenly. "And I won't tell you my name."

"Not any more, muchacho," Filomeno said as he dismounted and knelt beside the defiant boy. "I am Captain Filomeno Sanchez of The Mountain Riflemen. When I was a little younger than you, I was herding sheep one day, just as you were today and an Apache raiding party swooped down on me and carried me off to be raised as one of them. It took me four years, but I finally escaped and came to live under the protection of Don Simoñ Gomez on his hacienda. My entire family was killed on the day of that Apache raid and I was left all alone. This man whom you accuse of being a bandito is really Simoñ Gomez, patron of the hacienda where I live. You do him an injustice by accusing him so.

"He has organized a troop of Indian fighters to patrol the mountains to protect your village and the others. I was selected by him to lead that patrol and the men with us are those Indian fighters and this is our first patrol."

The boy raised his head slowly and looked Filomeno in the eyes for the first time as embarrassment and shame began to show on his face. "I'm sorry, Señor Filomeno, do you think the patron will forgive me?"

Filomeno stood up and looked at Simoñ and Simoñ said quickly, "You are a brave boy and I am very proud of you. You showed strength of character and courage in the way you fought those Indians alone. Of course I forgive you."

The boy ran toward Simon and threw himself into his arms and Simoñ gave the boy a fatherly hug as he thought, why is it taking so long, America? This boy needs you now.

The boy pulled away and asked, "Did you say something, señor?"

"I may have been thinking out loud, hijo (son). We still don't know your name."

"It's Eleberto Chavez," the boy answered with a smile.

"Well, Eleberto, what village are you from, El Cojo?"

"Si, señor."

"How far are we from your village?"

"It is just over that first hill, señor," Eleberto pointed to the west.

Simoñ glanced at Graciano who said, "We had better hurry."

"Jose," Simoñ said to one of the riflemen, "give this Indian fighter a ride."

"It will be my pleasure," Jose replied as he extended a hand to Eleberto and pulled him up behind him. The boy protested, "Aren't we going to bury my dogs?"

"First things first boy, we can bury the dogs later," Jose told him gruffly.

A short time later, the riflemen were sitting on a ridge looking down on the little village of El Cojo. It nestled in a deceptively peaceful small valley below them. An Indian attack seemed to be the farthest thing from the minds of the people as they went about their chores. Some of the women were busily washing clothes in the small creek and men could be seen working in the irrigated fields and others near the stock pens. As the riders looked down, they saw the Utes moving slowly and cautiously on foot, in the direction of the village, closer and closer they moved.

"You're the Indian fighter," Simoñ said softly to Graciano, "give the order."

"Si." Graciano turned in his saddle to instruct the men and when he had finished, the men dismounted and began to spread out and made their way swiftly and silently down the hill.

"I've told the men to position themselves as near as possible to the Indians and when I open fire, they will follow my example."

Simoñ and Eleberto followed down the slope on foot also, careful not to dislodge a rock which could alert the Utes. When Graciano judged that his men would be in position, he raised his rifle to his shoulder and fired. The noise ricocheted off the mountain walls, as its echo reverberated down the valley and then other shots could be heard. The villagers, upon hearing the gunfire, scurried for cover, not knowing that it was needless, for the few Utes who hadn't been killed in the first salvo hurriedly disappeared in surprise and confusion into the trees. When enough time had elapsed, Simoñ permitted Eleberto to go ahead into the village to explain what had happened. and when he finally appeared in the open, waving his arms, the Riflemen entered the village on foot. Those left in charge of the horses would bring them down once they realized the threat was over.

The men were greeted with cheers and shouts as the people tried to show their gratitude. Young children clung to their mothers' skirts shyly as they stared at the strangers. A grizzled old man hobbled forth wielding a juniper cane as he hastened to greet them. "Welcome to our humble village, Señor Gomez." The old man wore a broad smile as he removed his sombrero. "Our homes are yours, please accept our thanks for your timely visit!"

"I assure you, the pleasure is ours also," Simoñ replied with a smile.

My name is Martine Silva," the old man told them. It is I who received your gracious permission to bring my family and a few friends here to El Cojo to begin our village years ago. We here at El Cojo are eternally grateful to you for granting us that joy."

Simoñ walked forward and extended his hand to Martine and the two grasped hands tightly as they gazed into each other's eyes. Finally Martine said, before he released Simoñ's hand, "Muchas gracias."

Simoñ could see tears forming in the corners of Martine's faded blue eyes and he answered quickly, "De nada, de nada, mi amigo."

The Mountain Riflemen were invited to eat and stay the night and at first Simoñ declined the invitation and then went on to explain the future duties of the Riflemen. He introduced Graciano and Filomeno and they in turn introduced their men amid shouts of approval from the villagers.

"How far is it to Montoya?" Simoñ inquired of Martine.

"Three to four hours ride, Don Gomez," Martin told him,. "It will be dark soon, won't you reconsider and spend the night with us?"

Simoñ hesitated and looked at Graciano questioningly. Graciano grinned cheerfully and said softly, "It would be more comfortable here and the pobladores would feel they were returning, in a small way, the favor of our driving the Utes away. And besides," he looked down at Eleberto, "don't forget the dogs. We must bury them with honors."

"We'll stay," Simoñ said to Martine, smiling warmly as he spoke.

"Gracias, Señor Gomez, gracias," Martine replied in delight. We will remember this day for many years."

The pobladores scattered to make preparations for feeding and housing the Riflemen. Three lambs were butchered and while the men began to roast them over an open fire, the women busied themselves in their homes preparing the food to go with them. The ever present frijoles simmered in the pots and with tortillas and sopapillas, and honey the visitors would be fed royally.

Before the meal was served, Martine invited their guests to visit the small church for a short service.

The church had a dirt floor and the few benches would not furnish seating for everyone, so they were reserved for the visitors first, and the villagers stood at the back and around the walls of the church as the Hermano Mayor (the chief brother of the Third Order of Saint Francis of Assisi, or as it was sometimes called, The Brothers of Light, or more commonly, the Penitentes) walked to the front of the church, knelt before a crudely carved wooden statue on a crucifix, crossed himself, and then turned toward the congregation and spoke "As you can see, we have yet to complete our church. We have no altar or confessional, but we will, with God's help, have our church completed some day soon. God knows that this is His house. We are building it for His children and He blesses and watches over all of those who come here to seek Him out. Some day He may send a priest to us, in the meantime we remember Him in the best way and the only way that we know how, we pray. Let us pray, then." The Hermano Mayor bowed his head.

The next morning the Mountain Riflemen saddled up and left El Cojo, heading for the village of Montoya, and as they rode, Simon turned to Filomeno and asked, "Do you know the origin of the Penitentes, Filomeno?"

"I think so, patron, but I am not sure."

"Where did you learn about it?"

"From my grandmother, señor."

"Would I be prying too much if I asked you to share what you know of the history of the Penitentes, Filomeno? I do not wish to pry, so if you do not want to talk about the Brotherhood, I'll understand."

"I do not know much, but what I do know, I'll be more than happy to share with you," replied Filomeno politely.

"Please," answered Simoñ.

"Our Holy Saint Francis of Assisi was its founder many, many years ago when Spain wasn't even a country yet. My grandmother told me that the Saint organized two orders, one for the men and the other for women. The men's order was called The Order of Saint Francis of Assisi and the women's order was called The Franciscan Order of Poor Ladies. From the first order came the so called Third Order of Saint Francis which we now call Los Hermanos de Penitente. That is all I know about the history of the Brothers of Light," concluded Filomeno. "I wish that I knew more, but that is all I know, señor."

"Thank you for telling me that much, Filomeno" Simoñ knew full well that Filomeno probably knew much more about the Penitentes, but would rather not discuss it. He would respect that reticence. He knew that the Penitentes filled the vacuum left by the absence of a priest to minister to each little flock. We are a religous people, Simoñ thought to himself, and we are going to show our love for the Lord whether there are enough priests or not. I wonder sometimes whether there really is a shortage of priests or whether they don't want to be assigned to small isolated villages high in the mountains. Surely the Church realizes that our sick and dying need a priest here just as much as do the people in Santa Fe or other more populated places. We want the last rites administered to our dying as much as do the others. Our young people need the blessing of the church as they marry, and the baptisms need the sanction of the priests. The Penitentes are here when the people need them, they comfort the sick and bury the dead. The people will not easily forget the Brothers of Light, nor should they.

"Montoya should not be far ahead now," Graciano's comment interrupted Simoñ's thoughts.

"And Hondo? How far is it from Montoya?"

"Montoya and El Cojo are on the west side of the mountain, as you know, and Hondo is about eight to ten miles from Montoya. Osha is below Hondo perhaps five miles."

"Who gave Osha its name, Graciano?"

"Serapio Sanchez, the first alcalde," Graciano replied. "He named it that because of the wild celery which grew near where he first made camp. Wild celery, if used properly, will cure many ills."

"So I have always heard," Simoñ replied. " Did you know that the shepherds carry the root of the osha with them to ward off rattlesnakes?"

"I've heard that," said Graciano gravely. "Do you think it really works?"

As the riflemen edged along the mountainside, they came upon a long, slanted slope which tilted down into a area which resembled giant gopher mounds. Each mound had a few adobe structures clinging to it and on the mound near the center was seen a torreon.

The seven hills of Rome," Simoñ said with a chuckle.

"The seven hills of Rome?" Filomeno wore a puzzled expression on his face when he heard the words spoken by Simoñ and he turned to look inquiringly at Simoñ.

"The original city of Rome was built on seven hills, Filomeno," Simoñ explained.

"Si, señor," Filomeno replied, "but Montoya is no Rome for it has only five hills! I wonder why the people selected this place to found their village?"

"Water, Filomeno, there are a number of large springs here, which provide the people with an abundance of clear, cool water all the year around. The springs have never run dry and the people catch the water in a huge rock tank which they built below the springs. The tank furnishes them with the water to irrigate their gardens and small fields."

Graciano now pointed and said, "See over there? You can see the Acequia Madre, the mother ditch."

"And they have a large torreon from which to defend themselves when attack. The people of Montoya have planned well," observed Simoñ.

"I've heard that the founder, Felix Montoya, the first alcalde, spent a good part of his life fighting Indians down in Mexico. During one of these fights, he questioned the stragegy of his superiors and for this he was exiled to the frontier. His sentence could have been death, but because of his earlier unblemished military record, the judge sentenced him to exile instead," Graciano told them.

"He could be of invaluable aid to you and your men," Simoñ commented to Filomeno.

"He's no longer alive, Don Gomez," Graciano said. "He was killed by Apaches only six months after he founded the village which bears his name. But he did live long enough to plan his village."

The loud clanking sound of metal clashing against metal ricocheted off the mountainside and the riflemen pulled in their horses abruptly as they searched for its cause.

Graciano explained, "It's the village alarm system warning the people that strangers are approaching."

We'll wait until they know who we are," Simoñ decided. "You are familiar with the village, Graciano, perhaps you'd better ride in ahead of us."

"Si, patron." Graciano rode away from them and down the hillside.

"Everyone is rushing toward the torreon." said Filomeno.

"Si," said Simoñ anxiously, "I hope they recognize that Graciano comes in peace."

Voices could be heard as Graciano reached shouting distance, and two men emerged from the torreon carrying muzzle loading rifles. They yelled something back at Graciano who continued to ride toward them until he had reached the two men. They watched as he talked to the men and then turned in his saddle to beckon them in. As the men rode down the hill, the villagers began to exit the torreon.

"Welcome to Montoya," one of them called as the riders drew nearer. "My name is Fermin Montoya. Please get down, all of you."

Simoñ dismounted first and introduced himself to Fermin as he extended his hand.

"Forgive our hostile welcome. We did not know who you were," Fermin said with a grin.

"We understand, for it's better to be overly cautious than not cautious enough," Simoñ assured him. "Are you related to the founder of this village?"

"Si, he was my grandfather, Señor Gomez," said Fermin promptly.

"You should be very proud of him."

"We are," Fermin answered. "It is ironic that he was killed by Apaches, for he was court martialed because he was trying to prevent his superiors from completely anniliating an Apache village, including women and children. Later, the officer who brought the charges against my grandfather, was, with his entire contingent of soldiers, ambushed. They were killed to the last man by Apaches who happened to be away from the village which my grandfather had tried to protect."

Simoñ told Fermin about the reason for their visit to each of the four villages and Fermin was delighted. "That will make the villagers happy and thankful, Señor Gomez. Lately the raids have been getting more intense and more frequent."

"Excuse me, Fermin," another villager said as he approached the alcalde. "

"Si, what is it, Tomas?"

"It's Porfidia, she's worse," Tomas said worriedly.

"Worse! Please excuse me, Señor Gomez." Fermin said as he turned quickly and followed Tomas in the direction of one of the small adobes.

Simoñ looked over at Graciano and suggested, "Perhaps we can be of some help. Let's go see if they need us."

"Bueno," Graciano agreed, and they both hastened to follow Fermin. When they reached the house which Fermin had entered they found the door closed. They both paused for a few seconds in front of the door and then Simoñ slowly raised his hand and knocked lightly.

"Come in, Señor Gomez, come in," Fermin's muffled voice called out from within and as Simoñ and Graciano entered the house they saw Fermin leaving the bed where Porfidia lay. The woman's mother and father were at her bedside and looked uneasy.

"Is there anything we can do?" Simoñ asked in a helpfull tone.

"I do not think so, señor. It is a infermendad puesta (a curse placed on her by a witch). Only the witch can help. We need to find her and convince her to remove the curse if we can, before it is too late," Fermin told them.

Simoñ turned his head so that Fermin could not see his expression and looked at Graciano raising his eyebrows in disbelief as he did. Then Simoñ asked as he walked toward the bed, "May I ask Porfidia a question?"

"Si, if you think it would help, Señor Gomez." Fermin answered.

Simoñ leaned over as he asked softly, "Porfidia?"

She turned her head and stared up into his face, startled to see the strange face.

"Has any meat been stolen?" Simoñ whispered. He waited intently for her reply.

Her eyes widened as she stared up into his face, but she did not answer. She just stared up at him with unblinking eyes. Not discouraged, he asked, "Were you visited by a lady before you became ill who had her face painted white and her long hair hung loosely about her shoulders?"

"No, señor," Porfidia answered weakly and then said, "I hold my stone for protection against a yiapana and besides she never visits anyone except in January and this is April. No, there is no yiapana, for I was not put to sleep and there was no meat missing. My sickness is infermendad puesta. I am sure of that."

"Where do you hurt, Porfidia?" Simon asked in a comforting voice.

Porfidia touched her stomach with her fingers and her eyes turned in that direction also.

Frowning, Simoñ placed his hand on her forehead gently and withdrew it quickly, exclaiming, "Holy Mother, the poor woman is burning up with fever!"

He turned to Fermin and asked, "Do you or anyone in the village have any yerbaluena?"

"Yerbaluena cannot cure infermendad puesta, Señor Gomez," Fermin protested in a weak respectful voice. "Only the person who cast the spell on her can break that spell."

Simoñ turned to Graciano and motioned for him to follow him to a safe distance from the others and whispered, "Do you know yerbaluena when you see it?"

"I think so," Graciano replied, "isn't it a mint?"

"Si," Simoñ answered. "See if you can find some in the village. Ask the women, especially the older ones. And ask for some mastranzo also. It is an herb which has a similar effect on people as yerbaluena when eaten. If you can find both, mix them and bring them to me. If not, ask them where you might be able to find some growing in or near the village. If they don't know where there is any, ask them about osha. I'm sure they must have some of that. I know it grows wild around the village of Osha just a few miles from here."

"Si," Graciano hurried away.

Simoñ then motioned for Fermin and asked, "Tell me about Porfidia. Is she married?"

"No, señor." Fermin was puzzled at such a question at a time such as this.

"Does she have a boy friend?"

"Tito is her boy friend, I think," Fermin said hesitantly.

"What do you mean, you think?"

"Maria claims Tito is hers also," explained Fermin.

"Stay with Porfidia, I want to speak with Tito. Where will I find him?"

He was sitting just outside the house when we came in," Fermin said. When Simoñ stepped outside, he saw a young man sitting on the ground, his back braced against the adobe wall of Porfidia's house, with his head bent over his knees.

"Are you called Tito?" Simon asked as he took two steps toward the young man and then stopped.

"Si, señor," the young man jerked his head upward when he heard his name spoken and quickly jumped to his feet asking eagerly as he did, "Is she going to be all right?"

"I think so, but tell me where Maria lives, will you please, Tito?"

"That is she watching from the door of that house," Tito pointed at Maria, who upon seeing the two men looking in her direction turned and disappeared instantly into the darkness of the doorway.

Simoñ approached the house and as he neared the door, Maria reappeared. "Do you know who I am?" Simoñ asked.

"Si," Maria curtsied, "You're the patron."

"That is correct, Maria," Simoñ replied in a soft voice. "Now I want you to listen to me carefully and do as I say."

"Si, patron."

"I want you to go to the person who placed a curse on Porfidia at your request and ask her to remove it."

"But señor," Maria began to protest and then abruptly halted her protest, when she remembered whom she was talking to, and she then said softly, "Si, Señor Gomez."

She hurried away at a fast pace not turning once to look at Simoñ and after Simoñ watched her for a few seconds she changed her fast pace to a trot. He then returned to Profidia just as Graciano came around the corner of the house with some green yerbaluena in his hand.

"All I could find is the yerbaluena. Will this do?"

"That will do," Simoñ took it from Graciano's hand and disappeared into Porfidia's house.

When he reached Porfidia's bedside, he gave the herb to her mother and advised her to boil it and have Porfidia drink some of the liquid. The woman glanced doubtfully at her husband, waiting for him to give his aproval of Simoñ's request. He nodded his head twice at her as his eye met hers and he whispered, "Do as he says, mi amor." She quickly did as Simoñ asked and then returned.

"But señor," she spoke respectfully as she looked at Simoñ and began to protest, but before she could continue, Simoñ interrupted by assuring her, "I have asked that the curse be removed and it will be done soon. The herb will also help her. Please give it to your daughter."

Porfidia looked up at her mother and opened her mouth obediently.

Simoñ and Fermin then left the house and when they were outside, Fermin motioned to a bench and asked, "You have located the witch and she has promised to remove the curse, señor?"

"Si, Porfidia will be much better by tomorrow morning. We must be going now for I wish to spend the night in Hondo, then visit Osha and start back to headquarters. Easter will be here soon, and I want to be with my family then."

The people of Montoya gathered to wish their patron a safe journey and Simoñ promised that he would not forget them and that he would be back soon to visit with them again.

As they rode toward Hondo, Graciano looked at Simon curiously, "Do you believe in witches, señor?

"Let's just say that I believe in treating both the mind and the stomach," Simon said with a smile.

Several miles from Montoya, as the riders rode through a pass and out into a little park-like meadow, they came upon a large flock of sheep and its shepherd who knelt a few feet from the nearest of his flock with his head bowed and eyes closed. As they drew nearer, they could hear him murmur as he clasped his hands together. He was startled when he heard them and jumped to his feet. The riders were even more amazed when he ran screaming toward his small tent.

"What on earth is wrong with him?" Simoñ glanced, mystified at Graciano and Filomeno, and then rode toward the tent, calling, "Do not be afraid. I am your patron, Señor Gomez. We will not harm you."

The shepherd came out of the tent hesitantly and began to walk toward Simoñ and when they met in the meadow, Simoñ asked, "What is wrong?"

The shepherd looked up at Simoñ beseechingly and faltered, "I not a bad man, Señor Gomez. I, Daniel, try to live a life which Christ would approve." He crossed himself nervously and then he went on pitifully, "I do not want to die."

Simoñ dismounted and took Daniel by the shoulder, shaking him slightly. "What is it Daniel, what is wrong?"

"Señor Gomez, less than ten minutes ago, I saw eight Ute warriors come riding down the hill, through those trees over there." He pointed to the trees, "They rode right through my flock without the sheep seeing them, or being disturbed in any way. Their horses' legs passed right through the bodies of the sheep as if they were ghosts and the sheep continued to graze, unaffected by their passing. The sheep did not see them, Señor Gomez. When I saw the Utes, I begged for my life and one of them said, `Dead warriors cannot kill. We are unable to harm you, for we are spirits of dead warriors. We are on our way back to our people to warn them that the four villages are protected by Mexican warriors.' The ghosts then rode right through the trees, disappearing into the forest." Daniel shuddered as he slumped to the ground with his face in his hands. The Indian fighters displayed great concern and crossed themselves hastily, as did Simoñ. "They must have been the spirits of the Utes whom we killed at El Cojo," Simoñ said thoughtfully. "This could be God's way of showing that he approves our protecting the poor defenceless villagers." Simoñ crossed himself once more and dropped to his knees for a brief prayer.

The riflemen followed suit and when they all rose to their feet, they looked wonderingly at the trees through which the Utes had ridden. Simoñ turned to Filomeno and told him soberly, "God has given his blessing to your mission."

"Si, Simoñ Gomez, I am honored to lead His crusade on behalf of His children," Filomeno said humbly.

Simoñ now asked Daniel, "Will you be all right now?"

"I will be all right now that I understand God's message." His face shone with fervor as he reassured his patron.

"Good, we must be on our way," he patted Daniel on the shoulder comfortingly and mounted his horse and his men did also and they headed once more for Hondo.

Daniel watched as they disappeared down the valley and then he took up once more the care of his flock.

"Who is in charge in Hondo, Don Simoñ?" Filomeno looked inquiringly at Simoñ as he asked.

"Roberto Sanchez, who is also the leader of the Penitentes," Simoñ replied.

"Why is the leader of the Penitentes also the leader of the village?"

"For some reason," Simoñ explained, "he has been able to keep his village immune from Indian raids. The people believe that it is because of his deep faith."

"The Hermanos seem to control all of the villages in northern New Mexico," Graciano observed. "No one moves without their approval, even the Alfonso Montaños at El Cojo, or the Fermin Montoyas at Montoya. The same will apply at Hondo, for they all do the bidding of the Hermano chief."

"Do I detect a bit of skepticism concerning the Penitentes?"

"No, patron," Graciano replied quickly. "I believe in the Penitentes. They fill the religious void created by the absence of priests."

"I see," Simoñ said in a low voice. "Some time we must talk more about this, Graciano. I'm not a Penitente either."

Graciano looked at his patron and nodded slightly. Hondo and Osha were visited without incident and the riflemen turned towards home. When they reached the headquarters, Simoñ instructed Filomeno to recruit five more men, train them, and begin regular patrols of the area surrounding the villages.

Graciano and his men resumed their duties with the buffalo segment of the far flung Gomez Hacienda.

CHAPTER XII

One evening Simoñ waited quietly in his library to be called to the evening meal. He was glad that Modesto and his wife and family would be eating with them that night.

When the evening meal was over, Simoñ asked Leandro, "What news do you bring back from Missouri?"

Leandro considered and then began, "I suppose the most important news to the people back there is that President Houston of Texas has threatened that if the United States does not annex Texas soon, he will invite all of the southern and western states and northern Mexico to join with Texas to form a new nation."

"Form a new nation?" Modesto raised his voice, "Does he think that northern Mexico would join in such a confederation? No, I do not think so. He realizes that the Texans and Mexicans have developed a deep distrust and hatred for one another ever since Texas declared her independence. He's just saying that for American consumption so that she will annex Texas."

"I think you're right, Tio Modesto, but if the United States does not move soon, the people of Missouri, at least around Westport Landing, are ready to follow such a plan," Leandro said soberly. "The people I've talked to there think it is a good idea. They don't think much of the northeast anyway. New Englanders aren't their kind of people, to them they are more like the English. After all, Texas has been refused admittance into the Union three times now, and the Texans feel insulted. If they are refused a fourth time and this new nation idea does not materialize, they may offer themselves to another country."

"With talk such as that, something surely will happen soon," Doña Maria commented.

"I'm afraid you're right," Simoñ said slowly.

"Why does the United States continue to refuse the Texans' request?" Ignacio looked at Leandro curiously.

"It's all because of the slave issue, little brother, "Leandro explained.

"What does that mean?"

"If Texas becomes a state, she will permit slavery within her borders," Leandro told him.

"And why is that so bad?"

"It will tilt the balance of power in the United States Senate in favor of the pro-slavers by two Texas senators. The pro and anti-slave states are evenly numbered in the senate at the present time," explained Leandro.

"Oh," Ignacio replied. He turned to his father and asked, "If the Americanos conquer New Mexico, how will that affect our peons whom the Americanos may consider as slaves, father?"

"Our peons are not slaves, son," Simoñ told him.

Ignacio glanced over at his mother and grandmother, but said nothing.

"What Ignacio is trying to ask," Doña Maria interjected, "is why does Mexico permit the institution of slavery to flourish unhindered in Mexico?"

"You two have been educating him about Mexico and the United States, haven't you?" Simon smiled his approval.

"Si," Sylvia replied promptly. "That is what you asked me to do, isn't it? Except for ours here on our hacienda, some of the people in Mexico are slaves and others are treated as slaves. Take the peons as an example. The ruling class does not see anything wrong with the peonage system and they also own thousands of Navajo slaves which were and still are, purchased for the sole purpose of using them as slaves. You yourself have visited many of their haciendas and seen the use of Navajo slaves as house servants. What do you do to the Mexican girls that our Comancheros get from the Comanches?"

"I free them so they can become part of our hacienda," Simoñ replied. "That is if we cannot find their parents and return them."

"But what happens to those who are traded to other Comancheros?"

"That is another question," admitted Simoñ, "and something over which I have no control. Those traded to other Comancheros can be sold into slavery, and the poor girls, especially the attractive ones, can be sold for immoral purposes," he finished in disgust.

"That is what your son is trying to ask," Sylvia told him.

"Does that mean that we are opposed to slavery, father?"

"With all my heart, my son."

Ignacio smiled and said, "Thank you, father, you make me proud. Discrimination seems so senseless. Why do people discriminate?"

"Some people need to feel superior to someone else, I suppose," his father said slowly, "but people are people, regardless of race or whatever religion they profess. Some day everyone may accept that fact, and see others as individuals entitled to consideration on their merits, and not be divided into Anglos, Mexicans, or whatever. As I see it, it is more likely to happen in the United States."

He asked as he looked at Leandro, "What do you hear about a possible war between Mexico and the Americanos?"

"Everyone back there seems to think it will come, father."

"Let's not talk of war during Holy Week," Doña Maria reminded them.

"Tomorrow is Holy Thursday and the Penitentes on the hacienda are making preparations. I heard someone practicing on his pito, (the flute) and the solemn tune gave me goose bumps."

The Hermano Mayor at the hacienda was Casimiro Benividez and he performed the necessary rituals in the absence of the priest.

Simoñ and Modesto had decided that they would participate in the celebration at the lower morada that evening. When they reached the little building, a number of men were already kneeling there in prayer, and they joined them. A number of large wooden crosses were leaning against the outer wall of the morada, placed there by those about to do penance. The sounds of chanting floated through the still evening air and it was accompanied by the eerie sounds of the pito. Together they contributed to the atmosphere of spiritual peace.

Suddenly, the Hermano Mayor emerged from the doorway of the morada carrying a crucifix of Christ, and a few steps behind him walked the rezador carrying his open prayer book. The rezador gazed down upon the dimly lit pages of the book as he chanted. Two men walked to either side of the rezador carrying lanterns to provide light for him, and they also joined in the chanting, as they cautiously chose their steps in the semi-darkness.

The pito player followed on the heels of the rezador as he continued his mournful tune. After the pito player stepped through the doorway, seven men who were clad only in white shorts, emerged. They each carried a whip made of cactus and their backs already ran red from the blood which dripped from wounds which had been self inflicted earlier. They continued their flagellation as they trudged in single file behind the rezador.

Now came several men who wore black hoods on their heads. It was these men who took up the large crosses, placing them on their shoulders, and joining the procession which moved toward the creek and the site of the Campo Santo, which was located about one hundred yards north of the creek.

The chanting grew lower as the hooded men began to drag the heavy crosses along the worn path. Those who hadn't been able to enter the crowded morada, now also joined in the low chanting, and walked with reverent faces and bowed heads. Behind the cross bearers rolled the Carreta del Muerto, the wooden cart which bore on it the carved wooden statue of death. The statue carried a wooden sword in one hand, and a lance in the other, both symbols of death. At the foot of the statue could be seen several other instruments of death, including an old musket loader, parts of other guns, a rusted sword, and two knives. The face of the statue of death was painted white and it was clothed in a black satin garment.

The penitente who pulled the carreta did so only with great effort, for the wheels of the carreta were locked into place so that they would not turn, thereby making a rut in the path. The drawing of the cart was his particular penance.

Now the rest of the congregation fell in behind the carreta, and with lanterns swinging, they trudged chanting toward the Campo Santo. The silhouettes of the crosses against the skyline were visible as the procession slowly and laboriously made its way toward the creek.

Although the sound of the flagellants' whips could be heard above the low chanting, no sound of pain escaped their lips.

As Simoñ and Modesto took their places unobtrusively in the line they could hear the clanking of chains and they turned, startled, to see a man behind them flogging himself with a chain.

They crossed the creek and began the upward climb toward the dry stone wall which enclosed the Campo Santo. As each supplicant reached the wall, he knelt, crossed himself, and continued to chant. The flagellants, however, did not stop at the wall, but continued their mechanical trudging through the small arched wooden gateway. They moved toward the large cross which had been erected in the Campo Santo. The pathway from the gateway to the cross had been littered with cactus and other sharp objects and the suffering men fell on their knees and proceeded along the path thus. The flesh on their backs had by now been torn open in many places and blood ran profusely down their backs, turning their white shorts almost completely red. Two of the men were fatigued to the point that they might not be able to make the trip back to the lower morada, for they moved slowly to the foot of the cross on their knees. Their prayers finished at the foot of the cross, they began their painful journey back to the little gate, still on their knees. Reaching it, they regained their feet with difficulty, but resumed their flagellation as they moved on toward the upper morada.

The services over, Simoñ and Modesto started back down the hill toward their homes, and Modesto asked, "Will you attend the services on Good Friday night when they tie one of their members on the cross?"

"No," Simoñ said decidedly. "I don't want to be present, if by accident, the man who is selected to be fixed on the cross should die."

"That is very unlikely for it has never happened here."

"There is always a first time," Simoñ answered somberly.

"The candidate is only suspended on the cross until he passes out, which seldom exceeds fifteen minutes, from what I've heard," commented Modesto hesitantly.

"We, at this hacienda have had no fatalities, as you say, but there is always a first time for everything and I don't want to be present when the first candidate does not make it. Would you, Modesto, want to be assigned the gruesome duty of bringing the dead man's shoes to his family, thus symbolizing his death on the cross?"

"Of course not!"

"Neither would I," Simoñ told him. "Which is why I will not be present at Friday night's simulation of the crucifixation of Christ. And besides, I am not sure I approve of some of the things the Penitentes do and it does not seem to me that the Church should either."

"It doesn't, but old ways die slowly," conceded Modesto.

"Surely Saint Francis did not intend for the Penitentes to carry their religious zeal and faith to this extreme. At least I don't believe that he did. He surely didn't practice such rituals when he was alive," Simoñ said emphatically.

"That is probably true, but don't be too hard on the Penitentes, Simoñ. The peons cannot be blamed for the shortage of priests. They are doing the best they can to show that they are faithful and in my opinion, they are not doing a bad job of it under the present circumstances."

"Perhaps you are right, Modesto, there is no other nation in the world more catholic than Spain and if Mother Church cannot be everywhere to support the faith, the people will do their duty as they see it to preserve God's word. That is an admirable trait of Spanish speaking people."

When they reached home, Simon said, "First thing in the morning, I'd like to talk with you about sending some sheep and cattle out on the Llanos."

"Because tomorrow is Good Friday, don't you think we should wait to talk about this later?" asked Modesto.

"You are right, of course," admitted Simoñ. "Monday morning it will be."

Modesto hesitated before he turned in at his gate. "I do think that pasturing herds of cattle and flocks of sheep out on the Llano Estacado could be the most rewarding of all of our enterprises thus far."

"I'm glad you feel that way, because I agree with you," Simoñ replied as he gave a wave and continued on toward his house.

When Simoñ came to breakfast the following morning, only his mother waited for him.

"Where is Sylvia?" Simoñ asked.

"She had a few more instructions for the cooks," Doña Maria told her son as she sipped on her hot chocolate. "You have a guest who will join us for breakfast shortly."

"And who might that be?" Simoñ gave his attention to the hot dishes which the servant placed before him.

Doña Maria only smiled and asked, "Whom do you think?"

"Oh?" Simoñ smiled as he began to eat his breakfast. "We're going to have a guessing game this morning. All right, I'll play. Is it my good friend, Kit Carson?"

"No," Doña Maria replied as she concentrated on her chocolate.

"One of the Bent brothers?"

"Wrong again!"

"Beaubien?" Simoñ tried once more.

"No."

"I give up, who is it?"

"You give up too easily," Doña Maria smiled sweetly at her son. "Try again."

"All right," sighed Simoñ. "James Magoffin, the Santa Fe trader whose wife is related to the governor?"

"Good morning, Simoñ."

Simoñ turned quickly to see the owner of the loud voice and saw Justin. He rose quickly and extended his hand for a handshake as he said enthusiastically, "It is good to see you, old friend, what are you doing in New Mexico? Are you with a wagon train?" He motioned Justin to a seat across the table.

Justin bowed to Doña Maria as he seated himself and said, "Good morning, Doña Maria."

Doña Maria nodded, smiled, and replied, "Good morning to you, Señor Justin. I hope you slept well."

"I was very comfortable, thank you, Doña Maria."

Then Justin turned to Simoñ and said, "Leandro asked me to come, for he wants me to handle the trains to Missouri. It is my understanding that he wants to spend more of his time developing the trade with Santa Fe, Albuquerque, El Paso, and Chihuahua."

"That's Leandro, all right," Simoñ smiled proudly. "He's always one step ahead of me." He turned to Luis, who had just entered the dining room and asked, "Would you send someone to ask Señor Polaco to join us for coffee?"

Within a short time, Modesto entered the room, greeted Justin warmly and seated himself expectantly.

"Have some breakfast, Modesto," Simoñ motioned to the side board. "Or at least some coffee or chocolate?"

"No, thank you, I've had my breakfast, but I will have some coffee."

"Modesto why don't we call for a full meeting of all department heads after you and I have set up an agenda? In this way, we can get reports from all of them as to how things are going?"

Modesto smiled. "When you begin, you do it with a vengeance, don't you?"

Doña Maria asked, "Is this the Llanos thing again?"

Modesto looked at her and smiled as he said, "And what else does your son have on his mind?" He then looked at Simoñ and asked, "What time do you want the meeting set?"

"Let's plan on nine o'clock on Monday morning." Simoñ suggested.

Modesto excused himself and left the room preparatory to informing those concerned to be in the office the day after the Easter celebration. He realized that it would be appropriate timing for they would all be at the headquarters for the Easter celebration.

CHAPTER XIII

Everyone was seated at the huge table in the center of Simoñ's office when he entered hurriedly on Monday morning. They ceased visiting when he sat down and he noticed that each mayordomo also had his agregados (assistants) seated behind him.

Simoñ smiled to himself as he noticed his youngest, Emilo, sitting very erect behind the cow boss. He had finally found what he liked, thought his father. The mayordomo had assured him that Emilo had taken to caring for cattle as a duck takes to water.

Ignacio was busying himself helping Marcello place the necessary papers on the table and he smiled down at his father as he said, "Good morning, padre."

"Good morning, son."

Simoñ leaned forward now and glanced around the table and then, at his son, Leandro, who sat opposite him. Next to Leandro Simoñ saw Ramon Prudencio with his brothers and Carlos sat with them. Filomeno, dressed in a new buckskin shirt, was present, as was Graciano and his agregador. T. P. Nuñez, the sheep mayordomo, sat with his hands folded on the table in front of him, and behind him sat two of his caporales, (overseers).

Modesto, the segundo, sat at Simoñ's right hand. Flomingo Chavez, the acequia mayordomo, was there also, as the hermano mayor of the Penitentes, as well as the mayordomo of the maintenance crews, and those in charge of the orchard and house servants.

When he saw that everyone was represented, Simoñ spoke in a commanding voice, "Shall we begin?"

He then proceeded to speak of his plan for the Llano Estacado, and when he had finished, he looked at Benigno Trujillo, and asked, "How many head of cattle do we have now, Benigno?"

"Over seven thousand, señor," Benigno told him.

"What do you think of dividing them into small herds, around three hundred to a bunch and putting them out on the Llanos with enough men to keep track of them, more or less?"

"More or less may be the problem, señor, if we do not lose too many to the Indians, wolves, and the weather, we could do well with them out there. Of course Ramon is always trading for cattle with the Comanches and in this way we can count on an increase in our herds that way also."

"Do we have enough qualified agregados to handle..." Simoñ glanced at his fingers, "roughly twenty-five different herds?"

Benigno spoke without having to consider, "No, señor, I can tell you that we do not have, unless we include some of the youngest vaqueros."

"What if we reduced that figure to fifteen herds?"

Benigno thought for a moment and then replied, "I think we can handle that. That would make each herd around five hundred head."

"All right, Benigno, begin planning to move the herds out onto the Llanos soon."

"What about the buffalo, señor?"

"The buffalo?"

"Si, señor, if the buffalo herds come too close to the cattle, they could mingle with them and carry them away as they move on."

Simoñ glanced at Graciano who said, "That is true, Señor Gomez. Once the cattle are mixed with the buffalo herds, it will be extremely difficult to cut them out."

"How likely is that to happen?"

"One cannot predict with any degree of accuracy how likely it is to happen, but the possibility will always be there as long as there are large herds of buffalo migrating over the Llanos.

"If a herd threatens us, could it be stampeded away from our stock?"

"They are easy to stampede...that is no problem, but in which direction is unpredictable. And remember the cattle will be scattered and if they missed one bunch, they might easily take another with them."

"What if we used outriders to watch for the buffalo herds? Would it be possible to move the cattle out of their path?"

"All we can do is try," Benigno finally said, "But I'm not sure that it will work. What do you think, Graciano?"

"This is new to me, also," Graciano admitted. "I'd have to go along with you, Benigno and say we can try and see how we do."

"Let's give it a try then," Simoñ said confidently.

"Bravo! Bravo!" The men around the table welcomed the opportunity to try something new.

Simoñ now turned to T. P. Nuñez. "How many sheep would you estimate that we have now, T. P.?"

"In the vicinity of seventeen thousand," Señor Gomez."

"Can we do the same with them as we plan to do with the cattle?"

"How many do you want to a flock, señor?"

"What do you think would be a fair size, taking into consideration safety and manpower?"

"No more than one thousand per flock and perhaps less, with one shepherd and three dogs. We'll just have to experiment," he mused.

"Do that, T. P., and have the maintenance people modify some wagons for the shepherds to use for shelter instead of tents. The Llanos is not the mountains, and wagons can be used out there and will be much warmer and more comfortable. The carpenters can build in a bunk and have plenty of room for storage and cooking facilities left over."

T. P. glanced at Cruz Flores, who nodded.

"Aren't you forgetting the Indians?" Filomeno asked doubtfully. "One flock of a thousand sheep, with only one shepherd and three dogs guarding it, could be an enticing target for a raiding party, let alone the danger you place the herder in."

Simoñ didn't answer immediately, but glanced at Graciano, T. P. and on to Benigno.

"There will always be danger from the Indians. We cannot escape that problem, whether it be here at the headquarters, or at El Cojo, Montoya, Osha, or Hondo, or with the wagon train," Benigno pointed out.

Filomeno disagreed. "The target would be easier for the Indians to take with almost no risk to themselves out on the Llanos, especially with a small number of men covering such a large area."

"Not if we strike back swiftly and make them pay a heavy price for their misconduct," Graciano argued.

"Are you suggesting that we organize another riflemen unit for the Llanos, Graciano?" Simoñ looked with interest at Graciano.

"Not unless you want one," Gracianao replied. "But if you gave me five more men, armed with the best rifles, we could do the dual job of hunting buffalo and protecting the vaqueros and shepherds as well as rescuing those unfortunate enough to be taken captive. If we do our job right, the Indians will hesitate to attack too often."

"What do you mean, if we do our job right?"

"Swift reprisals...make them pay a heavy price." Graciano replied. "I don't believe that the Comanches will give us any problems for we are on friendly terms with them, are we not, Ramon?"

"Graciano is correct on that score, patroñ. I'll talk to each chief of the various Comanche bands just east of us before we move out onto the Staked Plains with the stock. I believe we can count on their cooperation. But I can't speak for the chiefs farther south. After all, a lot of the stock we'll be pasturing out there is that which we got from them originally or their descendents. It would defeat their whole purpose if they rustled our stock. No, they won't bother us, but the Apaches and Kiowas are a different story altogether," Ramoñ concluded.

"Those two give us trouble already so it can't get any worse," put in Graciano.

"Perhaps the question is, do we have enough men who are willing to take the risk and face the dangers which can be expected out there?" Simoñ looked at Modesto as he posed the question.

"Your people on the hacienda consider themselves very fortunate, Simoñ, and I believe that they'll not hesitate to do your bidding, regardless of the danger. They are loyal and dependable and will face whatever you ask of them."

"We'll do it then," Simon decided. "But first I'd like you and your men to take me on a tour of the Llano Estacado, Graciano. I want to see more of the land first hand, see more of that ocean of open grass land."

"When do you wish to go?"

"Will tomorrow morning be all right with you?" Simoñ grinned as he looked at Graciano and then added more soberly, "Then we'll have another meeting after I return."

The following morning Simoñ and Graciano and his men who were followed by their pack mules, rode out of the gate of the compound and headed eastward toward the plains.

"Do you feel like a pioneer?" Graciano smiled as he jested.

"What do you mean?" Simoñ grinned cheerfully. "We are pioneers, aren't we?"

"Not to me, we aren't. At least I don't feel like one."

Graciano adjusted his saddle as he pushed down on his right stirrup and then turned to glance behind at his men who followed at some distance.

"You don't feel like a pioneer? Why not?"

"No, señor, I've been riding the Llanos ever since my father took me out on my first buffalo hunt when I was only fifteen. I've been living on the Llanos ever since, you might say."

"Then I chose the right guide."

I know it like the back of my hand, better than any other part of New Mexico," Graciano replied simply.

"Graciano, I've been thinking, I'd like it better if we addressed one another in a less formal way. Eventually, when the Americanos come, it will be that way, so why don't we begin now to call each other by our first names?"

Graciano glanced at Simon for a moment in surprise and then said quietly, as he looked straight ahead, "It will be difficult, but if it pleases you señor, I will try."

"It would please me," Simoñ replied earnestly "You know, Graciano, when the Americanos sent their delegates to Philadelphia, to draw up their present constitution, those delegates decided many issues, one of which was what title they would confer upon their president. Such titles as `Your Holiness' and `Your Majesty' were proposed, but one sensible delegate reminded the others that the president would be selected from among the citizenry and once selected, should not be set aside as an annointed one. And that is why they address him as `Mr. President'."

"These Americans sound as if they are really sincere about what their constitution says about equality, don't they?" observed Graciano.

"Let's hope they continue to live by it," Simoñ said before he turned his attention back once more to the Llano Estacado. "Is there plenty of water out there, Graciano?"

"If you know where to look."

"And you know where to look, right, mi amigo?"

"Si, Simoñ, I know where to look. You won't find that the land out here resembles the lands around Las Vegas, for instance, some of which are marshy meadows nourished by the Gallinas River."

"I suppose not," Simoñ mused. "I'm sure that the abundance of water was why Don Luis Maria Cabeza de Baca selected that location as the center of his empire."

"Cabeza de Baca's empire was short lived," Graciano said. "It could have become a reality if he had been more realistic."

"What do you mean?"

"He should have found a way of dealing with the Comanches. If he had, his family would still be there. You have only four sons, but he had seventeen."

As Simoñ considered this, he made a promise to himself that the Gomez Hacienda would continue to flourish, even out on the Llanos, and he asked, "Tell me something of what I can expect to see out there on the Llano Estacado, Graciano. This time I will be looking at it from a different perspective."

"Well, first of all, Simoñ, after we pass the mound which is shaped like a wagon, we run into the Canadian River, which, as you know, rambles its way south until it runs into Cañon Largo. Then it breaks out of that cañon and continues its southerly flow until it comes to an ideal location for a marsh, where many wild birds migrate for the winter. As you know, the Canadian is fed from many rivers and creeks. Our own Ocate Creek is one of them, and many others also run into the Canadian. Rivers such as the Vermijo, the Mora, Cañon Largo Creek, Conchos River and many others contribute their share to the Canadian. The area north and east of the Canadian is broken country, some of it difficult to cross, and covered with mesas, wooded areas, hills, canyons, and arroyos. Some of the canyons and arroyos are so deep and jagged that they are almost impossible to cross. It is also blanketed with vegetation that one would expect to find in a semi-arid land, from mesquite to prickly pear, to juniper and pinon, buffalo grass, and of course the black grama grass which is so nourishing to our stock. And there are plenty of springs for those who know how to find them."

"Then how is it that we hear of men perishing out there of thirst?"

"Because those who perish don't know the Llanos and what to look for," replied Graciano. "You can be sure that the Comanches know the location of every spring out there. There are even small lakes out there and the location of these springs and lakes will be of prime importance when you stock part of the Llanos."

"I can see that you and the buffalo hunters will be indispensable if my dream of grazing stock out there is to be realized."

"That is what I meant earlier when I said that you can succeed while Don de Baca failed. You are a realist and he was not. He was a dreamer, that is true, and so are you, but you temper your dreams with reality and he did not," Graciano hesitated before he continued. "You are a born leader of men, Simoñ, and understand the complex nature of men."

"Be careful, Graciano," said Simoñ with a grin. "Or I will believe that I don't need a horse with which to travel, that I could walk on air!"

Graciano chuckled as he said, "I recommend that you disperse your herds of cattle and flocks of sheep below the Ceja, Simoñ."

"Below the eyebrow? Are you suggesting that we bypass the area between the Ceja and the hacienda? Not stock it? How many miles would you estimate it is from the Ceja to the hacienda?"

"A good hundred miles or more to the tip of the Ceja, I'd say. That's the beginning of the real Comanche nation, but the country is less broken and better for stock."

"We can't have that much empty space between home and the stock, Graciano," Simoñ protested. "They would be left completely on their own and that would be asking too much of our people."

Graciano smiled and when Simoñ saw that smile he asked, "You are testing me again? Go ahead, out with it. What do you want to say this time?"

"It is my opinion, also, that a hundred miles is too much unoccupied territory to be left between the hacienda and the flocks and herds."

"Continue."

"A small number of plazas (villages) should be established on the route to the Staked Plains or Llano Estacado below the Ceja. These small plazas would funish protection to your people as well as provide a sense of security. They could just be line camps, but it seems to me that they will be necessary in the opening up of the Llanos. Without such places, your dream could join that of de Baca, and end in something which people lament about around the warm fires during the cold, lonely winters."

Simoñ said slowly, "It will take time, but if we are to succeed, we will need to establish such camps or plazas, as you call them. I had planned something of the sort, but perhaps closer to the herders. My idea was to construct them in a square, with a courtyard in the center so they would be easily fortified."

"That is why I called them plazas instead of villages," Graciano replied. "If we call them plazas from the beginning, the people will build plazas and not develop villages with no plan or pattern for defence. Adobes built in separate locations, and scattered in all directions would invite trouble. The word plaza conjures up in the minds of the people, a certain type of village, the proper and safe kind."

"You would make a good tactician, Graciano. Santa Anna or Armijo had better not tangle with you," Simoñ said with a chuckle.

"I am a hunter of the ciboleros (buffaloes) and a follower of such an occupation must be a tactician among other things, or he doesn't last long out here on the Llanos. The buffalo is also a tactician and a man would have to be a fool if he did not learn from what he hunts."

"I value your friendship and your counsel, Graciano," Simoñ said earnestly. "We must add to the ingredients which contribute to our success, the good advice from people such as you with all of your experience behind you."

"De nada," Graciano said. "Loyalty and advice are given easily when one has a patron such as you who cares and shows compassion for others."

"Speaking of buffalo, tell me more about your hunts."

"I take my men to the north edge of the Ceja and turn east, keeping below the Ceja until we reach the Palo Duro Canyon country. Usually between the Ceja and the Palo Duro, we find all of the ciboleros we want. If we shouldn't, we sometimes climb the Ceja at El Puerto de los Rio Abajenos, and head for the plains of the lower Estacado. It is there that we can always be assured of finding the ciboleros. It is there, also, that we find the Comanches. You know they are the ones who drove the Jicarilla Apaches off the plains and into the mountains of northern New Mexico and southern Colorado, and they did not stop there, but pursued the Mescalero Apaches, who are south of here, and the other branches of the Apache nation, until they, too, were driven from the plains to the mountains. They were able to keep all other tribes off the Llanos easily because they had superior weapons which they traded for with their friends and allies, the Wichitas, who are east of here.

"Apparently the Wichitas got them from the Americanos and the French. The Apaches didn't have this access to the newer weapons so they had no choice but to retreat before the better armed Comanches. The early Spanish soldiers respected the Comanches also, and the Comancheros managed to trade and maintain friendly relations with them. In fact they have developed a unique relationship which holds to this day."

"It was to their mutual interest to be friends," Simoñ reminded him.

"Whatever you choose to call it, it still exists to this day."

The men rode for over a week through the Llano Estacado north of the Ceja, until Simoñ thought he had the feel and lay of the land, and then they turned southward toward the lower Llano Estacado.

It was still early one morning as they rode that Simoñ pointed and asked, "What's causing that dust cloud up ahead?"

They reined in their horses and sat watching and then Graciano muttered, "Whatever it is, it is going away from us."

After a while, Simoñ said, "It looks like a small train of carretas."

Graciano continued to stare in that direction before he finally agreed, "I believe you are right, it is a train of carretas."

"Do you suppose they could be hunting buffalo?"

"I'm sure of it...let's join them."

They put their horses into a lope and when they neared the train, four men on horseback turned to wait for them. Each of them rested a muzzle loader across his saddle and remained leary until they realized that the approaching riders were Mexicans.

As Simoñ and Graciano and the rest of their men approached, Simoñ called, "Where are you headed?"

"Out onto the Staked Plains, to hunt the ciboleros, eventually," came the answer.

"What do you mean, eventually?"

"We hope to find other hunters camped on the Ceja whom we plan to join, that is if there are enough of them."

"And if there are not enough?"

"Then we wait until there are enough, or we might have to go alone."

"May we join you?" Simoñ glanced at Graciano to see what his reaction might be and Graciano nodded in agreement.

"The mayordomo is up front, ask him. His name is Luciano Candelaria."

"Muchas gracias," Simoñ said as he and his men spurred their horses toward the train. They were followed by the four buffalo hunters. When they neared the head of the seven carreta train, a man reined his horse back to meet them.

"Buenos dias, señores," he greeted them.

"Buenos dias," Simoñ replied. "Are you Luciano Candelaria?"

"Si, can I be of assistance?"

The men introduced themselves and Luciano said that they would be grateful to have more men join up with them.

Simoñ asked, "Where are you from?"

"Sapello," Luciano answered. "And you?"

"From the Gomez Hacienda."

"You wouldn't be the patron, would you, señor?"

"Si, but I don't wish for the others with you to know that," Simoñ replied.

"As you wish, Señor Gomez."

When the train approached the Ceja, a number of carretas could be seen up ahead. They had made camp and the smoke from their fires drifted slowly into the turquoise sky.

"I wonder how long they have been waiting?" Luciano said.

The oxen drawn carretas from Sapello pulled up not far from those who had already pitched camp and immediately yells could be heard from the men as they recognized old friends among them who came to give them a hand in setting up camp.

"El Pordiosero!" Luciano called a greeting as he quickly dismounted. He had recognized an old friend and the two met with a bear hug. "How have you been, compadre? It's been a long time," Luciano told him.

Most of the men knew each other and they moved about, happily shaking hands and getting caught up on the news of their families.

"Who is the large, bearded man dressed in buckskins whom Luciano yelled at?" Simoñ asked Graciano as he looked with interest at the stranger.

"Him? He's the greatest cibolero hunter of them all," Graciano told him. "He is called El Pordiosero because everyone wants to go with him when he goes out." Graciano grinned, "They'll even beg if they have to, to be given the privilege of going out on one of his hunts."

"He must be good," Simoñ commented as he watched the newly arrived hunters gather around him to shake his hand.

"He's the best," Graciano repeated. "As you can see, everyone is happy that he is here. No doubt he'll be made mayordomo of the hunt."

Simoñ glanced around the camp and asked, "Are there enough men here now to begin a hunt?"

"I'd guess that they'll wait a few more days to give others a chance to arrive. Meanwhile the ciboleros will be located and it is my guess that men are already out there looking. It's possible that there's no herd within hunting distance, and this entire camp will have to wait for a herd to come close enough. Everyone will believe that El Pordiosero will bring good luck, and that a herd will be located soon."

"While they are waiting, why don't we ride out after a while and take a look around?" Simoñ suggested.

When they ridden a few miles away from the camp, they drew up and sat gazing in all directions. "It's unbelievable," Simoñ finally commented. "Nothing but mile after mile of grassland. It's like an ocean from horizon to horizon. What a wonderful thing it would be if we can graze it."

"Before you get too excited, Simoñ, remember that others have prior claim to it, the Comanches and the buffalo, and the hunters, of course, just to name three of them. And mother nature speaks up every now and then, and believe me, when she speaks, people listen intently."

What they did not know as they rode leisurely across the Llanos was that Apaches were watching the buffalo hunters, and awaiting the proper time to strike. And that Comanche scouts had detected the unsuspecting Jicarilla Apaches and were preparing to intercept them.

While this was unfolding, two wagon loads of merchandise were rumbling toward the Comanche village of the Yap-eaters, the northern most village of the Comanche nation. The wagons were from the Gomez Hacienda and Ramon and Elmon Prudencio were in charge, with Carlos Gomez accompanying them.

Back at the Ceja, the hunters had gathered around Luciano Candelaria and heard him say, "I believe there are enough of us to begin to plan our hunt. If others arrive before we leave, we'll invite them to join us. The first order of business is to elect a mayordomo of the spring hunt. I, myself, feel that we are very fortunate to have with us the most celebrated hunter of them all. He needs no introduction because he is known by all of us here. It is my privilege to nominate El Pordiosero as mayordomo."

"I second the nomination," Alberto Salas tossed his hat into the air as he spoke.

"Are there any other nominations?" Luciano glanced around the circle.

"Oh, let's get on with it," Sosa Martinez from Trujillo, yelled. "We all know El Pordiosero is the best and no one else would even want to have his name placed in nomination when we have El Pordiosero with us. I move that we elect El Pordiosero by acclamation."

With a unanimous cheer, the men proclaimed El Pordiosero the mayordomo and Luciano turned to the newly elected leader and said with a grin, "It's all yours, my compadre."

"I want to thank you for electing me your mayordomo." El Pordiosero walked to the center of the circle and placed the butt of his musket on the ground, resting his arm on the barrel. "I need not remind any of you that from this point on, my word is law." Although he grinned as he spoke, the men knew that he was deadly serious. Some of them began to seat themselves on the ground, preparing to give careful attention to his words.

"I expect everyone to obey my orders, to carry them out to the letter. I won't ask for your votes of approval as to my choice of agregados, for I'll choose them for myself right now."

He turned to inspect each of the men around him and then said, "I believe there are enough of us on this hunt to form four killing groups. Arturo, you will be my agregado for group number one. Caesar, for number two, Romulo for number three, and Luciano for number four. Arturo, your leader will be Joaquin. Yours, Caesar, will be Eloy. Yours, Romulo, will be Daniel, and yours, Luciano, will be Catarino. The duty of the bleeders will be to follow behind the buffalo killers and bleed them once they are down, of course."

These assignments taken care of, El Pordiosero continued, "No saddles will be permitted on the kill, only pads. I don't want anyone dragged to death by a frightened horse, and stirrups have a way of doing that. I also expect each of you to carry a long lance. Do you all have lances?"

The men all nodded and he continued, "I assume you all have the standard length, from five to seven feet and with steel points. Are there any who do not?"

Again no one answered, and he nodded his approval. "Now I'll go over the procedure which we will use on the hunt. The lancers will ride on the herd first, of course, followed by the bleeders. Then my agregados, with their carretas, will go out on the plains and skin and cut up the buffalo and bring them back to camp. The rest of you will do the butchering. Don't waste any of the fat, for we will use it in the making of tallow. Back home we'll need the tallow to make candles and use in cooking, as you know. The hides are not prime at this time of the year, of course, so we don't need to worry about using them as robes. But they'll be kept, of course, for making leather goods, such as reatas, boots, saddles, and for many other uses. I don't want the wool from the neck and shoulders to be left behind either, for it, too, can be used for spinning the yarn for weaving. It also can be used for stuffing mattresses and pillows and cushions, as you all know. Are there any questions?"

There were none and once more he continued, "The buffalo move into the wind, so right now we can expect them to be moving toward the southwest. The scouts are expected back at any time so be ready to move out soon afterwards."

Not very far from the Mexican camp below the Ceja, a few miles to the east, the Jicarilla Apaches had made their camp under the leadership of Laughing Coyote. They, too, were making plans. Laughing Coyote stood in the center of the seated circle of warriors, at the same time that El Pordiosero was speaking to his men. The Apache leader was saying, "Our scouts are keeping a close watch on the Mexicans. They will return when the Mexicans begin their hunt and then we'll position ourselves for the battle. The Mexicans will leave their muskets at the main camp when they ride out to hunt with their lances. They should be easy prey for you, Stone Arrow, and for your warriors who are equipped with good rifles.

Walking Bear, your duty is to attack the agregados, the bleeders, and the carretas. That could be more difficult because they will probably have their muskets, but their muskets should be no match for your better rifles. You will have the added element of surprise in your favor. You should be able to kill many of them before they realize what is happening."

He turned to Stone Arrow and said, "When Walking Bear strikes, you close in on the lancers."

Stone Arrow acknowledged his instructions by grunting and Laughing Coyote said, "The rest of you will be ready to fall on the camp at my command. It should be all over very quickly and we will be riding back to our people before our enemy, the Comanche, realizes that we are in his nation. Now everyone should see to his horses and weapons."

At the Yap-eaters or Yapain village, their chief, Broken Arrow, along with his villagers, was patiently waiting for the arrival of the Gomez comancheros, when a brave galloped into camp and pulled his horse to an abrupt halt in front of Broken Arrow's tepee. He vaulted to the ground and yelled to his chief. The flap of tepee was immediately pushed to one side and the chief emerged. The people of the village began to converge on the two and within seconds, the chief shouted, "Apaches!"

The people just as swiftly scattered once more, the warriors gathering their weapons and the women caring for the children.

The warriors hurriedly brought in their favorite war ponies from the pony herd and began to paint both themselves and their ponies with war paint. Not a motion was wasted for they were eager to meet one of their ancient enemies. Broken Arrow had summoned a war council to meet in his tepee for the purpose of planning the attack and when they were assembled, they sat in a circle around his fire.

Broken Arrow then turned the council over to the war chief, Wind in the Face, who nodded gravely at Broken Arrow and then turned to face the others. "I propose we circle behind the Apache dogs and move upon them when they begin to ride down on the Mexicans. In this way, the Apaches will be giving their full attention to the Mexicans. What they believe will be a surprise attack on the Mexicans will turn out to be one on them. Now depart and prepare to leave immediately."

....

Graciano pulled his horse in and looked down at the ground in silence.

"What is it?" Simoñ reined in and sat watching.

"Look here," Graciano dismounted and fell to one knee as he studied something. Simoñ dismounted and knelt beside him as he asked, "Indian sign?"

"Si," Graciano answered softly as he continued to study the sign. In front of them was a small clump of grass, part of which had been twisted several times until it resembled a ponytail and tied in a knot. Graciano glanced around sharply and then pointed, "There's another one over there beyond this one."

Simoñ asked curiously, "What do they mean?"

Graciano at first said nothing, but finally suggested, "Let's follow them."

They walked their horses slowly as they bent to watch for any similar signs and after a few seconds, Simoñ pointed. "There is another, but it looks different from the others."

Graciano dismounted once more and studied the grass clump closely, finally saying, "Although this is tied in a knot as were the others, the top of the clump of grass is broken so as to tilt the part above the knot toward the north. Which means that they want their followers to turn here and head for the Ceja." He bent closer and then said quickly, "See those lines drawn in the dirt? Let's see...there are thirty-one lines, which means thirty-one warriors are in the war party."

"Who is doing the signaling and why?"

"It's my guess that it's Apaches. Comanches would not need to leave signs in such a way."

"What are they up to, Graciano?" Even as Simoñ spoke, he knew. "The hunting party! We must warn them."

The sense of danger had alerted Graciano's other senses and he quickly reconnoitered the horizon with his keen eyes and said, "There is something south of us. See that spot barely visible on the horizon?"

"No," Simoñ replied as he strained his eyes toward the south, but within a few seconds he said in excitement, "Yes, I see something now. Whatever it is, it's not very large. Could it be Comanches or Apaches?"

"No, neither," Graciano decided. "It must be wagons."

"Comancheros," Simoñ's eyes widened in fear. "Would the Apaches be after our Comancheros?"

"No, I don't think so," Graciano considered. "If they were the target, the Apaches would have taken them by now and they are not worth the risk for the Apaches out here in Comanche country. No, I think the hunters are the target."

Graciano kept his eyes trained on the distant objects which seemed to move very slowly. Finally he said, "It's two wagons, with a horseman accompanying them. It also looks as though two horses are tied to the back of the wagon."

"Are you sure they are not carretas?"

"I'm positive, the white canvas wagon covers are too large to be mistaken for carretas."

Now the outline of the wagons began to take shape as they moved eastward along the horizon and Simoñ agreed, "You're right, they are wagons, wagons just like mine. It could be the Prudencios and Carlos. My God, I must warn them about the Apaches."

"What about the buffalo hunters? They are in more immediate danger than those wagons out there, if it isn't too late already?"

Simoñ calmed down and asked, "What do you suggest?"

"I'll ride to warn the hunters and you ride to warn the wagons." Graciano was already in motion as he spurred his horse into a gallop.

Simoñ sat watching for a moment and then he, too, spurred his horse and leaned over his neck to yell to him as he raced toward the distant wagons. When Ramon spotted the rider racing toward them, he turned to call to Elmon and Carlos who were driving the wagons. They picked up their rifles which rested on the seat beside them, checked them calmly and pulled their wagons to a halt. Ramon rode to where they waited and the three watched the approaching rider.

"He rides like father," Carlos said as he rose to his feet and studied the rider for a few seconds. "It is father!" He waved his sombrero over his head.

When Simoñ reached them, Ramon asked in alarm, "What's wrong, what are you doing out here all alone without a guide?"

"Graciano is with me, but he rode north to warn a party of cibolero hunters of an Apache ambush," Simoñ shouted, out of breath.

"Ambush!" Ramon yelled in surprise.

"Leave the wagons and come with me. If we hurry we may get there in time," Simoñ ordered.

Elmon and Carlos had their horses saddled within minutes and the four raced northward at top speed, as they held their rifles in readiness and leaned forward into the wind.

....

The Comanches had ridden eastward until they reached the Ceja, well ahead of the buffalo scouts. They descended from the rim rocks of the Ceja in single file, in complete silence, and when they reached the floor below, they continued to ride swiftly northward, through the thick mesquite brush and trees. The trees and brush were just beginning to bud out, the delicate leaves barely hinting their future color. Quietly, the single file of braves followed their leader, Wind in the Face, until he raised his hand. Without a word, the chief pointed to one of the warriors and then motioned to a higher elevation which was topped by a rocky ledge. The warrior rode as close to the ledge as he could and then proceeded cautiously, finally dropping to his stomach and moving forward until he could peer over the ledge. He stayed there watching for a few moments and then reversing his procedure, was soon back before his chief. He whispered of what he had seen, and the chief then pointed to fifteen warriors, one at a time, and again pointed at the ledge. The designated warriors rode toward the ledge as Wind in the Face rode on accompanied by the remainder of his warriors. When the Comanches were in place at a safe distance from the Jicarillas, they waited for the Apaches to make their first move. Both Apaches and Comanches were as still as the surrounding rocks. For over an hour there was no sign of movement from the ranks of either of the Indian parties, until almost without prior notice, the Apaches slid upon their ponies and waited for the signal from their chief to attack. The Comanches mounted their ponies also and when the Apaches fired their first shots, the Comanches opened up also. For awhile, the Apaches couldn't fathom why their warriors were falling, because the Mexicans had not yet had time to respond. When the Apaches realized the dilemma they faced, they fled the field of battle and dashed westward.

Graciano saw the Apaches riding toward the west as he rode toward the buffalo hunters so he turned and rode back toward Simoñ and the others. The Apaches fired a few snap shots at him, but continued their flight to the west, leaving only three of their number to race toward him. These three needed to vent their frustration on someone and they strived to lessen the distance between themselves and Graciano. When Graciano turned to fire back at them, he was amazed to see them veer away and ride after their fellow warriors. He looked back and was enlightened as he saw Simon and the others galloping toward him.

The New Mexican cibolero hunters were completely confused as to what was happening and braced themselves for an attack which did not come. Only

El Pordiosero perceived what had probably happened and he called out to his confused men what he thought had taken place, and asked them if they had seen the second war party follow the first. He then issued orders for them to circle the carretas and prepare for further trouble.

They obeyed his orders and then were surprised to see Graciano, Simoñ, and the Comancheros riding toward them calmly at a trot. An hour passed as they maintained a careful vigilance until finally El Pordiosero shouted, "Here they come."

They concealed themselves as best they could and waited and then suddenly Graciano yelled, "They are Comanches, hold your fire!"

Ramon jumped to his feet, ran to his horse, mounted and rode at a gallop toward the approaching Comanches.

"Where in hell is that damn fool going?" one of the buffalo hunters yelled in disbelief as he jumped to his feet.

"He knows Wind in the Face, the chief who is leading them," Carlos said angrily. "So don't do anything foolish."

The buffalo hunters looked from Carlos to one another in surprise and Elmon rose from his concealed position and joined Carlos as they watched Ramon ride toward the approaching war party.

Carlos was a striking figure with his typical Mexican pantaloons, the sides unbuttoned showing his knee high, black leather boots. He wore a buckskin shirt and a low crowned, wide brimmed hat with an eagle feather tucked beneath a bright red hat band. He turned to Elmon and said, "There are a few women with them."

Elmon replied calmly, "The Comanches permit women to join men on a raid or a war party if they so choose. Make no mistake about it, the few squaws who join the men are just as fierce as the warriors."

Elmon was also a colorful figure, for he wore buckskin trousers which were tucked into his knee length moccasins. His shirt was of homespun wool over which he wore a colorful vest which was decorated in Indian designs. His hat was crumpled and pushed back on his head.

One of the buffalo hutners muttered to another who stood beside him, "They look half Mexican and half Comanche as far as their clothing is concerned."

Carlos and Elmon could hear the remark, but merely glanced at one another and grinned and then turned their attention once more to Ramon and the Comanches, who were much closer now. The Comanche chief rode a prancing snow white war horse around whose eyes he had painted red circles, and a red hand print decorated one of the horse's shoulders. The lance which the chief carried boasted several eagle feathers. His buckskin clothing was fringed and decorated with colorful beadwork. His bull buffalo hide shield was round and it too, was hung with a number of eagle feathers. Two long braids fell to his waist. He made an impressive and warlike figure as he talked gravely to Ramon. The two friends then made the sign of friendship and the chief wheeled his horse, and followed by his braves, trotted away.

Ramon spurred his horse into a lope and rode back toward the carretas to join Carlos and Elmon who stood out in front of them. "What's happening, Carlos?" His father walked up to stand beside him as they waited for Ramon.

Ramon answered instead as he pulled his horse in by the three men. "The Comanches are returning to their village." He grinned cheerfully, "I told them that we had two wagons full of trade goods with us and that we would follow their trail so if it's all right with you, Señor Gomez, Carlos, Elmon and I had better get back to the wagons and take them on to the village."

"You are running the operation, Ramoñ, do what you think best."

"Thank you, señor." Ramon said and then turned to Carlos and Elmon and said," Let's ride!"

Simoñ turned from watching the three ride away and said to Graciano who had stepped up beside him. "What do you say we head back to the Hacienda? I think I've gotten a good idea of the Llanos country." He broke off and looked to the east when he heard sounds. "What was that?"

"What was what?" Graciano looked puzzled.

"There, I heard it again," Simoñ said, "don't you hear it?"

"Now I do," Graciano replied "it's coyotes, probably hundreds of them. You can tell by their highly pitched barking, and coyotes mean cibolero and that also means wolves, for both follow the large herds. The wolves attack the old cows and bulls who lag behind. They feast on them and leave what they don't eat for the coyotes."

"Well, I guess the hunters will have a good kill," commented Simoñ. "It must be a large herd, if the coyotes' yapping is any indication."

"Don't you want to stay and join in on the hunt?"

"Yes, but I think I'd better get back to the hacienda and tend to business. Let's say our goodbyes to the hunters and head for home."

"You're the boss," Graciano said as he tried to hide his disappointment.

A few minutes later they and Graciano's men were heading westward and Simoñ remarked, "I hope you know the way back because I sure don't. How can you tell where you are? Everything looks the same to me."

"The person who is familiar with the Llano Estacado learns to spot certain geographic phenomena which guide him homeward," Graciano chuckled, and then continued, "These phenomena are not readily noticeable to the infrequent visitor to the Llanos, the rise of a low hill, a dip along the skyline, certain clusters of one kind of vegetation like sage brush, these things and others, a buffalo hunter or other traveler learns to spot and use as a compass. And of course the wind which largely blows from the southwest can play tricks on you. I suppose the stars are the most reliable guides." He pointed ahead and said, "See those two long, rolling hills which run north and south of us but don't quite meet, leaving a gap between them?"

"Yes, but I wouldn't distinguish them by calling them hills," grinned Simoñ. "They 're more like giant snakes stretched out in the hot sun."

"They may look like that to you but not to me. Look about three or four miles north of the gap. What do you see?"

"Three small knolls which look like three graves, from this distance," Simoñ said after studying them for awhile.

"There are many sleepy snakes, as you call them, out here on the Llanos, but others don't have those three knolls on their northern end. At the gap where the two long hills almost meet, there is a spring of cool water. I have never known that spring to go dry. That's where we are headed now. We'll refill our canteens and rest there. We'll let our horses water and graze and then go on when it's a little cooler. We will even have time for a siesta, if you like. Don't worry about the horses straying from there, for there's good lush grass all around the spring."

As they neared the water hole, they spooked a large bunch of antelope who were drinking and when they saw the men they ran off at their approach. As always the men marveled at the speed and grace of the shy beasts. They scattered like a bunch of doves although some of them ran as if in double harness as they disappeared into the distance.

"What are all those trails leading to the water hole?" Simoñ asked as he looked at Graciano with interest and began to unsaddled his horse.

"Buffalo trails," Graciano replied. "And that's another way you can find water. If you become lost and don't know where to find water, hide near a buffalo herd and wait. Sooner or later one of the cows will lift up her head and begin to walk slowly toward where the water is to be found and the others will follow her."

Their horses hobbled, the men lay on their stomachs and drank and splashed their faces with the cool water. Suddenly Graciano paused and listened, and Simoñ listened also but he could hear nothing strange and he finally asked "What's the matter?"

"Shhh," Graciano remained absolutely still before he said, "Put your hands on the ground and see if you feel anything."

Simoñ did as Graciano suggested and finally said, "No, I don't feel anything. What am I supposed to feel?"

"You can't feel any vibrations?" Graciano cocked his head to listen again.

"No, I don't feel any vibrations. What are you expecting to hear?"

"It's a buffalo stampede," Graciano said in explanation. "The hunters have begun their kill, and in the process they have stampeded the herd."

The men quickly saddled their horses once more and rode to higher ground to take a look. "You can hear them now, can't you?" Graciano asked.

"Almost like thunder, isn't it?" Simoñ asked.

"Do you see any clouds, Simoñ? And since when is thunder continuous? There is a stampede and we'd better head for the Pecos River to get out of their way."

The two men, with the others close behind them, galloped in the direction of the Pecos. They looked over their shoulders occasionally to see if they could see any sign of the herd, and as they did the noise made by the thousands of hooves began to grow louder and Simoñ yelled as he glanced yet another time behind him, "That dust cloud which they are making is still miles away, so we ought to be safe."

"Not as far as it looks, and not far enough for me. We need to reach the other side of the Pecos and then we'll be all right!" Graciano called grimly.

"How far away is the river?"

"Can't you smell the water?" Graciano gestured ahead of them and said, "See the trees up ahead? They line the banks of the Pecos."

He glanced once more behind them and checked to see if his men were still keeping up the hard pace. The sound of the stampeding herd was louder now and the great dust cloud which their hooves were churning up was almost over them.

"Can we make it to the river before they reach us?" Simoñ shouted.

"If we don't we'll never live to tell about it," Graciano yelled back. "And where is that southwest wind when we need it?"

Their horses were beginning to falter now, and only their fear lent them the strength to keep on running. By now it became a life and death race between the riders and the fast approaching herd. The ground began to shake and speech was no longer possible, as the men leaned forward on their horses' necks urging them onward. By now the buffalo had closed much of the gap between the riders and themselves, but before them, the trees which bordered the Pecos loomed through the dust. They extended for perhaps a quarter of a mile on either side of the river, and their protection would slow the herd down somewhat, Simoñ hoped.

When they reached the river, Graciano's horse refused to jump into the water and for a moment tried to turn back, but the riders behind him, pushed him in as they came up to the river's edge. Simoñ's horse plunged into the river gladly and began to swim to the other side as eagerly as Simoñ. Simoñ had slid out of the saddle, grabbing his horse's tail, hoping to be less of a hindrance that way.

When they had all reached the riverbank on the west side they mounted their horses once more and sat watching as the first of the herd came to the trees, and swerved southward, paralleling the river. The noise was deafening and the dust so thick the men could hardly see each other and could no longer see the herd.

Their horses were wild eyed with fear and the men finally turned them away from the river and rode into the trees. Sounds of the stampede were fainter now and the trees filtered the dust somewhat.

Graciano finally pulled up and asked with a slight smile, "Was that close enough for you, Simoñ?"

"Let's do it again," Simoñ grinned.

Graciano grabbed off his hat and slapped Simoñ on the shoulder as Simoñ continued, "Well, it has certainly taught me something."

"And what might that be?"

"I won't send my herds or flocks east of the Pecos River or below the Ceja. The buffalo are just too plentiful. They could carry the cattle away, trample the sheep, and cost lives also. We'll stay in the broken country north of the Ceja. The mesas, hills, canyons, and arroyos, will furnish protection for the vaqueros, and herders and livestock."

"I think you're making the right decision, Simoñ, and you are right about the number of buffalo. There are too many of them out here now to make it either profitable or wise. There is plenty of pasture north of the Ceja to graze on, but remember the ciboleros also roam north of the Ceja, although not in the large numbers they do below it. I think it would be more profitable to graze the northern area, especially if you have enough riders searching for the buffalo, and once spotted they could be encouraged to return eastward."

Simoñ glanced back at the riders who followed them at some distance and saw that they were laughing and talking among themselves. "They certainly have taken this experience in stride. Why do they keep their distance from us at all times?"

"Because you are the patron, Simoñ, and they don't feel comfortable with you. They like you and respect you, but there is a barrier between you and them which stretches back for generations. Better leave it alone," Graciano said soberly.

"This trip has been an eye opener for me in many ways," Simoñ said with a sigh.

CHAPTER XIV

The month of June began with a warm, dry breeze from the west which dried even further the arid conditions on the Gomez Hacienda.

Simoñ had just finished his breakfast and he bent to kiss his wife Sylvia before he left the dining room. "I'll be in the office for a little while if you need me. When I leave there, I'll tell Marcello where I can be reached."

His tone was grave and Sylvia looked up at him in concern, "Is everything all right? Something is troubling you, what is it?"

"It looks as though we're in for a drought. I hope not, for dry years can sure hurt the stock. It couldn't have come at a worse time. Although there is never a good time, I guess."

"It will rain, Simoñ, it always has," Sylvia said in an effort to cheer her husband.

"If we wait long enough, it will!" Simoñ replied with a chuckle. "But the mayordomos have reported that the grass out on the Llanos is very dry. The ground is beginning to crack and some of the lakes and springs are beginning to dry up. It doesn't look good for my five year experiment in sending stock out there. One bolt of lightning from our first shower could set the Llanos ablaze. Have I offended God in some way and He is punishing me? Is He trying to tell me to bring our stock in off the Llanos?"

Sylvia was alarmed as she realized how gravely Simoñ viewed the situation, and attempted to comfort him once more as she rose to hug him and said, "No, my husband, if anything, the opposite is true, He is testing your will and resolve. God will send you rain. I will go to the church this morning to pray. I am sure He will hear my prayers and send rain. God is trying to tell you that good things are not easily come by." She leaned back to look up into her husband's face and smiled cheerfully. "You just wait and see."

Simoñ returned her smile and held her close for a moment before he released her and said, "I must be on my way, little one, Marcello is waiting for me."

As he entered the office he asked the busy Marcello, "Have you received any reports from the mayordomos concerning the weather?"

"Not since yesterday, Don Simoñ." Marcello looked up from the work on his desk.

"Where is Ignacio? He's not still in bed, is he?"

"He is up and out on an errand."

"When will it rain, Marcello?" Simoñ asked skeptically as he sat down behind his desk and began to glance over the papers before him.

Marcello grinned wearily, "We know it will rain next month, for it always has. But we need it now."

"I'm glad we didn't send any stock out below the Ceja for the Cañon del Agua hill south of here is still getting a little run off from the mountains by way of the Gallinas River and its tributaries, so we can take advantage of that water if we need to do so. They haven't sent word that they may move some of the stock in that direction, have they?"

"No señor, I don't think the need is that pressing yet, for they say that there is still plenty of grass along the river bottoms. As you know, there is subsurface water along the Mora and Canadian rivers in many places."

"Perhaps I'm becoming a worrier, Marcello. There should be enough grass until it rains and worrying certainly won't help any."

He leaned his head against the tall back of his chair, and mused aloud, "That's sure a beautiful sight east of Wagon Mound. The landscape is so varied with its mesas, shallow valleys, rolling land and high country covered with juniper and pinon trees and a carpet of grama grass everywhere. I'm sure that Cabra Spring will have water, for it never dries up. Its source of water must come underground all the way from the Sangre de Cristos. That spring has the best water I've ever tasted. I guess the wild goats which gave it its name knew good water when they drank it."

Marcello also leaned back in his chair and joined Simoñ in his musing. "I like the Bull Canyon area also for its beauty. Perhaps even more than the area east of Wagon Mound. He put his hands behind his head and stared into space. "The brilliant red color of the rocks and soil is so striking, especially in contrast to the yellow and tan colors of the rocks and dirt of the canyon's walls. We live in a beautiful country, Señor Gomez."

"It would be even more beautiful if it would rain," Simoñ rose and walked to the window and stood looking out. "What are the field hands doing? A number of them are walking toward the church. Come and look, Marcello."

Simoñ and Marcello watched as the men entered the church and shortly thereafter they came out and the man in the lead carried a Santo in his hands.

Marcello smiled and said, "They're taking one of the Santos out of the church so he can see how dry it is." He and then Simoñ crossed themselves as they watched.

"They'll take it to the fields and orchards so it can witness the dry soil and then they'll pray to the Santo, asking him to send rain." He turned and walked back to his desk once more and then the two men worked in silence until Simoñ suddenly raised his hand and asked, "Did you hear thunder, Marcello?"

Marcello stopped his work and cocked his head as he listened and then a second distant rumble was heard. Both men jumped to their feet and rushed to the door and stepped outside. Smiles came to their faces as they looked up at the dark purple clouds which were beginning to blow their way from over the Sangre de Cristo Mountains. "It looks as though we could get a cloud burst and that could mean flash flooding," Simoñ said.

"The men are already preparing for just that eventuality," Marcello observed as he saw some of the men running. A few large drops of rain began to hit the dry, powdery dust at the feet of the two men and small puffs of dust floated upward as the drops stirred it.

"It looks as though the drought will be broken," Simoñ said in relief as he turned to reenter the office. The raindrops increased steadily until it was raining so hard that he had to yell at Marcello to make himself hear.

The ground quickly soaked up the water and the surplus began to accumulate, forming puddles, and before long the whole area began to assume the appearance of a large lake.

"There goes the acequia madre (mother ditch) and all the smaller acequias," yelled Marcello as once more he stood at the open door watching the storm. The nearby arroyos and canyons began to rise rapidly and before long the force of the water began to carry rocks and boulders before it, creating a roaring sound which grew greater and greater by the minute until it seemed the end of the world was eminent. Debris from the torrent of rushing water in the arroyos and canyons was deposited in the open areas at their mouths. And then, just as quickly as it began, the rain stopped and the sun broke through the clouds. A fresh, clean scent of pine filled the air, inviting the people to breathe deeply, cherishing it while it lasted. The roaring water from out of the mountains, continued, however, and would as long as the smaller tributaries contributed their runoff.

Modesto stuck his head through the door of the office, grinning. "No more worries about a drought."

"Let's hope those worries are over," Simoñ said with an answering smile. "Have a seat, Modesto." He glanced through his papers and asked, "Do we have enough men to adquately care for the stock out on the Llanos?"

"Si, we have enough, and they are some of the best, I might add," Modesto replied as he sat down in the large chair in front of Simoñ's desk and removed his hat. "We'll never have a shortage of good men, for there are many out there who would gladly become indebted to you because of your compassionate reputation."

"It is sad when so many of our people are willing to sell themselves and their families into peonage," Simoñ said soberly.

"There's another way to look at it, Simoñ. There are thousands and thousands of people all over New Mexico who have reached the bottom rung of the economic ladder. There is no way that they can become any poorer than they already are. Most are unskilled, uneducated, and unwanted. Those people would be more than happy to receive employment on this hacienda and would go out onto the Llanos without giving it a second thought. Poverty is a great motivator for courage, and empty bellies drive people to face any danger. As long as the rewards are adequate food, shelter, and security of a kind. And that, my friend, is what no other hacienda offers more than yours. Your reputation in that regard is unsurpassed, and employment here is what most New Mexicans desire and dream about. What else is there for most of them to do except herd sheep or become vaqueros? Take those peons who live and work here, they rise in the morning at sunup, have breakfast and work at whatever task they are given until noon, then at that time they go to their casas to eat. They have their siestas, and then go back to work until the sun disappears over the Sangre de Cristos. The rest of the evening is theirs and they know how to enjoy themselves, how to get the most out of life." He smiled as he thought fondly of the people and their infinite capacity for enjoyment, much of it centered around their music.

"I wish we had better methods of treating the sick, however," said Simon with a sigh. "I know we have age old remedies using herbs and other plants, but sometimes they are of no avail. Praying sometimes seems to be the final solace. When all else fails, that never fails to sooth both the ill and their worried families."

"With only one doctor that I know of in all of New Mexico, and he is in Santa Fe, we are all dependent on our own remedies," reminded Modesto. "Don't forget our squaw tea, as the Indians call it, or Canutillo as we call it, does much to ease the suffering of the kidneys. Snake weed or yerba de la bibora is another concoction used often for arthritis after it is gathered green and boiled. Strained and rubbed on the skin, it has properties which penetrate the flesh and relieve the pain. And of course, the yerba del manzo is believed to cure many stomach problems and there are lamb's quarters which are very nutritious." He paused and then smiled and said, "Necessity and mother nature have provided those who need them many cures for their ailments."

"And don't forget osha, which is good for toothaches," Simoñ reminded him. "But I know what you mean, what you are trying to tell me, my friend, is that the peons have a drab and dreary prospect, that they can have very little hope for improvement in their lifestyles. I understand and agree but what worries me the most is that most of them have accepted their stations in life and it will take years, many years before they become convinced that they are capable of doing anything other than working with their hands or in the fields."

"When the Americanos come, our people will continue to accept that low station in life which we patrons have so successfully allocated to them. They will have a tendency to accept the Americanos as their new patrons. Change, I'm afraid, will come slowly for our people. More than one generation will have to pass before they will begin to adapt to the Americano style, and free themselves from what they perceive as their social position in life.

"Our people have placed themselves unknowingly in a small jail from which it will be difficult to escape."

Modesto said nothing for awhile and then mused, "And whom will they blame for their misfortune? The Americanos, of course, and it is possible that they will deserve the blame to a degree. But the blame will, in truth, lie with both peoples, if everyone were honest about it. This rift which is happening in Texas right now, will surely not enhance good relations, and if war should break out between Mexico and the United States over the Texas issue, that too, will add to the tension and ill feeling which already exists.

War has a tendency to bring out both the best and the worst in people, but the ill feeling which succeeds a war can linger for many years."

"But while we are assessing the blame for the condition of the peons as a class, we must not fail to examine our own part in it," Simoñ said. "Once a person has accepted a station in life, however inferior, it is almost impossible to change his attitude and he may become inferior in practice."

"And what of the poor who don't live on a hacienda? Many of them are worse off than those who do. I do think that the people who live in the mountain villages have attained a dignity which comes from their feeling of self reliance," said Modesto. "Your policy in regard to the villagers has done much to improve the quality of their lives. The common practice of carrying off the children to become members of the Indian tribes, has almost disappeared, thanks to your Mountain Riflemen. Before that, a child who grew up with a tribe, has been known to attack that same village without ever knowing it was his ancestral village. You can be proud of what you have accomplished so far, Simoñ."

"But there is much more to be done," Simoñ said slowly. "They are a hardy people, strong in heart and mind, deserving of much more than our poor efforts have attained. But when we are part of the United States, they will realize finally their full potential, God willing."

"I agree whole heartedly with what you are saying. See what you have done to me with that dream of yours!"

"I hope it is not merely a dream," said Simoñ soberly. "Will it really happen? Will our people join with the Americanos in dedicating themselves to what is good and decent in life?"

"We will not see the end result of that reunion, I'm afraid, but it will come, Simoñ, it will come. I feel that God has a hand in this venture and with His help, how can we fail?" Modesto rose from his chair and continued, "It is time for lunch and I'd better not be late."

"You know you are welcome to join us," Simoñ told him and he also prepared to go to lunch.

"Thanks, Simoñ, but today I must eat at home. My wife has promised me one of my favorite meals."

Marcello also straightened the papers on his desk and commented drily, "You both have given me much to think about. I did not mean to eavesdrop, but it was impossible not to hear what you were saying."

"If we had wanted to keep our thoughts to ourselves, we would have gone elsewhere," Simoñ said with a smile.

CHAPTER XV

How many miles do you judge it to be from here to Socorro?" Simoñ asked.

"Around two hundred and fifty miles, padre," Leandro replied. "Socorro would be a good place to open another trading post for our American goods. It should do well, because the location for the new store is right on the plaza."

Simoñ looked up from his meal and asked, "What do you think of Leandro's idea of opening a trading post in Socorro, Sylvia?"

Doña Silvia touched her lips with her napkin and then returned it to her lap as she replied, "His business judgment thus far has been flawless." She turned to her son and continued, with a twinkle in her eye, "I have complete faith in him."

"Thank you, madre."

"What are mothers for?" She smiled at him fondly before returning her attention to her plate.

Simoñ now looked at Doña Maria and asked, "And you, my dear mother, do you agree?"

She smiled and said merely, "I have complete faith in both my son's and grandsons' judgment."

Simoñ glanced farther along the table at his only daughter and asked, "Josephine?"

"Si, padre?" Josephine answered.

"Do you have an opinion?"

"An opinion on what, padre?" She wore a broad grin and she glanced up at Simoñ.

"Oh, now we are playing games," Simoñ surrendered with a laugh. "It seems you have planned well, Leandro. You have rallied your troops and have them in place." He gave a quick glance at the women." You win and you have my blessing. I cannot fight women."

"We are not women!" Carlos, Ignacio and Emilo all spoke at once and then burst out laughing, as Carlos finished, "But we agree with the girls."

"Oh, so it's girls, now," Simoñ glanced first at his mother and then at his wife who both smiled sweetly at the boys and then returned to their meal without saying a word.

Doña Maria finally broke the silence by suggesting, "Maybe you should go with Leandro to see what he has done and is doing."

Simoñ looked at Leandro and said, "I'm sorry son, perhaps I have not shown enough interest and appreciation for the hard work you have done in developing the trade end of our enterprises. I know you have done an outstanding job and if I didn't think that, I would have interfered long ago. However, that does not excuse my insensitivity in not acknowledging your accomplishments. I do so now, tardy as it may be."

"And?" Doña Maria said with a smile of approval.

"And what?" Simoñ glanced at his mother who was turning her eyes to the other boys.

"This is confession day, I see." Simoñ grinned broadly. "I guess I have just taken it for granted that all of you knew that I was proud of all of your accomplishments. That I shouldn't have done and I stand corrected. And now that I think about it, I would like to accompany you, Leandro, on that trip to Socorro, that is if your plans are flexible enough?"

"I would like that, padre."

"When do we leave?"

"Early tomorrow," Leandro answered.

"Let's ask Modesto to go with us. Heaven knows he could use a change." Simoñ glanced at his other sons and continued, "And when I return from the trip to Socorro, I will go with you to the cow and sheep camps and also on a trading trip to the Comanches. I have kept myself too close to headquarters in recent months."

Rosita entered the dining room and said hurriedly, "Please excuse my intrusion, Don Simoñ, but there are Comanches approaching."

Carlos rose to his feet and as he dropped his napkin on the table he said, "It's all right. I'm sure it's not a raid, and Ramon and I will take care of it. As a matter of fact, we have been encouraging them to come to the hacienda to trade. It would save us much time and effort if they came here when they have enough trade goods rather than our having to search for them. Often, when we go to them, they haven't enough goods to trade. In this way we know they'll have enough."

"Good thinking," his father said approvingly.

"Please excuse me, madre and abuela (mother and grandmother,") the tall young man said politely before he turned to leave the room.

He passed Modesto in the hallway and the rest of the family could hear their hurried exchange before Carlos continued on his way.

Modesto entered the room and saluted the women in a courtly manner before he seated himself at the table. "I see you have been told that the Comanches are less than two miles from here."

"Si, and I have Carlos' assurance that they have come to trade in peace.

Now that you are here, I have a proposal to make. How would you like to leave for Socorro tomorrow? I plan to accompany Leandro and would like for you to go with us."

"Opening another store?" He accepted the cup of coffee which Rosita handed to him and continued, "If you don't watch that son of yours, he'll be driving the merchants of El Paso del Norte and Chihuahua out of business, and they may retaliate!"

"While they may try to drive him out of business, they'll never be able to do that," Doña Maria said complacently, "but they might try to interfere by enlisting Mexican officials in Chihuahua or Santa Fe."

Modesto grinned cheerfully. "Leandro will handle them, for he's the politician in the family. He'll out maneuver them somehow, never fear."

"Thank you for the vote of confidence, Tio Modesto," Leandro said, pleased by his uncle's words, but slightly embarrassed by the sudden attention.

Simoñ's face was lit up with pride as he watched his oldest son, and then to help him out of the embarrassing situation, suggested, "Can we be ready to leave tomorrow?"

"I don't see why not, padre. I'll go see to it. Please excuse me, everyone." He rose hastily and was through the door before anyone could answer.

As he left, Modesto turned to Simoñ and said, "Yes, my very good friend, and brother in law, I would like very much to accompany you and Leandro to Socorro, that is, if you don't think we are getting too old for such a trip."

"Then it is time we were out on the trail once more," said Simoñ. "Before we are indeed too old to enjoy it. We will leave Ignacio in charge while we go south."

Leandro arrived at the corrals early the following morning and saw that the pack mule was ready, as well as the horses which they would take. When he saw his father and uncle approach, he called out exuberantly, "Everything is ready!"

"Do you think we could travel to Socorro by way of the Jicarilla Mountains, Leandro?"

"Any particular reason for that route, padre?"

"Si," Simoñ replied. "I'd like to drop in and visit my old friend, Reese, who lives at the Nat Cochran ranch. If you remember, it is situated in the foothills of the Jicarilla Mountains."

"To the Jicarilla Mountains it will be then," Leandro said as he swung into the saddle.

"Reese is a special friend and I will never have a better opportunity to see him than now," Simoñ added as the two older men stepped up on their horses with more restraint.

As they rode out through the main gate, Simoñ went on with his thoughts. "Perhaps you were joking about our age, Modesto, but we won't be making as many long trips as we did and since Reese is older than we are, we had better see him on this trip. I just hope we're not too late."

The men rode three abreast and Simoñ asked, "Which way do you intend going, Leandro?"

"If we're going by way of the Jicarillas, we'll turn at Romeroville and ride toward Villanueva, on the Pecos River. Then on to Palma, Negra, Pinto Wells, and shortly after that we should be on the Cochran Ranch."

The first part of their journey was routine, uneventful, until on their first day out of Villanueva, Leandro said, "I think we're being followed."

To his surprise, his father and uncle both nodded in agreement, and his father said, "And it is not Indians who follow us, so it must be banditos. Don't let them know that we suspect anything."

"I agree," said Modesto. "And I estimate that there are eight or ten of them."

"What are they waiting for? But I know without asking. They will wait until we are away from any chance of help from others and then they will strike," said Leandro grimly.

"Well, we can't handle ten of them," said Simoñ impatiently. "Any suggestions?"

"They won't bother us until we are well away from Palma and since we have no proof of any hostile intentions on their part, we can't have them arrested in Palma. I'd say we just keep going and be prepared to act when it is to our advantage," said Modesto.

"What else can we do?" Simon shrugged and then grinned. "After all, although there are more of them, we are probably better armed and if we add surprise and skill to our plan of attack, we should be able to handle them."

....

Five Apaches sat their horses as they gazed down on the scene below. The leader of the small party of braves, Snow Hawk, turned to the others and said, "There were many white eyes who deserved to die, but not that one."

"Why was he different from the others?" Broken Limb looked his scorn at such reasoning.

"Because he was as much one of us as one of them," Snow Hawk said as he continued to stare below, "Thunderbolt, Evening Star and their sons knew what I mean, and I applaud their courage in going to the friends of the dead white eyes to make ammends."

Broken Limb asked once more, "Who was this dead white eyes and why did he deserve special treatment?"

"He deserved special treatment," said Snow Hawk softly, "by all who cherish dignity and honor and love Usen and wish to do His bidding. Because that one was as close as anyone to being the messenger of Usen. His name was

Reese, I am told. I never had the pleasure of meeting him, but that was my loss. See they still honor him, perhaps on the anniversary of his death. See the man who is standing at the head of the grave reading from their holy book? He is not a medicine man, and his name is Nat, but the Comanches called him Vlach. He was like a son to the dead white eyes. "The woman who stands at his right side is called Snow Skin. Her mother is all white eyes as is Thunderbolt's woman, Evening Star. Snow Skin is Nat's woman. Her mother is there also. You can see her standing next to the Comanche who is Snow Skin's brother. The tall man who stands beside her is the Macedonian."

The other four braves looked at one another with expressions of surprise and reverence when they heard that name. Snow Hawk continued to talk softly as he stared down at the little group of people who stood around the grave. "Yes, he is the Macedonian. That is why I said before that while there are many white eyes who deserve to die, those down there do not, for they are honoring the friend of all Usen's children."

The five braves continued to watch as they leaned forward on their ponies' necks and no one broke the silence until Snow Hawk spoke once more. "All tribes have misfits and outcasts and those who attacked and killed Reese were misfits and outcasts. Evening Star, I am sure, explained that to the white eyes many years ago. Everything was explained and at least those white eyes down there have not blamed the rest of the Mescaleros for the misdeeds of some of our outcasts. They have been told that the Mescaleros have no jails in which to put criminals and rather than feed and clothe our undesirables at the expense of all good, law abiding Apaches, we do what our laws say, and that is to cast them out of our band."

The sound of galloping horses could be heard and the Apaches turned quickly from watching the white eyes and saw one of their own riding toward them.

"Mexican bandits," the warrior said as his horse slid to a halt in front of Snow Hawk.

"Where?'

"They have left Negra and are headed toward Pinto Wells."

"How many?"

"Ten, they are following three other Mexicans, and I'm sure they intend to kill and rob them. The three Mexicans are from the Gomez Hacienda."

"How do you know this?" Snow Hawk asked quickly.

"Because Leandro Gomez is with them. I've seen him in Socorro, for he's getting ready to open a store there."

"Describe the two who ride with him."

When this had been done, Snow Hawk merely said, "They are the ones." He sat in deep thought for several minutes until finally one of the others asked curiously, "What do you mean, they are the ones?"

"They are the two who set me free from El Alambrero, the slave camp, at great risk to themselves, many years ago. I must help them as they helped me. Let us ride toward Negra."

On the following morning, the six Apaches halted their ponies and began to don their war paint in silence. When they were finished, each carefully adjusted a specially designed, unique headband. They were two inches in width and were made of soft deer skin.

"Now camouflage yourselves," Snow Hawk ordered. They hid their ponies and then themselves, so successfully that they blended into the landscape completely. Let the three Mexicans pass in safety and when the bandits reach this location, I want every yucca, every bunch of greasewood, mound of dirt, or whatever to turn into Apache warriors. I want all the bandits dead within one minute after we strike."

....

"It is very quiet," Modesto said with misgiving. "I don't like the feel of it." He glanced constantly in every direction.

"There is a stillness in the air which makes me feel uneasy," agreed Simoñ, as he, too, looked about with apprehension.

"The horses are beginning to shy away from yucca and other vegetation and even from mounds of dirt," said Leandro worriedly. "They seem to be looking for something at which to spook."

"We had better be especially alert for something is afoot, you can be sure of it," his father told him. "Do you suppose the banditos are closing the distance between us?"

"I think so," Modesto said as he turned around to face the road before them. "They're not making any effort to hide the dust they're kicking up any longer."

"Which means they will be attacking soon," Simoñ said grimly. "Let's find a good defensive position and wait for them."

They decided to make their stand among some huge boulders which stood among some junipers. They tied their horses securely and then waited quietly for what would come, as they watched in every direction. They waited for what seemed longer than it was and finally Simoñ said softly, "What are they waiting for?"

"They must be close," Modesto whispered. "I can't hear even a bird call."

Now they could hear a faint sound coming from the direction from which they had ridden.

"Some one stumbled over a rock," Simoñ guessed softly.

It became quiet again and then they heard a moan, accompanied by the sound of footsteps. Nothing else was heard for what seemed like hours to the three crouched men and then more moans were heard, so close together that they could have been mistaken for one. Next came a frightening yell and the word 'Apaches'! filled the air.

Gunfire was heard and one bandit dashed at full speed toward the north. He disappeared into the junipers, and his horse's hoofbeats could be heard for several moments before they died away. It was quiet once more and then the silence was broken by a bloodcurdling scream, and then once more, silence. A silence broken only slightly by the soft sighing of the junipers as a breeze sprang up.

"What is happening?" Leandro leaned closer to whisper to his father although his eyes continued to search in all directions.

"Speak, Simoñ Gomez!" The voice came from beyond the trees.

The three men glanced quickly at one another, but remained still as they held their rifles ready. Then Simoñ called, "What do you want?"

"We want proof that you are Simoñ," the voice answered.

"That is the voice of an Indian," Modesto whispered in surprise.

"Who are you?" Simoñ asked and waited for an answer.

"Who were the captives at the El Alambrero slave camp?"

Simoñ's eyes widened as did Modesto's and Simoñ called back his answer. "Two Comanches, one Cochiti, an Acoma, and one Mescalero Apache."

"I am that Mescalero Apache," Snow Hawk called back.

"How do we know that this is not just a trick?"

"You are a smart man, Señor Gomez," Snow Hawk replied. "How many banditos have been following you?"

"At least ten," Simoñ answered firmly.

"Don't shoot and I'll expose the bodies of the ten banditos."

Movement was heard from all areas in front of the hidden men and the sound of bodies being dragged could be heard. Shortly one dead bandito after another was rolled into a clearing in plain view of the men from the hacienda. When the banditos were all exposed, Snow Hawk called out, "There are your banditos. Do not shoot and I will step out into the open so that you can see that we are Apaches and not banditos." He stepped out from behind a juniper tree and held his empty hands before him. "I have done this in return for your setting me free from the slave camp. I am now called Snow Hawk."

"Where are the rest of your braves?"

"There are only six of us," Snow Hawk replied. "Don't you believe me? We don't want to be tricked either. I have never exposed myself to so much uncertainty. Never! I do this because I know that you are Simoñ Gomez. Why don't you believe me?"

"First of all," Simoñ said as he rose from his crounched position and rested his rifle against a boulder, "you are an Apache and Apaches are well known for their cunning and deception. I do not want to pay with my life to find out that I am correct. We have a rifle pointed at you, Snow Hawk, and any trickery and you'll be the first to die."

"No trickery," Snow Hawk grinned as he walked toward Simoñ. The two men met face to face and stared into one another's eyes. After a few seconds of silence, Simoñ extended his hand and said, "You are the Apache from the slave camp."

"I am a little older, but the same," Snow Hawk replied as he grasped Simoñ's hand firmly.

"I, too, have grey hairs," Simoñ laughed. "Thank you for coming to our aid. He turned and beckoned to Modesto and Leandro. "You remember Modesto and this is my oldest son, Leandro."

Snow Hawk shook their hands, also, as the other Apaches came out from concealment with their rifles pointed toward the ground, a sign of non-hostility.

"It is good to see you again, Modesto," Snow Hawk said.

Modesto grinned as he said, "It is nice to see you again, especially under the circumstances!"

"Aren't you taking a dangerous route to Socorro, my friends?"

"How did you know we were going to Socorro?"

"We are Apaches," Snow Hawk said simply.

"Si, we are journeying to Socorro but we came this way to see an old friend," Simoñ admitted.

"Who is your old friend?"

"He is called Reese and he is supposed to be with a party of people who have settled in the Jicarillas," Simoñ answered.

"I'm afraid you are too late," Snow Hawk spoke regretfully.

"Too late, what do you mean, too late?"

"He was buried by his friends, many summers ago. He was killed by renegade Apaches. Apaches outlawed and cast out of our tribe. I am very sorry that it happened. Come, I will take you to his people."

"Before we leave, tell me how you were able to kill all but one of those banditos, without losing a single man," Simoñ requested.

"That is easy," Snow Hawk answered with a grin. "We are Apaches, the superior people."

"That is not an answer," Simoñ replied respectfully. "That is only a statement."

"Close your eyes, Simoñ," Snow Hawk ordered.

"Close my eyes, why?"

"All of you, close your eyes and count to fifty and then open them and see if you can locate us. That is the quickest way that I know of to answer your question," Snow Hawk replied.

The three men glanced at one another, hesitated, and then said with a grin, "This will be a test of our faith in you as well."

Snow Hawk grinned back as he retorted, "Don't worry, you will not be harmed. I give you my word."

"I've been told it is suicide to trust an Apache," Leandro said cautiously.

"I hope you were also told that under Apache law and custom, once an

Apache accepts a favor from a stranger, that stranger becomes an adopted member of that Apache band and is entitled to all of the benefits of a member," Snow Hawk said gravely.

"No, I never heard that," admitted Leandro.

"Well, it's true, and because I accepted help from your father and uncle in my escape from the slave camp, I consider them as members of my band, and as their relative you are safe, also."

Upon hearing this the three men closed their eyes and began to count aloud and when they reached fifty, they opened their eyes and could see no Apache in sight. It seemed as though they had vanished, leaving no trace of themselves, not even tracks.

"Where did they go?" Leandro turned in every direction, mystified.

"It is amazing," said Modesto. "They have vanished, completely vanished."

Simoñ turned slowly in a complete circle and was taken by surprise as one of the Apaches rose up from his very feet from a shallow grave. Another rose from the ground right before their very eyes. His camouflage was such that when he was perfectly still, he blended into the ground completely. Another rose from behind a clump of sacatone, still another from behind a clump of yucca.

Simoñ laughed as he conceded, "You have answered my question. How do you do that?"

"It takes years of practice to learn how to become completely invisible," Snow Hawk told him. "But here, put some of this on your skin." He opened a small leather pouch. "Rub some dirt and some green needles of the juniper over it before it dries."

Simoñ did so and was astonished at the result. "That is how we killed the banditos," Snow Hawk told him.

"Now let us be on our way. We will guide you to the people who were the friends of Reese."

They mounted and headed southward once more and after several hours of steady riding, Snow Hawk motioned for a halt, saying, "I think it is best that we make camp here for the night, and ride to Nat's headquarters at mid morning tomorrow." He slid from his pony as he spoke.

The next morning when they were within a few miles of Nat's ranch headquarters, Snow Hawk pulled in his pony and said, "This is as far as we go. Some day we will meet your friends, but not on this occasion."

The men from the Gomez Hacienda thanked the Apaches once more, said adios and sat their horses as they watched them disappear into a thicket of cedar and juniper before they continued on their way.

Leandro was the first to speak as they rode on. "That old saying that the Apache can be seen only when he wants to be seen means a whole lot more to me than it did."

They trotted along in silence and then Simoñ pointed ahead, "Up there on that little knoll. We are being watched."

"They're well armed," commented Modesto drily.

"They need to be out here, they are probably Reese's friends," Simoñ added. "It wasn't too long before the men from the knoll rode up and one of them asked, "Where did your Apache friends go?"

"Could it be that I am addressing Señor Nat?" Simoñ asked.

"Who are you and what do you want?" Nat spoke gruffly as he kept his rifle ready.

"My name is Simoñ Gomez and this is my son, Leandro and my brother-in-law, Modesto Polaco. We are friends of Reese and I promised him that I would visit him one day. But the Apaches told us that we are too late."

"Why were they riding with you?" Nat wore a sombre expression as he asked the question.

"That is a long story, which I'd be more than glad to tell at another time, but for now I can assure you that they were not the ones who killed Reese. They are more like Thunderbolt and Evening Star, good Apaches."

Nat glanced at Leandro and Modesto and asked in surprise, "What do you know of Thunderbolt and Evening Star?"

"Very little, only what those Apaches told us," Simoñ admitted.

"If you are from the Gomez Hacienda," Fernando, who was the only Mexican riding with Nat, asked, "who is the doña of the hacienda?"

"My mother is called Doña Maria and my wife, Doña Sylvia," Simoñ replied promptly. He smiled and then continued, "The Prudencio brothers are my Comancheros and Marcello is my bookkeeper. Do you want more names or will knowing Otto Muller in Westport Landing convince you of who we are?"

Nat urged his horse closer as he said, "You can't blame us for being careful, especially now with a war between our two countries eminent. Please forgive our caution, but I'm sure you understand under the circumstances."

Simoñ extended his hand to Nat as he said, "Your caution is understandable, señor. We would like to visit the grave of our friend, Reese, now, if that would be all right with you."

Nat reined his horse and led the way to the grave and then led his men a short distance away to give the men from the hacienda some privacy.

Simoñ, Modesto, and Leandro dismounted slowly, walked to the grave, and knelt, making the sign of the cross as they did so, and bowed their heads. Watching them, Nat realized once more how many friends Reese had made in his lifetime.

When the three men finally mounted their horses, Nat escorted them to the headquarters where they were introduced to the other members of the American Team, as they called themselves.

They were Jim, the Macedonian, and his wife Spirit, her daughter, Snow

Skin, who was Nat's wife, and Spirit's son, Three Tongues. Fernando, Fidela, and their children and Nat's and Snow Skin's children combined to make a small community in themselves.

The men from the Gomez Hacienda stayed for two days visiting with the American Team and during those two days, a strong friendship began to develop between them, mainly because of their shared memories of Reese.

"Reese would have been proud of the part that he played in bringing our two peoples together," Nat commented on the last evening the men from the north were to spend with them.

"That he would," Simoñ said as he rose to his feet, raised his glass of wine and said, "I give a toast to our good friend and wise confidant, Reese Marquette."

The other rose to their feet quickly, saying, "Here, here!"

They all downed their drinks and as everyone sat down once more, Simon continued, "I would like for all of you to come to visit us someday at Ocate whenever it is convenient for you. I want our friendship to blossom into full maturity, especially between our children. We like and admire your kind and because in the not too distant future we will be fellow countrymen. It is most desirable that we cultivate our friendship."

Spirit answered, saying what was in all their hearts as she said, "Good friends are hard to find and loyal friends are even harder to find. You, our New Mexico friends, soon, I hope, will be our American friends."

"Thank you for those generous and kind remarks, señora, we too wish that we will become Americans very soon, for in our hearts we are already Americans. We will always have, however, a soft spot in our hearts for our mother, Mexico. But not for her system of government. Our philosophies, yours and ours, seem identical. Let us hope that our children and children's children will work together in harmony to develop a broad understanding of the true meaning of Americanism. One for all and all for one, indivisible, united, and indestructable. I suggest here and now that our two families plan a reunion to renew our faith in our friendship and in America, periodically."

"Perhaps we can widen the group to include our Apache friends," Jim, the Macedonian, said.

"That is truly in the tradition of the Macedonian spirit," Three Tongues said gravely.

"Fine," Nat said. "Let us decide on a date for our first reunion after we have had time to study the matter."

"Can we call it 'Reeseunion'?" Young Henri looked around the circle eagerly.

"Your Uncle Reese would be proud of you, Henri," his mother, Snow Skin said, "in that way he will be present at the Reeseunion also."

"Reeseunion, it is," agreed Simoñ heartily.

"Now that that is settled, may I ask where your journey takes you from here, Señor Gomez?"

194

"I'd be happy to tell you, Fernando. We travel to Socorro to establish a new store," Simoñ answered.

Fernando was interested. "Do you plan to open another at Mesilla or maybe Las Cruces?"

"We have no plans at the present in that direction," Leandro replied, "although that is a colorful and historic area."

"What makes that area especially historic?" Spirit leaned forward with interest.

"According to history," Simoñ told her, "Mesilla was once an Indian settlement and later, when Don Juan de Oñate, who colonized New Mexico, passed by there on his journey up the Rio Grande, he founded the town and called it `Trenequel de La Mesilla.' Later it was shortened to La Mesilla. A tribe of Indians called Monos lived nearby although some people called them Sumas. The entire area is referred to as Doña Aña in honor of a little girl who died there as her parents passed through with one of Don Juan de Oñate's supply trains. Las Cruces is a new village, you know, as compared to La Mesilla and it was named after a large group of Taoans who were killed there by Apaches. Many wooden crosses were erected on the graves of the dead who were buried at the scene of the disaster. Because of the crosses, people began to refer to it as Las Cruces, the city of crosses. As you will find, the longer you live here, New Mexico's history is very long and interesting. Many brave Spaniards lost their lives in the service of the twin majesties, the church and the crown, and we people of Spanish ancestry remember with honor and respect those brave people."

He smiled wryly and continued, "Although the Indians remember them quite differently. They remember them as conquerors and enslavers, destroyers of their culture and religion. Don Juan de Oñate colonized and named New Mexico in honor of Mexico City, not Mexico, as so many believe. Mexico did not receive her name until after the Revolution of 1821.

"We, here, have been called zealous Christians, some say in fact that the Spanish Catholics are more Catholic than the pope. Because we could not tolerate any other religion, the Indian's religion had to be destroyed. But we didn't succeed in its destruction, however hard we tried. We tried many disciplinary measures, even going to the length of hanging anyone caught worshiping his own god. Indians were forced to live at missions, the better to control them. We used the encomienda system which was merely a legal term for slavery, and although it was established in order to indoctrinate the Indians into the Spanish way of life, it tended to keep them as slaves."

Simoñ sighed as he contemplated some of the practices which he deplored, and then resumed speaking. "While we didn't have a Martin Luther and a reformation, as other Europeans did, we did suffer the Inquisition, the Holy Office, a sort of retrogression, as I regard it, in the church. If we had had a reformation, perhaps many things would be different today. Quien sabe?"

"But we are an ingenious people and have proven capable of adapting to all kinds of hardship. Why, when draft animals became scarce in Santa Fe, we captured deer when they were fawns, and later taught them to pull our carts!"

"Perhaps we have not been properly appreciative of our conquistadore ancestors, many of whom were disposed of by greedy men who had the ear of the king. Many of them died in disgrace, and many were executed by their replacements, but they all fought, conquered and died for God, glory, and king. They are remembered with fondness by the people, if not by the kings and their courts.

"We are also a stoic people and can suffer hardship and still do, but we, too, have our faults. We Spaniards detest labor, that is why we enslaved the Indians and later brought the Negro over to do the hard work, against the wishes of the church and the king, I might add. We fear nothing and even court danger, which is one reason why we love the bull fight."

Nat asked, "How was the the Palace of Governors built?"

"How else? With slave labor of course. It was built on the ruins of an old pueblo by order of Governor Peralta. Although the Catholic church objected strenuously to the use of Indian slavery, its wishes were ignored. In fact when one of the priests appeared before the governor and argued against using slaves, the governor is said to have drawn a pistol and fired it, missing his target, but wounding another priest who was nearby, as well as a civilian. Such squabbles between the Church and the military authorities began to erode the faith of the people in both the church and the government and perhaps was the beginning of the erosion of the Spanish empire, at least in New Mexico. That erosion has continued to this day, which is why I look to the Americans with such hope. But I am talking too much, let someone else speak for a change."

"I'm sure I don't just speak for myself when I say that I find your history of much interest," said Jim. "Perhaps you can enlighten me about something. You say the church opposed the practice of using the Indians as slaves. From what I have heard, some of the individual priests were not above the practice. What can you tell us of that?"

"Have you heard of the Acoma Pueblo?"

When Jim nodded that he had, "Simoñ continued, "As you know, then, Acoma is situated on a solid rock mesa which rises more than three hundred feet above the desert floor. It is located southwest of Albuquerque. A priest, one Fray Baltazar, forced the Acoma Indians to rebuild his church and even bring up soil from the plain below to enable him to have a garden and an orchard. From what I have heard, the Indian women were assigned the task of bringing the water from the cisterns to water his little orchard and vegetables. During a time of drouth, this must have posed a hardship for them. Baltazar must have lived like a king on his mesa with the Acoma Indians as his serfs. Whether or not the church officials were aware of his and other priests' abuses and turned its head, I do not know, but whatever the situation, both representatives of the Church and of the government have abused the Indians. And now I should stop and we should get some rest, for we have a long journey to resume tomorrow."

"We must meet again soon, and continue with our history lesson," Nat said earnestly. "It will be our history soon, perhaps."

"Yes, we must get together soon," agreed Simoñ. "Please come to our hacienda whenever you can and consider it your home. It would give me much pleasure if you would do so."

The members of the American Team watched the men from the Gomez Hacienda ride off in the direction of Socorro the following morning and were pleased to have their friendship.

"They are good people," Leandro said as they rode away. "But they are different from us, aren't they?"

"Different?" Simoñ glanced at his son in surprise. "How different?"

"I don't know, but they just seem different," Leandro said, for he was puzzled.

"I know what you mean, Leandro," his uncle said slowly. "You can't put your finger on it, or put it into words, but they are different. They are more open, more self reliant, perhaps more independent. They haven't had to worry about some corrupt government official coming to visit them unexpectedly with harsh demands. They seem to be a government unto themselves, don't they?"

"More free, more self assured, is that what you're trying to say?" Simoñ asked eagerly.

"That, too," Leandro told his father. "It may be many years before our people can develop that kind of temperament. It's a completely new way of life, a completely different way of looking at things. Do you think we will ever become that self assured, Tio Modesto?"

"You probably will, for you are younger than your father and I," Modesto told him. "We grew up in a closed society where most decisions were made for us, whereas in American society, the individual must rely on his own wit, his own initiative, his own instincts, where no decisions are made for him. In the American society, the government stays out of peoples' lives as much as possible, while in ours, it is the reverse. We are regulated, we are intimidated, we are forced and conjoled to follow a behaviour pattern that has been set down by those at the top. "While your father and I have gone our own way, more or less, still that system, for better or worse, is engrained into our souls and it is going to be difficult for many of us to make the change. Some may never make the change and will continue to look to the government to do for them what they should do for themselves. It will take many years before we will become one people."

Simoñ, Leandro, and Modesto were present at the opening of the Socorro store and then they returned to their hacienda.

CHAPTER XVI

A few weeks later, Simoñ accompanied Filomeno and his company of Riflemen on a tour of the mountain villages. The Riflemen had been successful in protecting the villages from indiscriminate raiding by the Apaches and other tribes, for the most part. They had not been able to put a stop to the raiding altogether, but the training in self defence had enabled the villagers to withstand attacks which occurred when the Riflemen were not in the immediate area.

"Did you ever run into that Abeyta boy?" Simoñ glanced at Filomeno as they rode along.

"No, patron, I fear even if we do find him now, assuming that he is alive, he may not want to return to his family in Hondo. It has been nearly ten years since the Apaches took him."

....

While the light of the full moon was still contending with the early light of dawn for supremacy, a member of the Abeyta family tossed and turned in the straw bed which he shared with his brother, Ruben. Roberto's murmuring in his sleep awakened Ruben and he rose on one elbow to look over at his brother. Roberto's eyes were shut and his face was covered with perspiration, and he tossed his head this way and that restlessly. Ruben reached over and placed the palm of his hand on his brother's forehead and then leaped from the bed and rushed to his mother and father. "Mama, mama!" He shouted as he shook his mother's shoulder. She opened her eyes drowsily and looked up at her son and then sat up hurriedly and asked, "Que parsa, Ruben?"

"It is Roberto, mama, he is burning up with fever."

She slid out of bed and rushed to Roberto and when she reached his side she grasped a three legged stool which was within her reach and slid it beneath her and as she sat she stretched out her hand and gently laid it on his forehead and when she touched him her eyes instantly rose to meet those of her husband who by now had also reached the young man's side and she whispered to him, "Alonzo, he has a high fever again. Go to Stella and tell her to build a fire and boil some of the yerba del manzo, pronto!" Alonzo did not say a word but turned and hurried away, and as he disappeared through the doorway his wife rushed to get a pan of cool water and a small towel. Within minutes she returned to her son's side and as she did she placed the pan on the floor and lifted the towel from the water and twisted it until she could not squeeze any more water from it and she then laid the damp towel on her son's forehead. The soothing feel of the cool, wet towel awoke Roberto and he opened his eyes and murmured, "It's the ulcers again, mama, and they sure do hurt." He rubbed his stomach fretfully.

Now Stella entered the room in a rush and said softly as she reached her mother's side, "Here is the yerba del manzo, mama." She stooped and held out the cup filled with steaming liquid.

"Drink this, Roberto," Prestina said softly as she raised her son's head and placed the cup to his lips. "It will take away your stomach pain and the fever as well."

Roberto slowly drank the concoction and then lowered himself painfully.

"Now rest, muchacho." She then turned to Ruben and said, "you will have to take the sheep out to pasture today. Your brother is too sick."

The others now retreated to the kitchen and Prestina began to prepare breakfast.

"It's because of Julio that Roberto is sick again, isn't it mama?" Ruben stared worriedly at his mother.

Alonzo answered before his wife had a chance to speak, "It must be, Ruben, for ever since the Apaches carried Julio away, Roberto has had these attacks."

"How old would Julio be now, padre?"

"Seventeen," Prestina quickly interrupted with the answer. "That is if he is still alive," she added somberly. Tears rushed to her eyes as the thought of her oldest son assailed her. She shook her head to dispel such thoughts and went on, "He will be seventeen next month," she said firmly.

"Roberto blames himself for what happened to Julio," Alonzo reminded Ruben as he picked up another tortilla and spread honey on it.

"But why? It was not Roberto's fault."

"No, it was not Roberto's fault, but he thinks it was. He left Julio alone when they were with the sheep in the high country to come home for more food. When he returned, Julio was gone and so were most of the sheep. Roberto followed the pony tracks until he spotted the Apaches in the distance. There were ten of them altogether, and all well armed with rifles. Roberto rushed back to tell us what happened and we knew that we could not rescue Julio without help, for if we had tried, we would have been killed, so we sent for help to the hacienda."

"But Don Simoñ and his Riflemen could never find Julio or the warriors who took him. Do you think they really tried to find him?" Ruben looked disgusted.

Alonzo hastened to tell his son once again that the Riflemen from the hacienda had done all in their power to find Julio. "They were gone over two weeks, but they could find neither Julio nor the Apaches, nor even the sheep. The rains which occurred shortly after he was taken made their efforts almost doomed to failure, but they did their utmost. Never forget that, my son."

"Do you think my brother is still alive?"

"Only God knows for sure," Alonzo crossed himself and then uttered angrily, "and those heathens who stole him away."

Prestina looked across at Ruben and said slowly, "You know it is possible that your brother has grown into a full fledged Apache warrior by now and has even taken part in raiding his own people. One cannot be raised in an Apache environment and not be affected by it. It has been over ten years since we last saw him. You were not even born when the Apaches took him from us."

"Why hasn't he escaped and returned to us?"

"I don't know the answer to that, my son," Prestina replied, "perhaps he did try on many occasions, but if he did, it's obvious he didn't succeed. Perhaps as the years went by, he accepted those who adopted him as his parents and forgot us, heaven forbid."

She crossed herself and sat silently, staring down at the hardly touched plate before her.

"So what you are saying," Ruben said painfully, "is that my brother, Julio, could be a Jicarilla Apache warrior by now."

"Si," Alonzo said slowly, "that is what your mother and I are trying to tell you."

"And that you will never see him again, and I will never see him at all." Tears ran down his cheeks as he looked imploringly at his parents.

"Si, we must face the facts, my son," Alonzo told him gently.

"It should not be difficult for me to accept that fact, because I do not know my brother and would not recognize him even if I saw him, or he me. It should not be difficult not to miss a person you've never seen or lived with, but I can't accept that. I cannot forget that I have another brother. I cannot give up hope. I know that some day I will see him and persuade him to come home."

"You forget, my son, that it is quite possible that he feels at home where he is. He may not want to leave the Apache band of which he is a member and return to live under Mexican rule. He may think that the Apache way of life is superior to ours," Prestina said sadly.

"But he is a Mexican, one hundred per cent, he is not an Apache!" Ruben spoke angrily. "How could he forget that?"

"He may have chosen to ignore his heritage for something which he believes shows more promise," his father reminded him.

"Well, then," Ruben shouted as he rose to his feet abruptly. "We are just going to have to change our system of government to make it more acceptable to Julio and the rest of us. Aren't we?"

"Ruben, Ruben!" Prestina rose and gathered her son into her arms and kissed the top of his head. "Do not torture yourself."

"You have both said more than once that the patron believes that some day we will be Americanos. When the day arrives, things will surely change. That might bring Julio home. Wouldn't it?" Ruben looked up into his mothers's face as he fought back tears.

Prestina looked across at her husband helplessly as she tried to comfort her little son. Alonzo stared at his wife and son for a moment and then turned wearily and left the room.

"It might, Ruben, it might," Prestina whispered comfortingly.

Ruben pulled himself away from his mother's arms and said, "I'd better take the sheep out to pasture now."

As he stepped out into the cool morning air, his dog greeted him exuberantly, barking and running toward him. "Hello, Pepe, you will help me today instead of Roberto." He bent to pet the sheep dog and then walked on toward the pens where the sheep were bleating anxiously as they waited to be released. The enclosure was constructed of small juniper limbs, hardly bigger around than the seven year old boy's arm. They stood upright and were perhaps six to seven feet in height. Ruben removed the leather thong which looped around the gatepost and swung the gate to one side. "Get them out of there, Pepe."

The dog dashed into the corral barking as Ruben took up the long sheep staff which rested against the pen, and watched as the dog drove the sheep toward the hill pasture.

When the dog had succeeded in his task the boy whistled to him and upon hearing his master's signal the animal abruptly turned and raced back to join the boy. Ruben smiled at the dog who was now by his side and reached down and petted him on the head saying as he did, "That's enough, Pepe, we'll let them graze as they go."

The dog gave him the smile which was so familiar to the little boy and his brother. "Good boy, Pepe," Ruben repeated and rewarded him with a number of pats and a tortilla which he had brought from the house.

By the time the sun was high overhead, the flock of sheep, shepherded by the boy and the dog, had wandered up through the forest and the thick underbrush, eating the vegetation which they most liked. Ruben spotted a large rock and walked toward it. "Let's rest a little while, what do you say, Pepe?" He sat down on the rock and continued to talk to his companion who lay down contentedly by his side. "It sure is a quiet day, isn't it, Pepe? The leaves are hardly moving."

Pepe, whose head had been resting on his paws, suddenly raised his head and his ears perked up. He listened for a moment and then bounded to his feet and running behind Ruben, barked furiously. Ruben quickly rose to his feet and as he turned, he saw six Apaches sitting their ponies at some distance away.

They said nothing and did nothing, but sat there studying the boy. Ruben called Pepe to his side without taking his eyes off the Indians. He placed both hands on his staff in such a way as to be able to swing it as a club. Still, the Apaches sat silently until the boy, in a terrified voice, yelled, "Stay away from me. Go away. Leave me alone!" Ruben spread his feet apart to balance himself better and prepared to give battle.

One of the Apaches had a light beard and Ruben focused his eyes on him and yelled, "You're not an Apache. You're a Mexican. Indians do not have beards."

That seemed to irritate the Apache who raised his rifle and pointed it at the boy.

"No, Julio," one of the Apaches yelled. He rode up beside Julio quickly, pushing the barrel of his rifle into the air. "He shows too much bravery to be killed. He would make a good Apache."

"Julio?" Ruben gasped in a whisper upon hearing the name and he slowly lowered his staff to the ground as if in slow motion, keeping his eyes fixed on the one called Julio as he did and tears sprang to his eyes. This response caught the Apaches off guard and they glanced at one another, puzzled.

"What is this?" Julio stared with hostility at the small boy. "You call my name?"

"Is that your name?" Ruben brushed the tears from his cheeks with his right hand and then with his left.

"Apaches use their Apache names only when the law requires. Other times they use their Mexican names. My Mexican name is Julio."

"Who gave you the name, Julio?" Ruben asked with emotion.

Julio became more confused and he looked around at his fellow braves and then turned his eyes again on the small boy and asked, "Why do you ask such a question?"

"I ask," Ruben told him, "because I had a brother named Julio who was taken from us in an Apache raid years ago when he was small. Could that Julio be you?"

Julio drew himself up angrily and retorted, "My father is Yellow Cougar and I am an Apache!"

"You are Julio, an adopted Apache," an older Apache said as he stared without emotion at Julio. "You were born a Mexican, but raised as an Apache by Yellow Cougar and Cactus Flower. This boy could be your brother."

"No, I was born and raised an Apache," Julio yelled in defiance.

"Such actions will not change the truth for the boy is right, you are Julio, a Mexican, his brother," the older warrior said sternly. "I was present on the raid when we carried you away."

Julio wore a baffled, hurt expression as he muttered resentfully, "It does not make any difference."

The Apaches were so engrossed in the predicament with the boy, that they failed to realize that the men of Filomeno's Riflemen had positioned themselves behind them. The cocking of their rifles alerted the attention of the Apaches and they whirled, prepared to give battle.

"No!" Ruben yelled as he ran in front of Julio. "He is my brother, please do not shoot!"

No one fired a shot, but it was obvious that the Apaches were ready to fight to the death. Finally Filomeno asked in frustration, "Which one of you is Julio?"

"The one behind me, but the others are his friends and comrades. Please do not kill them! Let them go in peace," pleaded the boy. He looked at them beseechingly and then continued, "Let not this happy reunion be marred by bloodshed and death. It is an occasion for celebration and happiness, not for hatred and suffering. Please, Señor Filomeno, let the Apaches leave unharmed."

"This is the voice of Simoñ Gomez, the patron of the hacienda, speaking." Simoñ rode out of the forest as he spoke, "It is a sad day when a young boy is the only one who speaks wisdom and with courage. He shames the rest of us. His wishes will be obeyed, and the Apaches may leave in peace. As for you, Julio, you must decide for yourself who you are, whom you wish to be with, the Jicarilla Apaches or your family."

All was quiet as Julio looked at his brother Apaches in arms and then at his brother by birth. He then rode over to the old Apache warrior who earlier had prevented him from killing Ruben and talked with him in a low voice. At the end of the conversation, Julio sat his motionless pony and faced toward Ruben, his legs dangling, as the other Apaches reined their horses and rode away, occasionally turning to look back at the warrior they left behind.

Now the Mountain Riflemen rode up to join Julio and Ruben, and Simoñ introduced them and extended his hand for the customary handshake to both Ruben and then to Julio. Ruben shook it gratefully, but Julio refused the friendly overture and said with hostility, "I know who you are." He stared at Simoñ coldly. "It is people like you who keep my father in bondage, a life that a dog shouldn't have to live. I will not live such a life. I'm not a dog and I refuse to be treated as one."

"Why didn't you ride away with the others then?" Simoñ asked.

"If I had, we would all be dead now. You and your men would have shot us. This way, at least they are free to return to their people."

That is honorable, to sacrifice your life for them," Simoñ told him.

"They would not hesitate to do the same for me. That is the Apache way," Julio said proudly.

"Why do you wait? Why don't you do it now? I am ready." Julio asked as he drew himself up.

"Do what?" Simoñ was confused.

"Kill him," Filomeno interpreted.

"So that is what you think we will do with you? I hate to disappoint you, Julio, but we are not going to stoop to Apache ways," Simoñ said angrily. "You are free to go."

Julio said nothing for a few seconds, but only stared into empty space stolidly as he waited for the shot which would kill him. It was Ruben who spoke next. "Please, Julio, do not anger the patron, let us go home now."

"That is no home, that is a jail, my brother. I have had a taste of freedom and I know what a precious thing it is. You talk foolish, you talk like a woman. The Mexican aristocrats will never control me again! I refuse to return to that hopeless life, that life of dispair and ignorance. I've been as free as an eagle and I will return to that life or die."

Irritated as he was, Simoñ felt compassion and understanding for the young man and finally asked, "Would you accept a partido contract from me?"

Julio said nothing but continued to stare into space and Simoñ asked impatiently, "Well, will you?"

Julio turned toward Simoñ and looked him straight in the eyes and neither spoke for a long time until Julio asked in wonder, "You are serious aren't you? But what is a partido contract?"

Simoñ smiled in relief and said, "Of course I'm serious. You may sign a contract with me and move as many people as you like out on the Llanos. Your family and as many more as you want!"

Julio glanced at Ruben who wore a broad smile from ear to ear, his white teeth sparkling. A plea could be seen in his shining eyes.

"But I have no security to offer. Surely your kind will not permit one such as me to sign a contract without a person of worth to vouch for me."

"You must remember that I have known your family for many years and I trust their son," Simon said simply. "Which do you want to take, sheep or cattle?"

"Would you give me five hundred two year old ewes?"

"Sounds fair enough," Simon answered quickly without hesitation. "The usual return is twice that many back within five years. Is that agreeable with you? You may want to talk it over with your father first, of course."

Julio wore a much more friendly expression as he now extended his hand for Simoñ to shake, and Simoñ said as the two men's hands clasped, "All right, we have a deal, if your father agrees. I'll keep my end of it and I hope you will."

"An Apache never lies or breaks a promise, and neither will this Apache-Mexican," said Julio soberly.

"Good," Simoñ said with a friendly smile. "Go with Ruben to see your family and later come to the hacienda when you are ready. I'll have the partido contract ready for you to mark, partidario! You will not be a peon for long now. When you get your first crop of wool and lambs you can take them to Las Vegas or a place of your choosing and trade them for money, clothing, or whatever you choose. When that happens, you will know that you are truly free!"

Simón reined his horse away and yelled, "Let's go home, hombres, we are through here."

Ruben and Julio watched the men ride away and when they could be seen no longer, Julio reached down from his pony and Ruben grabbed his hand and Julio pulled him up on the pony behind him. Ruben wrapped his arms around his brother's waist as he laid his head against his broad back and tears of joy ran down his cheeks.

"Get that dog to working, little brother," Julio said softly. "We need to get these sheep home. I left them out here over ten years ago and I know that papa wants them returned."

"Pepe! Let's bring the sheep home," Ruben yelled jubalently.

The dog jumped eagerly to his task, circling and nipping at the reluctant sheep. Within a few minutes the sheep were moving down the slopes of the Sangre de Cristo Mountains toward home.

As they rode back down the slopes of the great mountain range, Ruben told Julio of the sickness which Roberto suffered from and Julio asked about their parents and Stella. "I can remember them now," he admitted. "Perhaps I didn't want to remember until now."

Prestina watched with anxiety as she saw the sheep coming home early that day, and then she saw that an Apache accompanied them. But where was Ruben? Her relief was great when she saw that Ruben rode behind the Apache on his pony. Riding behind an Apache? And then with a great happiness she knew! "Alonzo!" She screamed and turned and rushed back toward the little adobe casa, shouting her husband's name over and over again as she ran, so fast did she run that she almost stumbled twice. "Roberto, Stella!" she screeched, "Julio has come back to us!"

Roberto awoke to the sound of his mother's voice and leaped from the bed in one bound. In another he was out the door and shielding his eyes as he looked up the hill at the approaching sheep and those who accompanied them. He was at the sheep pens along with the rest of the family when Julio and Ruben arrived there with their charges, and great was the rejoicing as the family was once more united.

CHAPTER XVII

When Simoñ, Filomeno, and the Riflemen reached the hacienda head quarters, they saw much activity going on around the church. One group of people were whitewashing the outer walls and others could be seen entering and leaving the church with cloth of many lengths and colors draped over their arms. There was an air of happy excitement in the atmosphere and Simoñ smiled as he told Filomeno, "The priest must be coming. He will perform many marriages and baptisms."

"And offer masses for the dead, too," Filomeno added, as he held his horse in check.

"Your horse seems to think it is a time for joy and merriment," grinned Simoñ as he glanced at the prancing animal.

"More likely that he thinks he will soon be given the grain he can expect when he reaches his stall," Filomeno smiled as he reached forward to pat his horse on the neck affectionately.

"Those from the nearest haciendas will also be making preparations to come here to join in the festivities. There will be much activity as they polish the carriages and harnesses and make ready. And I see some of the women already preparing the hornos to bake squaw bread. We got home just in time," said Simoñ as they dismounted at the stables.

Filomeno had waved at his wife and daughter who were busily doing something in the shade of the trees by their casa. "The priest comes in two days!" His wife wore a happy smile as she waved and then turned to continue with her work.

"Which priest will come this time, I wonder?" Filomeno glanced over at Simoñ as they began to unsaddle their mounts.

"I hope it will be Father Gustamantes," Simoñ replied, "but whoever comes, he will bring much news. I have been wondering what has been going on since we last heard. What the Americanos and Santa Anna may be doing by now? Surely the Father will know something. We may be at war and not know it!"

Father Gustamantes arrived about noon on the following day, amid the pomp and celebration which accompanied him wherever he went, so gladly was he always welcomed.

Doña Sylvia and Doña Maria had worked unceasingly for several days, supervising the many preparations which must be made for the celebration. Doña Sylvia had overseen the kitchen activities and Doña Maria had taken responsibility that the rest of the large house was in perfect order and ready to receive their honored guest. The peons on the hacienda had labored unceasingly to make the celebration one which the Father would remember as having an abundance of faith, piety, and reverence for the Holy Church.

They were rewarded for their efforts, for immediately upon his arrival, the old priest blessed all of those present on behalf of the Church and the archbishop. Mass the following day would be the paramount reward for their days of toil.

Father Gustamantes was made welcome by the Gomez family with the courtesy befitting his station. He was first escorted to his room so that he could refresh himself and rest after the long, dusty journey from Las Vegas. The evening meal had been prepared with the most lavish pride, using only the best and tried and true recipes of generations gone by.

After the evening meal, they retired to the long sala for an evening of relaxation and discussion and to sip the best wine from the Gomez cellar. The dons and doñas from the neighboring haciendas contributed to the color and festive mood, amd when they were all settled, Simoñ could restrain his curiosity no longer and asked eagerly, "What news do you bring us, Father?"

The benign expression which usually graced the countenance of the old priest changed dramatically as he growled, "Those infidel Americanos and their dreams of manifest destiny are not news, but are likely to cause us much trouble. Hah! The only destiny they will have is that which our president permits them once he reaches Washington, D. C. with his army and raises the Mexican flag over their capitol. The United States will then be annexed to Mexico, and maybe then Mother Church can bring the lost sheep back into the fold, by force of arms, if necessary!"

The old priest sank back in his chair and took a sip of wine with which to sooth his temper. At his age, it wasn't good for him to become so agitated.

"Mohammed tried that once and it did not work," Simoñ offered politely as he toyed with his wine glass.

"Ah, my son, but it did work. All were threatened with death by the sword if they did not submit to the Islamic faith. Because of this tactic, the Islamic religion today has more followers than does our Church."

"We Spaniards did not leave the church under threat of death when the Moors invaded and conquered Iberia, but rather, many of us died by the sword, defending the Holy Catholic faith," Modesto reminded them. "The sword is not always the best instrument that can be used."

"That will be the only instrument that can be used against the Americanos," Father Gustamantes said. His eyes flashed with determination and he glared at Modesto.

Simoñ glanced at Modesto and then back at the priest and asked, "Are the views you speak of also those of the archbishop of the Church or are they yours solely?"

"I speak for myself as a good Catholic and they are the views every good Catholic should have! Do I sense a difference of opinion, my son?"

"I only seek news and information, father, I do not seek confrontation."

"And what news do you seek, my son? Do you seek news that President Tyler of the United States, an expansionist, I might add, sought for and did not get the necessary two thirds vote of their senate to approve a treaty to annex Texas into their country? That his expansionist followers did, however, force through both houses of their Congress a resolution to that effect? Such a resolution requires only a majority vote, which he got. Is that the kind of news that you wish to hear, my son? Or do you perhaps wish to hear that President Tyler's entire cabinet resigned in protest against the annexation of Texas, which if accomplished would undoubtedly mean war with Mexico?" The old priest leaned forward and stared at Simoñ accusingly.

"Why did the senate vote against him, Father?"

"Why to prevent a war with Mexico, which they cannot possibly win, that is why."

"Or to prevent the spread of slavery?" Don Trujillo leaned forward in his chair inquiringly from the opposite side of the room in defence of Simoñ.

The others turned to look at Señor Trujillo as the priest released a barrage of cold, unfriendly stares at the don. The doña placed a slender white hand on her husband's sleeve in an attempt to warn him to refrain from further statements which would only enflame the priest.

"We are pleased to have you with us, Father," Doña Maria told him in a conciliatory tone. "Let us talk of more pleasant things."

The old priest turned to Doña Maria, the dowager of the hacienda and smiled, "You would make a very good mother superior."

"Thank you, Father." Doña Maria nodded gravely.

The priest placed both hands on the arms of his chair, and said, "I am fatigued and I have a full schedule tomorrow, so I must retire." He rose and everyone in the room also rose and bowed their heads as the priest made the sign of the cross and said, "Bless you all and may He watch over you and guide you in your decision making in the trying days ahead." He strode from the room, much to the relief of the other guests. Now the women rustled into the parlor to discuss their families and whatever domestic crises might have occurred since they last were together, and their menfolk sat down again to carry on the interrupted conversation.

"Well, we know where Father Gustamantes stands," Don Trujillo said with a light laugh.

"I had no intention of irritating the Father. I only wanted to know the news," said Simoñ ruefully. "Shall we continue our discussion or would it please you also to retire for the night?" He waited and saw that no one had any intention of leaving so interesting a conversation.

"Who wishes to go first?" Modesto glanced at their friends who were seated comfortably around the room, some of them smoking now that the women were absent.

Simoñ turned to Don Trujillo and asked, "You said something earlier about the spread of slavery, my friend. Would you please expand on that statement?"

Don Trujillo leaned forward and spoke earnestly, "Most of the anti-slavery people in the United States oppose admitting Texas into their union, not because they fear us, but because they know that Texas would become a slave state and the institution of slavery would then be spread farther west. Father Gustamantes cannot be faulted in his zeal to defend the Church. The American Catholics are not as docile as we are and if we should be defeated and New Mexico annexed, churches other than our Church would be permitted. Father Gustamantes can rightly fear that this could be a challenge to the supremacy of the pope."

"Can our army drive back the Americanos or defeat them?" Now Don Chavez leaned forward eagerly.

Everyone was silent as they pondered the liklihood of this happening, and finally Modesto spoke. "It would be extremely difficult to contain the Americanos."

Don Trujillo straightened in his chair and predicted, "Polk will win their next election, ex-president Jackson will see to that."

"Go on, my friend," Don Chavez urged him, "you are among friends."

"Just that while Polk is not a member of the Whig Party as is Tyler, he is also an expansionist."

"So the Democratic Party is in the hands of the expansionists, then," Simoñ said "is that what you are saying?"

"From what I have heard, most of them are," Don Trujillo told him calmly.

"Can the expansionists lead their country into a war against Mexico?" Don Chavez looked unconvinced.

"Andrew Jackson is seventy-seven years old and is blind in one eye and almost so in the other. He has been bedridden because of poor health for a long time, but he believes so strongly that Texas should become part of America, that the old war horse has gotten out of bed and is campaigning for his friend, Polk. Jackson has been quoted as saying that if Texas is rejected, `the glory of the United States has already culminated. A rival power will be built up'. Because of Jackson alone, I believe Polk will win," Don Trujillo said, "and we will be at war with the Americanos, if we are not already."

"Already!" Don Chavez rose from his slumped position in his chair and sat up straight as an arrow. "Do you have information which you are keeping from us?"

"As you may know, my son returned along the Santa Fe Trail just days ago from Westport and I know only what he heard while there. He heard that an American army was sent to take up its position on the north side of the Rio Grande."

"Oh, my God," the Americanos have invaded Mexico!" Don Chavez began to pace the length of the room, puffing vigorously on his cigar.

Don Trujillo watched him with amusement, "Not in the eyes of the Americanos, they haven't."

"The Nueces River separates Texas from Mexico and if the Americanos have taken up a position on the Rio Grande, then they are in Mexico," Don Chavez retorted angrily.

"There is a revolution in Mexico again," Don Torrez added his voice to the heated discussion, but endeavored to speak calmly.

"Revolution?" Simoñ was surprised at hearing this development.

"That's what I have heard," Don Torrez told them. "And Polk has already been elected, by the way, and has sent a John Slidell to represent him to Santa Anna to offer him twenty-five million dollars for all of Texas, New Mexico and California, and all of the other lands we claim above those areas."

"Will Santa Anna accept or will he fight? That's the question," said Don Chavez soberly.

"Let me finish," broke in Don Torrez. "No one on either side in Mexico City would receive this Slidell representative of the president of the United States, so he returned to his country empty handed."

"Then it is war," Don Trujillo said.

"It could be more like capitulation, rather than war, as far as New Mexico is concerned," Don Torrez commented.

"Capitulate? Without a fight? That doesn't sound much like Santa Anna," said Don Trujillo thoughtfully.

The other men watched Don Torrez closely, waiting for him to expand on what he was implying. He finally continued, and he spoke slowly, consideringly. "From what I have heard and they are only rumors, mind you, James Magoffin, the Americano trader who married a cousin of our governor in Chihuahua has been having secret meetings with Armijo and the talk is that Magoffin is trying to persuade him not to resist."

"Do you think Magoffin will succeed?" Now it was Simoñ who rose and began to pace the room excitedly.

"If he brought enough money with him, he will," Don Trujillo assured him wryly.

"But that would be treason and Santa Anna would have him shot," Don Chavez said in outrage.

"Santa Anna will have to catch him first," Don Trujillo added ironically.

"Manuel is a sly one, and he'll survive somehow," Don Torrez told them softly.

"I suppose you are right," Modesto agreed. "If anyone can burn the candle at both ends and survive, it's Armijo."

At that point, Luis came to the door and said, "Excuse me, patron, but Graciano is here and he wants to talk with you. He says it is urgent."

Simoñ excused himself and went to meet with his buffalo hunter, and upon finding him in the patio, Simoñ smiled and extended his hand, "How are you, my friend?"

"Fine, and you?"

"Sit down and tell me what is on your mind," invited Simoñ.

"An American general by the name of Kearny is at Bent's Fort with an army. He made a speech saying that New Mexico is now part of the United States. He is preparing to leave the fort and will come down through the Raton Pass to Las Vegas. It is said that his ultimate goal is California," Graciano concluded excitedly.

"There must have been a declaration of war, then," Simoñ decided. "Mexico and the United States are at war."

"It would appear that way," Graciano replied, "or else the American army would not be coming."

"Thank you for bringing me this news," Simoñ said. "Get some rest now."

Simoñ rushed back to his guests and told them of what Graciano had said and they all immediately decided to leave for their haciendas.

"Simoñ protested, "But it is night, why don't you stay the night and leave at sunup?"

Don Trujillo spoke for them all when he said, "Don Simoñ, you are here at your hacienda and we need to be at ours."

Candlelight could be seen at all windows as individuals hurriedly set about preparing for departure. Word had been sent to the peons of the various haciendas to pack and be ready for departure.

Father Gustamantes joined in the confusion as he, too, prepared to go, wanting to return to Las Vegas as soon as possible. His blessings of the previous day would have to suffice until he was again at the hacienda.

It was a cool, moonlit night, a quiet night, before the hacienda exploded into a hive of activity. The sound of commands, of children crying and horses neighing added to the confusion as the frantic preparations for departure went forward. When each individual entourage was ready, they said adios and Vaya con Dios hurriedly and drove off into the night until they had all gone, leaving behind an uneasy peace as Simon and Modesto, along with their wives, stood for a moment before returning to their houses. The silence was broken by Doña Sylvia who asked, "What will happen now?"

"We'll wait and see what happens," her husband replied calmly as he placed his arm around her. "Armijo may not put up any resistance and if that is the case, there will be no bloodshed. I'll send Graciano to Las Vegas later, to see what happens when the American general arrives there."

Now the peons of the hacienda began to gather before the house of the patron, fear on their faces, and Simoñ, with Modesto beside him, attempted to calm their fears. "It appears," Simoñ told them, "that the United States and Mexico are at war."

A loud murmur of voices followed this announcement and then Simoñ continued, "There is nothing to fear at this point. If we are at war, the war will not come here, it will be fought elsewhere, if at all, and it is highly possible that there will be no fighting at all."

One of the peons spoke up now and said fearfully, "Some Indians have told people in the villages in the Sangre de Cristos, that the Americanos will carry us off into slavery. They say we will be sold like animals and that our families will be divided and sold separately. That we will never see one another again. Is that true, Don Simoñ?"

Simoñ murmured to Modesto, "It appears that someone wants to fight and it isn't our governor." Then he answered firmly, "That is not true for I know these Americanos and I know that they would not do such things. Believe me and trust me. I will protect you. You have nothing to be afraid of. Now return to your homes and wait until you hear from me directly. Don't listen to what others may say."

The crowd of peons began to disperse to return to their homes, confident that their patron would protect them.

"Well?" Simoñ turned to Modesto. "It is testing time. It is time to test the will of the Americanos to live up to their reputation, their constitution and their faith in mankind. The days ahead are going to be long and tedious, but a new beginning is at hand. We are Americanos now, Modesto, and our future and that of our children will be as Americanos. We may find the sky is the limit according to our industry and imagination."

"The war is not over yet, my friend," Modesto said soberly. "It has just begun."

"What are you driving at?"

"There are many Mexicans who are still loyal to Mexico City. I suggest that we be doubly careful and keep a close watch for assassins and renegades from now on. There will be some who seek to exact revenge upon anyone they consider disloyal and figure this time of confusion is ideal for their purposes. We are not out of the woods yet. We may not be for years to come," Modesto concluded gloomily.

While not accepting completely Modesto's dour assessment of the situation, Simoñ suggested, "Why don't we call in Graciano's buffalo hunters and also ask

Filomeno and his men to stay here at the hacienda for a few days until we see what happens?"

....

High in the Sangre de Cristo mountains east of Chacon and a few miles west of Guadalupita, a party of banditos huddled around a large fire, trying to keep themselves warm. Many of them wore beards which covered most of their faces and their clothing was shabby and unkempt. All but one of them wore the customary wide brimmed, high crowned Mexican sombrero and some wore colorful serapes wrapped around their shoulders, while other wore ponchos. They were heavily armed with pistols and rifles and a close observer could have seen that each also wore a knife at his belt.

"If we work together, we can pull this off and we will all be rich." The speaker had pushed his sombrero back to let it dangle on its cord against his back. He wore a wide grin as he studied the others gathered around the fire.

A large man who sat next to him grunted in derision as he asked sarcastically, "And I suppose you will lead us, Flavio?"

"It was my idea to bring together the three largest bands of banditos in all of northern New Mexico for this job. Why shouldn't I lead?"

The big man spoke calmly and ignored the glare directed at him. "I lead my men, Edmundo's men take orders from no one but him and your men follow only you, so what makes you think our men will follow your orders?" The big man, whose name was Victor, chewed the stub of a cigar as he stared back at Flavio.

"If I do not lead, then I am pulling out," Flavio threatened, as he rose and started for his horse. His men rose in a body and prepared to follow him.

"Don't be in such a rush, Flavio, Edmundo called after him.

"Victor said his piece, but I have not said mine. Don't I have that right?"

Flavio turned on his heel and returned to the fire, standing there impatiently. "Well, what do you have to add?"

"I want to hear your plan first, and then I'll let you know if I want in."

Somewhat pacified, Flavio began to explain. "It is a simple plan. We ride to the Gomez Hacienda, led by one of our men who will carry the Mexican flag. We tell Simoñ Gomez that we are partisans and that we are fighting the Americano invasion, and that we want to spend the night there to rest our men. When he lets down his guard, we will take over and carry away anything we want."

"What makes you so sure that he will believe you?" Edmundo wore a dubious expression as he stared into the fire, thinking.

Flavio spoke persuasively, "He's a Mexican aristocrat, isn't he? His kind has everything to lose if Mexico does not win the war. Why wouldn't he give us shelter and food and any other help we need?"

Edmundo turned to Victor and admitted, "It could work, Victor. Will you join us?"

Victor countered, "Do you want him to lead your men?"

"What is there to lead? We all ride to the hacienda headquarters as a body of men and when the time is right, we strike. There need be no leader. Your men ride with you, mine with me and Flavio leads his."

"Who will try to convince Gomez that we are Mexican partisans"?

"Flavio is the best of the three of us for that job and I suggest that he be given that job. Surely you and I are not equipped to do it."

Victor hesitated and then demanded as he realized that he was outnumbered, "I lead my own men and all that we take will belong to us. We do not want to share what we take with anyone else. If that is acceptable with you two, count me in."

Edmundo glanced at Flavio and said, "That suits me fine, how about you, Flavio?"

"If that's the only way it can be done, then I'll go along," Flavio said angrily.

"How many men ride with you, Victor?

"Eighteen, Edmundo," Victor replied crisply.

"I have fourteen," Edmundo said, "and how many ride with you, Flavio?"

"Twenty."

"That makes fifty-five of us altogether, then," Edmundo figured. "That should look like an army to anyone. Surely under the best of conditions, Gomez couldn't match that many, especially on short notice. We should have little trouble. He will have to surrender to us or risk the slaughter of many of his people. I feel sure that he will not resist."

Not far from where the banditos plotted their raid, the figure of a Jicarilla Apache slipped through the darkness of the night and disappeared. Later he appeared within hearing distance of Julio's home and began his bird calls. Julio awoke and lay quietly as he listened to the calls, then slipped out of the house, careful not to awaken anyone else. He stopped outside and listened, waiting for a repeat of the whistles. When it came, he bagan to move with caution in that direction. When he joined the Apache who concealed himself in the junipers which grew near the sheep pens, the Apache told him about the plot against the hacienda. In a few minutes, the Apache slipped away and Julio returned to the house to awaken his family to tell them what he had heard.

"What do you plan to do, Julio?" Alonzo rubbed the sleep from his eyes and looked at his oldest son.

Prestina lit a fire in the fireplace and they all seated themselves at the crudely constructed table which stood near it. She whispered, "Let's not wake your sister."

"We must warn the patron," Julio said softly.

"Roberto and I will go with you," his father said. "Señor Gomez might need our help."

"What about me, father?" Ruben looked hurt at being left behind.

"You are too young to be of any help," his father said impatiently.

"I can surely be of some help! I want to go."

Julio looked across at his father and said, "We can't sit here and argue, let's all go."

Prestina said eagerly, "We could be of some help, too, and besides, I don't want to be left here alone. Especially if that army of banditos chooses to come this way. We will be safer if we all stick together."

"Mother is right, father," Julio admitted.

"All right," Alonzo relented. "Wake Stella and let's be on our way."

It was a little after five in the morning when the Abeyta's reached the hacienda headquarters. Alonzo walked to the front door and banged on it with his big fist, yelling, "Patron? Patron! Do you hear me? Wake up patron!" He continued to pound on the door until he saw the gleam of the candle through the narrow windows beside the door. Simoñ's shadow was cast on the white adobe walls as he hastened toward the door. When he flung open the door, he did not recognize Alonzo at first.

"We must speak to you, patron, it is urgent."

"Who are you?"

Upon seeing the confusion, Julio dismounted and ran to the door.

"Julio? What is going on?"

Julio explained what he had heard from his Apache friend, and Simoñ broke in hurriedly, "Run to the church and ring the bell while I get dressed."

When the people of the hacienda had assembled in response to the ringing of the bell, Simon told them about the impending attack by the banditos, and then ordered, "Filomeno, you post your men on the east and south side of the battlements and conceal yourselves. I don't want the banditos to have the slightest idea that you are there. Modesto," Simoñ continued to give orders rapidly as he turned to his trusted friend, "get everyone into the compound and then take charge of the twelve pounders. You buffalo hunters man the north and west sides of the battlements."

The men ran eagerly to get ready to repel the banditos, and the women, under the direction of Doña Sylvia, Doña Maria, and Josephine shepherded the house servants inside and instructed them to prepare hot coffee and also lay out supplies to care for the wounded, if, Heaven forbid! wounded there might be, before this was over.

While they were doing this, Simoñ had instructed Leandro and his brothers and also the Prudencio brothers to arm themselves and report back at the house as soon as possible.

In less than an hour, everyone was in place and all was quiet as they watched and listened. Suddenly Leandro said, "I can hear hoofbeats!"

Simoñ listened and Ignacio spoke up, "He's right, they're coming!"

As the line of riders came into sight, Simoñ gasped, "That's an army!"

"And they are carrying a Mexican flag," Carlos said with scorn. "They are desecrating our flag!"

"With what they plan, that is a small thing to them," Simoñ said grimly. "When they arrive, I want all of you to remain concealed. I will talk to them."

"Don't go too far away from the door," Modesto cautioned.

When the banditos pulled their horses to a halt in front of the house, Flavio fired a few shots into the air and yelled, "Señor Gomez!"

After a few moments had passed, Simoñ stepped out onto the veranda. "Si, what do you want?"

"Are you Señor Gomez?" Flavio sat his horse arrogantly, his rifle butt resting on his thigh.

"Si, I am Señor Gomez," Simoñ replied calmly.

"We are with the Mexican Army, but under the direct command of Governor Armijo. Some people call us partisans. We have orders to cut the Americano supply line between here and Raton Pass, and we would like your cooperation. Will you help?"

Simoñ had to admit to himself that the request sounded plausible and gave thanks silently that they had been warned. He asked politely, "What help can I give you?"

"By permitting us to set up camp here," Flavio answered.

"I cannot do that," Simoñ said.

Flavio's face darkened and he thundered, "Are you refusing to help the Mexican government in its war with the Americanos?"

"That's enough talk," Victor yelled as he raised his rife to point it at Simoñ.

A shot was fired from within the house and Victor slid from his horse and fell to the ground and lay motionless. Simoñ quietly stepped back into the house.

"Flavio!" Edmundo yelled and pointed his rifle northward where at least twenty Apaches could be seen sitting their horses in a single line on a small rise, perhaps two or three hundred yards distant. They did not move, but sat their ponies silently and the banditos could see they carried rifles, good Americano rifles.

"Apaches? What are Apaches doing here?" Flavio looked uncertain now, unsure of what to do.

Edmundo rode over to his side and muttered, "Maybe they have the same idea we have."

"Let's find out." Flavio yelled, "There is plenty for all of us. We will leave some for you. Give us an hour and then we'll leave."

In reply, one of the Apaches pointed to the east with his rifle and the banditos turned quickly in their saddles and looked where the Apache pointed.

"Oh, my God!" Flavio shouted, "Comanches!" He turned back toward the house imploringly and yelled, "Gomez, you can't leave us out here to these savages. Let us into your compound!"

"You had better leave with your banditos," Simoñ called back from inside the house, "before it is too late."

"We are not banditos, we are Mexican soldiers," Flavio yelled in desperation. He raised his rifle and fired into the house.

Simoñ and the others responded as the banditos opened up on the house and immediately fire came next from the ramparts of the compound and many of the banditos fell to the ground.

"It's a trap, everyone for himself!" Flavio wheeled his horse sharply and galloped southward. The rifle fire from the compound continued, with many of the banditos falling from their saddles and the rest scattering in several directions. Those who fled toward the west were pursued by the galloping Apaches and those who rode south were chased by the Comanches.

"Where did the Apaches come from?" Simoñ was surprised, but elated as he and the others stepped out onto the veranda.

"They came to help Julio, I imagine," Modesto said with a grin.

"Who told the Comanches, then?"

"They were probably coming in to trade and happened to arrive at the right time," Carlos also wore a wide grin.

"It was the right time, all right," Simoñ said. "It seems we have more friends than we thought, Modesto. We must be doing something right after all."

Later that morning over coffee, Simoñ told Modesto, "I believe before long we should go to Santa Fe to show our support for our new government."

Modesto nodded and mused, "I wonder who our new governor will be?" He glanced at Simoñ and said, "Charles Bent would be an admirable governor. Governor Bent has a nice ring, doesn't it?"

"That is true, and it is only common courtesy that we present ourselves to the new governor in the presence of his assistants and governmental representatives and declare our loyalty to our new government and country," Simoñ urged.

CHAPTER XVIII

Some time after the skirmish at the hacienda, Simoñ and Modesto rode to Santa Fe and found it a different city from their last visit. American flags could be seen everywhere and the American soldiers guarded the Palace of the Governors. They made their presence seen elsewhere in the old city as well.

The señoritas, at least, seemed to welcome the newcomers, for they could be seen visiting with them on the sidewalks of the busy city. They were welcoming the strangers and dressed in their best finery, their hair worn in the Spanish style, and held in place with ornate combs. They had not been sparing with the extensive cosmetics, either, Simoñ noticed as they rode down the street. Their bright and colorful gowns looked like flowers around the plaza. Simoñ also noticed the displeasure on some of the faces of the older, more conservative ladies, who were shocked at the forward behavior of some of the younger senoritas.

As they tied their horses on the south side of the plaza, the two men gazed around and noticed that however displeased the older women might be, the Mexican men who went about their business seemed even more disapproving, and cast short, quick glances of caution at the flirtatious young women and girls.

If Simoñ was any judge of human nature, the young women would be scolded properly when they returned to the privacy of their homes.

"Let's see if we can get an audience with our old friend, the governor," Simoñ suggested as they began to stride across the center of the plaza. They had been correct in their conjectures concerning Charles Bent. "He could be too busy to see us," Modesto cautioned.

When they reached the palace, their way was blocked by soldiers who were posted at the entrance. "Do you have business with the governor?" The young soldier spoke politely but with authority.

"We would like an audience with Governor Bent," Simoñ told him.

"Just a minute, sir." The soldier said as he turned to enter the palace. He came back almost immediately and said, "His secretary will see you. Take the first door to your left, please."

"Thank you sergeant," Simoñ replied politely and he and Modesto walked into the palace and entered the office of the secretary. Governor Bent was there, talking with his secretary when they entered, and upon seeing his old friends, the governor smiled broadly and extended his hand. "What a pleasant surprise.

It is good to see you both again, mi amigos."

"We were hoping to get an audience with you Governor Bent, if you have a minute," Simoñ told him.

"I have an office full of aides at the moment, and I am extremely busy trying to organize the territory. Could you come for supper?"

"It would give me great pleasure if I could address the officials who are gathered in your office. I promise I will take only a moment of your time. We would like to declare openly our loyalty and show our support for you and the United States," Simoñ told him earnestly.

"That is government business and that's the business we're in," the governor said heartily. "Please follow me."

The governor's office was full of officials, both civilian and military and they turned to stare inquiringly at Simoñ and Modesto as the governor ushered them into the room.

"Gentlemen," Charles Bent said as he led his friends to the front of his office. "I would like to introduce to you two old friends of mine. As you know, we are indebted to people such as these two, for they made it possible for the annexation of New Mexico into our union without bloodshed. Gentlemen it is my pleasure to present to you Don Simoñ Gomez and his friend and brother-in-law, Don Modesto Polaco."

The men in the office applauded and listened attentively as Simoñ began to speak. "Thank you for that kind and gracious introduction, your Excellency." He bowed to Governor Bent and then turned to face the room full of officials. "Please, señors, permit me a minute of your time. I know that you are extremely busy and I ask your forgiveness for our interruption. Please indulge a new American a moment to express his thoughts on your arrival.

"The guns of war are silent today. The war with Mexico is over and New Mexico and her people are now citizens of the United States. I stand before you as an illustration of that conquest. Many of us dreamed for many years that this day would come. We dreamed of freedom, we dreamed of equality, we dreamed of justice and we dreamed much more, we dreamed of acceptance. We dreamed of understanding, we dreamed of fruitful cooperation between our two peoples.

"We, as a people have much to contribute to the making of the new man, the American, of which your country so bravely conceived and gave birth. This new man does not stand alone, nor will he. He is but one of many. Some to be born within your borders, and some to be adopted as full and equal partners of your family.

"Your revolution lit a small flame in every man's heart throughout all lands and nations. A flame that is to grow until it will engulf his whole being, his whole existance, his reason to live. Let my people join you in fanning that flame of dignity, that flame of hope, of which dreams are made.

"We are ready to join hands with our adopted country and march proudly by the side of her sons and daughters as full and equal partners in placing our footprints beside yours in the sands of time. Thank you for your time and for giving me the pleasure and honor of addressing such an august body." As he concluded, Simoñ bowed and the men bowed in return, amid the thundering applause.

Charles Bent followed Simoñ and Modesto out of the Palace of Governors and once outside, he turned to the two and said, "That was an excellent talk that you gave back there, Simoñ, and it should go a long ways toward healing the wounds which can happen at such a time. Have you heard some of the rumors which are already circulating?"

"We've heard some," admitted Simoñ. "And we did not hear them all in Santa Fe, either."

"Where did you hear them?"

"Before we left home, some of our peons who live in the Sangre de Cristos, told us of what friends of theirs from Taos and Mora are saying. Do you have any idea who is starting the rumors and why?"

Governor Bent was grave as he replied, "I think I do know one of those who is behind them, but I don't think many of the people will believe him."

"Don't count on that," Modesto warned. "Most of the peons are uneducated to the ways of the Americans, and they are suspicious enough to be swayed easily."

"Perhaps you are right, especially if one uses that superstition to arouse fear in the peons. Especially if that one happens to be a priest," he mused. "He could put depth to the rumors."

"A priest?" Simoñ was startled and he glanced at Modesto in shock.

"Well, that's my problem, my friends. I don't want to burden you with it, anyway. I believe things are quiet enough now, for me to pay a visit to Taos."

....

Simoñ and Modesto were never to see Governor Bent again, for an uprising was, even then, being plotted against the Americans in Taos, as well as in other northern New Mexico villages. One of the first casualties of the plot would be Governor Bent himself.

The rebellion would be crushed by the American forces with great cost in lives and property to the ill equipped native New Mexicans. It was to be the last great effort by the mostly pueblo Indian rebels to rid their ancestral lands of the white man. With the crushing of this revolt, the long, long slow healing process between the three cultures was to begin. The eastern melting pot had finally arrived in New Mexico.

SUNSTONE
PRESS

Send for our **free catalog**

and find out more about our books on:

- ❖ The Old West
- ❖ American Indian subjects
- ❖ Western Fiction
- ❖ Architecture
- ❖ Hispanic interest subjects
- ❖ And our line of full-color notecards

Just mail this card or call us on our toll-free number below

_____
Name

_____
Address

_____
City   State   Zip

Send Book Catalog _____ Send Notecard Catalog _____

Sunstone Press / P.O.Box 2321 / Santa Fe, NM 87504
(505) 988-4418   FAX (505) 988-1025   (800)-243-5644